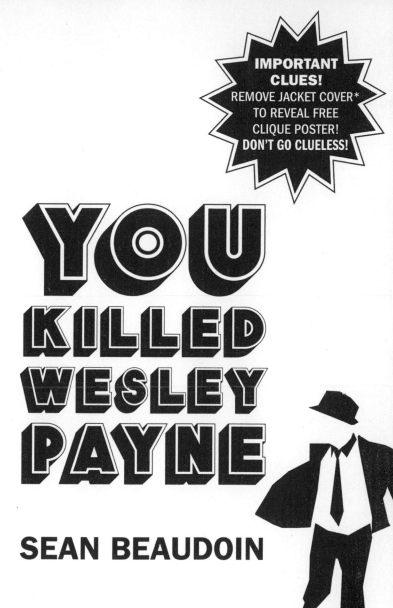

IMPORTANT CLUES!
REMOVE JACKET COVER*
TO REVEAL FREE
CLIQUE POSTER!
DON'T GO CLUELESS!

YOU KILLED WESLEY PAYNE

SEAN BEAUDOIN

Little, Brown and Company
New York   Boston

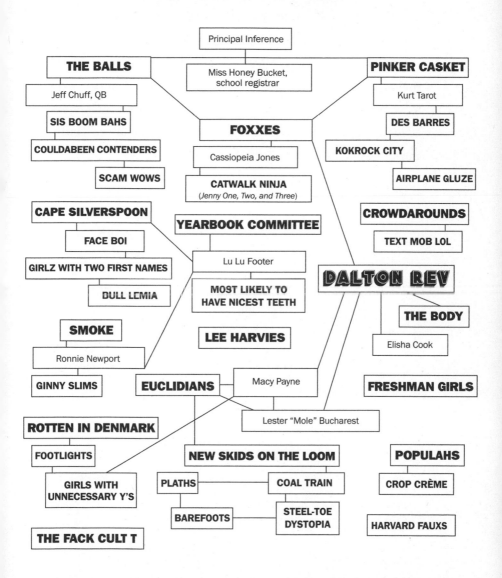

SALT RIVER HIGH
CLIQUE CHART

Principal Inference

Miss Honey Bucket, school registrar

THE BALLS

Jeff Chuff, QB

SIS BOOM BAHS

COULDABEEN CONTENDERS

SCAM WOWS

PINKER CASKET

Kurt Tarot

DES BARRES

KOKROCK CITY

AIRPLANE GLUZE

FOXXES

Cassiopeia Jones

CATWALK NINJA
(Jenny One, Two, and Three)

CAPE SILVERSPOON

FACE BOI

GIRLZ WITH TWO FIRST NAMES

DULL LEMIA

YEARBOOK COMMITTEE

Lu Lu Footer

MOST LIKELY TO HAVE NICEST TEETH

CROWDAROUNDS

TEXT MOB LOL

DALTON REV

THE BODY

Elisha Cook

SMOKE

Ronnie Newport

GINNY SLIMS

LEE HARVIES

EUCLIDIANS

Macy Payne

FRESHMAN GIRLS

Lester "Mole" Bucharest

ROTTEN IN DENMARK

FOOTLIGHTS

GIRLS WITH UNNECESSARY Y'S

THE FACK CULT T

NEW SKIDS ON THE LOOM

PLATHS

COAL TRAIN

BAREFOOTS

STEEL-TOE DYSTOPIA

POPULAHS

CROP CRÈME

HARVARD FAUXS

TURN TO PAGE 360 **RIGHT NOW** FOR THE FULL CLIQUE DOWN-LOW.
DEEPER SLANG! **MEANER GOSSIP! WHACK-EST RACKETS!**
ONLY TOTAL FISH STICKS WOULD WAIT UNTIL THEY'VE READ THE WHOLE BOOK!

ACKNOWLEDGMENTS:

The author would like to thank the following excellent people: Alvina "Rock" Ling, Connie "Roll" Hsu, Becca Hannon, Kristine Serio, Victoria Stapleton, Steve Malk, Alex Wang, Martha Clarkson, Mike "Chezbollah" Nesi, Daryl Miller Salomons, Emma Larson, Maria Behan, Angelo Gianni, Pie Truck Bauer, Henry Kyburg, Curtis Mayfield, Mary Love Maddox, Pamela Gruber, Melanie Sanders, Barbara Bakowski, Christine Ma, Alison Impey, Shawn Harris, Hayley Foster, Scott Hale, and Sally King.

....

Little, Brown and Company

Hachette Book Group
237 Park Avenue, New York, NY 10017
Visit our website at www.lb-teens.com

Little, Brown and Company is a division of Hachette Book Group, Inc.
The Little, Brown name and logo are trademarks of Hachette Book Group, Inc.

First Edition: February 2011

Library of Congress Cataloging-in-Publication Data

Beaudoin, Sean.
  You killed Wesley Payne / by Sean Beaudoin. — 1st ed.
    p. cm.
  Summary: When hard-boiled, seventeen-year-old private investigator Dalton Rev transfers to Salt River High to solve the case of a dead student, he has his hands full trying to outwit the police, negotiate the school's social hierarchy, and get paid.
  ISBN 978-0-316-07742-2
  [1. Mystery and detective stories. 2. High schools—Fiction. 3. Schools—Fiction. 4. Cliques (Sociology)—Fiction. 5. Humorous stories.] I. Title.
  PZ7.B3805775Yo 2011
  [Fic] —dc22   2010008639

10 9 8 7 6 5 4 3 2 1

RRD-C

Book design by Alison Impey

Printed in the United States of America

DEDICATION
For Cathy

TURN TO PAGE 318 FOR
MEGA-RUDE
SLANG GLOSSARY!
ABSOLUTELY FREE!
NOW WITH TONS OF BONUS GLOSS!

CHAPTER 1
HOW DALTON CAME TO SCHOOL

Dalton Rev thundered into the parking lot of Salt River High, a squat brick building at the top of a grassless hill that looked more like the last stop of the hopeless than a springboard to the college of your choice. His black scooter wove through groups of students waiting for the first bell, muffler growling like a defective chain saw. In Dalton's line of work it was vital to make a good first impression, especially if by good you meant utterly intimidating.

He parked away from a pool of mud, chained his helmet to the tire, and unzipped his leather jacket. Underneath was a crisp white dress shirt with a black tie. His work uniform. It tended to keep people guessing. And guessing was good. A few extra seconds could mean the difference between being stomped to jelly or not, some steroid case busy wondering, *What kind of loser wears a tie with steel-toe boots?*

Dalton did.

He was, after all, a professional.

Who'd come to do a job.

That involved a body.

Wrapped in duct tape and hanging from the goalposts at the end of the football field.

THE PRIVATE DICK HANDBOOK, RULE #1
People have problems. You can solve them for cash.

Dalton needed to figure out why The Body was at the morgue instead of snoring its way through algebra. Then he'd get paid. But until a big wad of folding green was tucked safely into his boot, he was Salt River's newest transfer fish.

"Nice tie, asshat!" someone yelled. Kids began to crowd around, hoping for a scene, but Dalton ignored them, turning toward a chrome sandwich truck in the corner of the parking lot. His cropped hair gleamed under the sun, dark eyes hooded with a practiced expression. Long hours of practice. In the mirror. Going for a look that said *justifiably ruthless*.

Or at least ruthless-ish.

THE PRIVATE DICK HANDBOOK, RULE #2
Be enigmatic. Be mysterious. Never explain.

The sandwich truck's awning sagged. The driver sagged with it. There were rows of chocolate donuts that looked like they'd been soaked in Ebola. There was a pile of cut-rate candy with names like Butterfingerer and Snuckers and Baby Ralph. A big sign on the counter said NO CREDIT—DON'T EVEN ASK!

"Hey," Dalton asked. "Can I get an apple on credit?"

The driver laughed like it was his first time ever. "What-canIgetcha?"

2

"Coffee. Black."

"That'll be twenty even."

"Cents?"

"Dollars."

Dalton considered not paying—ten minutes on the job and already over his expense budget. But people were watching. He grabbed the cup, flash-searing his palm, and took a sip. It tasted like coffee-colored ass. People laughed as he spat it out in a long, brown sneeze.

"It's a seller's market," the driver admitted. "No one eats in the cafeteria no more."

"Why not?"

"Caf's Chitty Chitty," answered a kid who seemed to have materialized out of nowhere, hair poking from his scalp as if it were trying to escape. He cocked his thumb like a pistol and fired off a few imaginary rounds. "As in *Bang Bang*?"

"You serious?"

The kid selected a donut. "Or, you know, maybe the food just sucks."

Dalton needed to check out the crime scene. First stop, football field. The kid followed, plump and sweaty, huffing to catch up. He held out his knuckles for a bump. "My name's Mole."

Dalton didn't bump back.

Mole sniffed his fist and then shrugged. "So, you affiliated, new guy?"

"Independent."

"Ha! That'd be a first. You must be with *someone*, yo. No one transfers to Salt River alone."

Dalton pushed through dumped girlfriends and dice nerds,

hoodie boys and scruffy rockers twirling Paper Mate drumsticks. People mostly made way, except for an expensively dressed girl who towered over her speed-texting posse.

"Who's that?"

"Lu Lu Footer. Your basic Armani giraffe. Also, she's head of Yearbook."

"That a clique?"

"They're all, *Hi, my book bag's shaped like Hello Kitty!* They're all, *Hi, I crap pink and green polka dots!*"

Lu Lu Footer glared. Mole ducked as they passed a circle of large girls in black. "Plaths," he explained. "Total down-in-the-mouthers." He pointed to a girl in hot pants. "But check her out. Used to be a Plath and now she's flashing those Nutrisystem legs like no one remembers last semester."

Dalton rounded the edge of the building and stood under the goalposts. They were yellow and metal. Tubular in construction. Regulation height. There were scratch marks in the paint that could have come from a coiled rope. Or they could have just been scratches. Dalton wanted to consult the paperback in his back pocket, *The Istanbul Tryst and the Infant Wrist*. It was a Lexington Cole mystery, #22, the one where Lex solves a murder at a boarding school in the Alps. But he wasn't about to yank it out with people around.

"You ready to bounce?" Mole asked nervously. "We're not really allowed to stand here, yo."

Dalton wondered what he was looking for. A map? A videotaped confession? Lexington Cole would already have intuited something about the grass, like how it was a nonnative strain, or that its crush pattern indicated a wearer of size six pumps.

"Yeah, see, this whole area, it's sort of off-limits."

Music blared as football players emerged from the locker room. They slapped hands and joked loudly and ran into one another with helmets clacking. Except for the ones not wearing helmets, who banged skulls anyway. Some of them weren't wearing shirts at all, just shoulder pads. Their cleats smacked the pavement in crisp formation.

"I take it that's the welcome committee?"

Mole dropped to one knee, retying his shoes even though they had no laces. "Don't look directly at them!"

"Who are they?" Dalton asked, looking directly at them.

"The Balls. Between them and Pinker Casket, they pretty much run the show."

"Balls?"

"Foot*ball*. Your Salt River Mighty Log Splitters? Their random violence level is proportional to the number of points surrendered the previous game. And, guy? We got stomped last week."

"Your vocabulary has mysteriously improved. What happened to the 'yo, yo, yo' routine?"

"Comes and goes," Mole admitted.

Dalton turned as the Balls busted into a jerky line of calisthenics. "Who're you with again?"

"Euclidians."

"The brain contingent?"

Mole gestured toward the picnic tables, where kids sat reading biology texts and grammar worksheets. The girls wore glasses and sensible skirts; the boys, sweater-vests and slacks. "You can't swing a Siamese around here without smacking a nerd in the teeth, but, yeah, they're my people."

"Thanks for not saying *my peeps*."

"Fo sho."

"Looks like your peep could use some help."

One of the players, built like a neckless bar of soap, yelled "Chuff to Chugg...touchdown!" as he pushed a Euclidian into the mud. The kid struggled to get away, slipped, and then knocked over a shiny black scooter. Other cliques were already jogging over to see the action.

Dalton looked at his watch. "Well, that didn't take long. Nineteen minutes."

Mole grabbed Dalton's arm. "Seriously, guy? You want to leave those Balls alone."

It was true. Dalton wanted to go home and lie in bed and pull the sheets up to his chin. He wanted to eat pretzels and sweep crumbs with his toes. But then he thought about Lex Cole. And the fearless pair of stones Lex Cole toted around in his impeccably ironed slacks. He also thought about last night, counting up the money he'd managed to save so far. Twice. And how both times it wasn't nearly enough to save his brother.

"Stay here."

Dalton pushed through the crowd, working his way past assorted pleather windbreakers and nymphets in yellow cowl. The football players turned as one, like it was written in the script: *Test the New Guy II*, starring Dalton Rev. He stood before a glistening wall of beef, a collective four dollars' worth of crew cuts. The shirtless ones showed off their abs and punched each other's shoulder pads like extras from a version of *Mad Max* where no one shaved yet.

Dalton waved. "Hi."

Just like the Spanish Inquisition, no one ever expected friendliness. The players stared, chewing mouthpieces in unison, as a girl emerged from the crowd and began helping the Euclidian up. She had a blond pixie cut, a tiny waist, and a tinier skirt.

"Leave him alone, Chance!" she told the player doing the pushing. "Please?"

Dalton liked her voice, low and calm. And her eyes, almost purple. Sharp and intense. She stood with her hips forward, like a chorus girl who'd come to the city with a suitcase full of spunk, ready to do whatever it took to save Daddy's farm. It was one very cute package. Actually, in both Dalton's professional and decidedly unprofessional opinion, she was beautiful.

THE PRIVATE DICK HANDBOOK, RULE #3
Doing free things for beautiful girls is never the smart play.
In fact, it's always a colossal mistake.
Avoid doing free things. Avoid beautiful girls.
Continue to charge maximum fees and take cold showers.

"This is none of your business, Macy," the largest Ball said, getting up from a lawn chair. Dalton had thought he was already standing; the guy looked like a giant walking Krispy Kreme, one big twist of muscle. His head was shaved. A simian hairline hovered just above his eyes, radiating a hunger for raw veal. He was clearly the one person, out of Salt River's entire student body, to be avoided at all costs.

Dalton walked over and helped Macy help the Euclidian up.

"You okay?"

The kid spat mud, then ran toward the school doors, trying not to cry. Macy mouthed a silent thanks and followed him on adorably sensible heels.

"You're standing on *my* field," the Krispy Kreme growled.

Dalton turned. "That make you the groundskeeper?"

The crowd drew a collective breath. A few of the more brazen laughed aloud. The Krispy Kreme flexed, dipping to show the name sewn across the back of his jersey: JEFF CHUFF, QB.

"Impressive."

"You got a problem, new fish?"

"Your Ball is mistreating my ride."

The Crowdarounds turned, looking at Dalton's scooter lying in the mud.

THE PRIVATE DICK HANDBOOK, RULE #4
Never let anyone mess with your ride.
Conversely, feel free to mess with theirs, especially
if there's a chance they'll be chasing you on it later.

Chuff laughed. "So? Have your mommy buy another one."

Dalton lifted his crisp white button-up. Underneath was a T-shirt that said THE CLASH IS THE ONLY BAND THAT MATTERS. When he lifted that as well, everyone could see the worn grip of his silver-plated automatic. The hilt was wrapped with rubber bands to keep it from slipping down his pants, a little trick he'd learned from chapter 6 of *The Cairo Score*. Just like the scooter, the gun was shiny and mean-looking.

"You're strapped?" Chuff wheezed, stepping back. "That's bloshite. Ever since The Body, we got an agreement."

"Like one of those abstinence ring things?"

"A *pact*. All the cliques. Us and Foxxes and Yearbook. Even Pinker Casket. No guns."

"Huh," Dalton said, fingering his gun. "Or what?"

Chuff's eyes scanned the rooftop. "When Lee Harvies find out you got a pistol on campus, they'll let you know or what. You're lucky, only your leg'll get ventilated."

"It's true," Mole said, appearing out of nowhere. "Lee Harvies aim to keep the peace."

Dalton shook his head. "Let me get this straight. You got a clique that keeps other cliques from carrying guns by shooting at them?"

"Used to be cops in the lot four days a week," Chuff explained. "Hassle this, hassle that, badges and cuffs. Calls to parents. We *all* realized it was bad for business."

"So you have an agreement," Dalton said. "What I have is a scooter in the mud."

"And?"

"And it needs to not be there anymore."

Birds tweeted. Bees buzzed. Grass grew.

"People lose teeth talking like that."

"People get shot talking about other people's teeth."

Chuff looked around. The rest of the Balls shrugged. Dalton flicked the safety.

"I got a full clip. You factor in a miss rate of twenty percent and I am still about to seriously reduce your available starters for next practice."

Chuff rubbed his oven-roaster neck, then grudgingly lifted the scooter with one hand, setting it upright.

THE PRIVATE DICK HANDBOOK, RULE #5
The thing about tough guys is they tend to be as tough as you let them be.

"Now wipe it off."

Chuff didn't move. His jaw worked like he was gnawing shale.

"It's a bluff!" Chance Chugg yelled.

Dalton whipped out the automatic. The Crowdarounds panicked, pushing backward as a big-haired girl stood on the fringes with a cigarette in her mouth fumbling for a light. He stuck the gun in her face and pulled the trigger. A wail went up, followed by a raft of curses and screams.

But there was no bang.

Instead, a small butane flame licked out of the end of the barrel. Dalton held it steady, lighting the girl's cigarette. The crowd roared with relief and giddy laughter.

"It's a toy?" Chuff yelled, already running forward.

Dalton began a mental inventory of the Lex Cole library. At this point, the bad guy usually made a series of threats, gave a face-saving speech, and then walked away. Except Chuff wasn't walking away. He was picking up speed.

Um.

Nine feet.

Um.

Six.

Um.

10

Three.

Pang pang pang!

Shots spattered through the dirt. Chuff veered wildly left, crashing into bags of equipment. From the roof came the reflection of a scope blinking in the hazy morning light.

"LEE HARVIES!" someone yelled, and there was chaos, more shots picking up the dirt in pairs, friends and enemies scattering. Plaths formed a black beret phalanx. Sis Boom Bahs circled like tight-sweatered chickens. The Balls dragged a groggy Chuff into the locker room as everyone shielded their heads, ducking into the relative safety of the school.

"Run!"

Dalton didn't run. He knelt among the churning legs and slid his finger over a bullet hole in the grass. There was a streak of sticky red. It could have been blood. It smelled a whole lot like vinegar. He stood and scanned the rooftop, catching a glimpse of a bright white face. It wasn't a face, it was a hockey mask. A Jason mask. The mask looked down at him, just a plastic mouth and nose, black eyes surrounded by silver anarchy symbols.

It was totally, utterly, piss-leg scary.

The rifle rose again. This time Dalton covered his head and ran inside like everyone else. Even in *One Bullet, One Kill* Lexington Cole hadn't thought it smart to go mano a mano with a sniper.

CHAPTER 2
A BUCKET HALF EMPTY

Dalton found the administration office and waited in line. When it was his turn at the desk, the enormous woman behind it adjusted her nameplate—MISS HONEY BUCKET, SCHOOL REGIS-TRAR—and gave him a frown. "Classes have already begun." She patted her black beehive and smoothed her terry-cloth jogging suit, before handing Dalton his schedule. "You're a month late signing up."

"Sorry about that."

Honey Bucket pursed her sluggy lips. The birthmark on her cheek pursed with them. "Sorry doesn't wash many dishes, young man."

FIRST PERIOD	CALCULUS I
SECOND PERIOD	CALCULUS II
THIRD PERIOD	ADVANCED CALCULUS
FOURTH PERIOD	CALCULUS SEMINAR
FIFTH PERIOD	NO LUNCH/CALC LAB
SIXTH PERIOD	CALCULUS ON ABACUS
SEVENTH PERIOD	FUN WITH CHAUCER

Dalton fished three twenty-dollar bills from his pocket and slid them across the desk.

"Quick learner," Miss Bucket said. "That'll come in handy around here."

"So would an ATM."

She smiled. "I heard about your…performance. In the parking lot. Very impressive."

"Already? From who?"

Honey Bucket flapped her arms without generating anywhere near the requisite lift. "A little birdie."

"That little birdie happen to be on your little payroll?"

"My job is to know what there is to know. When people sing, I listen." Honey Bucket looked both ways. "There's a calm before the storm, but the storm is definitely coming."

"What's that? Haiku?"

"Rockers or jocks. A new fish like yourself would be smart to pick a side."

Dalton thought about Chuff. For about two seconds. "I'll take rockers for a hundred, Alex."

Honey Bucket laughed, folding Dalton's cash into her waistband before handing over a new schedule. This one had a normal class load. She filed his paperwork behind a stash of contraband with handwritten prices. There were brass knuckles and some cheap nunchucks. There were also comics, celebrity magazines, naked celebrity magazines, sugared cereals, duct tape, and NoDoz.

"See anything you like?"

Dalton's answer was muffled by a loud *bang*.

"No shooting in the hallway!" Miss Bucket called, waving away the noise with splayed fingers. A few kids ran past, chased by a few other kids. They were carrying balloons. One of the balloons popped. *Bang.*

Miss Bucket shrugged. "Honestly, around here you never know."

In the other direction walked the girl with the blond pixie. She wore a butterfly barrette with tiny emeralds embedded in the wings. Dalton tried to catch her eye, but she gave him a blank look and kept going.

"I think you struck out there, stud. You want some advice? I'd say lose the tie, for starters. You look like a politician. Or an undertaker."

Dalton tightened his Windsor knot. "Is there a difference?"

"Just make sure you stay current on your reading." Honey Bucket handed him two pamphlets. The first was called *Violence and Salt River and You.* The second was called *Not Calling the Cops: Keeping Trouble In-House.* "In the meantime, you need to saddle up and see the principal."

"Why?"

"All new students do. School policy. Second door on your left, just past the Fack Cult T Lounge. Welcome to Salt River."

◎

The frosted pane read PRINCIPAL INFERENCE. Dalton turned the knob. Locked. He knocked. No answer. At the end of the corridor, Honey Bucket was typing with her back to him, pecking one finger at a time. Dalton slipped his mother's old credit card from his boot and edged it between the bolt and the socket, pulling on the handle to keep a steady friction. Amazingly, the knob turned.

He closed the door quietly and began knocking on the walls with his knuckle. You were supposed to be able to hear if it was hollow or something. He looked in a fruit bowl, lifted up the rug, and checked the file cabinet. Just police reports and minutes from Fack Cult meetings. He checked Inference's desk. Erasers, test scores, detention slips. The largest drawer, at the bottom, was full of makeup and tampons. Dalton picked up a tampon and marveled at it. He knew what it did, but wasn't entirely sure *how* it did what it did. He dropped the thing back among its wrappered cousins as the door clacked open. Principal Inference backed in balancing a coffee, a leather purse, a lipstick, and a hand mirror. She jumped as he tried a preemptive ass covering.

"You wanted to see me?"

The coffee slammed to the floor. Principal Inference stared. Red hair ran down her back in a glistening wave. She was wearing a tight red dress that showed off considerable leadership talents. He could tell she was trying to decide if she should explode or play it cool. Cool won.

"Ah, Mr. Rev. Have a seat."

Inference said nothing as she closed her obviously rifled desk drawer with one knee. Dalton was about to try out something suitably ruthless-ish, when he noticed a man in a blue pin-striped suit staring in the window. When he blinked, the man was gone.

"I know why you're here, Rev."

"Valuable life skills. And if I study real hard, maybe even a diploma."

Inference clacked a few keys before turning her computer screen. A website blinked: DALTON REV, PRIVATE DICK—I SOLVE YOUR PROBLEMS.

15

"You and I, Mr. Rev, are now having what's known as a Student Diagnostic." She began scribbling on a take-out menu. "There. It's done. I've officially diagnosed that this school is not for you. The exit's down the hall to your left."

Dalton unfolded the Tehachapi High transfer papers stuck in a compartment in his tie. They were in triplicate, signed and notarized. Inference poked through them and then sighed.

"You're wasting your time. Wesley Payne was a suicide. The case is already closed."

THE PRIVATE DICK HANDBOOK, RULE #6
Always speak Truth to authority.
If you have no idea what the Truth is,
speaking Obnoxious to authority sometimes works too.

"The case is closed when I close it."

Inference's eyes narrowed. "We don't like that tone of voice around here."

"So don't use it."

She filled out a demerit form with big, looping strokes. "Very clever. You can now spend the rest of the semester investigating the mysteries of detention."

"Thirty percent."

Inference looked up. "Of what?"

"The money that was stolen out of your office. The hundred grand. Deal I'm offering is: I find it, you give me thirty percent. Plus, while I look into The Body, you keep the Fack Cult out of my way."

"How do you know about the money?"

"It was a rumor," Dalton said. "That you just confirmed."

A drop of sweat carved a runnel through Principal Inference's blush. Dalton could tell she was trying to decide if she should let loose a real smashed-lamp hair-puller, or be all *I have no idea what you're blah blah blahing about.*

"Six percent."

"Seventeen."

"Ten. That's as high as I go, Rev. Ten is sheer gravy."

Dalton needed that gravy. Bad. But it meant he'd only have till the weekend to find a killer *and* a stack of cash. He'd spent six months setting up a deal for his brother. After Saturday at midnight it was going to turn into a moldy pumpkin.

"Deal."

Inference settled somewhere between pissed and relieved as Dalton gestured to the painting behind her, an amateurish job of a jowly man in a cheap suit.

"My father. Hannibal Inference."

"I take it the cash was stuffed behind him?" In *Another Day, Another Dahlia*, Lexington Cole had found a missing diamond stiletto concealed by an heiress's portrait.

She frowned, then got up and pulled the hinged frame aside, revealing a small wall safe. Next to the dial were freshly drilled holes, corkscrews of metal filings resting on the sill.

Dalton crossed his legs. "So, okay, you've been squeezing cliques for a weekly skim of their rackets. No surprise there. What I don't get is how you didn't figure sooner or later one of them was going to decide it'd be easier to hit your stash than spend the semester stealing Euclidian lunch money."

Inference's eyes flashed. She leaned forward to rest her

17

chin on the steeple of her fingers, her face about six inches from Dalton's. "Did I mention, by any chance, Mr. Rev, that I called your parents this morning?"

"You didn't."

"I did."

"You wouldn't."

"I would."

They stared at one another. Parents, like libraries, sporting events, and little sisters, were off-limits.

"Nice woman, your mother," Inference continued, pressing her advantage. "She's worried, unsurprisingly, about your grades. Your father is of the opinion that if you'd only apply yourself more, you could be college material."

THE PRIVATE DICK HANDBOOK, RULE #7
The weaker the play, the weaker the bluff.
Also, never trust a redhead.

"There are dogs barking in your hallways, Inference. Balls on one side, Caskets on the other. That leaves you in the middle, cashless. Why call my parents and risk extra heat? The way I see it, you didn't call anyone. And while you weren't calling, you didn't say shite."

Principal Inference played with her bangs. "Well, you can't blame a girl for trying."

"Yeah, you can. You can blame a girl for just about anything."

Principal Inference stood, a foot taller and forty pounds heavier than Dalton. Even so, he could see the man in the blue pin-striped suit over her left shoulder. The suit ducked behind a tree as Inference punched something into Dalton's gut. "You're late for class. Here's your permission slip."

He took it and walked to the door, trying to breathe.

"One more thing, Rev. Crack the books. You talk a good game, but that's not going to help if you fall below a C average. You go below a C and you're out of here, like *that*."

Dalton took one last look out the window, but the pinstripe was gone.

As soon as the door closed, Principal Inference punched the intercom.

"Miss Bucket?"

"Cute, isn't he?"

"Get Kurt Tarot out of class. Now."

Honey Bucket gulped. Something dropped from her desk and broke. "Out of class? What should I say?"

Principal Inference looked at the portrait of her father, Hannibal, who stared back with marked disapproval.

"Tell him we have a problem that needs immediate fixing."

CHAPTER 3
EYES LIKE BURNING FIRE.
AS OPPOSED TO THE OTHER KIND.

As soon as the door was closed, Mole materialized out of nowhere, slapping Dalton's back. "I'm telling you, crackstar, that action with the scooter was classic." He did a western six-shooter routine, spinning imaginary Colts on his fingers. "Huffing up to Chuff? Trust me, *no one* huffs to Chuff."

"I just hate when there's mud on my helmet."

"Whatever, Johnny Rambo!" Mole held out his knuckles for a bump. "What do you say we head over to the biology lab and free some POWs?"

"Maybe after lunch," Dalton said, bumping back.

"So what do we do now?"

"We?"

"Okay, what are you doing now?"

"I need to go see my client."

"Who's that?"

"Whoever pays."

"What if I paid?"

"Paid for what?"

"To be your sidekick."

"You want to *pay* me to hire you?"

Mole pushed his glasses up his nose. "Everyone needs a sidekick. Even Aquaman had a sidekick."

"He did?"

"Squid Boy. Crab Boy or whoever. Helping unbeach whales and foil polluters. I could do that."

Dalton held out a hand. "You're hired. That'll be two hundred bucks."

Mole pretended to search his pockets, coming up empty. "Do you take checks?"

Dalton turned toward his next class. The hallway of Salt River High was exactly the same as every other school: dirty tile, broken lockers, porcelain water fountains, and walls covered with handmade posters for events that had happened years ago. They entered the slipstream of students, forced to the edge, shouldering into couples mid-grope, the cinder-block walls wet with smoochy condensation.

"It must be spring; there's love in the air."

Mole smirked. "Yeah, the Pilgrims called it necking. In the fifties it was making out. Goths say suck-facing. At Salt River it's just between classes on a Monday morning."

"You make that up or read it in a magazine?"

Mole tapped his temple three times. "Thank Bob I'm a Euclidian."

They passed a janitor mopping up something red. It could have been blood. It could have been a spilled smoothie. Near the janitor was a skinny kid with a newly bandaged thumb.

Some other kids surrounded him, all of them asking "You got shot?"

"No, I got a blister," he kept saying.

Dalton found his locker. It was blocked by cliques showing off their wares: stolen test scores, fake iPods, and rodent cashmere. A few Face Boi were selling soda bottles from a cooler, the name RUSH handwritten over the old labels with a Sharpie. "Got an important quiz to study for? Buy it now—I only got six left!"

A pale kid handed over a twenty and twisted the top open, pupils immediately pinned. He let out a manic whoop and ran in place for a minute, spit caked in the corners of his mouth, before taking off down the hall. A line quickly formed, pushing and shoving until the last bottle was gone.

"They say Rush is made out of Euclidian blood. It's supposed to make you smarter."

"Who says?"

Mole shrugged, tracing a rectangle in the air with two fingers. "Check it, new bumper sticker: Guns Don't Kill Kids, Rush Kills Kids."

"And you believe it?"

Mole pulled at his goatee hairs, considering. "Some people say that's why they did Wes Payne. Drained him for his sangria. Since he was, you know, the smartest dude in school."

As Dalton fiddled with his locker, a hatchet-faced kid slid in front of him. "Here's my offer: Five bucks to open it for you now, or, twenty a month to remember your combination on a permanent basis."

"I'll pass."

The kid shrugged, already latching onto another prospective sale.

"Scam Wow," Mole said. "Guy would steal your liver, sauté it with onions, and charge you extra for rice."

Dalton's locker banged open. Twenty inches of banana peels, gym shorts, and old quizzes moldered at the bottom. He closed the door as whispers swelled down the hall, building like an electrical storm, little buzzing clouds forming under the asbestos ceiling panels. Bull Lemia stopped hawking goods. Silverspoon stopped giggling at private jokes. Dalton turned as they all parted, a girl suddenly owning the hallway like she'd just grabbed the mic at center stage. She was Asian, with dyed pink hair, thigh-high leather boots, and legs that went on practically forever.

She was absolutely smoking.

She was disco atomic.

She was Fat Man *and* Little Boy.

Dalton recognized his cue. It was the exact moment Lexington Cole would have turned on a Cuban heel, walked over without a word, and crushed his lips against hers. He'd done it to Minka Lynx in *There Are No Corners in a Rubber Room*. He'd done it to Calumny Ride in *Who Isn't Buried in Trotsky's Grave?* Lex would have smoldered her silly, and then pulled back, saying something like *You taste like doom, baby.*

Dalton, instead, did nothing.

Mole made an imaginary rectangle with his fingers. "Check it, new bumper sticker: Your Kid May Be on the Honor Roll, but That Chick Is a Whiskey Lick."

"A whiskey what?"

"Dude, that's Cassiopeia Jones. Head of Foxxes."

"Fox's?"

"Dos equis. Two *x*'s. New clique in town."

"What's their angle?"

Mole shrugged. "Aside from handing out dagwoodies like Halloween candy? Half the guys in school with rodneys at attention twenty-four/seven? Got me."

Cassiopeia sauntered over. Her black lipstick glistened.

"Gossip said there was a new fish around. Said some real hard case row, row, rowed his boat down the Salt River."

Dalton eyeballed Cassiopeia's outfit. "You look different. What's with all the war paint?"

"You *know* her?" Mole asked.

"You mean biblically?"

"Yes. That's exactly what I mean."

"More like Judas."

The Crowdarounds laughed, their numbers swelling as Text Mob LOL texted the play-by-play to the rest of the school. A tall, thin teacher came around the corner, urging everyone to go to class. They ignored him. He alluded to detention. Someone slipped him a five and he went away.

"Go away, Lester," Cassiopeia said.

Dalton raised an eyebrow. "Lester?"

Mole looked down at the pineapples on his shirt, a purple pattern that hung over his protruding belly. "Mole. *Molester.* Hilarious. Say it a few times. Get it out of your system. Can we move on?"

"Yes, you can," Cassiopeia said, snapping her fingers. A dangerous-looking girl with a single blond braid stood at Mole's elbow. He instantly faded into the Crowdarounds.

"Dalton, Dalton." Cassiopeia sighed. "Still with the detective routine?"

"It's not that complicated. Add killer, subtract body, solve for x. What can I say? It's a career."

"You're not even eighteen. You're failing algebra."

"And you killed Wesley Payne."

Cassiopeia didn't even blink. "I suppose I could have. But honestly? I'd have to say no."

"Then enough with the junior varsity patter. This interview is over."

Cassiopeia twisted the silver ring in her eyebrow. "Listen, we both left some messy things behind at Tehachapi, okay? I just didn't know that messy thing would follow me here."

"I had no idea you transferred to Salt River."

Cassiopeia bent closer. She smelled like an extra hour of daylight. "Dalton, what happened to us?"

"What *us*?"

"So I got tired of waiting around! So I went to the prom with someone else!"

"Yeah, some haircut. What was his name? Keith?"

"Keith was nice. Keith bought me a corsage."

"Sounds like a keeper."

"Why do we talk like this? It makes me feel empty inside."

Dalton fished in his pocket for some change. "So open your mouth. I'll drop in a quarter and we can all listen to it clang around for a while."

The Crowdarounds roared with laughter.

THE PRIVATE DICK HANDBOOK, RULE #8
Never fall for a girl named after a constellation
or a European city. Especially not twice.

"Whatever, Rev," Cassiopeia snapped, sashaying away. "Losers are as losers do. Just see if you can keep from grabbing too many others on your way down with you."

The bell rang. As the crowd reluctantly broke up, Dalton wiped his forehead with his tie, wondering if he'd been able to hide how impressed he was with Cassiopeia's new look.

CHAPTER 4
WHEREIN DALTON GOES TO THE SHOP FOR A MAJOR TUNE-UP

When Dalton finally found his second-period class, he was late. He put his hand on the doorknob as a Scam Wow zipped up behind him, looking like a sideways ax. "Pssst."

"What?"

"Here's my offer: School pass. Totally legit. Fifty bucks."

He held up a piece of paper signed by Inference and Miss Honey Bucket.

"No thanks."

"Okay, forty. Only forty bucks."

Dalton walked into the room. The teacher, a tiny Kleenex of a woman in an enormous cable-knit sweater, said nothing. There was an empty seat in back, right next to the girl with the blond pixie. Dalton sat and took out his notebook, listening as the teacher recounted the short, flaming arc of the Etruscan civilization. They were good with pottery, but not so hot at predicting the behavior of volcanoes. As the class settled into its first layer of bored despair, someone cut a One-Cheek Sneak. There were giggles and moans as it hovered like a rogue weather pattern. Some kids moved closer to the windows. Macy used the commotion to hand Dalton an elaborately folded note. It said, in her adorably proper handwriting:

—*It's you, isn't it?*

Dalton took out his pen and wrote:

—*Yeah, it's me.*

They continued to pass the note back and forth.

—*Thank Bob you're finally here.*

—*Not sure Bob has much to do with it. Speaking of money, do you have my deposit? I've already had a few… expenses.*

Macy wrapped the butterfly hairpin in the next note. Dalton had mailed it to her so he'd know who his client was, an idea that had actually worked. It was going straight in the Private Dick Handbook.

—*I'll pay you after class.*

Dalton pocketed the butterfly and wrote back.

—*Good. Also, I need you to pull my coat on some things before I can get to work.*

—*Pull your coat?*

Dalton gave her a sideways glance to see if she was kidding, but Macy was staring straight ahead, cheekbones lightly shadowed in profile, eyes betraying nothing as the teacher glanced over. God, she was cute.

—*Give me more information. You were right about Inference's safe. Someone jacked it for sure. And I need to see the suicide note.*

—*Oh. I guess we can meet out at the bus stop after school. But be careful. You really made an impression on Jeffrey.*

Dalton nodded. It was disconcerting to be sitting next to her after all the nights they'd spent IMing, talking about the case. Her mostly talking him into taking it. At first he'd refused; articles in the *Salt River Courier* made it sound like the police had it pretty much sewn up. A suicide. But then she'd mentioned Inference. And the rumors about Inference's safe. It was more cash than he'd ever had a chance to sneeze at, even on a percentage basis. Dalton already felt like he knew Macy. And he could tell she felt the same. The flirty shorthand they'd developed had made it just that much harder to refuse.

—*Don't worry about Chuff. Anyway, you can tell me all this later.*

—*But where do we go? What if someone sees?*

Miss Splonge turned around mid-ramble, knee-deep in the origins of Dionysian cults. She stared directly at Macy. She stared at the note. She stared at Dalton. Then she went back to writing on the board.

—*Don't worry about it. I'll give you a ride. You can pose as my tutor.*

—*I'm not very good at posing.*

—*Yeah, but you're a Euclidian, aren't you? Perfect cover story. Besides, I really need to get my grades up, or I'm not going to be around long enough to do you any good.*

—*Okay. I meant to mention, by the way, there's someone else you need to watch out for. A bunch of someone elses.*

—*Who?*

—*Pinker Casket.*

—*What's a pinker casket?* Dalton wrote, as the paper was torn away. He fished for his wallet, ready to slip Splonge a twenty, but it wasn't Splonge. It was a tall rocker with permed hair and a cheesy leather jacket. He had rings in his lip and eyebrow and nose. He had studs punched in his ears. He wore a shirt that had a picture of a pink casket and said PINKER CASKET SO TOTALLY ROCKS!

"Love notes?" The guy laughed, reading in a flowery voice: *"Oh my darling, even one minute is one minute too long to be away from you...."*

Dalton grabbed the paper back and palmed it to Macy, who slipped it into her skirt.

"Hey, Miss Splonge?" the rocker asked. "How did this purse get in here?"

The teacher turned from the chalkboard. "Mister Freeley, please sit down."

"Call me Mick." He smiled as the second rocker got up and stood on the other side of Dalton. His shirt said PINKY TUSCADERO DIES TONIGHT. He also wore black lipstick and looked like he'd woken up in the middle of a middling Victorian novel.

"Yeah, maybe this dangle found his way into the wrong class, Miss Splonge!"

"I don't think—"

"This probe could have taken the wrong hallway! He could have, you know, even taken the wrong highway exit."

"Please, if you—"

"This knob could have gotten the wrong schedule! Check your master schedule, Miss Splonge! He might even be enrolled in a totally different school!"

"Yeah, like that one across town for motards!"

"Boys?" the teacher asked. "Can you sit down? Please?"

The door banged open. A lo-fi buzz filled the room, as if someone jammed a nail clipper into one of the sockets. A Plath whimpered. A New Skid joined her. Out of the shadows emerged a third rocker, taller than the others, with a black sheaf of hair gelled up off his forehead. Tattoos ringed his neck like chains, except the links were Latin cursive. Dalton knew enough to half-translate, something about trees and the blood of tyrants.

"I'll need to see your pass," Miss Splonge said. The rocker handed it to her impaled on the end of a long black fingernail. Out in the hallway, a Scam Wow was bent over, holding his bleeding mouth.

"Your papers seem to be in order, but you're tardy."

"Funny," the rocker said. "I don't feel tardy."

People snickered uncertainly as the rocker walked down the aisle, cowboy boots clacking, until he stood directly in front of Dalton. His T-shirt said THE CASKET OF AMONTADILDO. Up close, he was ugly and handsome at the same time, with a long face and ludicrous sideburns, looking either eighteen or fifty depending on the light, like Rasputin's younger and older brother simultaneously. He looked like he'd spent six straight months on a tour bus without seeing the sun, or maybe six straight months in prison sharpening his teeth with a chunk of concrete.

THE PRIVATE DICK HANDBOOK, RULE #9
Does a showdown with this character
smell like hospital time followed by about
ten thousand dollars worth of Freudian analysis?
Um, yeah.

31

"I'm not getting up," Dalton said. "If that's what you're waiting for."

"He don't want your desk," Mick Freeley said.

"Duh," the other rocker said. Dalton squirmed, finding it hard to believe he'd let himself get flanked so easily. What old-school Dick lets himself get boxed in like a two-dollar Happy Meal? It was the girl. Macy. He was paying too much attention to her. To her cute neck and her cute hands. Totally unprofessional.

"I'm Kurt Tarot," Kurt Tarot said, his accent pure industrial mishap. "But since this is *my* school, you can call me *zir*."

The word *zir* echoed around the room, which was otherwise entirely silent. Everyone waited for Dalton to respond. To get up and throw spinning kicks. To bust out the perfect line. To radio in air cover.

"Please don't drink my blood, sir," he finally said.

No one laughed.

Except Kurt Tarot. He waved his fingers at Miss Splonge, who gulped and went back to writing on the board. The other rockers pinned Dalton's legs beneath the tiny desk. There was nowhere to go, no way to make a move. In *Forty Leagues Under Berlin*, Lex Cole had been trapped in a German pillbox with nothing but a spoon. In *Right Cross, Mob Boss*, he'd fought off a gang of hopped-up Zoot Suiters with a leather wing tip. Neither scenario was much help now. Kurt Tarot leaned over and began to whisper. His tongue was pierced with a huge silver skull. The skull had two ruby eyes that blinked with each word, the hunk of metal forcing a *z* sound each time it caught on his glottal downslope.

"Word is you're here about The Body. I wonder who it was

azked you to come around, get all nosy in everyone's business, Dick? I know it wasn't me, Dick. And if *I* didn't ask, Dick, then *you* shouldn't have come, Dick."

"Totally shouldn't have," Mick Freeley agreed, his eyes lined with mascara and the desire to hurt.

The rest of the class had already gotten up and leaned against the walls to watch. Some kids came in from the hallway. The Scam Wow, with a handful of folded bills and a swollen mouth, was taking action. Odds on Dalton? Long. The Scam Wow slipped some bills under the apple on Miss Splonge's desk, and she turned back to the board. Macy stood by the door. Dalton was amazed by how expressive her face was. Just a slight lifting of her chin clearly said, *Should I try to get someone?*

Dalton shook his head. *Who?*

Her eyes flashed. *I'm sorry I got you into this.*

His eyes flashed back. *I got myself into this.*

"So who waz it?" Tarot asked, the skull making an insect *click* against the back of his teeth. "Some parent hired you? Somebody for some reason thinks they have a conzcience?"

Dalton shrugged. "Sorry, Count Chocula, but I've got zero clue what you're yammering about."

"Time to play you a knuckle song," Tarot said. Mick Freeley kicked the desk leg, causing Dalton to sprawl onto the floor.

THE PRIVATE DICK HANDBOOK, RULE #10
Knuckle song?

Dalton tried to get to his feet. Kurt Tarot spun around and got him into a headlock, forearms like steel cable from playing endless power chords. The other Caskets began to punch and kick, wearing heavy rings that dug between Dalton's ribs. He yelped in pain, managing to catch Mick Freeley in the gut with his heel. There was a satisfying *hurk*. Dalton pulled the jeweled butterfly from his pocket and stuck the pin deep into the second rocker's hand, which made him jump back and swear like he'd been stung by a wasp. Kurt Tarot bore down, his breath like copper pipe and spot-welds. Dalton could hear a Splongey voice above it all: "*Mwah, mwah, mwah,* pottery *mwah,* cartography *mwah,* Zeus *mwah*…"

"I know…where the…hundred thousand is…"

Tarot's grip lessened for a second. He put his teeth right in Dalton's ear, like he was getting ready to gnaw it off.

"*Where?*"

"You…killed…Wesley…Payne."

Tarot's arms clamped harder. A gurgle rose in Dalton's throat, stayed there.

"Everyone has to pick a side," Tarot whispered. "Even if it's suicide."

Dalton's face tingled from a lack of oxygen. A little cartoon vampire appeared on the tip of his nose and did a little cartoon jig, adjusting its cape with a deep bow. Just as Dalton passed out, he swore he heard a *bang, bang, bang.* It could have been gunshots. Or it could have been his vertebrae snapping.

CHAPTER 5
YES, IT'S A FLASHBACK

Dalton stuck out his thumb. Landon laughed and plopped his little brother onto the back of his motorcycle. Then he plopped the helmet onto Dalton's head, a few sizes too big, so that he looked like a skinny, pimply lollipop. It was the middle of Dalton's freshman year, Landon was a senior. It had been a great few months, at least as far as Dalton was concerned. Being the younger brother of the star running back of Tehachapi High's football team sucked in some ways, like constantly being reminded that you not only weren't a star yourself, you didn't even play because your mother thought you were too skinny. And that she was right. Dalton joined the chess team instead, and even though he was the strongest player, it was still like saying you were the least Assy out of a van full of Assbournes. On the other hand, being Landon's younger brother meant an endless train of sexy girls laughed and flirted around the house in their tight outfits and complicated perfumes and giggle-twisted bangs. Dalton got to hang out while Landon and his friends goofed off in the backyard, listening to music, punching each other's arms and saying "No effing way! Get outta here! She did *what*?"

Landon's friends all called Dalton "little bro." They didn't tell him to leave them alone, didn't squeeze the loose skin on his chest and twist, didn't push him to the ground and laugh like what happened most days at school. After games, Dalton's father would replay the entire thing aloud from memory, adding in details and comments, smacking the steering wheel every time Landon faked some kid half out of his jock. Dalton would be in the back, next to Turd Unit's child seat, playing a parallel fantasy reel in which he was the one barreling through the secondary, while his mother endlessly searched the radio for an acceptable song.

Landon strapped on his football helmet, since they had only one real motorcycle one, and got on the bike as well.

"When are they going to make you captain?" Dalton asked, unable to fit his arms around his brother's muscular back.

"Don't want to be captain."

Landon fiddled with the choke, jamming the kick start and trying to get his old Kawasaki to cough to life. They were going out to the lake together, Landon having talked Dalton into ditching school.

"Why not?"

"I dunno," Landon said, getting off the bike. He had long-ish hair, which the coach hated but didn't dare give him crap about, and was always flipping it out of his eyes. "Unless it's Captain Kirk, *captain* just doesn't feel all that cool, you know?"

"Not really."

Landon fiddled with the bike some more and then gave up. "I guess we're not going anywhere, dude. Sorry."

Dalton slid down and took the helmet off. "That's okay."

"Didn't really want to go swimming anyway."

"You didn't?"

"Nah. Wanted to talk to you."

"*Really?*"

"Yeah, really. Something important we gotta get straight."

Landon sat in the grass and Dalton joined him, not liking the way it pricked the underside of his legs. His brother peeled a tall weed and stuck it in the corner of his mouth. Dalton thought about doing the same, but didn't want to be a copy-cat, and also sort of worried a dog might have taken a piss there.

"I hitched up."

"To who, Donna? Or wait, that redhead? Mary?"

Landon laughed, throwing his head back. His teeth gleamed. "No, dude. Hitched up with the jarheads. I'm going Full Metal Marine."

Dalton stared at his brother, his face suddenly cold. "You're leaving?"

"Guess so, man. Unless they're gonna let me do boot camp in the backyard."

Dalton nodded, just able to make the urge to cry stop in time.

"When?"

"Four months. Soon as I graduate."

"Huh. How come?"

Landon kicked off his boots and stuck his toes into the dirt.

"Maybe you hadn't heard, but there's a war on. The Front called and I answered the phone."

"Why?"

"Had to make a decision. No scholarship coming. Jobs around here? What, like delivering pizza? Landscaping? No, thanks."

"What about football?"

"Sure, in a small town like this. In college? Those bad boys'd eat me for breakfast. Too small, too slow. Besides, even if I thought I could make it, no one's offering. Except the military. They're offering plenty."

"Offering what? To get you killed?"

Landon's eyes narrowed. He pulled a long string off the frayed end of his shorts. "Anyway, broha, what I wanted to talk about was Mom and Dad."

"Okay."

"I'll be making decent money, sending some home. But, obviously, I'm not going to be here to deal. That falls on you. Kicking in a little extra with a job, plus helping Mom out with Captain La-Z-Boy."

"What about him?"

"You know what about him."

Their father had been laid off from BoxxMart, hurt lowering forty-pound tubs of applesauce by hand after a forklift had broken down. They'd pulled his insurance and pink-slipped him for not filling out the right forms.

Dalton frowned. "When his back is better he'll find something else."

Landon spat out the blade of grass and selected another one. Birds flew over their heads in a ragged V.

"There's nothing wrong with Dad's back."

"What do you mean?"

"What I mean is, he doesn't need that brace anymore. He needs that brace like he needs another remote control."

Dalton looked down at his lap. An ant crawled across his thigh. He thought about mashing it and then just flicked it away.

Landon tapped his forehead. "It's nothing you need to get all uptight about, but Dad's not going to be leaving the house much any time soon. Dad's going to be sitting in the dark a lot, cause that's where his head is at. In the meantime, Mom's gonna need you to get up off your ham. You hear me?"

"Yeah," Dalton said.

"Good."

"But, like what do I do?"

"Pudding Patrol, for one."

"So I bring dessert."

"It's not just pudding, it's his meds. Mom crushes them up; he won't take them otherwise."

Dalton nodded, understanding for the first time there was an entire drama being played out in his house that he didn't have tickets to. "I'll make sure."

"Outstanding," Landon said. He stood and stretched, the ropy muscles along his neck kinking.

"Landon?"

"Yeah?"

"You gonna kill people?"

"Nah, brohman. I mean, I'm gonna get trained and get lethal, sure. But then I'm gonna get assigned stateside. Fix helicopters or something. Drink beer and lie on a cot. No shooting for me."

"No shooting for you," Dalton repeated, as their mother's car pulled into the driveway. She jumped out, furious. The school had called, both of her boys playing hooky. Sherry Rev laid into Landon, giving him a lecture. He took it for a while, and then eased onto the Kawasaki, which, amazingly, started with the first kick. He tore out of the driveway without his helmet or even his boots, leaving Dalton alone with his mother. She held her purse against her forehead for a minute before grabbing the extra skin on his chest and yanking him into the house.

CHAPTER 6
A SNOUT'S WORTH OF TLC

Dalton was lying on a cot. A nurse was gently dressing the cut above his eye, wearing white nylons and a white cap with a red cross on the front. When she was done, she pressed his dressing firmly and stood to the side. There was a little swipe machine on her belt. She turned it on, swiped Dalton's credit card, slipped it back into his sock, and handed him a receipt. A hundred even. Near the gurney was a tip jar. She looked at it meaningfully. Dalton sighed, pulled a few bills from his pocket, and tossed them in. The nurse nodded, giving him a little smile. Next to her was a vending machine. Instead of snacks, it was filled with gauze and tape and cough syrup and Band-Aids. The nurse took some bills from the tip jar, fed them into the machine, and pressed N-9. The machine whirred, a metal coil inside turned, and a prescription for antibacterial ointment fell into the slot. She pulled it out and handed it to Dalton.

"Hey, lady, can I get some treatment too?" asked a kid dressed in black. The nurse ignored him. He had long greasy hair, big leather boots dangling from the gurney's edge.

Dalton half sat up, wincing, ready to fight. Or at least fight him off. "Who're you with?"

The kid smiled. "Take it easy, chief. I'm Kokrock City. We're a few levels down from Pinker Casket."

"Good choice." Dalton exhaled, lying back again. "Those Pinkertons are too nice for their own good."

"They're a bunch of knobs," the kid said, toying with his bangs. "And their band blows. But what're you gonna do, play football? At least Kokrock's got some style."

Dalton looked at the kid's wound. There was blood trickling from a small round circle on his calf.

"What's that all about?"

"Ah, nothing. Poked myself with a pencil."

"A pencil, huh?"

The kid picked at his wound absentmindedly. "So who're *you* with?"

"Independent."

"Oh, shite," Kokrock said, his default frown suddenly a wide-open O. "No wonder you got tuned up! Are you the dude from this morning? With the *scooter*?"

"I guess so."

Kokrock whistled. "Word in the halls is you're not going to make it to the end of the day. Word is you're toast by sixth period."

"Where did you get that?"

"Oh, man, I heard *all* about you."

"So did we," said two burly Snouts, slamming the already-open door against the frame. Detectives. One blond, whose visitor pass said ESTRADA, and one Hispanic, whose tag said HUTCH.

"Just in the oink of time," Dalton said.

Kokrock City laughed.

"Take a sniff," Hutch told him coolly, scratching neck stubble like he was in a procedural show where the cops examined microscopic evidence and spotted little clues that less attractive and less perceptive cops somehow missed.

"But my leg hasn't even been dressed yet!"

"So shut up and bleed," Hutch snapped, like he was in a drama where cops had angry wives and cross-dressing sons and a taste for cheap scotch that they took out on groveling informants. "But do it somewhere else."

"Guess I got no cash anyway," Kokrock muttered, but didn't move, staring at the nurse, who was now turning the pages of a magazine.

Hutch squeezed his hands together, all armpit-stain and gym reps in a cheap polyester shirt. "Do I need to tell you again, or am I dragging you into the hallway by your short-hairs?"

Kokrock City got up, bumping knuckles with Dalton. "Be cool, brother," he said, before limping through the door.

"You need to leave too, ma'am," Estrada told the nurse. "Police business."

The nurse held out her hand. Estrada stared at it. Hutch stared at it. Estrada finally pulled out his wallet and laid a wrinkly five in her palm. The nurse gave him two aspirin and left.

Hutch slid the deadbolt like he was in a show about dirty cops who took cash from the mob and used it as down payments on their dream fishing boat, until someone named Jimmy the Nose came and visited in the middle of the night.

"Just what kind of Dick you think you are, kid?"

"The kind that doesn't taste like pork?"

Hutch turned his squat torso in one motion, giving Dalton a left cross to the chin. Things went dark. A company of cartoon pigs did a production of *Swine Lake* on his chest. Dalton woke up, staring at tongue depressors spilled on the floor. He counted them. Twelve. He counted them again. Eighteen.

"...did you have to hit him for?" Estrada was saying in his weary cop voice. "Now we're going to have to file a 46-20, and if the kid's hurt, we..."

Dalton sat up, massaging his back teeth with two fingers. "Don't worry. No one's filing charges."

Hutch had Dalton's pistol on his lap. "Some kids pack lunch, you know," he said, then cracked it open. The barrel was empty. No bullets. No firing pin. Hutch aimed the gun at himself and pulled the trigger like he was in a show about cops who are too dumb to breathe, holding his finger over the tiny flame until it burned. "Ouch! Em eff!"

Estrada handed Dalton a towel and some ice. "My partner tends to get carried away."

"Forget it," Dalton said. His face hurt, but not too badly. He'd pretty much been waiting his whole career to be roughed up by the Snouts, and it had finally happened. He was determined to take it like a man. "So what's the rumpus?"

"Listen, son, we know why you're here."

"So do I. You killed Wesley Payne."

Hutch circled his ear with one finger, the universal symbol for *I'm not creative enough to come up with a new way to suggest that someone's crazy.*

44

Estrada cleared his throat. "Bottom line, we, ah...we don't need you stepping into the middle of an open investigation."

Dalton dabbed his lip. "The investigation's still open? I thought it was closed. Or are you talking about your investigation into the stolen hundred grand?"

Hutch glared. He straightened a paper clip and began cleaning under his fingernails like he was in a show about psychopath cops with a fetish for sad-eyed runaways trying to enroll in secretarial school and get their lives back on track.

"Anyway," Estrada said. "Consider this an official warning. It's time you leave things to the pros."

Dalton considered agreeing the case was sewn up. Or that there was no case at all. For one thing, it was probably true. A kid wrapped himself in duct tape and went all INXS in the end zone? It could happen. Of course, it meant the kid had been truly twisted. It meant he needed help and none of the Fack Cult, from Inference down to the guidance counselors, did shite about it. *You want some guidance? Here's a tip: Shut your mouth and suffer alone.* Besides, even Lex Cole got tired of being punched after a couple hundred pages.

THE PRIVATE DICK HANDBOOK, RULE #11
Keep pissing cops off. A pissed cop is a sloppy cop.
A sloppy cop is a font of information.

"Sorry, Estrada. I never back off a case once I start it."

Estrada shook his head wearily. "This thing was a suicide, okay, son? There *is* no case."

"Plain as a bell," Hutch said. "Clear and simple."

"The family's suffered enough."

"Cut and sealed. Pasted and dried."

"And if that doesn't sound good, we may have to call your parents."

Dalton gulped, forcing himself into The Best Defense Is a Better Offense mode. "Fine. Answer me one question straight, and I'll leave it alone."

Estrada nodded.

"Were Wesley Payne's arms free? Under all that duct tape? You bother to try and work out how he got himself up on that post?"

"That's three questions," Hutch said.

"We're still looking into it," Estrada said. "Doesn't change anything."

"Okay, then what about the suicide note? You guys really farcked that up, huh? I mean, I hear it's missing."

Hutch managed to push his way around Estrada far enough to swing a right hook, which half connected. Dalton wiped his mouth with his tie, as a kid with slicked-back hair popped into the room. He had a mean-looking camera with a huge black lens, the flash going off, *bang, bang, bang.* Hutch held his cheap sports coat up in front of his face. Estrada didn't bother.

"We'll see you soon," Hutch warned.

Estrada pocketed Dalton's gun, slamming the door behind him.

"Thanks, Slim," Dalton said.

"Ronnie." The kid shook out a smoke and lit it in one practiced motion. "Newport."

"Ronnie. Right."

Newport looked at his lens, wiped off some dirt that wasn't there, took one more picture of Dalton, and slipped out of the room. A minute later, the nurse came back, fingering her credit card machine.

"You okay, hon? Need some more treatment?"

Dalton felt for his wallet, then looked at his watch. "What time do the buses leave?"

"Twenty minutes," the nurse said, examining the new bruise blossoming on his cheek.

"I need to meet someone."

"There's plenty of time," the nurse soothed, tearing open a new Band-Aid. "Relax, slugger, this one's on the house."

CHAPTER 7
BLOOD EUCLIDIAN

Dalton found his scooter lying on its side, dinged up pretty good, a scratch here and there, some paint chipped away. Just like its owner. He unlocked his helmet from the wheel as a piece of paper fell out, fluttering to the ground. It was an index card with large block handwriting.

LOOK AT LEE HARVIES. LOOK CLOSE. AND THEN LOOK CLOSER. YOU STAY ON THE ROOF LONG ENOUGH, YOU EVENTUALLY SEE EVERYTHING.

DUH.

There was no name, no signature. Dalton sniffed it. No smell. He had a fingerprint kit at home, but no database to check it against, so unless he'd written the note to himself, there wasn't much point in dusting it. He grabbed the scooter's bent handlebars and righted the frame, driving over to where the buses queued. Most of them were gone, and there was almost no one around. He circled the Dumpster, for a second swearing he saw the man in the blue pin-striped suit peering from behind bags of garbage, but when he blinked, the man was gone. Dalton chalked it up to the fringe benefits of two beatings in one day, and did another loop, almost running up the back bumper of a van parked in the alley. It was an old, rusted-out Econoline covered with bumper stickers and graffiti. He knew even before pulling up alongside it was going to have a name spray-painted across the doors. And he was right. In ugly pink letters, next to anarchy symbols, curse words, and the last names of famous serial killers, it said *Whatever, Lesser, Joe Mama Besser.* And below that, in even larger letters, *Pinker Casket.* Dalton looked around. There was no one in the alley.

How incredibly stupid would it be to break into Tarot's van?

Dalton let his scooter idle, then gunned the engine. It made a loud *blaat*, coughed, and then *blaat*ed some more. No one looked around the corner. There were no sounds or sirens or yelling.

What if a Casket's in there, waiting for me?

Dalton cupped his hands against the glare, peering in the driver's side window. Empty.

What if I weren't such a pussy and stopped asking questions and just did what I knew I was going to do all along?

He went around to the back of the van, loosened the bolts holding the license plate, and then slid the plate into the driver's side door frame flat, shoving it into the gap between the window and the handle. In *I Wiped Something Off My Cheek and It Was the Floor*, Lex Cole had broken into a '66 Bonneville filled with stolen Krugerrands the same way. Dalton doubted it would actually work, but when he yanked the plate, the indentations from the pressed letters caught the lock. Amazingly, the knob popped up. Dalton replaced the plate, then stood with his hands in his pockets, whistling. No sound, no movement.

Quit stalling.

Inside, the van smelled like a lemur cage. The floorboards were filled with trash, fast-food wrappers, CDs, and clumps of napkins. He pushed aside the pink bedsheet that separated the front seats from the back. The hold was essentially a dorm room. A mattress, musical equipment, and a little fridge. Jars of hair dye, leather socks, rubbing alcohol, Q-tips, empty plastic bottles of hand-labeled Rush, rolls of duct tape, and a toothbrush that looked like it had been used to scrub down a crime scene. There were books, mostly Sun Tzu, Machiavelli, and Aristotle. There were biographies of Scipio Africanus and Mussolini. Under the books was a long rectangular box. Dalton nudged the lid aside. Ax handles. Hickory. Maybe two dozen. Old-school armaments. Caskets were ready for action, but apparently not ready enough to piss off Lee Harvies. Dalton turned, knocking over a hot plate full of canned ravioli. It was still warm. Which meant Tarot had just been here, and was probably coming home soon. Which also meant the back of the van was the last place in the world, aside from Jeff Chuff's jockstrap, that Dalton wanted to be. Especially holding what he was holding. The thing he'd just kicked with his foot. The thing he'd picked up, disbelievingly, and held in his hand. The thing that was unmistakable.

It couldn't be anyone else's.

Dalton fingered the strands of hair gently.

No.

It was sticky inside. Flaps hung down from beneath the hairline like pieces of scalp.

Please, no.

It was Cassiopeia Jones's pink wig.

Cassiopeia. With Tarot.

Bam.

Dalton dropped the wig as he heard a voice. There was a banging on the door. *Hey!* He picked up a heavy frying pan, grease dribbling down his wrist as he held it aloft.

The back door cracked open.

Dalton swung the pan.

And then stopped. Just in time.

Inches from mashing a nose completely flat.

A very cute nose.

Macy was staring at him, hair adjusted and new makeup applied.

"What are you *doing* in there?"

"What are you doing out *there*?"

"You were supposed to meet me. You didn't show, so I looked around. I saw your scooter."

"How did you get the door open?"

She gave him a funny look. "It was unlocked."

He tossed the frying pan on the mattress, next to the wig, then stepped into sunlight.

"Oh my Bob, are you okay?" she asked, examining the cuts and bruises on his face.

"Just business," he said, pleased with her concern, and even more that it gave him a chance to act like he didn't care. "You ready?"

"For what?"

Dalton picked up his helmet. There was no sign of Tarot, which meant, due to the immutable laws of bad movies and cowboy ballads, he would show up out of nowhere any second. Still, Dalton played it cool. He played it frozen. He was in full Deano at the Copa mode.

"You didn't, by any chance, leave me a note on an index card, did you? Like, stuck in my helmet?"

Macy looked confused. "Note? Um…"

"Never mind. Get on, I'll give you a ride."

She laughed, straightening her skirt. Her hair was fluffed up from the wind, the light freckles across her cheeks almost glowing. "There's no way I'm getting on that thing."

"Suit yourself."

Dalton put it in gear and moved a few feet with a rubbery chirp.

"Hey!"

"What?"

"Okay, I get it. My options are limited. But seriously, where are we going?"

Dalton gazed off into the distance as if he were scanning the shale formations for hidden Apache. "Only one way to find out."

Macy stuck out her tongue. Dalton didn't react. Macy gave him the finger. Dalton didn't react. Macy took a massive trigonometry book out of her backpack and slung all twenty pounds of it at his head, just missing. The thing crashed into the pavement, cover ripping off. It was a good throw. He was impressed.

"Can you translate that action into Euclidic, please?"

"All I know is it's going to cost me."

"What, the cover?"

"Yeah, the cover. Silverspoon has the textbook racket. It's almost impossible to get your deposit back as it is."

Dalton shoved the book into her pack, a scoliosis-inducing deadweight that had her practically listing starboard. "Consider it an object lesson in why studying is overrated. So are you coming or not?"

Macy swung her leg over the fender and put her arms around Dalton's waist. He handed her his helmet, black, with the face of his hero, Voltaire, painted on the side.

"Who's that?"

"Lead singer of Perv Idols."

Macy cocked her head. "Funny, I could have sworn it was Voltaire. You know, the guy who wrote *Candide* and died two hundred years ago?"

"Just put it on," Dalton said, unable to hide his grin.

"It'll ruin my hair."

"Hair shmair. We crash, that helmet could be the difference between Ivy League and community college. Even for a Euclidian with a great arm."

"Hilarious," she said, but plopped the visor down and tightened the chin strap. At the end of the alley, four figures in long black coats turned the corner, walking in slow motion like they'd just strutted out of the Moloko Milk Bar.

Better hit it, Pussanova.

"Hold on," Dalton said, snapping the clutch. The scooter *scree*d away, moving with each pound-per-square-foot a safer distance from any possible Casket fist. Or Pinker kick. Dalton leaned hard, perilously close to a concrete berm, before hanging a sharp left and roaring up Route 6.

"Where're we going?" Macy yelled into the wind. "Seriously."

"You'll see."

She hugged his waist tightly. If tightly meant wanting to unzip his leather jacket and climb inside. As if the speed scared her. As if *he* scared her. Dalton settled into the warmly satisfying, slightly queasy bath of inspiring fear. He could feel her breasts pressed against his back, her cheek pressed between his shoulder blades, her arms knotted around his rib cage. He liked it. A lot. *Idiot.* She smelled good too. *Fish stick.* She smelled good even though the wind was blowing, taking any possible odor fifty miles an hour away from his nose. *Weak bag of hair.* Dalton popped into neutral and gunned the engine, making the entire frame hiccup. Macy's arms gripped even harder. He was unable to suppress a grin.

THE PRIVATE DICK HANDBOOK, RULE #12
Stop grinning, Cardigan! Get ahold of yourself.
Pretend Aunt Brenda's arms are around you.
Especially since she's dead. And even when she was alive
she smelled like neck sweat and garlic raisins.
There you go. That's it. Concentrate!
Aunt Brenda in a rubber raincoat and mud boots
trudging out to the mailbox for her usual stack of
misaddressed envelopes and grocery circulars.
Leg hair! Varicose! Moldy candy!

The scooter slowed and took a hard right, changing directions. Macy must have thought he was taking her to the bridge or the lake, maybe out by The Point, something obvious and typical, because she seemed completely surprised when he pulled in front of her father's house.

"Are you...um...sure?"

"We have work to do," he said curtly, forcing himself into Just the Facts, Ma'am mode.

Macy got off, shoving the helmet into Dalton's belly. She took a few wobbly steps, brows angled together. They were on something more than client-Dick ground. He should have loaded up on some serious Lex Cole *Cold Shoulder*–brand cologne for men. The clock was running. His fee was unpaid.

"Ready?"

Dalton watched Macy watching him. He switched to his hardest street face. His Dickface Killah face. *Stand back and let me solve your problems, baby, because this enigma is all business.*

"Why are you making that face?"

"What face?"

"The one you're making right now. The one that looks like you've got dog shite between your toes."

Dalton tried not to laugh, and then did, reminding himself she was a Euclidian for a reason.

"Dalton?"

It was hard to keep envisioning her as Aunt Brenda when she was so close. So close she almost glowed. If she let her hair grow out and wore a little makeup, she could easily pass for a Silverspoon. If she put on a few pounds and some leather, she could maybe even be a Foxx. Her collarbones peeked from the wide collar of her shirt, sweater tied around her waist. She stood with one foot shyly in front of the other, hands behind her back, her white tights lovably rumpled across...*idiot!*

"You know that I charge by the hour, right?"

Macy appraised him coolly. "Fine. Let's go."

Dalton followed her over flagstone pavers that cut through the middle of an immaculate lawn. Before they even got to the top of the front steps, Macy's father, a heavyset, older-model Euclidian, stepped out the front door and gave her an enormous hug. He shook Dalton's hand. His blue V-neck perfectly matched his daughter's rolling eyes.

"You kids look thirsty. How about a nice cold drink?"

"Dad—"

"Sure," Dalton said. "Thank you, sir."

"Great!" Albert Payne laughed. "But don't call me sir. That's my father's name."

"Yes, sir."

Macy shot Dalton scimitars, while Albert Payne led them into the kitchen. A stainless-steel fridge hummed in the corner next to a spotless granite countertop. Macy looked like she wanted to slam her face into the center of it.

"Nice place."

Albert whistled a tuneless thank-you, placing three glasses of water on the table, each one topped with a healthy squirt from a bottle of Flavor Flavah, which suspended itself in viscous globs between cubes of ice. Dalton suppressed a gag.

"I don't make it like Macy's mother used to," Albert said wistfully. "But I do my best."

"It's terrific." Dalton pretended he was drinking without actually opening his mouth. Even so, he could taste the Flavah's molten sweetness as it clung to the edge of his lip. Macy took a tiny sip and put the glass down.

"So, did you kids meet at school?"

"Dad!"

Dalton smiled, feeling for his pistol to make sure it didn't slip out of the back of his pants. Then he remembered that Hutch had confiscated it in the nurse's office. "Let's just say I'm not doing as well as I should in math. So Macy has volunteered to tutor me."

Albert Payne slammed down the rest of his drink and stood up. Residue of the brown-red Flavor Flavah coated his chin like a shaving accident. "Well, I'll let you two get to studying."

"Yessir."

Macy stood as well, flushed just short of vermilion.

"Don't forget, hon," Albert said, walking over to the leather couch and turning on the television, a flat screen the size of Wyoming. He touched the remote, and a quiz program blinked and dinged into life. "Dinner's at seven thirty on the nose."

"Okay, Dad," Macy said, motioning frantically for Dalton to follow. She led him up a flight of stairs lined with pictures of a younger version of Albert Payne, grinning without reservation into the camera. The kid had a friendly, intelligent face and his father's generous features.

Wesley. The Body.

Macy pulled Dalton into her room, then locked the door

with relief. They could hear the booming hilarity of the game show through the floorboards. It sounded like someone was a big winner.

"Someone's a big winner."

"Yeah, you. Having a dad like that? Nice. Cares and all."

"He hasn't been the same since Wesley. Like clingy and sad and nostalgic all the time. I mean, my mom being sick was one thing, but that was ten years ago. After Wes—"

Macy stopped talking, her chin all scrunched up. Dust floated in the shaft of light coming through the curtains. The carpet was an immaculate pink oval. The walls were pink-white and without a single ding. She was waiting for him to hug her. He very much wanted to hug her. He would not, repeat, would *not* walk over, pull her into his arms, and hug her.

THE PRIVATE DICK HANDBOOK, RULE #13
You will not, repeat, will *not* hug her, Rev.
You unprofessional carp. You weak bag of hair.
Do your job! Collect your fee!

"I want to hear about Wesley," Dalton said, aiming for Professional Wheelchair Repossessor mode. "But there's something else first."

Macy dabbed her eyes with the corner of the pink bedspread, looking at him with relief. Looking at him, he thought, almost wantonly. At least that's what Lex Cole called it in *Ten Stories Up on the Windblown Ledge of Desire.*

"What is it?"

"My fee."

Astonishment passed over her like an infomercial for a slap across the cheek.

Good. Distance.

"I need the first installment. Plus expenses. Before we proceed."

Macy composed herself with difficulty. She got up and went to a pink desk. Above it were pictures of horses, and posters of some boy band Dalton barely recognized, five skinny kids in matching satiny outfits, each frozen in the middle of a different dance move, flashing the signature grin of breakers of twelve-year-old hearts.

Vanilla Donkey Ride? It was on the tip of his tongue. *Hot Cinnamon Twist?*

"Do you like Kiss Me Cherry too?" she asked, with forced lightness. Dalton didn't answer, holding out his hand. Macy put four hundred-dollar bills in it. He turned the pink desk chair around and straddled the seat, keeping the wooden back between them. It was time to get busy.

"So, I talked to Inference. Not much help there."

Macy nodded.

"I also talked to the friendly neighborhood Snouts."

She frowned. "But they won't even return our calls anymore. How did you—"

"They came to see me," Dalton said, instinctively dabbing the cut on his lip. "Anyhow, they insist he…Wesley…took his own life. School insists also. So far, I'm inclined to think—"

"He was murdered. Without a doubt."

She'd insisted this again and again via e-mail, but refused to say exactly why. At least not until they were talking in person. In private.

"I agree it's unlikely someone could wrap themselves in tape and haul themselves up onto a goalpost. But, in cases like these..." *God, do you sound like a tool.* "In cases like these, the unlikely often becomes the only plausible explanation. To be honest, so far I haven't seen or heard anything that makes me think it's not possible."

"It's not possible."

Dalton found himself slipping into Sarcastic Disbeliever Advises You to Babble Your Crackpot Theories to Whoever's Unlucky Enough to Be on the Barstool Next to You mode. He sighed deeply.

"Yeah, and why not?"

Macy crossed her legs, peering at him beneath exasperated lashes.

"Because he was found hanging upside down."

CHAPTER 8
SOMETIMES A SEXY NOTION

"No shite," Dalton finally said. Hanging a body upside down was something a bat would do. Or a rock 'n' roll vampire. "For real?"

Macy gave him a look. "There was no rope around his neck. Just his ankles."

"Okay," Dalton said, impressed that she was able to be so clinical. "But how do you know?"

"It was a rumor. Going around the cliques. I didn't believe it at first. But Jeff told me it was true."

"How would Chuff know?"

"He wouldn't say exactly. I've done pretty much everything I could to get him to tell me."

"*Every*thing?"

Macy blushed. "Jeff is hard to...persuade."

"He'd know if he was the one who did it."

"He'd also know if he saw Wesley while he was out on the field practicing, right? Where the captain of the team would naturally be?"

Dalton conceded the point with a click of his tongue.

"Okay, so what about you and him? Is Chuff your boy-friend or not?"

Macy threw up her hands. "No. Yes. I mean, he likes me? A lot? And so sometimes we hang out. But we're not *together* together. It's more like he just decides he wants you around, and then suddenly you're around. And, anyway, after Wesley, I didn't want...to be alone. Even if sometimes he acts like—"

"A tool?"

Macy grabbed a pink pillow and put it in her lap. Then she mashed her face into it. Dalton could almost hear her blushing. Eventually she sat up again.

"Yeah."

"So why stay with him? It's such a *West Side Story* cliché. Ball meets cute Euclidian from across the tracks, the families don't like it, somehow they persevere, blah, blah, blah, here comes Rita Moreno with a rose in her teeth."

"Did you say *cute* Euclidian?"

Dalton almost blushed. Almost. "You know what I mean."

Macy leaned forward. "He's not what everyone thinks. He has a heart. He's...sensitive."

"Uh-huh," Dalton said, picturing Chuff's pig-rending fists and massive Easter Island head. "So why not get this sensitive guy to help you instead of me?"

Macy threw the pillow on the floor. "Every time I get a chance to ask, one of the other Balls shows up! It's almost impossible to be alone with him without that stupid Chance

Chugg running over. *Chuff to Chugg...inappropriate and creepy!* But it's not like I think he's lying...it's more like he's trying to protect me."

"From?"

"From Tarot. And what Tarot's about to do."

"Which is?"

"Isn't it obvious? Take over."

Dalton pursed his lips, which hurt, so he stopped. "The Snouts and Inference worked me over pretty good today so I'd swallow their suicide line. Which makes no sense if they found Wesley hanging upside down. Which means they either didn't find him that way, or this whole town's on the take. If that's true, we're farcked. If the cops know Tarot's involved and are letting it slide, there isn't enough money in anyone's safe to make it right."

Macy's face hardened a bit. "The motive, whoever did it, is chaos."

"Excuse me?"

"Wesley was a symbol at Salt River. He sort of kept things balanced just by being there. And now he's not. Balls and Casket are going to butt heads soon. Hard."

"Why?"

"Because that's what happens when you throw two alpha monkeys and one banana in a cage. It's been brewing since freshman year, and now there's a vacuum."

"What do you mean, symbol? I thought Wesley was a Euclidian. Based on those pictures in the hallway, he doesn't exactly look like—"

"Wesley was a Populah."

"He was popular?"

"He was the head of Popu*lahs*," Macy said, with an accent like the rich chick from a movie where some dowdy old matron is sentenced to share her mansion with three fat rappers. She reached over and handed Dalton an elaborate hierarchical chart drawn by hand, all the cliques and sub-cliques laid out in boxes, connected by dozens of lines. It was intricate and meticulous. Dalton traced the lineage from Balls to Fack Cult T, marveling at her handiwork. Populahs floated at the bottom, not attached to any other clique except a single box beneath them.

"Crop Crème?"

"Means exactly what it sounds like. Sort of a subset of Populahs, but even more exclusive. There's popular, and then there's, like, those kids off in the stratosphere."

"That's the first I've heard of it. If Wesley was so influential, why isn't anyone talking about him? Why no outrage, no memorial, no—"

"That's how it *is* at Salt River!" Macy snapped. "Or haven't you noticed? The only thing that matters is to act like you don't care. And don't say a word. Something really bad happens? Pretend it doesn't exist. Move on. Keep working the rackets. I mean, there's people shooting off the rooftops, for Bob's sake, and it's like, hey, just another day in geography class." Macy rubbed her eyes with the heels of her hands, making a squeegee sound. "Wesley was a Populah because he was the only kid in school not trying to be. He had no racket. He dressed like a dork and worked hard in his classes. He wasn't trying to move up or down the ladder. He didn't make fun of things in an ironic voice or wear shirts of angry bands. He was just himself."

"And that made him a threat?"

"Being comfortable with who you are is the ultimate threat!

It makes the cliques' constantly milking the rackets and putting everyone else down seem pointless in comparison."

"So, you're saying the entire school is a suspect?"

"No, I'm saying Wesley wasn't killed. He was sacrificed."

"Sacrificed?"

Macy picked at the bedspread. "Listen, half the kids at school want to be Jeff, right? So they can be the big football star. The other half want to be Tarot so they can be a rock god. But deep down, everyone knows those are just clichés. Wesley is who people really want to be, not just when there's cheering, but alone late at night. And on Sunday morning. And in the car with their mother."

"So, if a guy like Wesley kills himself, it's like, what hope does everyone else have? If Salt River becomes Stepford River, it's easier to control?"

"Exactly."

"Okay, but what happened to the Populahs?"

"They broke up after Wes's body was found. There were actually only five Crop Crème. A couple transferred to boarding schools. The other cliques absorbed the rest. Except Ronnie Newport. He went and founded Smoke."

"Newport was a Populah? Just last semester?"

"I know, right? After Wesley he started in with the Cigarette Enigma routine."

Dalton rubbed his chin. "If Wesley was a Populah, he must have had a girlfriend."

Macy nodded.

"Then why haven't we talked to her? Why aren't we talking to her right now?"

"I don't know."

"You don't know what?"

"Who she *is*. It sounds stupid, but he wouldn't say. He had her picture in his wallet, but he wouldn't show me. When I went to the police station with Dad to look at his effects, his wallet was gone."

"So you pocketed the suicide note?"

Macy blushed. "It should probably have been in a detective file or something, but there it was, with his other stuff. I was going to say something, but..."

"Let me see it."

Macy went to a little pink jewelry box on her dresser and pulled a carefully folded note from a tiny pink envelope. The writing was in pencil, shaky in places, heavy-handed in others. It had been erased and rewritten and erased again.

Two steps forward, one taken back
A walk through the forest, all in black
Life on the edge, on the edge alone
No one to talk to, mental dial tone
It's painless, it's painless
It's raining, insane-ing
Going 'cross the river to the
Place with no blaming
I'm free
I'm a black angel
I'm free
Burst like star spangle
I'm free
I'm me
Just me

Dalton finished, about to say something like *Hey, that wasn't really so bad*, when Macy snatched it back, shaking her head.

"*Such* bloshite, right? On a level of suck, it's an eleven out of ten."

"Definitely."

"It's because those are the lyrics to 'Exquisite Lies.' The Pinker Casket song."

Bam.

"I need to take a look in your brother's room."

Macy's face darkened. "I don't like to. I haven't gone. In there. Since."

"It's okay," he said gently. "Wait here."

The room was a monument to prepubescent bliss. Too innocent for a kid Wesley's age, no matter how nice he was. More like emotionally stunted. Cartoon posters, piggy banks, sports trophies, a rug shaped like a giant fuzzy duck. There were fourteen volumes of *The Pesterton Boys Young Gentleman's Tales*. Then there were copies of *Dragon Rider* and *Dragon Fire* and *Dragon Fist*. And, of course, *Return of the Dragon*, *Dragon's Friend Wizard*, *Dragon Goes Shopping*, and *Fist's Big Revenge*. Dalton poked under the bed. A few crumpled tissues, an old Li'l Egghead's 1,001-Piece Chemistry Set, some dust bunnies, and some board games, including Dragon Dice 2000 and Welcome to PesterTown! There was also the entire Slangy Fang trilogy, *Bite Me Twice as Nice* and *Bite Me Even Harder*, along with the well-thumbed third volume, *Bite Me Totally Neckless*. The closet was immaculately organized. In the back, behind nondescript dress clothes, hung a T-shirt. Dalton draped it over his chest. It said PINKERLOVE CASKETHURTS.

When he turned, Macy was in the doorway.

"Did you know about this?"

"Never seen it before," she said disbelievingly. "What does it mean?"

"It's just a shirt, right? Half the school has them."

"I don't."

"You're the other half."

Dalton poked through Wesley's desk. There were pencils and paper clips and a roll of tape. He looked through a few dresser drawers. Zip. He felt around the drawer bottoms. Nothing.

Except in the bottom one.

THE PRIVATE DICK HANDBOOK, RULE #15
It's always the bottom one.

The drawer's tacking pulled back with a tiny rip. Dalton coughed to hide the sound. Under the tacking was a thick paper rectangle. He slipped it in his jacket, then turned to find Macy standing right behind him, the last light of the day oozing through the window and framing her in a gauzy filmic white.

"Looking for something?"

She was less than an inch away. It was like a scene from a movie called *Guy and Girl About to Kiss in Idyllic Setting II*, starring Dumbass Rev. The orchestral soundtrack was about to swell. There was the danger of a slow-motion montage. Macy tilted her chin and closed her eyes. Dalton wanted to put his hands on her waist, feel the spot where her back ended. He wanted to let the warmth of his palms sink into her skin. He wanted to kiss her neck, gently, and then bite her earlobe a little too hard, feeling her body tremble against his.

THE PRIVATE DICK HANDBOOK, RULE #16

If the girl you're about to make tremble has a gigantic boy-friend who not only looks like he was genetically engi-neered to pull a rusty plow through miles of pavement but has already demonstrated himself to be one of the biggest dangles in school, and she's also your client, and her dad is right downstairs, and you're standing in the creepily nostalgic bedroom of her murdered brother, you'd probably be wise to holster your totally unprofessional lips and even more unprofessional rodney and begin seriously channeling mental images a whole lot worse than Aunt Brenda.

"No *way*," Dalton said.

"What?" Macy asked, flinching. Her eyes fluttered open.

"I don't farcking believe it."

"Believe what? What did I do?"

Dalton turned and ran. He ran down the stairs and out the screen door.

"Dalton?" Macy yelled. "Hey!'

"Everything okay?" Albert Payne yelled.

Dalton flung himself into the backyard, heading across the street, clomping through the grass like a halfback loose in the secondary.

Picking up speed and with each step...

Balling his fists...

Straight toward a leafy oak tree...

The exact same one he'd just spotted someone hiding behind.

Someone who'd been looking in the window, staring right at them.

CHAPTER 9
BINGO BANGO BONGO. DESTINY.

He reached the tree with three long strides, then almost fell while trying to stop his momentum, curling one arm around the trunk. There was no one there. He did a quick survey in each direction and saw a blue-clad leg disappearing behind the neighbor's house. Dalton took off after it. Dogs began to bark in volleys, one egging on the next. They snapped at the ends of their chains, teeth gnashing as he zipped past in a white-shirted blur.

THE PRIVATE DICK HANDBOOK, RULE #17
Run faster!

The peeper ran diagonally across the street, trying to make the next alley. Dalton took a shorter route through a bunch of lawn furniture, knocking over red-hatted gnomes as he propelled himself onto the peeper's back. Momentum carried them behind a Dumpster, the guy breaking down like a roped steer.

Dalton grabbed two handfuls of pin-striped collar. Blue pinstripe. It was the same guy who'd been outside Inference's window.

"You!"

He was, maybe, forty. Thin and pale, with a gray mustache. For an old man, he sure could run.

"Why the *farck* are you following me around?"

"I work…I work…"

"For Tarot? Huh? For *Inference*?"

"No," the man managed, struggling to breathe.

"Who then? The Snouts?"

"I work…for the university."

"What is that? Another clique?"

"Harvard University. I am Elisha Cook, head of the admissions department. I've been wanting to talk with you. About your application."

"My application?" Dalton said incredulously. "*What* application?"

Elisha Cook reached into his double-breasted jacket, pulling out a sheaf of paper. The first page had Dalton's name at the top. But it wasn't his handwriting. Even though the handwriting was familiar. Very familiar. *Unfarckingbelievable.* Dalton inhaled deeply twice, exhaled deeply once, and then got off the man's chest. He dabbed at his forehead with his tie, which was now too shiny to absorb much. He felt in his back pocket, half tempted to consult Lex Cole, but the pocket was empty. *Shite.* That one had been a first edition.

"May I stand now?"

Dalton stuck out a hand and helped him up. Elisha Cook did an odd little bow, brushing off his clothes and straightening his paisley tie with a degree of dignity.

71

"If you wanted to talk to me about some application, why didn't you just say so? What's with all the hiding behind trees? And why did you run?"

The man looked embarrassed. "You were charging at me like an enraged wildebeest. I was scared. Also, I wanted to be sure it was you. To be honest, from what I've observed so far, your campus posture doesn't seem very...literate."

"Very what?"

Elisha Cook removed the first page of Dalton's application. Beneath it was a stack of short stories. The stories he'd been writing since he was thirteen. The stories he'd never shown anyone. The stories he kept locked in a steel box under a loose plank in his bedroom floor. The lockbox no one knew existed. The lockbox with a combination only he had the numbers to. The lockbox filled with his Private Dick earnings. All his Private Dick earnings. All his writing. And some other, even more embarrassing things.

"You've been in my *lockbox*?"

Elisha Cook looked terrified. "*Excuse* me? Your what?"

Dalton could tell the man's confusion was real. He was ashen faced, and his hair was standing straight up. He looked ridiculous. Okay, so he hadn't been in the lockbox.

"At any rate," Elisha Cook continued, gesturing toward the two stories, "this 'The Leaves Always Scream the Loudest' is terrific. Really. Very advanced for a boy your age. Man. Young man. Teen...anyway, it shows true promise. The entire committee thought so. And although this one, 'The A to Z of Possible Gods,' was...somewhat more controversial, I personally found it to be very thought-provoking."

"Thanks. Even though you had no right to read it."

"You sent it to me."

Dalton tried to come up with a response and failed.

"Nevertheless, I think you would make a great addition to our program."

"What are you saying?"

"Even in light of this little contretemps, I'm offering you a scholarship. A full scholarship. To Harvard."

Dalton rubbed his neck, kicking a rock in the dirt. It was completely ridiculous.

"But why?"

"The strength of your work, of course. I think you're an extremely talented writer."

"Who put you up to this? Cassiopeia? I mean, you've really got to be shite-ing me here."

Elisha Cook coughed, spat dirt, and apologized, dabbing his lips.

"No. I am decidedly not...*shy-it-ing* you. I mean, there is also the matter of your extremely high scores on the SATs. And while at Harvard we don't necessarily put so much stock in standardized—"

The dog barking ratcheted up a notch. There was a low rumble coming from one end of the alley.

"Take a sniff," Dalton said, his voice becoming hard.

"Excuse me?"

"Go away, suit. You're complicating my play."

"But...but...do you not understand what I'm offer—"

"Do *you* not listen? That's a roll of fish wrap I'm not buying. So beat it. Now!"

Elisha Cook, his face still flushed, turned on one wing-tipped heel and walked around the corner, just as a jacked-up

'72 Nova idled over. The paint job was a combo of candy-apple red and rust-apple rust. The engine was incredibly loud. It made Dalton's scooter sound like an asthmatic goat. The driver had a camera slung around his neck and a slicked-back pompadour. Ronnie Newport. He lit a cigarette with the one he'd half finished and flicked the butt expertly past Dalton's left shoulder. The three Ginny Slims in the back laughed, lighting their own. The car smelled like a rolling ashtray and looked like the set from a forties Sherlock Holmes movie, wave after wave of smoke rolling in off the moors.

"Strange place for you to be cruising, no?"

"CRUISING FOR A BRUISING!" The girls yelled, then devolved into laughter. Their teeth seemed too big for their mouths. "HEY, ISN'T THIS CAR BOLSHEVIK? HUH? ISN'T IT? IT'S TOTALLY FREAKIN' *BOLSHEVIK*!" They slapped five and sucked in their cheeks and adopted modeling poses. Ronnie Newport slid the camera off his neck and pointed it at them, the flash incredibly powerful, *bang bang bang!* It shut the girls up. Newport lit another cigarette, this time flicking the old one over Dalton's right shoulder.

"So who's the suit? Snout? Or you joining the Fack Cult?"

"Neither. Guy's some old perv. A creeper. Wants to make home movies. Wants to know do I have any friends interested in free candy."

"GROSS!" the girls said in unison.

"It's an ugly world. I just live in it."

Newport nodded, the barest fraction of a smile skating across his lips. He kicked open the passenger door. "Get in. Chuff wants to talk to you."

"Seems like I talked to him plenty already this morning."

Newport shrugged. He revved the engine. The car practically swayed with pent-up aggression.

"What's he want to talk about?"

The wheels ticked in the heat. Two birds flew overhead. In *A Fistful of Cholera*, Lex Cole had taken out four rival dealers with a garden shovel in order to be accepted into the inner circle of the drug lord Genghis Tom. But Dalton didn't have a garden shovel.

Run. Now. Do it.

Newport stared straight ahead, like he couldn't care less either way.

Quick. Split. Go.

Macy was probably waiting for him to come back and explain. Macy was probably angry.

Bingo.

Dalton slid into the front seat and wrenched the door closed. The Nova immediately accelerated out of the alley at a nausea-inducing speed, leaving a patch for a hundred feet. Ronnie Newport took the corner with the flat of his palm, generating enough g-force to snap the necks of half the Apollo mission. The girls in the back braced themselves like pros, one hand against the roof, the other against the back of the seat.

"You work for Chuff now?" Dalton asked, as the car careened around slower traffic, which was pretty much every other car on the road.

"Smoke don't work for nobody," Newport said curtly, blowing through a stop sign. "My racket's transpo. Chuff asked me to give you a ride, so here you are. Chuff runs a tab. At the end of the month, Chuff pays. Same as anyone else."

"Who else? Tarot?"

Newport ignored the question, breaking into a long, sheering left that sent them onto the highway ramp. One of the girls pulled a bottle of Rush from her purse and took a swig. Newport grabbed it from her mouth and tossed it out the window. Then he pulled out a business card. It had a tiny picture of a jacked-up car spitting a long gout of flame. Above that it said:

Ron Newport
transpo
426-3690

"So tell me about Populahs," Dalton said, slipping the card into his wallet.

"About who?"

"You heard me."

Newport turned his head ninety degrees and looked at Dalton, not turning back even though he continued to accelerate.

Eight seconds.

Ten.

Twelve.

The car whined feverishly. Newport kept his eyes locked on Dalton, calm and dark.

Fifteen.

Sixteen.

Dalton finally broke away. Ronnie Newport looked back over the steering wheel just in time to yank it around a van whose tailpipe he was about to drive into.

"So, okay," Dalton said, swallowing hard. "You don't want to talk about Populahs."

"People talk a lot. People will tell you anything if you ask the right way."

"Did I not ask the right way?"

"You're not the right people."

Dalton gripped the dash with both hands. "You killed Wesley Payne."

"No," Newport said, in a way that made it clear why he'd once been a Crop Crème. "I didn't."

"Well, then who—"

"I tell you what. You don't want to go see Chuff? Pay me more than he does, I'll drive you somewhere else."

"How much is more?"

"Two hundred."

"I'll go see Chuff."

"Suit yourself."

The car roared into the fast lane, the horizon closer with every foot. Dalton pulled the roll from his pocket. "How about forty bucks to tell me who Wes Payne's girlfriend was?"

Ronnie Newport gave Dalton a disappointed look. After a minute he took the twenties and tossed them into the back-seat. "Why don't you ask the girls?"

There was a loud squeal. The Ginny Slims grabbed each other's wrists and necks and collars. The ones on each end secured a bill, while the one in the middle started to cry.

"Well?" Dalton asked the winners, who stared at him dumbly. "Who...was...Wes...Payne's...girlfriend?"

"OOH! *I* was!" the first one said. "*I* was Wes Payne's girl-friend!'

She closed her eyes and wrapped her arms around herself, imagining it.

"No! *I* was! *I* was Wes Payne's girlfriend!" the second one insisted.

"No! Me!" the one in the middle said.

Dalton gave up and turned toward the front. Newport laughed, if you could call his ossified bark a laugh.

"Thanks for saving my bacon in the nurse's office, by the way. Was about to get tuned up for the third time."

"Snouts," Ronnie Newport said, shaking his head.

"So, you take pictures for Yearbook, huh?"

"Yup."

Dalton pointed at the enormous camera. "Wouldn't digital be easier?"

"Digital's for purses."

"It is?"

"Also, one of the cliques stole all our computers last year."

"Going old school by force?"

"Pretty much."

For a while, there was just the hum of the car and the forward motion. Eventually, they hit the exit and began passing fast-food signs, causing the Ginny Slims to yammer, "RON-EEE!…WE'RE HUN-GREE!"

"Shut up," Ronnie Newport said.

And so they did.

CHAPTER 10
TWO HALF-BEEF PATTIES, NOT-SO-SPECIAL SAUCE

Ronnie Newport *scree*d into the lot of a Burger Barn. A huge banner above the red plastic roof said HOME OF *THAT PHAT BURGER* and NOW WITH *HALF THE PHAT!*

"Yay!" said the Ginny Slims.

"Silver door behind the Dumpster," Newport said, then pulled away, the girls squealing *"BUT RON-EEE!"* all the way down the street. Dalton took a second to check out what he'd palmed from Wesley Payne's drawer. The thick rectangle was actually an envelope. Dalton slit it open with his thumbnail. Inside was a sheaf of bills sporting Ben Franklin's bemused mug. Ten grand, easy. Taped to the first bill was a small key, like one to a foot locker. Or a lockbox that a person could, say, hide his once-private short stories in. Dalton pulled out his own key ring and compared his with the silver one. Nearly identical. Except this key had a number 9 stamped on it. In every book ever written and movie ever made, a locker was for hiding money in. Then coming back to get it later, right before you double-crossed the bad guys. So why should it be different now? Everyone watched movies, and almost no one had original ideas. *Yeah, a bus locker is exactly the place you'd stuff a stolen hundred grand.* But Wes Payne and stolen cash? Those two things didn't fit at all.

Dalton was thumbing the key's awkward groove when a blue van *scree*d up to where he was standing. The kind of van a band and its roadies and equipment and Aleister Crowley, lead singer, might be packed into. Dalton stuffed the money into his boxers and turned, prepared to swing or run or both, as a half dozen screaming kids got out and tooled by, arguing about what to order: *CreamCheeser! BaconBucket! AngioLoad! Der Meatmeister!* A weary mom rested her head on the hood for a second, rolling her eyes at Dalton before trudging by.

He walked around Burger Barn, looking in the greasy windows. It was half full — old couples pulling the pickles off their Deep-Breaded Bread-o-Filets, and kids shoving fries between vinyl seat cushions, where they would calcify for eternity. Dalton continued down the alley until he found a silver door with EMPLOYEES ONLY stenciled on it, and knocked.

The door immediately opened.

Chance Chugg and another Ball, both in full football uniforms, dragged him in. The door slammed. They were in a storeroom, metal shelving stacked from floor to ceiling with twenty-gallon mayo jugs and industrial-sized tubes of Flavor Flavah. On one wall was a bunch of coat hangers and employee lockers. Dalton pretended to trip, falling toward the lockers, landing between 8 and 10. He slipped the silver key into number 9's lock. It fit but didn't turn. While he was leaning there, the Balls took the opportunity to frisk him. "No cheater this time, huh?" Chance Chugg said, in his neck-free way. "Well, you're learning."

"I am a sponge for knowledge," Dalton agreed, slipping the key back into his pocket. Chugg punched Dalton hard in the stomach, then shoved him into a smaller room behind a wall of deep freezers. Jeff Chuff, QB, was lying on a throne made of burlap sacks. Around him, various Balls were doing push-ups or lifting gigantic pickle tubs like barbells. In the corner, several of them were running through plays and formations, using a frozen ham as a football.

"New guy!" Chuff called. "Take off your dress and stay awhile!"

The Balls all laughed, while Dalton stood against the wall, taking stock. There were ten of them, sweaty and worked up. Lousy odds. He'd been expecting just Chuff, which was bad enough, but half the team was ridiculous.

"Truth be told, I never thought you'd come."

"Wasn't sure it was that smart a play myself."

"Took a lot of stones. I mean, after this morning? Whew, crackstar, you made me look bad!"

Dalton nodded, kept an eye open for something heavy and swingable, just in case. He'd need something capable of doing major damage. Like a grenade. It wasn't there.

"Yeah, it's all good, though. You coming here without my having to waste time finding you, that tells me you're a man who understands how things work. And, hey, the deal with the pistol? Very clever, Dick. Bravo." Chuff clapped longer than his sarcasm required. "So, okay, we put on a little theater this morning. The aggro routine keeps student body knees quaking, lets the other cliques think we're real hard cases. The way I see it, it's good for the image."

Dalton, surprised, nodded. Chuff rubbed his huge belly counterclockwise as the players continued to practice formations around him.

"But running through *King Lear* is one thing. Actual fights and shooting? Uh-uh. No sir. That gets in the way of business. And that's bad for everyone. You feeling me, Dick?"

"If I have to."

Chuff frowned, his ape-face looking tired. "Okay, here's a for instance. Say I went ahead and took your earlier behavior, provocative as it was, personally? And then say, as a matter of revenge, I beat you half to death with a frozen T-bone instead of having this adult discussion. It's tempting, sure. But where's my percentage?"

"Let alone mine."

"Exactly. So, in place of a well-deserved bludgeoning with zero profit to be found, I have a proposal."

"I'm listening," Dalton said as the inside door banged open. He could see through the Burger Barn kitchen, all the way out to the front counter, where lines of people were waiting impatiently to place their orders.

"Mr. Chuff?" came a quivery voice. It was a bald guy Dalton figured was the manager, not only because he had a thin mustache, but because he was wearing a name tag that said NED WHIMPLE, MANAGER. "Mr. Chuff, your break ended one hour ago. Are you ready to come run the deep fryer? There is no one presently manning the deep fryer, despite multiple orders for both fries and onion rings."

"Onion rings," Chuff said, shaking his head with disbelief. "Who actually likes onion rings?"

"Are you working or not, Mr. Chuff? Do I need to call your parents and ask their opinion of your job performance?"

Chuff didn't get up, but he did start to tie on a red Burger Barn apron with a name tag that said JEFFREY pinned to it. The manager shook his head with exasperation. He mimed dialing a phone and talking into it. Then his heels clacked down the hall.

"Close the door!" Chuff roared.

The clacks came back. The door gently closed, and the clacks went away again.

Chuff looked at Dalton with an apologetic smirk. "The things a man has to put up with for a halfway believable cover, huh?"

"Not to mention easy access to registers with which to launder clique money."

Chuff smiled, touching his finger to the tip of his nose. "Anyway, the main reason I haven't stomped you to jelly yet, fish, is that I want to ask you a favor."

"You're about to go to war with Caskets. Meanwhile, profits are flagging. You want to take out Tarot first, and you think you can use me to do it."

"Damn, you're sharp! Hey, Chuggster, you hear that? Is this guy sharp, or what?"

"Yeah, totally," Chance Chugg said, practicing snaps with a bag of frozen buns.

"Why not just roll the dice? You've got the manpower for a frontal assault."

Chuff raised an eyebrow. "No, sir. That would not be a smart play."

Dalton raised an eyebrow back. "Why not?"

"What we have at Salt River is managed anarchy. The big cliques? Despite our ideological differences, we need to work together to survive. Or at least profit. Used to be Pinker Casket understood that. Used to be they provided a balance. East and West. Russians and Americans. Siegfried and Roy. It kept the small animals distracted. But Tarot? Tarot has forgotten the framework. Tarot has gone Caesar, taken his troops across the Rubicon and started fomenting insurrection. So our anarchy is no longer managed. We are on the verge of war. And it's one we will all lose."

"Right, because there isn't any profit in war, is there?"

"War's a racket," Chuff agreed. "No doubt. But it's a racket for the politicians, not the soldiers. You and me? We're soldiers. And during war, you tend to get paid like a grunt."

Dalton didn't feel like a soldier. He felt like a punching bag. A punching bag aware of exactly how scared Chuff was of Kurt Tarot. And how he was probably smart to be.

"So, here you come on the scene, right on time. A free-floating antibody who doesn't mind stirring the shite. A fresh thinker to inject insulin into the vein of this stalemate. I'm thinking to myself, Jeffrey, can that be a coincidence? And further, Jeffrey, would it be a smart play to ignore this coincidence in exchange for the simple pleasures of revenge?"

"As long as it's a coincidence that doesn't have your fingerprints on it."

Chuff touched the tip of his nose again.

"Dangerous assignment."

"True. But not as dangerous as saying no."

The Balls stopped practicing. They turned toward Dalton, chests heaving. Sweat trickled. Pipes ticked. In the distance, registers banged open.

"I'll need a healthy down payment. Also, five hundred a day, plus expenses."

"NO WAY!" Chance Chugg said, clenching his fists. "I swear I'll—"

"You'll do nothing," Chuff said, reaching under the burlap and lobbing a stack of bills. Dalton caught it with two hands, resisting the urge to whistle. Chugg's neck was purple as he turned in furious circles.

"I want a plan by Friday night. Big party at Yearbook's house. I want you there, telling me what it is my money just bought. I want it all laid out, line by line. Playoffs start next weekend, so that's when Tarot will make his move, when he thinks we're distracted. We need to make our move first."

"Got it."

"Good." Chuff got up and put his mainsail arm around Dalton's shoulders. "But you decide to get cute, crackstar, and I'm going to chisel Roman numerals across your face. I'll make you look like a walking tombstone."

"Fair enough," Dalton said. "By the way, who was Wesley Payne's girlfriend?"

Chuff licked his lips. "No idea. You're speaking Korean."

"You found him, didn't you?"

"Maybe."

"Was he hanging by the neck or ankles?"

"None of his BUSINESS!" Chance Chugg screamed. Chuff swung his leg backward in a vicious mule-kick. Chugg's eyes rolled sideways and he fell, holding his belly. Chuff snapped his fingers, and some Balls lifted Chugg onto the burlap sacks.

"Neck or ankles?" Dalton asked again.

Chuff sighed deeply, rubbing his Pliocene forehead. "Crackstar, crackstar, crackstar."

Dalton waited, saying nothing.

"Ankles."

"You call the Snouts?"

"No."

"Why not?"

"Never called any Snouts in my life, not about to start now."

"You cut Payne down?"

Chuff frowned. His eyes were yellowed. His breath was atrocious. "You think I'm stupid?"

"Way I hear it, Payne was a bigger player than people are letting on. But no one wants to say peep about the guy. The Balls never had cause to work with him? A little side business?"

"Payne was a Samaritan. A true believer. There was no money in what he was selling."

Dalton nodded, turning to leave.

"One last thing," Chuff said, reknotting his apron. "My girl wasn't on campus when I went to see her. She usually drops by during my shift, but she hasn't been here either. Why do you think that is?"

Um, how would I know? I haven't kissed her in at least an hour.

"Am I stuttering? Am I speaking Chinese?"

"No."

Chuff pulled an entire side of beef out of one of the freezers and began doing presses with it over his head. "See, the thing is (*whuf*), me and her? We're entrenched. Fully. And if she's hanging around with some probe (*uhh*), I'm gonna buy a mallet and (*rrrgh*) play his head like a two-dollar gong." Chuff dropped the beef, balancing it at his side. "So I'm asking again. You haven't seen Macy around, have you, new guy?"

"No, I haven't seen her."

"Yeah?"

"Yeah."

"Sure?"

"Sure."

"There's two things I can smell a mile away. One is burning hamburger and the other's bloshite."

"It's the hamburger."

Chuff nodded, then punched clear through the ribs of the beef. It was an amazing feat of strength. Dalton stared at the shattered marrow-hole in the frozen cow.

"You can go."

Chuff snapped his fingers again. Chance Chugg stood up, still green and bent over. He grabbed Dalton by the shoulders and escorted him out the back, tossing him into a pile of wrappers and empty MassiveGulp containers in the alley. "Chuff to Chugg...touchdown!" he yelled, before slamming the door.

Dalton brushed ketchup from his chin, then got up and walked out to the highway, sticking out his thumb.

CHAPTER 11

KNEE-DEEP IN NURTURE, NATURE TAKES A WALK

It took two rides before an ice-cream truck dropped him in front of Macy's house. Dalton worked on his explanation for a while and then knocked. No answer. There were lights on in the basement, but not on the upper floors. He walked around to his scooter, which started on the third try, and let the engine idle for a few minutes, hoping if Macy was inside she'd hear it and come down. He knew she was probably furious. No one likes to be run out on, no matter what your excuse is. A furious woman was a bad thing. A furious client was even worse. A furious client could mean late, or even delinquent, payments. Could she really be up in her room, hiding in the dark? Dalton revved the engine and left it keening at a high whine. Nothing. As he went to put on his helmet, a note fell out. An index card. The same handwriting as before:

RUMORS ABOUT WHO KILLED WESLEY PAYNE:

1. THEY DRAINED HIM FOR HIS BLOOD.

2. INFERENCE ORDERED THE HIT.

3. PAYNE AND CHUFF WERE PLANNING A TAKEOVER.

4. PAYNE AND TAROT WERE PLANNING A TAKEOVER.

5. THE FACK CULT KNEW PAYNE WAS GOING TO PART THE SALT RIVER AND THEN LEAD HIS PEOPLE TO THE PROMISED LAND.

6. PAYNE FOUND JIMMY HOFFA BURIED IN HIS DAD'S AZALEAS, RIGHT BENEATH O.J.

LOOK AT LEE HARVIES. THEN LOOK EVEN CLOSER.
A GUN CLIQUE. A MURDER. SEE A LINK? CLIQUE, CLICK, BANG.

DUH.

Dalton put the note in his pocket, then pulled a U-turn, gunning across town.

His parents' house, unlike Macy's, was lit up like a film premiere. Even though he was almost nine, Turd Unit was going through a phase where he was scared of the dark. Or, more likely, he was just pretending to be because he was bored. Either way, neither of Dalton's parents complained, even when the bill came every month and was sixty dollars more than they could spare. Dalton had been paying it himself for almost a year. He also covered part of the rent. Neither of his parents ever asked where the money came from, but they knew he wasn't doing lawns. Even before BoxxMart, Mom's paralegal salary wasn't cutting it.

"Hi, honey," Sherry Rev called as Dalton came in the door off the kitchen. She was in an apron, making dinner, frayed perm all over the place as usual, a food smudge on her forehead. She gave him a big hug, her elaborate braces gleaming. Dalton loosened his tie and sat down.

"Tough day?" Sherry asked, not seeming to notice the bruises on his face.

"Not too bad."

Turd Unit immediately started playing with Dalton's helmet, making faces at Voltaire.

"Don't play with my helmet."

Turd Unit swept back his lanky red hair. He was the only person on either side of the family, as far as anyone knew, going back many generations, to have red hair. He was a skinny, cane-hyper, crooked-smiling anomaly. It was as if a drunken Irish stork had been blown off course and dropped a four-foot insult-bomb into their laps.

"Where's Dad?"

Sherry Rev rolled her eyes, which meant *On the La-Z-Boy, where else?* Then she took a bowl out of the microwave. "Would you take him dessert?"

"Dad doesn't need any more of that pudding, Mom."

"How interesting," Sherry said, "that your new school has made you an expert on what Dad needs. What a diverse curriculum. I can't believe you didn't transfer earlier."

There was no point in arguing with Sherry Rev, who, despite her surface ditziness, had a tongue like a sassy prosecutor on a show where male lawyers were regularly sacrificed at the altar of her *oh-no-you-didn't* legal opinions. Dalton picked up the hot bowl, stopping at the doorway. "Tell Turd Unit if he messes up my helmet, he's going to wish he'd lived to see puberty."

"Eat it," Dalton's little brother said, putting the helmet on and scooping a spoonful of mac and cheese through the visor.

"Kirkland!" Sherry scolded. "Language!"

"Sorry," Turd Unit said, then gave Dalton a Velveeta smile.

Dalton's father sat in a back brace almost the size of his chair, watching the news. He watched about six hours a night, flipping channels, hoping for a clip from the Middle East Front, where Landon had been stationed for the last two years. A week after he was deployed, Dalton's father had been convinced he'd seen footage of Landon crouched behind a low brick wall, loading his rifle. Since then he'd been flipping around every night, hoping for another glimpse. Dalton was working on an illegal deal to buy body armor. Mostly because Landon wrote letters about once a month complaining about how bad the food was, but also how President Forehead was spending a million dollars a day to keep them in some other people's country—and making a billion dollars a day selling that country's oil to the rest of the world—but he couldn't be bothered to cut a check for Kevlar.

"You don't go to war with what you want, you go with what you have," President Forehead's advisor had insisted at a news conference.

"Yeah!" Dalton's father barked, almost throwing the remote at the screen. "And you don't stay home and get fat with what you *have*, you buy all the Hummers and Big Macs and Italian wing tips you *want*!"

The day Landon was promoted to leader of Alpha Unit, Kirkland proclaimed himself leader of Turd Unit and started conducting raids in the backyard. Sherry Rev printed up shirts that said TEAM LANDON and joined a Moms of Middle East Front Vets support group. Dalton started cramming cash away, taking any job he could get his hands on—from stolen bicycles to lost cats to the disappearance of a local ombudsman and a van full of municipal bonds. It had taken him over a week to figure out what an ombudsman even was, but he'd eventually found the guy holed up in a motel one town over. Even so, he was nowhere close to having enough to order a full set. So he came up with a website, making himself sound a lot more experienced than he was, and downloaded a fake Dick's license for a hundred bucks. Chuff's money would help. So would Macy's. But the real stuff, the triple-lined Kevlar with trauma plates and heat vents and spinal protection, wasn't cheap. Or easy to find. And now the dealer in Ukraine he'd been negotiating with for months said if Dalton didn't pay by Saturday night, they were selling his order to someone else. It would take forever to line up another deal, if he could even find a new seller willing to ship to the Middle East Front. Dalton had originally planned to get a jacket just for Landon, but he realized Landon would refuse to wear the thing if the rest of his unit didn't have one too. Landon was like that. Dalton wanted to be like that.

"Hey, Dad, here's your pudding."

Dalton's father took the bowl without looking up. He hated to be interrupted during the news. Dalton went back to the kitchen and leaned against the fridge, slipping into Reasonably

Prodigal Son mode. He made himself take a deep breath and modulated his voice. You had to come at Sherry Rev sideways, if you were dumb enough to come at her at all.

"Mom, here's a question for you."

"Umm-hmm?"

"Did you, by any chance, happen to send an application to this little-known college called Harvard a few months ago?"

His mother looked up, distracted. Then she smiled.

"Yes. I didn't think you'd mind, since you've been so busy transferring schools. Do you?"

"Oh, not at all."

"Good."

"I just, uh, thought maybe I might be needed around here instead."

"Instead of what?"

"You know, instead of off on a campus somewhere. Learning to protest Columbus Day. And studying about the evolution of kegs and stuff."

Sherry Rev said nothing, leaning over her recipe.

"Mom?"

"Umm?"

"Did you also, by any chance, send some stories of mine in with the application? Stories, I might add, no one has ever read, which were sitting harmlessly and privately on the thumb drive I keep in my lockbox? Stories there's no way you could possibly have known about, in a place that's professionally hidden?"

"Well, honey," Sherry Rev said, folding two quarts of heavy cream into a pan of sautéed beef and putting it on simmer. "I had to add *something* in lieu of an essay. As Principal Inference said over the phone, your extracurriculars are, frankly, not all that impressive."

Dalton coughed. "You talked to Inference?"

Sherry narrowed her eyes in an unabashedly data-gathering glance. "Yes. She called this afternoon to say how well you're adjusting. Is it true?"

"Stiff Sheets is adjusting!" Turd Unit yelled.

"Kirkland, pipe down."

"Principal Inference is nice," Dalton said, not wanting to distract his mom from her recipe. A distracted Sherry was a cross-examining Sherry. "School's nice. Everything's fine."

"In my experience, which is considerable, when someone says *everything's fine*, it means the exact opposite."

"Stiff Sheets is being an opposite!" Turd Unit howled, spitting melted cheese inside Dalton's helmet.

THE PRIVATE DICK HANDBOOK, RULE #18
**When Mom starts asking unanswerable questions,
toss an aerosol can into the flames.**

Dalton reached over and yanked his helmet from Turd Unit's head.

"Hey!"

"Hey, what?"

"Hey, hairy palm, knock it off!"

Dalton got Turd Unit in a sleeper-hold, rubbing his knuckles over his little brother's scalp. Turd Unit fought and clawed until he got tired, and then possumed, pretending to cry.

"No crying," Sherry Rev said. "Work it out."

Turd Unit kept crying. Dalton grabbed some macaroni off the plate and slipped one into each of Turd Unit's nostrils. Turd Unit sneezed, sending them across the room like Roman candles, where they stuck to the far wall. Sherry Rev didn't seem to notice. Dalton and Turd Unit burst out laughing. They slapped five. Then reloaded the macaroni cannon. Like everything else in the world, it never worked as well the second time. Still, they slapped five. And then slapped ten. And then fifteen, doing it harder each time.

"Butt plug."

Ouch!

"Renob."

Ouch!

"Shaft grip."

Ouch!

"Rimwipe."

Ouch!

"BOYS!" Sherry Rev yelled, then pointed to the big clock on the wall. It was almost nine. The diversionary tactic had worked flawlessly. Dalton slipped out of the kitchen while Turd Unit went into the living room to watch his favorite show, *Bull Snap*, where contestants had to knock cigars out of each other's mouths with a thirteen-foot braided leather whip for cash and prizes. Sherry Rev absentmindedly wiped a long stain across the front of her dress and then went back to her recipe.

Dalton went to his room. Above his computer was a shelf containing, in chronological order, all but one of the fifty-two

Lexington Cole Mysteries. On the far left was the very first, a copy he'd paid nearly a hundred dollars for—*Hammershot Panicsmith*. On the far right was the final installment, published posthumously, *Even a Blind Pig Finds a Truffle Now and Again*. There was an empty slot next to *An Open Mind, a Closed Fist, and a Bloody Mouth* where the edition he'd lost chasing after Elisha Cook should have gone. Even so, Dalton felt inspired by the multicolored spines, the collected wisdom, guile, experience, and steel balls of one man. It was too bad he was going to have to sell the collection. He'd already had it appraised at a bookstore in town. The clerk had given him a low whistle and a nod of appreciation when he'd seen the stack of first editions. He'd get less now, of course, because of the missing book. Still, he'd be that much closer to the body armor.

Dalton snapped on the desk lamp and began making changes to "The A to Z of Possible Gods." He spent an hour doing revisions, then checked his website. A bunch of hits, but only a few messages. Two people with lost animals, a cat named Jacques and a dog named Mr. Tibbs. One message from the arms dealer in Ukraine. Dalton took a deep breath before clicking it open. He'd been waiting for a reply to his last e-mail asking for a little more time. The response was curt and final. Saturday, midnight, or the deal was off. Then they called him a dildo in Cyrillic, which he had to run through a translator to confirm.

Shite.

There were four e-mails from Macy, *Call me!* and *What happened?* and *Did I do something wrong?* and *Why haven't you called me yet?* But when Dalton called, the phone rang and rang, no answer. He sent her a reply, *Pick up your phone,* but she didn't e-mail back. Then he took out his case notebook and wrote out some thoughts on Salt River. *Wesley Payne was a Populah with cash. But Macy said Populahs had no racket. Which probably means they were into something a Euclidian wasn't likely to come across while studying for quizzes about the Sino-Japanese War. It also means, no matter how great a guy he was, Payne had had some power. And someone wanted his power. Or wanted him not to be able to wield it anymore. At the same time, there was a missing hundred grand. Money was power. Inference had power, but a whole lot less with no money, so maybe it was a cash grab and a move to weaken her at the same time. And then there was the clique war. All wars were fought over goods or egos. Someone was trying to corner the market at Salt River, grab the rackets and every-thing else for themselves. Chuff was wrong about a balance. There was no balance, and there never would be. There was one big hand whose fingers were slowly closing over the whole school. But whose? The notes in my helmet insist it was Lee Harvies. Except Lee Harvies are a ghost. Tarot made the most sense but was also the most obvious. It could be the Snouts, desperate to move into new rackets with the economy gone to shite. Corruption from within. Corruption with a badge. Sounds good, but not likely. Or maybe Wesley's old Crop Crème buddies were lying low and getting ready to re-form? Could they be strong enough to actually make a move?*

Dalton sighed. He knew he was going in circles. He needed more information. And there was only one place to get it. At the source. You had to apply the principle of Occam's Sledgehammer: Pressure the most obvious suspect and find out who Wes Payne's girlfriend was.

Dalton closed his case file, prepared to do a solid hour of homework, when he realized he'd left his bag with all his assignments at Macy's house.

Tragic. Seriously.

He dialed her again. No answer. He fished Wes Payne's envelope out of his jeans pocket, recounted the money, and put it carefully with the rest of his stash in the lockbox. On top he laid a note that said *Mom—knock it off!* Just before closing the door, he noticed faint writing on the envelope, lines running all the way across the back. He held it under the light. The first half was an even more lightly penciled version of Wesley's suicide note, the lyrics to "Exquisite Lies." Beneath that was what looked like a poem, or another Pinker Casket song. It was called "The Ballad of Mary Surratt." Could Mary Surratt be Wesley's girlfriend? And why was he so obsessed with cheesy lyrics? Some of the words had been heavily erased, exactly like the suicide note, either crossed out or written back in, like he had worked hard at getting it right. Dalton put the envelope in his pocket and got in bed. After a little while his mom poked her head in.

"'Night, honey."

"'Night."

"Dalton?"

"Yeah?"

"There are broken dishes on your floor."

Dalton had taken to laying broken crockery in a circle around his bed in case anyone decided to get cute and sneak in while he slept. Every night his mom mentioned it, sort of as a running joke, but also, he figured, in the vague hope he would one time take it upon himself to explain why. Instead, he told her what he always did.

"Sorry. I'll clean them up."

She nodded and closed the door. It was quiet for a few minutes, before his father's snoring started its nightly gore through the thin walls. Dalton snapped on the bedside lamp and thought about what Elisha Cook had said about his short stories. Were they really good enough to get into Harvard? What he'd wanted, more than anything, was to be able to write like Barnaby Smollet, the author of the Lexington Cole series. It was why he'd tried writing to begin with. Again and again he'd held one of Smollet's books open and attempted to match his style: the short sentences, the terse phrases, the tough-guy posturing. It never worked. The stuff he wrote was laughably overdone and thinly considered. He went through a dozen first chapters, through multiple dissipated debutantes. Through detectives so crooked they had to screw their underwear on. Through inbred heiresses and heavily scarved fortune readers and pharmacists of ill repute.

He reached over and pulled a sheaf of paper from his notebook, holding the stories his mom had submitted in front of him. He licked his thumb and looked at the first paragraph, trying to imagine what Elisha Cook had seen in his words, trying to read it from his point of view.

HARVARD ADMISSIONS PROGRAM
Danielle Steel Creative Writing Scholarship Application
Story #1, "The Leaves Always Scream the Loudest"
By Dalton Rev

It was twelve o'clock on a Tuesday afternoon and the darkness was absolute. Ash felt his way across the bedroom floor until he found the bottle of brandy that Counselor Dan kept under the bed. He popped it open and took a long swig, coughing half back up. His throat burned and he felt queasy, so he forced down another gulp. Counselor Dan wouldn't mind. Mostly because Counselor Dan and Counselor Sue and all the rest of the adults had disappeared a week ago.

Along with the electricity.

And the sun.

There was a scream and then a crash. One floor below, the remaining campers scratched and tore and rooted around. "Mom!" they yelled, over and over. "Mom mom mom mom mom!" Pubescent baritones mixed with late bloomers' pinched sopranos, voices rising in agonized fifths. Most of them had stripped naked. And used the mud in the yard for body paint. And torn the furniture apart to make clubs and spears. And tied the fat kid caught hoarding Ring Dings to the desk in the lobby, the same fat kid who kept moaning and crying and begging to be released, or at least given some water.

Ash finished the brandy as banging resumed against Counselor Dan's door. At first it was just a few fists, and then a frenzied dozen. Voices cursed and railed, fingers grappling for purchase, chanting in unison.

"Ash Ash Ash Ash Ash! Kill Kill Kill Kill Kill!"

They slammed themselves against the oak door that Ash had long since secured with nails and seven of the nine arms of the teak statue of Shiva that had once dominated the lobby. But even that wouldn't hold much longer.

"Ash!" *Bam.* "Ash!" *Bam.* "Ash!"

It had been a week since the darkness fell.

"Kill!" *Bam.* "Kill!" *Bam.* "Kill!"

Or never lifted.

It had been seven full days since the entire camp had woken to an absolutely black morning, since the students and staff and faculty had been forced to admit that the sun had simply failed to rise.

And maybe never would again...

Dalton threw the rest of the pages on the floor. It was crap and he knew it. He couldn't write for shite. Like, seriously, not at all.

Somewhere, Barnaby Smollet was boiling over in his grave.

CHAPTER 12

TWO EGGS, CRISPY BACON, AND A UNIT OF TURD SLURPING CEREAL

The cracking of dishes woke him. Dalton was on his belly, face mashed into a pillow, arms splayed. In one quick motion he reached between the mattress and the wall for his broken golf club, ready to swing. Sherry Rev didn't even flinch at the brandished nine iron, apologizing for waking him so early.

"What're you *doing*, Mom?"

"I know you need your sleep, Arnold Palmer, but there's someone on our lawn. Behind the tree. Looking up at your window."

Dalton sighed, thinking what a total cardigan this Elisha Cook was, but also secretly relieved. Harvard? Had he really turned down Harvard? Dalton pulled on some pants and parted the curtain, looking out at the tree in the backyard. There were no pinstripes, no three-piece suit. There was only a belly. A big one hidden by the world's ugliest Hawaiian shirt.

"Why is there a rather chubby young man who has overdosed on hair gel picking his nose on the lawn outside our house?"

"He wants a bromance."

"Terrific! You made a new friend at school already?"

"I guess you could say that."

"Do you want to invite him in for breakfast?"

THE PRIVATE DICK HANDBOOK, RULE #19

Why do people hide behind trees? No one in the history of the world has ever successfully hidden behind a tree.

"He can stand there and make his own breakfast."

"Dalton."

"Yeah, okay, Ma. Let's fire up the waffle iron. But make me a promise?"

"Sure, Tiger. What is it?"

"No more mentioning, let alone showing anyone, my writing?"

"Deal."

"I'm serious, Ma. Do *not* tell Mole, or I'll never hear the end of it."

"Mole?"

"Mole. You promise?"

Sherry Rev looked her son in the eye. "I promise."

Mole sat crunching through his fourth waffle covered with Flavor Flavah, while Turd Unit sat next to him, spraying the can directly into his mouth. Dalton's dad just drank coffee.

"So...Mole," Sherry said. "Do your parents live around here? Would I know them by any chance?"

"You can call me Lester, ma'am."

"You can call me Turd Unit," Turd Unit said, imitating Mole's voice and stuffed-cheek delivery almost perfectly. Even Dalton's father laughed.

"Clever, little man," Mole said. "Do I think you have a future on the comedic stage? In front of a mic and a boozy nightclub crowd? Yes, I do."

"Is Lester," Turd Unit asked, still in Mole's voice, "by any chance short for *M-O-L-E-S-T-E-R*?"

"Kirkland! Knock it off!" Sherry said. Turd Unit cackled maniacally, now spooning in huge mouthfuls of his favorite cereal, Frooty Bobbers. Light blue milk spilled down his chin.

"Your parents, Lester?"

"My dad's gone. It's like, what dad? He took off a while back. Mom works up at Milton Friedman. The community college? Teaches economics. Invest here, don't invest there, add this column of numbers to that one. Night school housewives deserve to bring home the investment bacon too, am I right?"

"What's her name?"

"Who?"

"Your mother."

"My mother?"

"Yes. Your mother."

Mole waited a long time before answering.

"Buffy."

"Buffy?" Dalton's mom said.

"Buffy?" Dalton's dad said.

"*Buffy?*" Turd Unit said, turning his spoon around and staking a vampire waffle in the heart.

"Buffy Bucharest," Mole said, without his usual enthusiasm. "Ha-ha. Hilarious. Say it a few times. Get it out of your system. Can we move on?"

Sherry Rev began washing dishes, her prosecutorial zeal

sated. Dalton's dad went into the living room with a refill and turned on the news.

"You know a Mary Surratt?" Dalton whispered. "She in any of the cliques?"

"I don't think so."

"You got any idea who Wesley Payne's girlfriend was?"

Mole looked surprised. "I guess most girls in school wanted to be. Saw him with lots of them, but not like holding hands. That slick had his pick, pluck any tomato off the vine. Rumors, rumors, you know, but to be honest, I'm not el convincedo Wesley really had one."

"Macy says he talked about her all the time. And why are you speaking Spanglish?"

Mole shrugged. "Wesley didn't talk about this mystery spinderella anywhere that it trickled down. I'm thinking if he habla'd about it, sooner or later the el poop would've trickled down to me."

"Poop!" Turd Unit said, fishing the prize out of his box of Frooty Bobbers. It was a tiny plastic hot dog whistle on a lanyard. He put it around his neck and began to blow.

"Anyhow," Mole said, finishing off another waffle, "we're gonna be late for escuela."

"Where's your car?" Dalton asked, looking out the window.

"Moms dropped me off in the Kia."

Turd Unit tweeted in shrill bursts. "No car means boyfriends ride tandem on scooters! One boyfriend saying *That feels so good* in Spanish the whole way!"

"Kirkland!" Sherry Rev said, without much enthusiasm. When she turned back toward the sink, Mole yanked the plastic whistle from Turd Unit's neck and ground it under his heel.

"Mom, Bucharest crushed my wiener!"

Dalton flicked his brother's ear, hard. Turd Unit pretended to cry for a minute, saw that there was zero value in it, and then went back to scooping Frooty Bobbers.

"Let me find the extra helmet," Dalton said, turning on the basement light, an old fluorescent carpenter's lamp that mostly left it dark. He stepped carefully over junk piled along the wooden stairs. The damp concrete floor was covered with stacks of cardboard boxes, rusting machinery, and piles of long-moldered laundry. There were magazines tossed at random, headless dolls, wheelless tricycles, and Joes with very little G.I. left in them. Dalton picked his way to where he thought the helmet was stashed, nosing through garbage, when he realized he wasn't alone.

Something was in the basement with him.

Something big.

Farck.

Hadn't he ever seen a slasher movie before? Everyone knew you didn't go in the basement alone.

Dalton peered over a cardboard box full of Christmas tree parts. In the back corner, a large, dark shadow flickered, moving slightly. It was hard to tell if the thing was ducking between boxes, or if it was the effect of the bare bulb hanging over the utility sink.

The one that Dalton hadn't turned on.

Run. Scream.

There had to be a better option.

Pee pants?

Uh, no.

Think, guy, think.

He was about equidistant to the thing and the stairs, the top coordinate in a serial killer isosceles. If he ran, it meant turning his back while picking through garbage in the dark. He didn't want to turn his back. At all. The other option was to fight. Dalton thought of Landon and what his brother was probably looking at through an infrared scope right that second, before forcing himself into Grow a Sac mode. He picked up a piece of rebar from a pile against the wall, hefting it. Rusty, but solid. It hurt his palm, but in a good way. He looked back longingly at the stairs, a thousand pounds of junk between him and the bottom step.

Then the overhead went off.

Dalton faked left. The thing didn't move. He faked right. The thing didn't move. He crept sideways, figuring it would try to cut him off, but it remained stationary. He could hear Turd Unit's girly laugh through the floorboards.

THE PRIVATE DICK HANDBOOK, RULE #20

When you're scared, always run directly at the thing you're scared of. Never run away while looking over your shoulder like every dead slasher blond. Force the thing to make a decision, and just hope it makes the wrong one.

Dalton raised the rebar over his head and charged.

Six feet.

The thing didn't move.

Three feet.

The thing didn't move.

One foot.

You have got to be shite-ing me.

The rebar fell with a clang. The thing was hanging from water pipes threaded through the ceiling joists, right above a pile of folded towels and nighties.

Wrapped in duct tape.

Head to toe.

The Body.

It had big red letters spray-painted on its chest. I KNOW I DIDN'T KILLED ME. And under that, the word TERRUR.

"Let's go, Johnny Rambo!" Mole yelled from the top of the steps, causing Dalton to jump and bang his head. The Body shook wildly. The room spun for a second.

"Turn on the lights!"

The lights clicked on.

"What are you doing down there?" Mole asked. "We're gonna miss vital instruction. I have a GPA to maintain."

Dalton spat, trying to think. It was ridiculous. A frame job? But by who? And how did they sneak it in here? Lex Cole would have just soaked The Body with kerosene and burned the house down. So much for actionable evidence. In *Takin' Care of Witness*, he'd siphoned fuel from a lawn mower and torched a sweatshop full of bloody tartan. Not really an option in this scenario, though. There had to be a smart play.

Get rid of it.

How?

Call the Snouts, claim zero knowledge, let them deal.

No chance.

Call Macy?

Why? To tell her you found her un-missing brother?

Dalton reached down and pulled a strip of duct tape off the thing's face. Two red lips puckered behind the tearing sound, but didn't move. He fought off a gag. Wesley Payne's lips. Shouldn't they be decomposed? Or was he jacked from the funeral home still full of formaldehyde? Dalton sniffed. It smelled like potato chips. Sour cream and chive.

Do not puke. Just don't.

Dalton slipped back up the stairs and into the kitchen. His mother was finishing the dishes. "Honey, did you turn the wash over? Or do I need to?"

"I'll do it!" Dalton answered, slipping a cleaver from the knife rack and hiding it in his waistband.

THE PRIVATE DICK HANDBOOK, RULE #21
Why didn't you just tell her it was already done?

"Why did you just slip a cleaver from the knife rack and hide it in your waistband?"

"Um. I was going to clean the lint trap. It's all backed up."

"Stiff Sheets battles lint!" Turd Unit yelled. "Lint wins!"

Dalton ran upstairs. He slipped a business card out of his wallet and called the number at the bottom. Then he pulled his throw rug from under the bed, rolling it like a tortilla and dragging it down the basement steps. A minute later, Mole materialized from between stacks of boxes like he'd been stored there for a year.

"Dude, what the em eff?"

"I know."

"Is that Wesley Payne? That can't be Wesley Payne. He's, like, muerto already."

Dalton unrolled the rug.

"And why does he have that on his chest? *I know I didn't killed me*? What's *terrur* supposed to mean?"

THE PRIVATE DICK HANDBOOK, RULE #22
Explaining the unexplainable is like de-virgining a virgin.
It's like sewing hair on a goat.
It's like punching yourself in the face.
And liking it.

"It means help me with this so it doesn't make any noise when I cut it down."

Mole shook his head. "Don't want to."

Dalton was already supporting the weight with one hand while extending the knife with the other. "Don't want to what?"

"Touch him."

"Touch him?"

Mole nodded.

"Listen—" Dalton began, but was drowned out by a rumble that shook the basement window, followed by a squeal of tires. *That was fast.* Dalton let go of The Body, which jounced on its rope like a piñata. "Stay here and make sure my mom doesn't come down, no matter what."

"No, please," Mole said. "Don't leave me with—"

Dalton ran back up the stairs and out the side door.

The rumble wasn't coming from a Nova. An earth mover was parked at the neighbor's, a truck from a septic tank company angled out the driveway.

Farck!

Dalton turned, slamming into Mole. They lay in the grass for a minute, holding their heads.

"You're supposed to be in the basement," Dalton moaned. "In case my mom—"

"But it's wicked dark."

Dalton got up and pushed past the stacks of junk again, hurrying over to the utility sink. The laundry was there. The bare bulb was there. The rope was there.

But The Body wasn't.

It was gone.

"It's gone," Mole said over his shoulder.

Dalton ran back upstairs. He checked every door, every closet, making his way to the family room.

"Hey, Dad. Did you see anything weird go by?"

"No sign of Landon," his father said, turning up the volume. That left the kitchen. *Shite.* Dalton zipped through the saloon doors, losing his balance and slamming into the fridge. A bowl of oranges fell on its side, rolling across the floor. Sherry Rev and Turd Unit looked up quizzically. If a body had somehow managed to zombie its way by, they obviously hadn't seen it.

"Thought I lost something. Guess I was wrong."

"Dalton lost his mind," Turd Unit said, almost calmly, his blood sugar having leveled off. "Dalton lost his boyfriend."

"Aren't you going to be late for school?" Sherry asked.

"Already am," Dalton said, wondering if he should warn her, *Hey, um, Mom, if you happen to see a, y'know, dead body around, um, go ahead and call the cops right away, okay?*

Pass.

In the driveway, Mole stood mopping sweat from his neck. His Hawaiian shirt was soaked through. He smelled like a wedge of Gouda.

"Look at me," Dalton said.

"Why?"

"Just do it."

Mole turned reluctantly.

"It *was* down there, right?"

"Come again?"

"The Body?"

"Yeah, man. It was there. Whatever it was."

Ronnie Newport's Nova screeched up to the curb. The window rolled down. Newport aimed his lens and took three pictures of the two of them, Fatman and Blobbin, rumpled and defeated and confused. Then he kicked open the passenger-side door.

"Got the trunk cleaned out. What do you need to move?"

"False alarm," Dalton said. "Now we just need a ride."

"Salt River?"

"No, Tarot's."

"Tarot's?"

"Tarot's."

"But we're gonna miss school," Mole said. "I got a test in Splonge's after lunch. No way I can skip that."

"Slip her a twenty," Newport said. "You'll pass."

"Euclidians don't do it that way."

"What way do Euclidians do it?" the Ginny Slims asked.

"And, um, also? I could have sworn you just said something about Tarot. No way do I want to go near that vampire."

"You can walk," Dalton said. "You don't have to come."

"Walk? Okay, for one thing, that's exercise. For another, there's a dead body shuffling around. Lester Bucharest and dead bodies don't mix. You feelin' me?"

"I'm feelin' you!" one of the Ginny Slims called, grabbing Mole's wrist.

"No, I'm feelin' him!" the other insisted, holding out her arms for a motherly embrace. Dalton shouldered Mole in with the Slims and then got in front, slamming the door.

"School's shut down today, anyhow," Newport said, lighting a butt and flicking the old one past Dalton's nose and out the window.

"What for?"

"Contraband locker search. Snouts're in there with bolt cutters right now, working the rows."

"Snouts?"

"Snouts, Inference, whatever."

"They announce it?"

"Nah, sign on the doors said 'Danger: Radon Leak.'" Newport slicked back his pompadour with two fingers, staring straight ahead. He lifted the camera from around his neck, focused the massive lens, and took a picture of a bird pecking at an old candy wrapper. "Lot of cliques gonna lose their shirts today."

"What are you going to lose?"

"I lost way before I even started," Newport said, exhaling six lungs' worth of smoke.

"Then why take me to Tarot? Long as you're being existential, why bother doing it at all?"

"Cash."

Dalton wondered if it was an act, this purposeful slide into disgrace, or if Newport really had been ruined on some level by the death of Wesley Payne. "You know who Mary Surratt is? She a friend of Wesley's maybe?"

"How you spell it? She got an unnecessary Y?"

"No."

"Everyone was a friend of Wesley's. I never heard of her, but she probably was too."

"Take the long way around, Godot," Dalton said, handing over four twenties. "I need to think."

Newport lit another cigarette, as the Nova peeled from the curb.

CHAPTER 13
ALL ALONG THE DONGTOWER

The car broke down twice. First it was a blown manifold. Then a problem with the linkage. Newport tinkered under the hood while the Slims cackled and whined. Dalton stood on the side of the road thinking while Mole tried to escape, vainly, from the backseat. They had to drive across town twice for two different parts, and then wait while Newport tried to decipher the elaborately folded Korean instructions before installing them. It was late afternoon by the time the red Nova pulled into the parking lot of Archie Shepp Studios, dropping off Dalton and Mole.

The building was in the worst part of town, under the highway bridge and near the docks. The pavement was pitted and wet. Men in trench coats slept by the rail lines, or sat on beds of cardboard, picking at their damp toes. They watched as van after van of tattooed longhairs and tattooed skinheads loaded amps and cords and mic stands up and down the steel loading dock. The sound of dozens of bands rehearsing simultaneously funneled out the blast doors like a jumbo jet coughing bolts from its last engine. Dalton could feel the blister of dropped notes and chord changes and falsetto choruses against his face.

It was impossible to imagine how each band could hear enough to differentiate their songs from the rest of the primordial squall. In *From Crayons to Perfume*, Lexington Cole goes undercover playing harmonica in a gutbucket Kansas City dive that sounded like *Abbey Road* compared to this.

"Now what?" Mole asked, his smirk and lingo gone, his flow of patter down to a faucet drip, suddenly just a fat, scared kid in a ridiculous shirt. He was also covered with scratches and hickeys courtesy of the Ginny Slims.

"Now we wait."

"You let them paw at me. I feel so dirty."

"You paid your dues," Dalton agreed, wiping lipstick off Mole's elbow. "No doubt."

"Move it, hand gallops!"

A trio of tall bald men with black eyeliner pushed past. Stenciled on all their equipment was the name STORMING KABUL. The tallest one wore a T-shirt that said ACE STORMING. The shortest one's said BILLY KABUL. Dalton stepped out of the way, slipping into Yeah, I'm That Keyboard Player Everyone Says You Shouldn't Mess With mode. He cleaned his fingernails with Wes Payne's locker key, staring at the black maw of the loading dock as if waiting for the rest of his band to show.

THE PRIVATE DICK HANDBOOK, RULE #23
Abandon Most of Your Hope, Ye Who Enter Here

"I want to go home," Mole said.

"I know."

"Seriously, man. What am I doing here?"

"I dunno. You're the one who came to my house, remember?"

"That's cold, yo. I came for waffles. Instead, there I am rolling up my sleeves helping you with a dead body in your basement. And now we're scuffling around downtown Beirut looking for Transylvanian Elvis. This is so messed up."

Dalton nodded, but he wasn't really listening. He was trying to time the gap in bands as they came in and out of the giant front door. Eventually the traffic would slow and there'd be a window to slip through, sort of like walking over to your buddy Ed Lecter's wearing a pork-chop necklace. A-one and a-two.

"Where you going, guy?"

"Room sixty-six. Like Newport said."

"No way." Mole ducked behind a gold truck that had the name TRANNIE AND THE TRAWLERS spray-painted on the side. "Tarot snacks on small children and shites out knitted booties. He wants to stick a straw in me and turn me into the world's biggest can of Rush."

"I won't let him do that," Dalton said, not entirely sure *let* was part of the equation.

"*Let* is so not part of the equation."

"I could use some sidekick backup here. Time to stop sitting on your ham."

"That's what I'm *doing*," Mole said, thumbing his glasses in place. "Kicking some serious side. I'm just doing it out here. Way out here. Ham or not."

"You know what Newport told me on the drive over?"

"How to rebuild a carburetor with hair gel and cigarette butts?"

"Salt River's closed today because they're tossing lockers for contraband."

Mole's face blanched. He rubbed his eyes counterclockwise. "For real?"

"For real."

"Yeah, um, okay. I gotta split now. This was fun. I'll see you later."

"You're walking? You won't get home until Christmas."

"At least there'll be presents when I get there," Mole said, already at the edge of the lot. Dalton turned into the warehouselike darkness. The entire building was vibrating. It was like entering the lung of someone burning through two cartons a day. He asked for a pair of earplugs at the little booth in the corner that sold strings and straps and tuning forks.

"Thirty bucks."

"For earplugs?"

The woman manning the booth nodded. "Seller's market." Her lips barely moved beneath a layer of white makeup and purple dreadlocks.

"You remind me of someone. You know a guy who drives a —"

"Lunch truck? Yeah, that's Roach. My cousin."

"That makes you, what? Black Widow?"

"Everyone loves a crackstar."

"It's so not true." Dalton inserted one earplug, about to insert the other when she said "Strata."

"Huh?"

"My name."

Dalton held up Wes Payne's key. "Ever seen one of these, Strata?"

"I believe they call that a key."

Dalton slipped her an extra twenty. She put his money in a little pouch sewn inside her skirt. "There's lockers on every floor. End of the hall on your left."

Dalton walked around in the dark until he found the staircase, climbing to the next level. Each floor contained two hallways, both gauntlets of mayhem. Dirty rugs, jangling guitars, shadowy figures in black smoking and arguing through jolts of distortion as pure as fresh corn. Girls in skirts and heels ran squealing after each other. Drummers air soloed. A hair metal band seemed to be shooting craps in the corner. Behind them was a wall of blue lockers covered in graffiti. Dalton patted his pockets, acting like he'd forgotten his sheet music, and tried number 9. It fit, but didn't turn. He repeated the pattern with the lockers on the second and third floors with the same result. At the end of the fourth hallway was room sixty-six, the door shaking like it was about to be torn off its hinges and swept across the Kansas prairie. Dalton counted to twenty-three trying to summon Wronged Commuter Metes Out Subway Justice mode, settling for Not Really All That Tough, but at Least Not an Obvious Purse instead.

There were any number of people in the room sitting on old couches and broken chairs and a rug so dirty it had no color at all anymore. Caskets and Girlz with Two First Names sucked face. Kokrocks and Airplane Gluze and even some hipper New Skids groused furtively in the corners, sipping out of paper bags. Cape Silverspoon on the slum stood all capri'd and ponytailed, waiting for someone to tell them how *totally wild* it was they were here. They all more or less faced the stage, a plywood rectangle where Kurt Tarot stood in a lone spotlight, a cone of white punching into the darkness. Mick Freeley noodled away on a pointy orange Charvel covered in skull decals. *Playing makeup and wearing guitars.* Tarot wore a leather coat with a high collar. He held the microphone the way a cat holds a parakeet, nuzzling its feathers. Dalton looked around the room, at the eyes of the girls, most of them watching intently, completely hooked. Tarot's paradox was to be enticing and off-putting in equal measure. His voice had a vaguely Arabic, snake-charming lilt, droning the same words over and over again.

Kiss fist, eat floor
Bite my wrist and drink some more
Feed, feed
Feed my greed
Feel my pulse and
Taste the gore

Suck neck, hit deck
Look down my throat and read the lore
Rush Rush
Into the blush
Dethorn the rose and
Beg for more

Tarot suddenly stopped singing. He cocked his head to one side, staring out into the darkness. *Here it comes*, Dalton thought, but Tarot turned and made a sweeping motion with his hand. The band stopped playing, the song falling apart like a barrel of lamps.

Tarot reached out and slapped the bass player. The smack resounded across the room, quieting laughter and random arguments.

"I haven't had time to learn this part yet!" the bass player explained, holding his check, a big punker guy in an A-TISKET, A-TASKET, YOUR GRILLED SPLEEN IN MY PICNIC CASKET T-shirt.

Tarot straightened his guitar in an almost fatherly way.

"Don't get it wrong again."

The bass player took a deep breath, putting his hands on the strings. Everyone in the room watched as he ran through the first few bars, shakily at first, then stronger, almost having it locked in before flubbing a note. Tarot grabbed him by the neck and dragged him backstage. There was a scream. Tarot came back alone, gripping the mic with the points of his black fingernails.

"Anyone elze?"

A tall Casket ran onto the stage, beating out two others, and shouldered the bass. He slapped a funky little chord and then picked out the first ten bars of the song perfectly.

"Good," Tarot said, about to count it off, when he saw Dalton.

"I believe we have been infiltrated by a Dick."

Everyone in the room craned their cheap-jeweled necks and turned their dyed-hair heads. A tingle ran up Dalton's spine like a wet cliché. He never got a tingle. Sweat broke out on his forehead. He never sweated, or broke out.

"I'm here to ask you some questions."

Kurt Tarot laughed into the mic, his skull piercing banging into the windscreen. "And how exactly did you know where to find me, offizer?"

"Newport."

"Ah. The human camera lens. And why would he bring you here?"

"I paid him. Apparently, so do you."

"Liar. If anything, I would have paid him to take you farther away."

The Crowdarounds laughed while Dalton considered the possibility that Ronnie Newport was full of shite.

THE PRIVATE DICK HANDBOOK, RULE #24
Why are you here again?
Better get off your ham and come up with a reason.

A number of Pinker Caskets stepped away from the stage's edge and into the shadows. One slid along the wall with a bandage on his hand from being stuck with a butterfly pin. Others came through the crowd, cutting off the path to the door. Tarot stepped off the stage as well, dropping the mic with a horrendous screech of feedback. Some of the groupies cheered, nipping off plastic bottles, eyes lolling in their heads. Tarot held up the mic stand, swinging the heavy metal end like a rockabilly ninja. Dalton backed away as far as he could, which wasn't far. If he caught a mouthful of the stand it would be denture time. As he tried to retreat, an Airplane Gluze blocked his way. Tarot changed the arc of the rotating pole, picking up speed, and then let it fall with a dizzying whistle, collapsing the table in front of Dalton like a watered melon.

"No Mizz Splonge to rescue you now," Tarot said. "No reason to be here. No reason to *be* at all, really." He raised the mic stand again. "But we can fix that."

"Do it," yelled a bunch of Caskets. Others echoed them, starting a chant, "*Do it! Do it! Do it! Do it! Do it!*"

Dalton crouched, ready to slip under Tarot's swing and grab the metal shaft. In *Fjord of the Flies*, Lex Cole had fought off a pack of feral Norwegians with a broomstick. If he could wrestle the mic away, he might be able to clear a path toward the door.

"*Do it! Do it! Do it! Do it! Do it!*"

Tarot raised the stand high above his head, picking up speed.

"STOP!" Cassiopeia Jones said, smoothing her way through the crowd, which instinctively made way. She walked to Dalton's side, casually standing between him and Tarot. New Skid necks swiveled and Kokrock eyes bulged, the entire room staring. And they were right to. She was acetylene-hot in a one-piece leather bodysuit. Her boots were thigh-high with a pink spiderweb pattern scored into them, tapering to impossibly long heels. Her hair was dyed android blue. "He's here because I asked him to be."

"You're late," Tarot growled, not lowering the stand. "And why would you azk him to come here?"

Cassiopeia played with her cerulean bangs. "Because he can help us."

"*Us?*" Dalton whispered.

Cassiopeia ignored him, concentrating on movement within the crowd. Caskets continued to press closer as Foxxes took strategic positions around the room. Jenny One, or maybe it was Jenny Three, stood behind Cassiopeia. Caskets and their sub-cliques had numerical superiority, but the Foxxes looked smoother, sleeker, and more fierce. Compared to the slovenly Des Barres passed out or Steel-toe Dystopia petulantly kicking holes in the walls, they were smooth and efficient and frightening.

"What in farck are you doing here, Cassie?" Dalton asked, out of the side of his mouth.

"Foxxes go down whatever holes they want to, Dalton, honey. Besides, I sing backup with Casket now. So watch your mouth, or I'll sing a song all about you."

Cassiopeia stepped away from Dalton and casually walked to a couch, guys scrambling out of their boxers to get up and give her space. "Maybe you, me, and Dalty should go talk somewhere, huh, Kurt?"

If Foxxes and Casket had formed an alliance, Chuff was in major trouble. On the other hand, it appeared to be a delicate alliance at best.

Tarot jabbed at Dalton with a pinky nail. "This Dick I don't trust. I have no interezt in talking to him."

"Fair enough," Cassiopeia said, waving her hand dismissively. "I'm not sure I trust him either."

"Good. Then—"

"So let's give him a test. He passes, we'll talk. If not? Eh."

Tarot smiled cold chrome. The skull worked around his mouth like a lizard playing with the mantis it'd just plucked from the air. He turned to a Casket guarding the door. "Bring in the nerd!"

The assorted New Skids and Kokrocks clapped and cheered as two enormous Caskets came in holding Mole by either arm. They shoved him into a yellow recliner, spilling furious Des Barres into the trash on the floor. Mole looked at Dalton pleadingly while Tarot held out a microphone. It was live, giving off yips of feedback.

"What am I supposed to do with that?"

"You will zing us a song. All of us. Up on the stage."

"No chance," Dalton said. He didn't do stages. He didn't do microphones. Mick Freeley moved up behind him.

"I can't zay I like your chances of getting out of here with any teeth if you don't."

The melody of "Exquisite Lies" rode up Dalton's throat and plunged into his brain, driving out all other songs. It boomed around, canceling thought, rendering him simple-minded.

"I don't know any songs."

Tarot snapped his fingers. A Casket produced a huge sheaf of sheet music. Tarot pulled a chart at random, looked at it, and laughed.

"'Mustang Zally.' How appropriate."

Dalton looked at the papers.

"Go ahead and say it," Tarot dared. "Go ahead and say no."

Dalton looked at the microphone. The Crowdarounds booed, jeering wildly.

"Dalton!" Mole yelled, getting kicked in the stomach for his trouble. He lay at the edge of the stage, wheezing in pain. Cassiopeia inspected her nails.

Dalton took the mic and walked onstage. The lights gleamed in his face. There were more boos. Someone yelled "Freebird." Someone else yelled "Breadway to Unleavened." Caskets in

PRETTY IN PINK, UGLY IN FLESH shirts looked like they wanted to sink their teeth into Dalton's ankle.

Kurt Tarot waved his hand through the air, a downward chop that silenced the crowd. "Now or never."

The bass player and drummer started a backbeat, easing into the first few measures. Dalton set his feet apart and cleared his throat, squinting to read the hand-lettered lyrics sheet. His throat was rusted shut. He was deep into something he'd never experienced before—watery stage terror—which, in the end, was the least of his problems.

THE PRIVATE DICK HANDBOOK, RULE #25
This sucks hard. This sucks harder than suck
can handle. In fact, this totally glarks.

The music picked up, coming around again. The boos got louder. A few people threw shoes, one just missing his head. Dalton squinted. The first verse was:

Ooh, Mustang Sally
Dontcha think ya oughta slow that Mustang down?
Yow! Uh-huh uh-huh!
Now baby, you gotta stop
Cruising that mid-priced Ford around

Wilson Pickett could pull that off, sure. To Dalton, it was a bunch of arrhythmic gibberish. And half of it wasn't even the right words. But he also knew killing it onstage wasn't really about the lyrics, it was about the attitude. It was about being on a sunny street corner in tight pants with sideburns and a wallet full of cash, whistling at cute girls in convertibles. It was about Joe Strummer, in pegged pants and a greasy pompadour, daring Brixton to rise up and smash the aristocracy with a slogan or a paving stone. It was confidence. It was animal. It was innate.

Dalton closed his eyes.

When he opened his mouth, nothing came out.

The crowd was now throwing bottles, which broke in the corners. Dalton waited for the bass line to come around, like Lex Cole timing a leap between rooftops, and then started into the next verse:

You been running with the wrong crowd, whoo
Guess I better put your flat feet in
Orthopedic shoes, too
You been crying with your crying eyes
Sally baby, signifyin' lady
Are you sure driving so fast is wise?

His throat finally loosened. A warm tenor began to trickle out. He'd heard the song on Landon's stereo any number of times, Landon being a big fan of sixties soul. Dalton relaxed a little and settled in with the rhythm. The crowd relaxed as well, suddenly half as surly, looking at one another in amazement. As it turned out, Dalton had a pretty good voice. Actually, a better than good voice. It was a little scratchy, but earthy and in key. It had a bit of plaint to it, a weariness, but it was solid and true. By the repeated chorus —

All you wanna do is buy a vowel, Sally
Buy, Sally, buy

—the crowd was clapping and singing along. Dalton closed his eyes, stronger now, digging into the verses, playing with the melody. The band settled behind him, the drummer right in the pocket. The song was funky, riding along like it was meant to, like a red Cadillac on a hot day. Dalton, caught up in it, leaned back and hit a high note that had the girls squealing, just as the music went dead.

Tarot held the PA plug in his hand.

"ENOUGH!"

The drums and bass staggered to a halt.

"Thanks for coming, I'll be here all week," Dalton said to the silent room. "Oh, and the real reason school's closed is so Fack Cult can conduct locker searches."

There was a beat of shocked disbelief, and then a group surge for the door. Dalton tossed the mic toward some Dystopias in the far corner. Cliques pushed and shoved while Mick Freeley and a few Caskets tried to wade against the tide, rushing the stage. Mole was just getting to his feet, holding his stomach, when someone slammed him into the drum set. It exploded, cymbals flying against the wall with an incredible clatter. Dalton grabbed a pointy orange guitar and swung it in a wide arc. The nearest Casket ducked, and the guitar hit an amp. The neck separated from the body, which clanged onto the stage, leaving him with a handful of curled strings. Mick Freeley screamed and flew at Dalton.

"NO!" Cassiopeia yelled, having secured the mic, as Caskets and Foxxes squared off, eyeing one another rudely.

"He did what you asked him to do," Cassiopeia insisted, her voice steady. "He sang the song. A deal's a deal. Now it's time to stop acting like little boys and talk business."

"But…my guitar!" Mick Freeley moaned, holding it like a treaded cat.

Tarot seemed to consider his options, most of which ended in a brawl with Catwalk Ninja. Everyone in the room waited for his signal, balancing their weight. Tarot finally held up one arm and made a fist. Caskets reluctantly retreated into dark corners. Cassiopeia nodded, and Foxxes did the same.

"Zo we will talk."

Dalton followed Cassiopeia and Tarot out into the hall, trying to decide exactly what in farck it was he was going to say.

CHAPTER 14
THE MEETING AT YALTA

What he said was: "You killed Wesley Payne."

In the end, he couldn't help himself. Sure, it was Lex Cole's signature move, like drinking a certain kind of martini or wearing a porkpie hat. Cole did it at least once every book—straight up accuse a mark of the crime, right to their face, just to see what it shook loose. Dalton had adopted it. Actually, stole it outright. And he'd already pulled it on Tarot once.

THE PRIVATE DICK HANDBOOK, RULE #26
You need a new signature move. Maybe a blue
Windbreaker with a racing stripe, or a cool catchphrase
like "The proof is in the pudding—blood pudding!"

"Also, Jeff Chuff just hired me to find a way to get rid of Pinker Casket. Like, this weekend. Once and for all."

Cassiopeia whistled. Tarot leaned back against the painted cinder-block wall, affecting a chromium yawn, but his eyes were bright with interest. Mick Freeley spat on the floor.

"Put me on your payroll, and I'm your guy inside. I'll tell you about the plan before it happens."

"Why would I pay you?" Tarot asked. "When I could beat the plan out of you instead?"

"Studies show torture is a notoriously ineffective method of gathering information."

"But it feels zo good."

Mick Freeley snickered.

"Listen," Dalton said. "I came to Salt River to—"

"Solve a zuicide? Or snake Chuff's girl?"

"To make money. Wes Payne's a job, this is a job. They both pay. Chuff thinks I'm working for him, he pays too."

"Who can trust a man who works for everyone?"

"The man who pays me the most."

Kurt Tarot actually smiled, but his eyes remained flat, dark pupils swimming in murk. "Go on."

"Chuff's right about one thing, Salt River needs a new top dog. I've only been here two days and I've seen all the money you two are pissing away while you get ready to knock heads. Chuff thinks he's next in line to be boss, but he doesn't want to do the heavy lifting. So I'll help him put a coup in motion. When he realizes you've been tipped, it's too late, Pinker Casket's a Trojan Horse, and your guys pour out and wipe the floor with the Balls for good."

Tarot looked at his fingernails for a long time. "If Chuff needs *you* to do his planning, he's even more of a fool than I thought. That's assuming you're even telling the truth."

"You heard about what happened in the parking lot," Cassiopeia said. "Dalton doesn't want Chuff around any more than we do."

131

Tarot stared at Cassiopeia pointedly. "Yes, but what *else* does Dalton want?"

"He wants you to say 'Mississippi sassafras.'"

Tarot replied without thinking. "Mizzizzippi zazzafrazz."

Cassiopeia stifled a laugh. So did Freeley.

"What?" Tarot glowered. "What's so funny?"

"Nothing," they both said at once.

"The other thing Dalton wants," Dalton continued, getting comfortable with himself in the third person, "is to get paid. With Chuff gone, Salt River becomes a cash machine instead of a war zone. I start my own clique, cherry-pick one or two of Chuff's rackets. You can have the rest."

"What kind of clique?"

"I'm thinking of calling it Rope-a-Dope Misanthropes. Or maybe Jett Rinks. Your usual loners. Readers of the Beats. The terminally enigmatic. A bunch of us standing around shrugging and being distant. Sure, it'll siphon off some arty girls, maybe a few drummers. Nothing you need to worry about."

"I told you it was worth talking to him," Cassiopeia said. "He's a mercenary, sure, but do you have a better idea?"

Tarot did not volunteer a better idea.

"This guy's so full of shite!" Mick Freeley said. "You can't be seriously thinking we can trust—"

"How much?" Tarot asked.

"Four grand."

"Ridiculouz."

Dalton stuck out his hand. "Four grand buys you a thousand more reasons to trust me than Chuff has."

Tarot stared at Dalton's palm distastefully, then went into

the studio. He came back with a stack of money wrapped with a bass string and a CLOSE YOUR PINKER EYES, SPREAD YOUR CASKET THIGHS T-shirt.

"Classy."

"When do I get details?"

"I'm supposed to lay it out at Yearbook's party."

"We'll be there anyway," Mick Freeley pouted. "We're playing that bash."

"Good. I'll run the specs by Chuff. He likes it, I'll find you after your set."

Tarot cracked his neck, which popped with a grotesque loudness, and then stuck out his hand to shake. His palm was enormous, pale and flaky and calloused.

THE PRIVATE DICK HANDBOOK, RULE #27
Do not, repeat, DO NOT touch that disgusting thing.

Dalton reached out. Tarot's hand enveloped his, constricting the Venus Fly of his palm. They stared at each other. Tarot increased the pressure. Dalton's knuckles compressed like rusty ball bearings being ground together. His bones were beginning to fuse.

"Double crosses mean cemetery crosses," Tarot warned.

Dalton's hand burned red, and then white. The pain was unbearable. And then it got worse. He kept his face composed, but it was on the verge of cracking.

"It's on the level," he whispered, trying not to plead. "I swear."

Tarot counted out a beat, and then a few more, before letting go.

THE PRIVATE DICK HANDBOOK, RULE #28

Don't rub it. Don't acknowledge it hurts. Think of Macy.
Think of Landon. Think of your hand encased in a glacier.
Smile. It DOES NOT hurt. At least not until you're by yourself.
Then you can go ahead and cry.

"So we have a deal," Cassiopeia said, toasting an imaginary martini.

Kurt Tarot did not toast. He glared.

Dalton did not toast. He winced.

"Here's to Salt River's new big dog!" Cassiopeia said anyway.

Dalton pulled Wesley Payne's envelope from his back pocket and held it up for Tarot. "You recognize this?"

I watch the branches frame my head,
the flap of apron string
Shadows cross the wagon ruts, dangle in the wind
I dream of all the rumpled men who
slept beneath my roof
But their vengeance was not my vengeance
nor my cloven hoof

Sunlight on her face
Mary sways
Shadows dance below her
Mary sways

Down with tyrants, Booth cried to set the final act

Death songs swept my boardinghouse
and blew away the facts
Southern winds gust in haste on this winter's day
Wilkes is gone and gut shot
but his sins are mine to taste

Sunlight on her face
Mary sways
Shadows dance below her
Mary sways

Tarot nodded. "It's 'The Ballad of Mary Surratt.'"

"Those are *your* lyrics?"

"It's one of our early songs," Mick Freeley said. "An effing good one too."

"Who's Mary Surratt? Your old girlfriend?"

"Zome of the lines have been changed." Tarot pointed at the eraser marks. "The wordz are moved around. Why would you do that?"

"I didn't."

"Then who did?"

"Wesley Payne."

Tarot's face became hard. "That's not amusing."

"What's not amusing?"

"Mary Surratt was the first woman executed by the U.S. government."

"*What?*" Cassiopeia said. "They executed a woman? Why?"

"She was wrongly implicated in helping John Wilkes Booth azzazzinate Abraham Lincoln."

"You're shite-ing me," Cassiopeia said.

Dalton tried to swallow, but it wouldn't go down. "How was she killed?"

"She was hanged."

"By the ankles?"

Tarot frowned. "No."

Dalton turned to Cassiopeia. "I need a ride home."

Cassiopeia snapped her fingers. Jenny Two lifted a set of car keys from the depths of her bra.

"You're not going anywhere," Tarot said. "We're not done with rehearsal."

"Where's the opera?" Cassiopeia asked soothingly, rubbing Tarot's cheek with her ring finger. "We'll run through the set as soon as I get back. Besides, you need to walk your new bass player through the changes. I don't want to sit around while you tear that hotshot a new clasp."

"No."

"I wasn't asking permission," Cassiopeia reminded him, but nice and soft, still stroking his cheek. Jenny Two quietly slipped off her high heel and held the point of the stiletto by her side. Mick Freeley slipped two guitar picks out of his sleeves, each one shaped like a razor blade. He and the Catwalk stared one another down.

"Yes, yez," Tarot finally conceded. "Go. But don't forget—"

Cassiopeia started down the hallway. Dalton ducked back into the practice room and grabbed Mole with the hand that hadn't been reduced to jelly.

"C'mon, Aqua Boy, before they change their minds."

Mole let himself be led along without a word, dragging his

backpack like a sack of turnips. Between the hickeys and the bruises he looked like he'd just machete'd his way out of the Saipan jungle only to find that World War II had been over for years. They caught up with Cassiopeia and walked back through the incredible wall of noise, down the four flights of steps. As they passed the gear booth, Strata waved. Dalton took out his earplugs and held them up. "Can I get a refund on these?"

"Once a crackstar, always a crackstar," she said, playing with her purple dreads.

The parking lot was quieter, dark now, but still full of cars. Cassiopeia nodded toward a convertible Jaguar.

"I should have known. Sugar daddy?"

"I look like I need a daddy? Sugar or otherwise?"

"I guess that's a no." Dalton used his shoulder to push Mole's girth into the tiny backseat, then climbed in front. Cassiopeia cranked the engine before squealing out of the lot in a spray of beer cans and taco wrappers.

"Since when do you sing, Dalton?"

"I was going to ask you the same thing," he said, gently rubbing his knuckles.

"Since I decided it was time to come out of the shower and show the world what I've got. You can only play second fiddle for so long."

"The world already knows what you got."

Cassiopeia took a corner at twice the recommended speed. "Well, thank Bob for that, a compliment from Dalton Rev."

"So how deep are you with Count Chocula?"

"Is this about him hurting your hand? Hey, I'm sorry he hurt your hand."

137

"This is about him being the biggest freak in a thousand-mile radius. This is about him being a dangerous sociopath."

"Jealous?"

"More like nauseated."

"Can you tell me something, Dalton?"

"Sure."

"Why do you keep crowding my action?"

"What action?"

"I don't need you swinging by places I'm working to make sure I'm okay, okay?"

Dalton considered telling her a lie.

THE PRIVATE DICK HANDBOOK, RULE #29
The truth hurts. A lie metastasizes.

"I didn't. Swing by. I was on the level about Newport. He brought us there. I didn't even know you—"

"Oh," she said. "I thought—"

"Well, I didn't—"

"Because, in that case—"

"I mean, not that I meant—"

"Even if you did—"

"Why don't you two get a room already and get it over with?" Mole asked from the backseat.

Cassiopeia accelerated on a straightaway, the Jag bucking like it'd been spurred in the flanks.

"The mummy speaks," Dalton said. "Not very cleverly, but he speaks."

"Not to you. Not anymore. You're a bad influence."

"Sidekick is a dangerous job."

"Enough of the hard-boiled patter," Cassiopeia warned. "This is much bigger than you have any idea. Tarot is—"

"I know what I'm doing," Dalton interrupted.

"Do you?"

"I guess I'll find out at Lu Lu Footer's party."

"There is no plan, is there? None at all."

"There's always a plan."

"Like walking into that studio about to get yourself crushed by a mic stand?"

"Everyone plays a role. By encouraging suspects to be the most extravagant version of themselves, they reveal their secrets."

"Oh my Bob. Where do you come up with this bloshite?"

"From *The Cat with One Life, the Crook with Nine Fingers.* At least that line specifically. Chapter fourteen, page sixty-six."

"Do I have clue one what you're talking about? Do I even want to?"

"Probably not. Being head of Foxxes and all, you probably can't afford to have any extraneous information clanging around in your head."

Cassiopeia slammed on the brakes in front of Mole's house. The Jag slid twenty feet through gravel. "We're here."

"No."

"*No?*"

"Not going alone," Mole said. "Too scared."

Cassiopeia pointed across the lawn. "Lester, your house is right there."

The small, aluminum-sided A-frame squatted in a yard full of plastic toys and dog turds.

Mole shook his head, not moving.

"Euclid, get outta my car!"

Mole set his lip. "Not going alone."

"Going where? Your front door?"

"Yup."

"Fine, I'll take him in."

"You and I need to talk," Cassiopeia said. "Like now."

"I know, but what am I going to do?" Dalton gestured to the backseat. "You go. I've got something to take care of, anyhow. I'll talk to you tomorrow."

"Dalton—"

"Go," Mole said petulantly.

Cassiopeia's eyes were furious. "Stupid Euclidian. They should have drained you and made you into a six-pack a month ago!"

The Jag peeled away, leaving them standing on the edge of the lawn. Dalton took Mole by the arm and started to lead him in. Mole pulled away angrily. "Don't touch me."

"But I thought—"

"It was a ruse, you rube. Like I'm too scared to walk across my own lawn? I needed to get you alone before that tarantula spun more of her web. Not like you deserve my help, but I just did you a mongo favor."

"Yeah, what's that?"

"Maybe I didn't make it clear enough before, guy, but Foxxes are into some seriously evil shite. I thought it was just rumors, but that was before Classless-iopeia hooked up with Tarot. That's one girl you need to stay way away from."

"Mole, I don't think—"

"Yeah, that's just it, *Dalton*. You're thinking with your rodney."

Mole's eyes were intense. The clown act was almost entirely gone.

"Okay, I hear you. I'll watch it around her."

"Don't just watch it. Stay away. There's a difference. Get it?"

"Got it."

"Good."

Mole turned and walked up to his house. In a corner window was a flickering bluish light, where Buffy Bucharest was watching TV. The door slammed.

Dalton looked down the street. Mole lived about twenty blocks from Macy's. If he kept up a steady jog, he might get there before she got into bed. He needed to talk to her tonight. He needed to apologize. He needed information. But what he really needed, more than anything, was to get home before curfew or Sherry Rev was going to be pissed.

CHAPTER 15

SALT RIVER STEEL

Macy picked up on the fourteenth ring, annoyed.

"Hey."

"Hi."

"Listen, I want to talk."

"And I want to sleep. You couldn't wait until homeroom?"

"I could have," Dalton said. "Except that I'm downstairs and all."

"Downstairs?"

"Well, across the street at a pay phone."

"You're going to wake my father up."

"I'll be quiet. Promise."

"Yeah, until you decide to start slamming doors and then run out of the house without a word."

"Sorry about that. Seriously. I know I owe you an explanation."

"At the very least."

"Fortunately, I have one."

Macy didn't answer.

"Or," Dalton said, "I could just leave and walk home, but

then I won't be able to tell you what I found out about Wesley."

She still didn't answer. He was about to hang up, when she said, "Around back in five minutes. And don't make a sound!"

Click.

Dalton stood at the screen door, moths doinking against it. Crickets chirped and frogs croaked and mosquitoes flew sorties at his neck in waves. Macy, wearing adorable red jammies, eventually appeared on the other side. Her hair stood up at a pillowed angle. She had a tiny speck of toothpaste at the corner of her lip. Dalton turned the handle, but it was locked.

"I said back door. I didn't say you could come in."

The low bass of TV commercials thrummed from the interior. Dalton could see half of Albert Payne asleep on the couch, his sockless feet and plaid slippers dangling above a near-empty bottle of wine.

"Looks like your dad is safely medicated."

"Mind your own business." Her pajama top was stretchy and tight. She didn't appear to be wearing a bra, going free range on him. Dalton tried hard to concentrate on the microwave in the kitchen.

"You're not paying me to mind my own business."

Her arms were crossed, but he could tell she was wavering with the Deservedly Angry routine.

"He makes his own. In the basement."

"Huh?"

"Wine. My father bought some kit over the Internet. It smells like kerosene."

Dalton sniffed the air. All he could smell was her. Her skin and the bitter tinge of soap.

"Macy?"

She didn't answer.

"Macy?"

"*What?*"

He made an ape face, pressing it against the screen, hard enough for little squares of lip to bubble through the mesh. "I won't run away again if you give me a banana."

It was so stupid she unlatched the door and put her arms around his neck. There was a desperation to the way she clung to him. She was scared. He hadn't realized just how much up until that second, taking for granted that she'd come to terms with losing her brother. With being alone. With being surrounded by a school full of suspects. He'd been a jerk hiding behind the guise of professionalism, thinking about Inference's money and Landon's armor, but not how totally unmoored she must be.

"Listen, I'm sorry—"

Macy cut him off, pressing even tighter.

"You better have a *really* good reason for taking off like that."

"I do. Let's go upstairs and I'll tell you all about it."

◎

Sitting on the pink bed, Dalton tried to describe Elisha Cook and his curly mustache without the whole thing sounding too much like a cartoon. Out loud, it was beyond implausible. He told her how Cook had been behind the tree, staring in her window, and how he admitted he'd been following Dalton around school. Macy rolled her eyes and made little snorting sounds of disbelief, but he didn't try to convince her, which more or less eventually convinced her. They regarded each other across the mussed pink comforter.

"Harvard? That's...crazy. *I* didn't even bother applying to Harvard."

"What are you trying to say?"

She blushed. "It's just, you know. I study and all."

Dalton slipped the silver number 9 key out of his back pocket, half dreading showing it to her. It would probably get him kicked back out the screen door. On the other hand, he wasn't entirely sure why he hadn't shown her right away. Let alone the money in the envelope, or the lyrics on the back. He could keep pretending it was because he'd had to run after Elisha Cook, but it wasn't. There was something about the way her brother had hidden the envelope that bothered him. It didn't feel innocent. It was furtive. Like Wesley was holding it for some kind of leverage or racket. Or even blackmail. And if his key really did belong to a locker full of cash, someone was going to have to do a whole lot of explaining on Wesley's behalf. Like, for instance, the sister who idolized him. But did Macy need to know about it now, especially if it turned out not to be true?

THE PRIVATE DICK HANDBOOK, RULE #30
Object Lesson #489 in why you shouldn't even
consider making out with a client. Besides, just which
one of you are you really trying to protect?

Dalton held up the key. "Ever seen this before?"

"No. Why?"

145

"Could be a clue. Could be garbage."

"What's it to?"

"I'm not sure yet."

"It's where Inference's money is, right?"

Dalton's eyes narrowed. "Why do you say that?"

"Duh, it's a locker key. The only thing a locker's good for is stashing loot."

"Who says?"

"No one *said*. It's in every movie ever made. Stash the cash in a Greyhound locker and then all the colorful characters take turns shooting each other over the key, since cash is just too heavy and inconvenient for actors to carry around while saying clever lines and pointing silver-plated Colt .45's all the time."

Dalton laughed. "Yeah, true. But I'm not so sure about this one."

"So what are you sure of?"

"You."

Her face brightened in a way that made him want to be a better person. She licked the toothpaste from the corner of her mouth. "Me?"

"Yeah. I mean, I'm sure we're going to figure this out. Together. I'm sure we're going to find the truth."

What a cheesebag. Why don't you give her your inspirational coach speech about how you have to play all four quarters and give 110 percent too?

"Oh."

"And, also, the main reason I came is to let you know I've been to see Tarot."

The skin around her mouth became taut. She hugged her knees to her chest. "You did? Really?"

There's no professional reason you had to see her tonight, liar. No vital questions to ask, or information you absolutely had to get before morning. Bottom line, you walked all the way over here because you wanted to be next to her, just like this.

"He's hooked solid."

"On what?"

Dalton knew it was unwise to tell her everything. Sure, she was his client, but she also was still involved on some level with Chuff. Lex Cole would tear him a new clasp for being such a sucker. But, in the end, he wanted to impress Macy more than he wanted to live up to the dictates of Lex. "I've set something up for the party tomorrow night. The old-school Blah Blah Blagatha Christie method: Get all the principals in one room and see who flinches first. It'll be like Colonel Mustard in the den with the candlestick."

"What does that mean? You're being way too vague."

"You're not going to like it."

"I already don't like it."

"I think there's a chance Wesley was more involved in the rackets than you may have realized. I think he was somehow brokering a deal. You're right that war between Chuff and Tarot is the next logical step. It's the only thing every clique can seem to agree on. Either way, I'm going to accelerate the process. There's a good chance whoever grabs the reins is our killer."

"*That's* your plan?"

"That's my plan."

"What about the cash?"

Dalton blanched, thinking of Wesley's envelope. "Whose?"

"Um, Inference's? Um, the safe?"

He exhaled. "Money and murder are like peanut butter and jelly." *If that's not the name of a Lex Cole novel, it should have been.* "It'd be dumb to think Wesley's killing doesn't fit with the theft."

"Do you really think this is the right thing to do? I mean, having a hand in stirring up violence? What if someone gets hurt?"

"People are already hurt. And this is going to happen no matter what I do. At least this way it's for a reason. Besides, with Lee Harvies around, it can't get too out of hand, can it? Caskets and Balls are both terrified of Lee Harvies."

Macy nodded, dabbing her eye with the bedsheet. A bit of mascara ran into the material.

"Since when do you wear makeup?" he asked jokingly. She flushed maroon and he realized, *idiot*, she must have tossed it on before coming down to let him in. Embarrassed, and having no other idea what to do to make it right, and knowing that he totally wanted to anyway, he leaned over and gave her a soft kiss on the lips.

Why does every single thing you do contradict every single thing you say, or at least pretend to believe in?

"I want you to tell me why you do this," she said, licking her lips. "Besides the money, I mean."

"Kissing you? Good question."

"No, crackstar. Why are you doing this Bogart stuff? Walking around with a magnifying glass, snooping, solving problems. Who just cranks out a website and starts telling everyone they're a Private Dick?"

Dalton stared at his sock, considering. No way he was telling anyone about Landon until he was positive the shipment was on its way to the front. But Landon wasn't the only reason.

"There used to be a guy, right? When I was a kid. Always giving me shite. Always on my back. I was…shorter then. Quiet. An easy target for the right type of sadist. Anyway, this guy, he was always pushing my head in the water fountain. Slapping the books out of my hands so they went flying down the hallway, everyone stepping all over them, footprints on my homework. And I just took it. He was bigger and I was smaller, so that was that. It didn't even *occur* to me to fight back, you know? Put up your dukes? It's not like the movies when you're actually being punched. So one day this kid's chasing me around the playground, says he's going to pants me in front of everyone. Kids are standing around, everyone's seen it all before. But there's this girl. This girl I kind of liked. She wasn't popular, not really even that pretty. But I liked her and I saw her in the crowd and I figured at least she'd feel bad for me. Maybe say something to the kid, tell him to knock it off. But she didn't feel bad."

"How did you know?"

"Because she was doubled over laughing at what a loser I was. Her friends were laughing too. There I am running, thinking, hey, these girls should know better, right? I mean, they're the kind that get picked on themselves. They're the kind that get made fun of for wearing the wrong skirts or having the wrong hair. But they don't see the contradiction. And that's when I realized no one feels bad for anyone. As long as it's not you getting the stick, it's like, hey, great, everyone else is fair game, let's all crowd around and watch. None of us had any... what? Communion? Understanding? Nope, it's all pure survival. So I stopped running. Why did I care what any of them thought about me? And if I didn't care, like *really* didn't care, there was nothing to be scared of."

Macy grinned. "So you stopped and kicked the guy's butt, right? You taught him a lesson, and then that girl was all into you?"

"No. I stopped and balled up my fists and waited. Then he came over and beat the spleens out of me."

"Umm... I don't see how—"

"He kicked my ass. But while he was hitting me, we locked eyes. He really saw me, and I really saw him. And I knew he knew."

"Knew what?"

"That I wasn't scared, and I wasn't going to be, no matter how many times he hit me."

"So what happened?"

"Nothing. I wiped the blood off my shirt and went back to class. But I was filled with this incredible sense of power. The fear leaked away. Taking a beating? Sure, you want to avoid it. But getting punched is not that big a deal. It hurts for a little while, and then it stops. Just like anything else. And it's, like, once you stop being scared, once it all seems inevitable, that understanding comes off you in waves, like cologne. People start to step out of your way. Or at least look for easier targets."

"Okay, I get it. But how does that make you into a snooper?"

"After that, I challenged myself to find what I really was afraid of. That's what this is. Taking these jobs. Pushing myself into these situations. It's money, sure. But finding out what people don't want you to know may be the scariest, most addictive thing of all."

Dalton took a deep breath, surprised at himself. He'd never said it out loud. Actually, he'd only begun to truly understand while he was explaining it to her.

"Honesty is so effing sexy," Macy said, and started unknotting Dalton's tie. He let her but didn't move. When it was off, she loosened his collar and started pulling at his buttons. She saw the Clash shirt beneath and made a face. It was a line-in-the-sand moment. *You mean you don't like the Clash?* She reached over with an opinionless expression and raised the T-shirt, scratching her nails along the black hair running from his belt to the center of his chest. It somehow seemed like a highly non-Euclidian thing to do.

"Tell me more about Ronnie Newport," Dalton said. "He and Wesley."

"Now?" She reached her leg out back behind her and flicked off the lights with her toes.

"Newport lied to me," Dalton said, in the dark. "Maybe even set me up. He and Wesley were both Crop Crème. I can't figure out his angle, but he's involved for sure."

"He's a cipher now," Macy said. He couldn't see her but could sense how close she was. He could feel her warmth. The hairs on his arms stood up straight.

"Not that he ever said that much before. He came over a few times to hang out with Wes. They played dice games together, the dragon thing, writing numbers and casting spells.

I think he liked Wesley because he could let out his inner nerd when they were alone. At school, it was more like James Dean 2.0. But now, you know, being his own clique, the whole gearhead thing…all I know is it's creepy how he's always being followed by those girls. They're like a flock of crows."

"A murder of crows."

"What?" she said, inches away.

"Murder, Euclidian," Dalton whispered, almost right into her lips. "Not flock. Pod of whales, pride of lions, murder of crows."

"Smart is sexy too," Macy whispered back. "Me and you, Dalton Rev? I mean, I know this sounds stupid, but I knew right away we…clicked. Even after the first e-mail…"

"Cliqued?"

"…but I didn't know in person if it would, you know. Translate. And now you're here. In the dark. Flesh and blood and bone. And I trust you. And sort of like you."

"Sort of?"

"Sort of a lot."

Dalton had been ready to be disappointed with her too. The person you wanted someone to be online was never the one they actually were, even just the image you had in your head. Let alone actually being better than that image.

Macy reached back without a word and pulled off her little pajama top, then slid down and pressed against him, moving slowly in the blackness, brushing herself in widening circles like she was painting a canvas.

"What about Chuff?" Dalton asked, almost unable to stand it.

"Huff Chuff," Macy whispered.

It seemed like such incredibly, unbelievably good advice.

CHAPTER 16
CAUGHT DEAD-HANDED

Dalton woke in the middle of the night. Alone. He listened for sounds from the splashbox, maybe the sink running, but there were none. He sat up, reaching for his pants, ready to head down the stairs and scout around, when he saw Macy sitting at her desk. She turned to face him, holding a sheaf of papers.

"Sleeping Beauty awakes."

Her face was haloed by a tiny candle on the desk. Her eyes were sharp and her features stretched. She looked angry.

"What are you reading?"

Macy looked down with a smirk. "You left your book bag before. Remember? Way back a million years ago when you ran out without a word?"

"I guess."

"Well, since you didn't seem concerned enough to take your things with you, I took the liberty of poking through them."

THE PRIVATE DICK HANDBOOK, RULE #31
No one snoops on a snooper. At least not a good one.

"You looked through my stuff?"

"I think the lawyers call it a question of eminent domain."

"That's not what eminent domain means, it—"

"Who is this Rev guy I hired?" Macy interrupted, her voice getting louder. "That's what I asked myself. Maybe he's got something to hide, you know? This guy who so easily runs away?"

"I told you why I—"

"Maybe he has something revealing stuffed in between his unread algebra book and his unread chemistry book. And, as it turns out, I was right."

Before Dalton could answer, Macy began to read aloud.

THE A TO Z OF POSSIBLE GODS
By Dalton Rev

A. God exists, exactly like it says in the Bible. We'll all be judged in heaven when we die, and a certain percentage of us will be cast down to hell.

B. God exists, which is proven by the fact that I am here to write this sentence. He will welcome me in heaven whether I go to church or not because I am generally a good person.

C. God exists, but it turns out he's the one Amazon River cannibals worship. We've been praying to the wrong guy all this time, and Uglathuthlu is seriously pissed about it.

D. God exists but is some sort of floating electrochemical stew not capable of thought, emotion, or profundity. The Stew has no investment whatsoever in our lives.

154

E. God exists and is indeed a bearded old man on a throne, but that old man is cold, confused, and scared. He would very much like it if some cosmonaut flew up to heaven and told him what he's supposed to be doing.

F. God doesn't exist. The universe is vast and unknowable. Everything within it is cold brute logic. The fact that there is life on Earth is mere mathematical happenstance. Eventually the sun will run out of hydrogen, and our planet will freeze. Nothing awaits us but eons of silence.

G. We do not exist. Our nonexistent selves dreamed up our nonexistent god to make our lack of existence more palatable.

H. Alien gods showed up in 1952 in a pie-shaped landing craft to explain the pyramids, but the government killed them.

"Enough," Dalton finally said.

"You're quite the philosopher, aren't you? This is really cheery stuff. I can't believe there's half an alphabet to go. Or, really, that this got you into Harvard."

"It didn't. And I'm not. Listen, believe me, I know I can't write. At all."

"Oh, stop with the coy routine. It's boring."

"Fine."

"So, Mr. Philosopher, are you saying when we die we don't go to heaven? That it's all just a farcking joke?"

"I don't know. I mean, I was trying to make the point, I guess, that anything's possible. That if you believe in one thing, you know, by definition, you sort of have to believe in everything."

"So that really sucks for Wesley, huh?"

Dalton just looked at her.

Macy threw his story on the floor. "Um, remember my brother? Wesley? Who we buried a month ago? Remember what I'm paying you for? Your investigative skills, not to mention your overwhelming empathy?"

Dalton collected his papers and shoved them with his socks into the book bag. "I remember exactly why you're paying me." He pulled Wesley's envelope from his back pocket—*The one I tore open and took your dead brother's money from*—showing her the lyrics to "The Ballad of Mary Surratt."

"Any idea why Wesley kept this in his room?"

Macy wiped the corners of her mouth. "Are you trying to change the subject?"

"You're a Euclidian. Wesley was a Populah. Why is he writing down Pinker Casket lyrics? Not only these, but why would he use them as a suicide note?"

"Who knows? Because he was bored? Because he was desperate and not thinking straight? Because he had lousy taste in music?"

"I looked on the Internet. About this woman? This Mary Surratt? I couldn't figure out why Wesley—"

"You couldn't figure out *anything*!" Macy said mockingly. "Not about me and not about yourself. I mean, god, do you even know what a Dalton *is*?"

"No, but I know why you're mad."

"A Dalton! Duh! It's a unit that expresses the weight of proteins!"

"You're mad about us being together."

"And Daltonism is a form of color blindness otherwise known as protanopia!"

"I know last night was my fault."

"And John Dalton was the father of modern atomic theory!"

"So, if you want to blame me..."

"He printed the first table of atomic weights!"

"Go right ahead."

Macy threw up her hands in disgust. "Blame? What a stupid word. Is it going to make me feel better? Am I going to blame Tarot and suddenly everything's fixed?"

Dalton knew it was his fault. Coming over. The lead-up. The letting go of control. Flirting like he was some dumb kid on his first case.

What a knob.

But, mostly, the reason he should be blamed is that after a while of wrestling around under the covers, he'd told her they should take it slow.

God, how lame.

He hadn't pushed her away, exactly. But he'd made it clear she was a client. She was vulnerable. He wasn't going to take advantage of that, and he wasn't doing anything else, at least until the case was over. He'd tried to explain it gently, but she barely seemed to be listening. She'd turned over in disbelief, pulling her shirt back on and refusing to answer his questions. They'd both lain there, looking at the ceiling. He rehearsed things to say in his head, adding, subtracting, starting over, and at some point had fallen asleep. He'd sort of been counting on her waking up and realizing he'd been right to say no, that she'd be glad he'd been strong.

She didn't want you to be strong, she wanted you to be weak. To crack the facade and expose yourself, even a little. And maybe you should have. Weakness is at least honest.

"I was named after a bouncer," Dalton finally said. "Not the scientist. I was named after this actor with a mullet who beats people up in my dad's favorite movie."

Macy didn't say anything. She put her face in her hands. Dalton tried to touch her shoulder, but she jerked away. He could barely believe what he'd done himself. In every teen movie he'd ever watched, there was always a scene where the hero had some hot girl alone, and she wanted him, but he didn't go through with it for some infuriating reason, like suddenly growing a conscience. The girl had too much to drink, or she was his best friend's girlfriend, or he liked some unattainable cheerleader instead. So the hero turns her down, even though she's right there in front of him, mostly because the writers don't want you to think he's a jerk, and meanwhile every single guy in the audience is like, *That's bloshite! C'mon, dog, grow a sac! Get busy and tap that ass and stop making dumb excuses!*

And now he, Dalton, *was* that guy. The excuses guy. The totally ridiculous, inexplicably sexually inert, doomed-to-virginity loser.

"I heard about you and Foxxes," Macy said quietly. "That's what all this is about, isn't it? You're still in love with the leather queen."

"You heard *what*?"

"Well, do you have a better explanation? Is it just a coincidence that Cassiopeia Jones is your old girlfriend?"

"Yes. It is a coincidence. I had no idea she transferred here. And she's not my old girlfriend."

"Oh really? That's not what Mole said."

Dalton was tempted to finally tell Macy about Landon. How he was halfway around the world, right that second, in a place that had nothing to do with flirting and arguing and being dramatic. It was real life. People were dying. And Dalton was running out of time. It wasn't a game.

"This isn't a game."

"It isn't? It sure seems like you're a player."

"I'm not playing anything."

"What did you mean, in his room, by the way?"

"What?"

"That envelope. You asked me why Wesley would keep it in his room."

"Because I found it there."

"When?"

"The other day. I didn't tell you because—"

Macy's whole body began to tremble, her left eye blinking rapidly. She held her palm against it and pointed with the other hand toward the door.

"Get out. Now."

"Are you okay?"

"GET OUT!"

She's right, you should go. You deserve to go. Solve the crime. Find the cash. Get paid and get gone.

Dalton slipped on his boots and went down the steps, this time quietly and without slamming any doors. There would be enough slamming doors when he got home if Sherry Rev was still awake.

CHAPTER 17
CRACKSTAR NOIR

"As many of you know, yearbooks came out today," Miss Honey Bucket trilled, over the crackling loudspeaker, in the middle of class, interrupting Miss Splonge. "Just a reminder that they're only a hundred fifty a pop. Get them in the hallway at the booth manned by yours truly. Cash, check, or money order." There was a long bleat of feedback. "Ha-ha, actually, it's cash or nothing. You know what you can do with a check, and it isn't hygienic. That is all."

There were some kids who already had theirs, signing coded notes about bands they liked and pool parties they'd gotten drunk at and embarrassing people they'd made out with. There was the vaguely narcotic smell of a printing press and fresh ink hanging in the room. Crowdarounds crowded around, oohing and squealing at the candids while Miss Splonge plodded ahead with her lecture.

"So, really, it was the Phoenician ships and their ability to range farther than fifty miles from the Mediterranean coast that led to greater trade between—"

Dalton leaned over to the Euclidian across from him. "Why are yearbooks out already? The semester just started."

The kid looked at Dalton fearfully. Then he held a Robot Lion Fist action figure in front of his mouth, speaking through it in an android voice. "We. Get. Yearbooks. Early. At. Salt. River. Due. To. High. Student. Turnover…preeer preeer."

Dalton turned away and tuned out, scribbling in his notebook, trying to formulate the plan he was going to present to Chuff. He had zero clue. It needed to be just right: dangerous, possibly profitable, and marginally plausible. Essentially, what would lure a roach like Tarot into the light, let alone onto the linoleum, within easy stomping distance and at a severe disadvantage, without making Chuff suspicious it was a setup? Dalton found it especially hard to concentrate, since Macy hadn't come to class. He hadn't expected that. Miss Splonge said during attendance donation collection that it was the first one she'd missed all year. Dalton tried to decide if he was relieved. Or guilty. Or both. In the hallway, various Pinker Caskets had given him dirty looks, including Mick Freeley and his razor pick, but none of them did anything—the decree from Tarot seemed to be holding. At least until tonight. That meant he had six periods of relative freedom to find Inference's money, figure out who killed Wes Payne, figure out why they bothered to hang him from the goalposts, if they hung him at all, and maybe most confusingly, why someone hung either Wesley Payne or a convincing Wes Payne effigy right above his mother's laundry pile. And where the ersatz Payne took off to while he and Mole were out on the front lawn.

Piece of Lex. Like shooting Cole in a barrel.

Miss Splonge concluded her lecture and then announced a surprise quiz. The class moaned in unison. A Scam Wow began circulating up the aisles, offering to take the test for fifty bucks. A pair of Couldabeens handed over their papers and the cash. Dalton found his pencil and skimmed the ten questions:

1. Compare and contrast the utterances of the Delphic Oracle with the words of Ovid as they relate to the Greeks' concept of animism.

2. Write a short essay discussing the tactics of Alexander the Great in the battle of Tyre. Concentrate specifically on troop movements, logistical support, cavalry handling, and flanking maneuvers.

3. Interpret and elaborate on the meaning of the phrase "He who listens with ears, let him." Feel free to use the back of the page for extra space.

4. What is the frequency, Kenneth?

5. Who is John Galt?

6. Which South American country produces the most raw bauxite, to which countries is the majority exported, and what do the importing countries primarily manufacture from it?

7. Who reprised the Richard Widmark role in the 1989 remake of *Road House*, and what was his character's name?

8. What two generals met at the battle of Shiloh, who won, who crouched behind a rock wall during an artillery barrage and wept like a little girl, and why?

9. What is kwashiorkor and why is it my favorite word?

10. EXTRA CREDIT: Samuel Taylor Coleridge more or less founded the English Romantic movement and was a major influence on early American Transcendentalists, principally Ralph Waldo Emerson. Write a short essay about how all our lives would be different if Coleridge had never been born, or at least had been born untalented.

When the bell finally rang, Dalton waited for the line of grumbling students to drop off their quizzes. He pretended to be finishing some notes until everyone was gone, and then approached Miss Splonge's desk. She gave him a big fake smile, framed by wilty brown hair and profoundly thick glasses.

"You failed your quiz."

Dalton frowned. "But—"

"Principal Inference has you on academic notice, Rev. That means you've fallen below a C average for my class. Which means you're out the door on the next garbage barge."

"You couldn't have corrected it already."

Miss Splonge pulled Dalton's quiz from the pile, along with a red marker, and put a big red X next to each answer without reading it. She totaled them up, which came to a zero. "Like I said. You failed." She wrote a big red *F* at the top, the marker seeming to squeak with pleasure.

"What does Inference want?"

"Principal Inference thinks you're moving too slowly with your…investigation. She wants her money found. And returned."

"And what do you want?"

"I want a big ol' safe full of money to lose on my own."

Dalton sighed. He fished five twenties from his pocket and dropped them over the *F*. Miss Splonge tore up his quiz and then stuck the money into a rubber band around her wrist, pulling her heavy sweater back over it. "You had a question, I believe? Or, should I say you were about to try to stick your nose somewhere beige?"

Dalton laughed, looking down at the tiny woman.

"Listen, Splonge—"

"Spl*ahn*-jay. It's French."

"I understand Wesley Payne was in your class."

"Who?"

"The Body."

"Who?"

Dalton fished out three more twenties. Spl*ahn*-jay reached, but Dalton dangled them at carrot distance.

"Payne didn't say much," she admitted, not taking her eyes off the folding green. "Kept to himself. Straight As, but never raised his hand. Things clearly came too easily for that young man. It's a sign of weakness. He stared out the window mostly."

"But he was a Crop Crème."

She wrinkled her nose. "A what?"

164

"Nothing. You know what he was staring out the window at? Maybe a guy in a pin-striped suit?"

Splonge gave Dalton an odd look, waving halfheartedly toward the football field. "How should I know? He faced that way."

"Toward the goalposts?"

"Ironic, isn't it?"

"No. It's—"

Splonge's arm darted out faster than Dalton thought possible. She snatched the money from his fingers and tucked it in her sleeve before he could blink.

THE PRIVATE DICK HANDBOOK, RULE #32
The Fack Cult is as the Fack Cult does.
You can't trust one as far as you could kick a lemon pie.

The bell rang for the second time.

"You're late for your next class," Splonge said, dabbing her permanently red nose with a tissue that appeared from her other sleeve.

Dalton walked to the door.

"And he smelled."

"Excuse me?"

Splonge started writing with her squeaky chalk on the board, spelling THE TUNGUSKA EVENT in big block letters. "That poor boy always smelled like a bad tube of cologne."

Dalton stepped into the hallway and was almost immediately mowed down by three Plaths running in circles.

"NO WAY NO WAY NO WAY!"

"OH MY BOB, OH MY BOB, OH MY BOB!"

One dropped her yearbook, and the other began showing hers to passing students. It set off a chain reaction. New Skids began pairing off, talking in low voices. Girlz with Two First Names cried and hugged one another. Miss Honey Bucket stood at her booth, counting money, while random cliques ran up and grabbed the yearbooks, cracking them open without paying for them. "Hey!" she kept saying. "Hey!"

Dalton asked a Sis Boom Bah if he could look at hers. She let go of it and ran down the hallway with her hands over her mouth. The book fell open to the centerfold, a big glossy color picture.

"No farcking way."

It was a smiling school portrait of Wesley Payne with a caption saying he'd been voted "Most Likely Not to Succeed." There was a crude drawing superimposed over his face. Cartoon holes were bored into his head with straws sticking out like a fruity tourist drink. A fanged Kurt Tarot was drawn sucking greedily on one of the straws, with a dialogue box that said *"MMMM, Euclidian Blood. Tastes just like cherry cola!"*

Lu Lu Footer pushed against a flow of crying students like a salmon in tight couture, not quite running. "Give me that!" she yelled, a blur of orange skirt, snatching the yearbook from Dalton's hands.

"That's impossible!" she kept saying, licking her thumb and flipping pages. "That wasn't there. I sent the proofs in myself last week. The centerfold was our class picture. It was of everyone out in the parking lot. It wasn't this! I sent it in myself!"

No one was listening. Girls in tears huddled while guys nervously made dumb jokes, kicking locker doors, hands stuffed deep in their pockets. An angry mob began to surround Miss Honey Bucket, demanding answers. She smiled sweetly, zipped her terry-cloth sweat suit up to her neck, and then grabbed her money box. As the Crowdarounds closed in, she slipped back into her office and slammed the door, leaving the remaining yearbooks as a sacrifice. It was suddenly clear just how much Wesley Payne's death actually had affected the cliques. And how much they'd been hiding it. His defaced picture seemed to have torn open whatever unspoken denial they'd shared. Dalton wasn't sure if it was out of fear of reprisal, greed, or a thick coat of cynicism, but once it was broken it festered up from the tiles like Chernobyl coolant eating through reinforced concrete. And, as always, that grief expressed itself as unexamined anger. There were accusations and shoving matches. Airplane Gluze and Couldabeens grappled against lockers. A mini riot began breaking out.

"Who had access to the proofs?" Dalton asked, grabbing Lu Lu Footer's arm. She didn't answer, looking down from her dongtower. It didn't seem to be so much imperiousness as shock. Dalton lowered his voice and asked again.

"I don't know. All of them. Any of them. I don't care. About this place. Anymore."

Lu Lu dropped the yearbook, gliding back down the raucous hallway in a flash of leopard print. Almost immediately, the shoving graduated into a melee. Dalton pushed through it, heading to his locker, shaking off two Scam Wows already selling "collector's item" yearbooks for twice the price. A group of Steel-toe Dystopias mobbed a Coal Train and smashed his clarinet. Kokrocks grabbed a New Skid and pantsed him hard, then pushed him into a lungbox, holding the door closed as he coughed and begged to be let go. Dalton was about to free the kid, when three shots went off in succession—*bang pang bang*. Long streaks of red marked the floor tiles.

"LEE HARVIES!" a half-shirted Sis Boom Bah screamed, bouncing pneumatically, as cliques tore away in every direction. The New Skid staggered out of the lungbox, coughing as he ran.

Dalton didn't move. As chaos reigned around him, he walked to the center of the hall.

THE PRIVATE DICK HANDBOOK, RULE #33
If you have a theory, test it. If you have balls, use them.

Dalton stood like a buoy around which a current eddied, searching for where the bullets could possibly have come from. He couldn't see any perch or firing line. No open windows or missing ceiling tiles. As students crouched, he stepped forward and spread his arms. No sound. He closed his eyes and waited. No movement. He threw open his mouth and yelled, "GO AHEAD!"

Nothing happened.

"SHOOT! I'M NOT SCARED!"

There was no response.

The final bell rang.

Doors up and down the hallway slammed just as frantic students managed to slip through. Fack Cult peered from the side windows of their classes, rubbing their fingers together to indicate what it would cost any stragglers to get in. Dalton knelt down, examining the red streaks. Again, they smelled like vinegar. They could have been blood, but there were no bullet holes or broken tiles. He stood up and ran out the emergency exit, circling around the side of the building, scanning the rooftop. *A guy in a Jason mask with silver anarchy symbols painted over the eyes? How hard can that be to find?* In the alley behind a Dumpster was a rusted metal fire ladder above a steel toolshed bolted into the brick wall. Dalton pulled himself to the top, leaped, caught the bottom rung, and wrenched the ladder down. He heard the crunching of gravel above. *Gotcha.* Dalton clambered up the ladder, with each step feeling a greater sway. A rumble sounded along the side supports. There was a loud jerk as the bolts began to pull away from the mortar they'd been sunk into.

Farck farck farck farck.

He scrambled to the top, rolling over the lip of the roof and scanning the area in a tactical way he'd seen in about fourteen movies involving the use of SWAT personnel.

No movement.

The parking lot below was quiet. In the center of the gravel and sheet-metal rectangle was a grouping of air vents. It was the only place to hide. Dalton stood and heel-toed over as fast as he could while trying not to make any noise. If he was caught out in the open, he was dead. There was nowhere to hide and nowhere to run. The crunching of his feet got louder. He closed the last ten yards in a sprint, pressing his back against the closest vent. If the Lee Harvies was there, he was right around the corner. Three feet away. With his back pressed against the vent too. Except he had a gun. A really, really big gun.

THE PRIVATE DICK HANDBOOK, RULE #34
Just stick your head out and see.
It'll be like a cartoon and you'll get your hat shot off.
Except, oh wait, you're not wearing a hat.

Dalton slowly peered around. There was nothing there. No Jason mask, no shooter. Nothing but a small pile of garbage. The sort of pile a guy who spent a lot of time on a roof waiting to squeeze off some shots would make. There were a couple of empty plastic bottles of Rush cola mashed flat, some food wrappers, an old rifle tripod, and a single playing card. It was the jack of spades. Except the jack's face had been replaced by the picture of a beady-eyed man staring maniacally at the camera. Dalton pocketed the card. Then he wedged the tripod between two steel pipes and yanked it sideways, shearing off one leg and bending the column. He tossed the thing on the ground and climbed gingerly back down the ladder, hoping if it did pull entirely out of the side of the building, it would at least wait until he was far enough down to jump and only break one leg.

The ladder held.

The bell rang.

Just in time for his next class.

CHAPTER 18

MAMA, DON'T TAKE MY KODACHROME AWAY

Mole was waiting at Dalton's locker, rubbing his neck, a Diego Rivera mural of blue-purple hickeys.

"I've been looking for you, guy. Thought you made like an old-time mobster, turned state's evidence, and went into witness protection. I'm all like, okay, maybe Dalton's hunkered down with a new name in some Phoenix split-level watching the tube and waiting for a knock on the door that isn't the mailman, you know?"

"And yet, here I am," Dalton said as a bunch of Balls tromped cleat-heavy down the hallway. They gave him dirty looks but kept going.

Mole held up a copy of the yearbook. "Crazy, huh? Real Hong Kong Phooey. Wesley didn't deserve that. Lots of people don't think so. Whole thing has stirred up some serious ill will."

"People are not happy," Dalton agreed. He was running out of time. Three periods left to come up with a plan. Or a suspect. He had to get off his ham and down to the Arts Wing.

"Heard about you standing up to Lee Harvies. Legendary maneuver. *Go ahead and shoot?* That's, like, Cobra Cobretti action. That's, like, half the guys at school crying into their Frooty Bobbers, *Why can't I be that cool?*"

"You're already that cool, Lester. You just need to find a way to let it out."

"Oh, okay, coach. Thanks for the inspirational speech."

Dalton shook his head. "Sorry. That was total Dr. Phil cures your pain. But you know what I mean."

"Do I?"

"Look, Mole, I've got something to do."

Mole nimbly slid around and stood in Dalton's way. "Need some help?"

"No."

"No?"

Dalton sighed. He was wasting time arguing about it. "Okay, yes. I can't believe I'm saying this, but actually I could use a lookout. You coming?"

"Now?"

"Now."

"Right now?"

"Right now."

Mole considered for a minute, patting down his unruly bangs, which only made them more unruly.

"You don't think I will, do you?"

Dalton looked at Mole, searching for sarcasm. He didn't find any. "Fine. Let's go."

"Righteous," Mole said, not going. "I'm totally your boy."

"You're not moving."

"I'm not?"

"Which means, at the very least, you're gonna miss your next class."

"Bumptious," Mole said. "I hate my next class. My next class is such uddersuck."

"You're still not moving."

"Pimptous," Mole said. "I love danger. You know that. You've seen me in action."

"That's not a word. Pimptous."

"You should buy a thesaurus," Mole said.

"Will you *please* get the farck out of the way?"

Mole tapped his temple and closed his eyes.

"What are you doing?"

"Visualizing."

"Oh my *Bob*."

Mole opened his eyes and stepped aside. "Okay, I am now mentally geared. Ready?"

Dalton was already heading down the hall toward the Arts Wing.

With Mole stationed against the door of the janitor's room, watching at the L of two hallways, Dalton knelt in front of Yearbook's door, working a metal spoke into the lock. He raked the pins. It took exactly forty-one seconds for him to get the tumbler to pop.

"Just keep an eye open. Knock twice if there's anyone coming and then walk away like you're lost."

"Got it. But only if you show me how to do that lock thing."

"I'll think about it," Dalton said before closing the door behind him.

Half the room was a computer lab, except, just as Newport had said, there were no computers. There were terminals and power cords and broken keyboards, but the hardware had been carted off, probably to be cannibalized and sold in another wing. The other half of the room had been converted to an old-school photo lab. Dalton stepped into the darkroom, which was, amazingly, dark. A red safelight in the corner turned everything a barely visible hue, like being in a wine bottle. There were two long metal sinks filled with trays that were in turn filled with different-colored liquids. Chemicals. There were enlargers along both walls that looked like mini industrial cranes, and big plastic barrels labeled STOP, DEVELOPER, FIXER, and HYPO. The smell was odd, but not unpleasant, like sweet eggs.

THE PRIVATE DICK HANDBOOK, RULE #35
Splonge said, "That poor boy always smelled
like a bad tube of cologne."

There was a closet in the corner with spools of film hanging like snakes drying on a laundry line. Dalton scanned through them, mostly quickie snaps, kids grinning in the hallways or classrooms, waving and acting goofy or holding their hands up to the lens like celebrities doing the perp walk. There was a roll from a dance, and head shots of the various Fack Cult. Against the far wall were long tables laid out with different pages of the yearbook, scraps and mistakes and comps that had been discarded before the final version was sent to the printers. Behind the tables were a dozen tall file cabinets. Dalton opened the first. It was full of indexed contact sheets going back ten years. He rifled around until he found the current year, stuff from this semester, holding the sheets up to the safelight. It was mostly all the same kind of shots—smiling couples, hallway candids. And then there were some that were telephoto.

Ronnie Newport.

They were different from the rest in style, long shots of the cliques in the parking lot. Balls, Kokrock, Steel-toe Dystopia, Face Boi, Plaths. They obviously had no idea they were being photographed. There were shots of Ginny Slims that Newport had obviously taken from the front seat of his Nova. There was Dalton, sitting in the nurse's office. There were Dalton and Mole, sweaty and bedraggled outside his parents' house.

Dalton was about to close the door, when he noticed that behind the last file was a manila envelope with three contact sheets. It was sealed with duct tape. Dalton tore it open. The first one had grainy shots of the roof. Telephotos of a shadowy figure wearing a Jason mask and what looked like a rifle.

Boomshakalaka.

Newport had managed to take pictures of an actual, real-life Lee Harvies. Why hadn't he told anyone? The Lee Harvies was lean and rangy, wearing all black, not much to go on as far as IDing him. There were a few shots of the guy looking through a scope, which reflected light at the lens, partially ruining them. Then there were pictures of the empty roof and the parking plaza and a grassy mound beyond the small book depository that was off the library. The second sheet was of various Foxxes, some of Cassiopeia. Her talking to Jenny Two.

Or maybe Jenny Three. Her talking to Tarot as he loaded up his van. The last sheet had a bunch of shots of Jeff Chuff. In fact, all of them did. Except for the ones that Wesley Payne was in with him. The date at the top was from the week before Wesley was killed. The shots were like an action series, taken one after another in succession. Chuff and Wesley arguing on the edge of the football field. Chuff gesturing wildly. Wesley staring at his feet. Chuff actually shoving Wesley behind the porta-potty, like they were about to fight. Then just shots of the porta-potty alone. Four of them. End of roll. *BAM*.

Dalton heard a noise.

A silent click.

He didn't bother to turn around, quietly sliding the cabinet door shut, about to tiptoe away, as five strong fingers grabbed him by the back of the neck. *Very* strong fingers. They dug into the muscle fascia along his spine.

"Farck!" he said aloud as the hand pushed, forcing him across the room. He winced with pain, swinging his leg backward in some lame Jackie Chan maneuver that missed entirely. The fingers gripped harder, aiming him toward the long metal sinks. He struggled to pull free, but it was no use. The hand shoved him against the lip of the sink, knocking the wind out of him, and then forced him face-first over the trays. Dalton tried to straighten his back but was levered even farther. The end of his tie went completely into the chemicals, slowly followed by the rest of it. In *Nine Seconds Over Boise*, Lex Cole was almost fed into an automated peeler. He'd managed to escape by crowning the henchman with a petrified russet.

Terrific. Thanks, Lex.

There was nothing in the sink Dalton could grab on to

except sponges or tongs. In any case, he was using both hands to keep himself from going entirely over.

"Wait!"

The hand pushed harder. The fumes were horrible, wavering like heat coming off the desert floor.

"You…killed…Wesley…Payne."

The hand let go.

Dalton coughed, leaking snot and tears, choking in lungfuls of fresh air. He was blind, completely at the hand's mercy, positive it was about to grip him again, maybe even someplace worse, but it didn't. He pulled the tails of his shirt out and flailed around for a spigot, dabbing gently at his eyes until he was able to open them. At first he could just see a halo, someone standing there. Tall, a dark outline. A yellow outline.

It was wearing a yellow dress.

"What are you *doing* in here, Rev?" Principal Inference demanded. "This darkroom is for Yearbook use only."

"Mother of Bob, what's wrong with you?" Dalton spat. His mouth tasted like cat litter.

"My father, Hannibal Inference, always told me that when a puppy shites on the carpet, you push his nose in it, so he learns a lesson."

Dalton blinked. There was violence in the angle of her sinewy neck.

"I'm looking for your money," he said, in a higher and whinier voice than he would have liked. "Isn't that what you want me to do? Splonge said—"

"Forget Splonge. I know why you're in here, so cut the bloshite."

Dalton coughed, not wanting to contradict her when he

could still barely breathe. "Yeah, the pictures. The new year-book."

"What pictures?"

Dalton pulled off his tie, which reeked of developer, and threw it into the trash. "Wes Payne and the skull straw. Euclidian blood. Someone's idea of a joke. Had to check it out."

She looked at him blankly, adjusting her dress.

"You mean you haven't seen the new yearbook?"

"I've had a hundred thousand other things on my mind."

"Well, you should take a peek. It's ugly. Check out the centerfold, and then you'll know why I'm in here."

"Forget the centerfold. I want a status report on the cash. Now."

Dalton cleared his throat. "I know where it is."

"You do?"

"In a locker."

She inhaled sharply. "Which one?"

"I'm not sure."

Inference shook her head. "We swept every locker in school. Plenty of contraband, but no cash. So that's an F minus, Rev. You are now officially failing."

"The key has a number 9 stamped on the back. That mean anything to you?"

"Let me see it."

"I don't have it with me."

Inference eyed Dalton as if she were about to grab him again, hold him down, and search his pockets. He waited, try-ing to decide on a plan to fight her off. Or maybe just give it to her. There was no noise in the room except their ragged breathing. Then she blinked, taking a step back. Lipstick was smeared on her cheek, dried spit caked at the corners of her mouth.

"I'm sorry. I'm acting…very unprofessionally."

Dalton nodded, relieved. "It's a problem I run into a lot myself."

Her voice was low and measured, almost plaintive. "It's just that…I need that money back, Rev. You have no idea."

He did have an idea. He could hear exactly how scared she was.

"Do you know how many piglets I have on the Salt River tit? The mayor, the school board, the Fack Cult union, the PTA. It never ends."

"If it makes you feel any better, as far as I'm concerned, the deal still stands. I find your cash, I'll take my percentage. And I'll make sure you get yours."

"I'm going to get mine, all right."

Inference straightened her dress and her broach and her hair, then walked to the door, holding it open, her face hardening again. "You're running out of time, Dick. I'm beginning to smell an expulsion in your future."

"It wouldn't be my first."

"An expulsion, Rev, would only be the first item on a very long list of unpleasant things I could do to you."

The heavy door slammed in his face like a backfiring Winchester. A few kids scattered. Some just shrugged and rolled their eyes. Dalton blinked in the harsh light of the hallway. He could still see enough, though, to tell that Mole was gone.

CHAPTER 19
CLIQUE. CLICK. BANG.

Dalton locked the door of his room and lay on the bed, staring at the ceiling for almost an hour. He had one day left. He needed to go to the party, find Chuff, convince him, find Tarot, convince him too, and get home in one piece. He felt nauseated from breathing in the darkroom. He felt nauseated thinking about Macy. He had too many questions and no answers. It sucked.

Choices:

1. Quit.

2. Keep pushing until the guilty mug fesses up.

3. Develop an addiction to photo developer, start wearing all black.

4. Pack harmonica, buy canned chili, and hop last train to Clarksville.

5. Sit on my farcking ham until someone else handles it.

6. Invent steak knife home acupuncture kit, become insanely rich.

7. Develop killer sexting app, become even richer.

When it was almost six, Dalton got up, changed his crisp white shirt, exchanging it for a crisper white shirt, and put on a new tie. He called Macy six times. No answer. He called Mole six times. No answer. Turd Unit stuck a fork through the space between the door and the frame, popped the lock, then came into the room and jumped up and down on the bed. Dalton didn't have the energy to tell him not to. Instead, he twisted the skin on the back of his brother's arm until Turd Unit pleaded and swore, going "ow wow ow wow" even though they both knew it didn't really hurt. He pouted in the corner for a while, rubbing his arm. Dalton made a face. Turd Unit didn't laugh. Dalton whacked him with a pillow, a perfect shot. Turd Unit didn't laugh. Dalton finally sighed and stuck his hand in his armpit and made the fart sound his brother loved so much. This time, Turd Unit broke into raucous giggles, which gave way to breathless hilarity, writhing around on the carpet as though someone had poured kerosene in his underwear. Dalton chuckled while slicking his scalp with water and a tiny dab of gel. He shaved the hairs that had settled sporadically on his cheeks and chin, quietly wishing there were more of them.

"Stiff Sheets shaved all six of his hairs!" Turd Unit screamed, slamming around on the bed again.

Dalton knuckled his brother's belly, coaxing an exaggerated

181

"woof," then walked downstairs, past his father, careful not to step in front of the TV. The old man said nothing, keeping his death grip on the remote. Dalton checked in the basement for a body hanging over the laundry. Nope. Then he avoided the kitchen, slipping out the back door. His mother called, "Dalton, honey? Dalton?" but he pretended not to hear.

The scooter started on the third try. He lifted his helmet and a note fell out. Another index card.

CONNECT THE DOTS. THE MONEY HAS A MIND OF ITS OWN. IT HAS GONE WHERE IT FEELS WARM AND SAFE. WHAT GOOD IS A KEY IF YOU IGNORE THE LOCK?

DUH.

STICK IT IN AND TWIST.

Dalton stuck the card in his back pocket with the others and gunned the engine, letting the exhaust roar. Then he let go of the clutch with a guttural chirp, aiming the tiny rocket across town, arcing across the troposphere, the black machine ready to run down and plant its nose cone right in the center of Lu Lu Footer's party.

◎

It was a huge Doric-columned house, three slabs of faux-marble pretension, with a cobblestone driveway that wound through the trees. There were dozens of cars parked haphazardly, kids standing at the mouth of the garage, chasing each other in circles, boys pretending not to care and girls pretending not to want to get caught. They rolled in the grass or just talked. They smoked and spat and lifted red plastic cups to their mouths in unison, up and down every twelve seconds.

Dalton parked his scooter between a pair of Mercedes, one silver and one red, then locked the helmet to the back wheel. A pair of Face Boi leaned against the doors, arms crossed, wearing looks of satisfied waiting.

"Nice sweater," Dalton said. They didn't answer, but one adjusted the cashmere sleeve knotted at his chest.

"No, seriously. I could use a sweater like that. Where'd you get it?"

The first Face Boi lifted his foot and picked a nonexistent piece of dirt off his docksider. The other one examined his nails.

Dalton gave up and walked over to the house. The front door was locked. He rang the bell.

"Well, don't you look familiar," Lu Lu Footer said, immediately yanking it open. She seemed about fourteen feet tall in a tiger-striped dress that wound around her body like a wet paper towel.

"You seem to have recovered from before."

"What before?"

"In the hallway?"

"What hallway?"

They stared at each other.

"Hey," Dalton finally said. "That dress fits you like a million simoleons."

Lu Lu Footer's expression changed from haughty smirk to slightly less haughty smirk. Then she slammed the door.

Dalton rang the bell and waited.

She opened it, saw him, and slammed it again.

Dalton pressed the buzzer.

She cracked the door, arms crossed. "Whoever put that picture in the yearbook put it there because of you, snooper. Because you came here. If it wasn't for—"

"If it wasn't for me, it'd be easier for you to pretend Wesley Payne never existed, just like everyone else."

Lu Lu took a deep breath, about to slam the door again, but stopped herself. "You have a point. But I still don't want you in my house."

"Why not?"

"Because, snooper, I heard you were snooping in my darkroom."

"I thought you gave up on everything. I thought you didn't care about Yearbook anymore."

"That was four hours ago."

"I wanted to see if I could find out something about who put Wes Payne's picture in the centerfold."

Her face softened, but not much. "You don't think it was me?"

"No."

"Everyone else does. That's why no one even came to my party."

Dalton peered behind her. The house was packed.

She shrugged. "No one good, anyway."

"Have I mentioned how great you look in that dress?"

Lu Lu Footer laughed. A tiny bit. Then she stepped aside

and let him in. "But no going upstairs. It's off-limits. I'm not kidding. Am I kidding?"

"It doesn't seem like it."

"Good. I'm watching you."

Three girls ran by with champagne bottles in their hands. There were plastic champagne glasses on the floor. Dalton nosed one into a standing position and then flipped it upward with his boot, snatching it out of the air by the stem.

"So can I buy you a drink?"

"Smooth, Cary Grant," Lu Lu said, before starting to talk to someone in a better tax bracket. "But I don't drink."

Dalton pushed his way through the packed room. There was dancing in one corner, Kiss Me Cherry playing full blast from a very expensive stereo. Even though the party had just started, there were kids making out on the couch, a few already sprawled on the floor. There were other kids drawing with Sharpies on the ones who had passed out, and then Crowd-arounds leaning over to see what was going on, making suggestions like "Head Fish Stick!" and "Mission Accomplished!" and "Brainwashed by Fack Cult!"

THE PRIVATE DICK HANDBOOK, RULE #36
Whether you've had too much beer or are
merely suffering from bovine spongiform,
never ever EVER pass out at a party. Ever.

Dalton elbowed through a packed hallway and finally made it to the kitchen, where a bunch of Euclidians were playing a drinking game called Go Ahead and Stump My Ass! They were amped up, sharing a large plastic bottle of Rush. A kid wearing a sweater-vest dribbled some down his chin before loudly pronouncing "Suez Canal!" and slamming down his empty. The rest of the players groaned as he rolled the dice again, cackling like a maniac.

Dalton walked into the dining room, where Plaths were taking turns reading aloud. The sound of poetry filled him with a momentary terror, as it always did. He feared poetry because he didn't understand it, didn't like how it seemed to be the province of hysterical fifties housewives, and was, in any case, quite sure it was not approved of by Barnaby Smollet. The girl who was reading saw Dalton and stopped mid-iamb. The rest looked up expectantly, shyly stroking their braids or rolling their black socks.

"Hi."

The head Plath, a very pale, very thin girl with black tights and a pin-covered beret, said, "Hey, um, do you want to come in and—"

Three Balls ran laughing down the hallway, smashing each other with sticks and knocking over family pictures.

"You bet I do," Dalton said, stepping into the room and closing the door. The assembled girls waited. Dalton slid the book out of the hand of the one who'd been reading. She took her place as the other Plaths sat cross-legged on the floor.

"I love this one," Dalton said, opening to a random page, to a poem he'd never seen before. It was entitled "Snip." The first lines were:

Quite a bonus among the azaleas
My toe instead of a turnip freed

The captain of the ship removed with ease
Hoed into the dirt like a dirty lie.

Dalton realized, to his amazement, that this woman had written a poem about accidentally chopping her big toe off. It was totally unexpected, unabashedly gross, and really sort of excellent. His voice switched from a laconic resignation to raptly enunciating the words, wanting to find out what happened. When he finished the last stanza...

The way you paused to help me leap—
Pruned anchor, sneaker fodder, empty cleat
Dirty feckless boy
Careless gardener spills
Blood amongst the seasonal greens
Sow toe, reap stump
You lightheaded chump.

...the Plaths cheered wildly. Some leaped up and clapped.

"That poem rocks," Dalton said. "Seriously. I had no idea Sylvia Plath was so cool."

"Who?" the pale girl said, confused.

"Sylvia Plath? Isn't that who you guys—"

"Fred."

"Excuse me?"

"We study the poetry of Fred Plath. Her second cousin. 'Snip' is his poem. We feel, as a group, Sylvia was the far lesser talent."

The other girls nodded with reverence, looking at the

publicity photo on the back of the book, a blurry shot of a guy who looked like he really knew how to bowl. Then the pale girl pulled a beer from behind a pillow and took a swig. "Anyway, want one? If we keep going like this, it's gonna get ca-*razy* in here soon."

They all laughed.

"Totally tempting. I gotta say, you guys have been hiding your hipness under a turtlenecked rock, you know it?"

The girls looked at one another doubtfully.

"Definitely time to let it out. Way out. And Fred rules. But I've got some business downstairs I've been putting off."

"Poems are pentameter," the pale girl mused, leaning back. "They are rhythm. All of Fred's poems are like beautiful, syllabic math."

"Exactly," Dalton said. "I could totally hear that while I was reading."

Dalton waved good-bye and turned toward the basement door. He took a deep breath and then began walking down the stairs. If there was a basement, there was a keg. And if there was a keg, there were Balls. Time to face Chuff.

The concrete walls opened into a large rec room. About twenty guys played knock hockey and shot pool and pushed kids who tried to get near the keg, which sat in a blow-up kiddie pool filled with ice. Chance Chugg, decked out in eye black, a helmet, and shoulder pads, kept yelling, "He who rules the keg rules the universe!" even though fewer people laughed each time. He held on to the hose, trying to decide which cup to fill out of the dozen empties thrust toward him, finally picking a Euclidian's. The kid wore a grateful smile as the stream of frosty beer approached the brim. When he went to take a sip, Chugg smacked the kid's hand, spraying beer all over his face and shirt and pants.

"Chuff to Chugg...touchdown!"

The Euclidian left the cup on the floor and walked up the stairs, arms spread like bird's wings, dripping onto the carpet.

"He who rules the keg rules a universe of dangles!"

There was a big projection TV against the far wall with a game on, Balls sitting around half watching but mostly wrestling or running formations. Chuff wasn't with them. Dalton reached into a plastic sleeve of cups nesting on the floor and held one out. Chugg stared in disbelief. Dalton stared back. It got quiet in the room, someone turning the TV down. A few Sis Boom Bahs backed against the wall while other Balls stood and flexed and hiked up their belts in anticipation.

"You keep squeezing that hose like that," Dalton said, "I'm gonna start blushing."

Chance Chugg laughed, his big horsey teeth gnashing like he couldn't possibly get enough air, so everyone else did as well. Chugg held his belly and wiped his nose and eyes. Then he straightened up and asked the crowd, "Can you be-*lieve* this guy? The stones on this fish, *I SWEAR TO BOB!*"

He reached over and filled Dalton's cup. Most of the Balls sat back down.

"Don't push it, murse," Chugg hissed through his neckless smile, so only he and Dalton could hear. "Just 'cause I got word from above to be cool doesn't mean I might not get too drunk and stomp your teeth for you anyway."

Chugg was smaller and decidedly wider, and he had at least twice as many hairs on his chin as Dalton. He was too dumb to be of use for anything except brute intimidation and running into things full speed. His already limited purview would grow smaller within minutes of graduating from Salt River and continue to compress in on itself over years of unappreciated labor, miserable family Christmases, and beers with the guys on Wednesday nights until nothing remained but the vague odor of Chex Mix and a desiccated sweat sock. So it was hard to hate him too much.

"Where's the big man?" Dalton asked.

"He's here. Waiting."

"For what?"

"WE PLAY ONLY ONE SPORT AT SALT RIVER!" Chugg yelled, instead of answering. He held up his beer and counted on stubby pig fingers as the entire team stood at attention.

"Baseball?"

"FOR PUSSIES!"

"Basketball?"

"FOR PUSSIES!"

"Soccer?"

"FOR PUSSIES!"

"Can you dig it?"

"YES, WE CAN!"

There was a collective whooping and slapping of high fives before the TV went back on. Dalton brought his beer upstairs and toured through the remaining rooms. No Macy, no Mole, no Chuff. He walked out through glass doors onto a big wooden deck. Below him, Pinker Casket was setting up gear on the patio that would serve as a stage. It was made of heavy flagstone surrounding a large pool built to look like a natural lagoon.

Mick Freeley, testing a mic, *test test test one two*, saw Dalton, flipped him the bird, then went back to what he was doing. Dalton put one leg over the railing and dropped down next to him.

"Tarot around?"

Freeley, wearing a look of barely restrained violence to go along with his STEVEN PINKER IS A GENIUS T-shirt, gestured with his head toward the van parked on the lawn. Dalton walked over and knocked on the rusty metal paneling. No answer. He pulled the sliding door open with a creak. Tarot was lying on top of some girl, her red high heel poking out from beneath him. *Not Cassie*, Dalton thought with relief. *Cassie wouldn't wear shoes that cheap.* Tarot turned, furious, the metal skull in his tongue flashing. "WHAT?"

He relaxed when he saw it was Dalton. He adjusted his coat and sat up.

"Ah. Iz you. Well?"

A Sis Boom Bah pushed Tarot's leg off her and sat up as well, straightening her dress. There were red welts on her neck and wrists.

"What are you looking at?"

"Aren't you supposed to stick to the sporty types?"

The Sis Boom Bah gave Dalton the finger.

"Tell me the plan," Tarot said, the dark lines under his eyes thicker than usual. "Now."

Dalton hesitated, looking at the Sis Boom.

"Go to the ladies' room," Tarot told her.

"I don't need to—"

"Now."

The cheerleader made a face but got up, straightening her

uniform. She peered around the edge of the van, making sure no one was looking, and tiptoed into the house.

"I just talked to Chuff."

Tarot looked around, suspecting a trap. "He's here?"

"Sure, right upstairs." Dalton pointed vaguely toward the tree line. "Anyway, he likes my plan. Loves it. Swallowed the thing whole. He agreed to a meet tomorrow. Me, you, and him. No lieutenants. Anyone else shows but us three who isn't a civilian, the whole thing's off."

"Where?"

"Kids' playground. Swing set."

"Zo we're meeting," he said, the skull lolling like a chrome maggot on his tongue. "What's the actual plan?"

"I'll give you the fine print tomorrow. It's a truce. You and him. Working together."

"That's not enough. Not nearly."

"It's plenty. What better way to get close to him if he's convinced you're tamed?"

"And why would he be ztupid enough to believe that?"

"You're the lead singer of Casket. Being up onstage is an acting job. So act. Be convincing. You sell it to him now, you can sell the rest of him later."

The Sis Boom Bah came back and sat on the edge of the mattress. She had fresh white powder on her cheeks and a new layer of bloodred lipstick.

"The rest will be spelled out at the playground," Dalton said. "Two o'clock. Sharp."

Tarot was about to protest, but the Sis Boom Bah kicked the door shut. Within seconds, there was a bout of giggling from inside.

"You don't show up, I'm keeping your four grand," Dalton told the cracked paint job.

◎

Back upstairs, Ronnie Newport was sitting on a long velvet couch. His pompadour was perfectly slicked, and he wore brand-new jeans with the cuffs rolled about six inches. Newport looked at Dalton without even registering him. He was smoking a cigarette, holding it by the filter with two fingers, the butt facing straight upward, like he'd developed a whole new method of smoking and soon everyone else would be holding them that way too. And he was probably right. The big-hair girls sat on either side of him, nattering away.

Ask him now, straight out. Did you take pictures of Lee Harvies? Do you know who they are? And why did you lie to me about driving?

But there was something about Newport's placid look that made Dalton hesitate. Not to mention Lu Lu Footer was standing over him insisting there was no smoking inside. He didn't register her either, just kept puffing away. Soon the big hairs lit up as well, and the room was like a lungbox your cousin Ferdie was roasting marshmallows in.

"DALTON!"

Mole was in the room off the kitchen, hunkered with some other Euclidians. They had an elaborately engineered beer bong in the air, Mole pulling off it like a suckling while the rowdy Euclidians chanted "MOLE-LES-TER! MOLE-LES-TER! MOLE-LES-TER!" Despite all their high-fiving and sousy bravado, they scattered as soon as Dalton walked up.

"You think maybe you should slow it down a bit there?"

"The writer of proverbs!" Mole belched wetly. "The leader of cheers! The dozer of bulls! The jump-offer of high buildings and low bridges!"

"They make decaf now."

"Funny, guy. Funny. You, guy, are a funny guy. Like, seriously."

"Have you seen Macy?"

"No. No. No. No. And it's, like, tragic, 'cause—"

"Have you seen Cassiopeia?"

"Oh, yeah. She's in the pool." Mole put his hands over his mouth like a ringmaster with a megaphone. "That Whiskey Lick's taking a swim, boys, and she's wetter than Madonna at a Kabbalah wristband store!"

Crowdarounds started to poke their heads in to see what the rumpus was. Most of them poked their heads back out, but the exceptionally bored stayed, vainly hoping someone might throw a punch.

"Doing laps," Mole mused. "While half the guys in school pretend not to watch. It's a parade of half-thumbed rodneys out there, I swear. Get it? It's a parade, and she's the float!"

Dalton didn't see Cassiopeia in the pool. There were guys milling around, but mostly they seemed to be waiting for someone oblivious to shove in with all their clothes on.

"What do you need her for, anyway?" Mole asked. "Salt River's got all kinds of girls. And you being you, tough and cool and all, you can have your pick. You walk down the hall and they practically start ovulating in unison. For a geek like me? It's pretty much, hey, I got four years to find someone to let me kiss them once in a while. Four years and if I'm lucky, maybe sniff a random boob."

"Mole—"

"But don't get me wrong. I'm not greedy. That's really all I need. A boob and a lip and maybe a friend who understands my movie references. A guy I can maybe quote some Stallone with. I got those three things, I'm golden."

"At least until college."

"No kidding." Mole sighed. "Then it starts all over again. Then you're stuck in a dorm room with some knob who wants to play 3-D Tetris and quote Charlie Sheen all night."

"You were supposed to have my back."

Mole chugged backwash from a can of beer. "Huh?"

"Remember? Outside Yearbook's office? I got ambushed. Came out of the darkroom and you were gone."

"Oh yeah, that. Hey, I'm sorry. I'm—I'm so..." Mole's voice began to crack. His face fell, and he rubbed his eyes.

"You're not crying, are you?"

Macy walked into the room, taking Mole by the hand. She led him to a couch in the back and laid three pool towels over him. Mole rolled over and immediately began to snore.

Say something suave. Not too interested, not too distant. Funny, but not trying too hard.

"I thought you weren't here."

"I wasn't," Macy said. "Now I am."

Dalton pointed with his chin toward the deck and then walked to the farthest point along the railing. He stood for a moment, convinced she'd decided not to follow. Then she was standing next to him. Pinker Casket was finishing their sound check. The new bass player wore a NEIL YOUNG AND THE SHOCK-ING PINKS T-shirt. The pool was filled with Silverspoon and Face Boi showing off their bodies by pretending to reach for towels and lotion. A dozen Barefoots sat on a big woven Guatemalan blanket in the grass, passing around flutes and bongos, having been told they weren't allowed in the pool unless they showered off the patchouli.

"What's with Purple Rain?" Dalton asked, pointing to a bunch of kids in costumes standing around a makeshift stage. They were all wearing purple turtlenecks.

"Rotten in Denmark."

"Something caught in your throat?"

"No, that's their name. Rotten in Denmark."

"That a racket?"

"It's the theater clique."

Dalton winced instinctively.

"Exactly. They're doing *Death of a Salesman* in mime. Actually, it was Jeff's idea."

"You never said Chuff was an actor."

"You never asked. Besides, that was a long time ago."

Dalton wanted to grab her and shake her out of her weird reserve.

Or maybe kiss her out of it.

She gave him a shy look. "Dalton, why—"

"What a cute couple you guys make!" Cassiopeia Jones called brightly, walking over. "Oh, wait, my bad. Did I interrupt something?"

THE PRIVATE DICK HANDBOOK, RULE #37
Absolutely no way this ends well. Your only hope:
Say nothing, appear humble.

Macy and Cassiopeia eyeballed each other, wearing dual frowns like they'd just shared a mayo smoothie.

"Don't you have a show to do?"

"Soon. Kurt's in the van warming up his vocal chords."

"Warming up something."

"Why, Dalton," Cassiopeia said, "you've become a gossip."

"Stop!" Macy said.

"Stop what, honey?"

"Stop talking to him like you're in a Woody Allen movie. All witty and urbane. And meaningless. It's so annoying."

"Urbane? I was actually going for street sass. With maybe a dash of working-class righteousness."

"See?" Macy said. "See that? It's like some fat, lonely, junk food–eating former sitcom writer came up with that line and plopped it in your mouth. Except he's the only one laughing."

Cassiopeia put her hands on her hips and looked at Dalton. "You know what? I *like* her. Not afraid to speak that big Euclidian mind. We always have room over at Foxxes for a girl with some zest."

"Thanks, but no thanks."

"Cassie..."

"And she's right. You and me? We really could use a laugh track."

Macy threw up her arms in disgust. "It's like you think you're so—"

"So what, hon?"

Macy blanched. "That's my pin."

Cassiopeia ran her fingers through her pink hair. "Ex-*cuse* me?"

"That pin," Macy said, looking at Dalton, then back to the sparkly butterfly he'd sent her in the mail.

Cassiopeia put her hand on it and smiled, like a saleswoman showing off a new product. She angled her head so it glinted in the light. "Oh, this little thing?"

"Where did you get that?" Dalton asked.

"You gave it to me, Dalty, remember?"

Macy shot them both a malevolent look. Then she slapped Dalton. A nice open-hander that landed solidly. "You gave it to *her*?"

"Is there something wrong?" Cassiopeia asked, taking it off as if she were about to hand it to Macy, before refastening it even higher above her left ear.

Macy's jaw trembled. She turned and stormed off the deck, slamming the glass door hard enough to crack the foundation. Dalton watched her go, knowing he couldn't afford the time it would take to chase after her, and not sure if he wanted to. He needed to find Chuff.

"That wasn't nice."

Cassiopeia laughed. "She's in deep. She's got her nose wide open over you, Dalty. You're going to have to let her down real easy."

"Who says I want to let her down?"

"Hmmm," Cassiopeia mused.

"Where *did* you get the pin?"

"Found it in Kurt's van. Guess you must have left it when

you broke in and snooped around, huh? Good thing I found it before he did. Or, wait, maybe I didn't find it before he did."

"What are you saying?"

"You should have called me, Dalton. We needed to talk."

Kurt Tarot walked onto the stage. The drummer started to count out a beat while Mick Freeley chunked in a rhythm.

"Too late to talk now, though, isn't it? Oh, well. You had your chance."

"This song is called 'Light Sweet Crude,'" Tarot said in a hungry vibrato. "Dedicated to a zertain little blond out there who knows just the way a boy likes her to shake her poms. Yeah, baby, you know who you are."

"Gotta go."

"Wait," Dalton said, trying to grab Cassiopeia's hand, but in one lithe movement she levered herself over the railing, landing on the grass like a nine-lived minx and bounding onstage just in time for the first verse, coming in a fifth above Tarot's gravelly voice, blending nicely. The crowd cheered.

Dalton listened to a few songs, "Shaka Zulu Was the First MC" and then "The Friend of My Enemy Is My Enemy's Dead Friend." Dalton was surprised that they were actually almost good. Cassiopeia's voice and moves added a balancing presence to the dark testicularness of the Casket groove. Most of the kids in the party came outside and filled the lawn, the majority of them drooling in front of Cassiopeia. Face Boi pulled off their sweaters en masse and waved them over their heads like flags, bottom lips jutted in concentration, not quite in time with the music. Girls with Unnecessary Y's tried to dance alongside, somehow one Y away from being coordinated. Then Casket began a song Dalton recognized, even though he'd never heard it before. It was "The Ballad of Mary Surratt." Dalton looked down at Cassiopeia singing words to a grinding, dirgelike melody. As the chorus came around for the second time, he could have sworn she looked up and winked.

Dalton walked back inside. He poured out Chugg's flat beer and filled the red cup with water from the kitchen faucet. "Synod!" said the same Euclidian, still answering questions on the same turn. "Smedley Darlington Butler! The Nostromo! Baruch Spinoza! Centrifugal force! Ernst Lubitsch!"

Another Euclidian slammed his beer on the table. "That's incorrect! Lubitsch is wrong!"

"Yeah, well, it says it right here on the card."

"It wasn't Lubitsch, it was Wilder! Billy Wilder!"

"Lubitsch, fool. The card says Lubitsch!"

The two Euclidians got in each other's faces.

"Take a hike, mister!"

"No, you take a hike!"

"Do you think I'm monkeying around here? Is that it? Huh?"

"If it *walks* like a monkey, *talks* like a monkey, and *reeks* like a monkey, then, yeah, I do!"

"Oh, that's it. It's on. It is totally *on*!"

A half dozen other Euclidians streamed into the room, all of them going "Hey, hey, hey, hey, hey," attempting to break apart the two sets of steamed-over glasses. Dalton, pretending to wait his turn for the hall bathroom, used the commotion to sneak over to the staircase. A thick velvet rope blocked it off. A sign in large block letters said:

NO ACCESS! DO NOT GO UPSTAIRS!
AM I KIDDING?
JUST GO AHEAD AND FIND OUT!
—L. L. F.

Dalton peeled the sign away.

THE PRIVATE DICK HANDBOOK, RULE #38
Seems like Footer means it. Better not.

Then he raised the rope and tiptoed up the plush carpeted treads.

CHAPTER 20
THE REVENANT

Dalton pressed himself against the near wall, peeking back down the stairs. No one looking, no one following. No nine-foot Footer losing her shite. He could feel the vibrations of Pinker Casket in the floorboards and walls, a walking bassline thrumming through the Sheetrock and directly into his jejunum. If Chuff wasn't upstairs, he wasn't here. Which meant there was no meet tomorrow, and no plan with just a day to go.

Dalton stepped softly toward the first room to his right. The door was closed. He turned the handle a micron at a time, cracking it enough to peer in. Empty. If you didn't count the thousand stuffed animals on the bed. And on the floor. And on the shelves. Not to mention the computer equipment, printers, scanners, and remnants of yearbook layouts duct taped all over the walls. Dalton checked the dresser's bottom drawer first, coming up with a handful of granny-white panties, each about the size of a small yacht sail.

THE PRIVATE DICK HANDBOOK, RULE #39
**In terms of hiding things, you're better off stapling them
to your forehead than stuffing them under the mattress.**

Dalton lifted Lu Lu's mattress and reached beneath, pulling
out a stack of letters. He shuffled through them. Nothing particularly interesting, lovey-dovey stuff, maudlin and strict at the
same time. At least not interesting until he saw the addresses,
which just happened to be for various tiers at the state prison.
And then a big stack that was all the same tier, same name,
same cell. Dalton was a firm believer that every single person in
the world had a dark secret, and even a mediocre Dick could
find it after a while, no matter how well it was hidden. But in a
million years of snooping he wouldn't have figured Lu Lu for a
prisoner groupie. He reached under again and found some pictures, a guy with a bunch of tattoos and a few missing teeth
posing in his cell. Dalton put those back, groping farther. There
was something square and solid. His neck was pressed against
the box spring, shoulder joint subluxed, fingers barely touching
whatever it was, when he heard a sound down the hallway.

Farck.

Was it a footstep?

He held his breath and waited, arm too far in to pull it out
quietly.

But there was no more noise except the steady blare of
Casket. Dalton grabbed the object and slid it out. A yearbook.
From the year before. He flipped through the juniors, and
there was Wesley Payne's class picture, the one that had been
defaced, along with an inscription.

Dear Lu. I know we've been rivals for student council and I know we're hoping to get elected again to the same posts, but I also hope you and I can be friends next year. Okay? Real friends. After all, there's room for both of us in this school, isn't there? Real friends can sometimes even be real partners.

Best, Wesley.

Dalton turned the page and two sheets of lined essay paper fell out. The drawings that had been superimposed over Wesley's face. Holes in his head, straws sticking out, Kurt Tarot sucking blood. The originals.

Bam.

Dalton put the papers back and stuck the yearbook down the front of his shirt, one corner under his belt to hold it still. He reknotted his tie and looked in the mirror. His chest was square, like he'd swallowed a baking pan, but not so obvious he couldn't bluff his way through if questioned. He needed to talk to Lu Lu. He needed to squeeze her hard. But there was one thing to do first.

Chuff.

The hall was silent and empty, the thud of kick drum in the joists. The next room was clearly Mom and Dad's, a huge four-poster and an enormous flat screen on the far wall. Then the hall bath. The turning handle surprised a Bull Lemia in a gray sweater. She looked at Dalton guiltily. He apologized and gently closed it again. The next one was a little sister's room, full of Annoya the Explorer dolls and My Hairless Pony coloring books. Then a closet. Then a laundry room. There was one final door at the end of the hall. Dalton put his ear against it.

There was rustling. And low voices. He pulled the knob. The voices got louder, almost panting. A girl and a guy. He was going hot and heavy, doing a lot of "C'mon, baby, c'mon." She giggled, then resisted. They alternated, *yes, no, yes.* Finally, she became more adamant. "Enough. Stop. Stop it. Get off."

Dalton sighed.

"Stop it!" the girl said again. "You're hurting."

THE PRIVATE DICK HANDBOOK, RULE #40
When it's too late not to get involved,
stop thinking and get involved.

Dalton slammed the door open. The knob on the other side planted itself two inches into Sheetrock.

"All right," he said, "knock it—"

A huge male head turned with a mixture of smirkiness and rage. A much smaller female head peered from under him, wide-eyed with fear.

Chuff.

Macy.

Macy and Chuff.

Chuff on top of Macy.

Holding her wrists.

Her shirt unbuttoned.

His shirt off completely, huge belly practically distending to the floor.

"New fish!" Chuff said. "What a coincidence!"

Chugg was right. Chuff was here. Waiting.

Macy didn't even look at Dalton. She blinked frantically, levering herself out from under Chuff, pushing him away with one hand and holding her shirt closed with the other. She got up and grabbed her shoes, slipping under Dalton's arm and running down the hallway.

THE PRIVATE DICK HANDBOOK, RULE #41
Option one: Crush, kill, destroy.
Option two: Do the job now, destroy later.
Option three: Wish for more options.
Option four: What was the kill one again?

"Sounds like you weren't very convincing," Dalton said through teeth clamped so hard they practically fused. "Despite all your convincing."

"Ah, her." Chuff smiled. "Good riddance to uncooperative rubbish."

The doorknob snapped off in Dalton's hand. It was heavy, Italianate. He considered staving in Chuff's nose with it. Chuff himself seemed to be wondering what Dalton would do, but appeared only mildly concerned. Dalton tossed the doorknob onto the bed.

"You feel okay, guy? You look like you've gone and caught a dose of swine flu."

"I'm fine."

Pinker Casket was now between songs. They could both see a corner of the stage out of the tiny seaman's window where Mick Freeley was noodling through some scales, jumping up and down and hammering the strings while wearing a shirt that said STINKS LIKE PINK, AND BABY, IT SMELLS ALL RIGHT.

"You believe anyone wants to listen to that blather?"

Dalton didn't answer, listening for the sound of footsteps at the bottom of the staircase. There weren't any.

"Anyhow," Chuff said, rising to his full height and taking up most of the room, but not putting his shirt back on. His bulk forced Dalton into the corner. "I am ready to collect on my investment. I want a plan and I want it now. And I'm telling you what, Mr. Doorknob, it had better be good."

Dalton opened his mouth.

"No," Chuff said, putting one finger over Dalton's lips. "It had better be *outstanding*."

"It is," Dalton said, wishing it was. Or, really, that there was really any plan at all.

"Yeah? And?"

"You, me, and Tarot. Swing set tomorrow at two. I got him to agree to a truce. I got him thinking about you two going into business instead of knocking heads. He sees the profit motive light but wants to hear it from you and decide if it's on the level. We all stand in the sandbox and share our toys like good little boys, then I lay out the fine print."

"That's a start," Chuff said, pressing himself into Dalton and beginning to crush him against the wall. "And I'm impressed by your negotiation skills. But I'm not waiting until tomorrow. You lay the rest out for me now. Right now."

It was hard to breathe. The full weight of Chuff was like a sweaty bison. The music coming from outside was frenetic. It pounded and tore and spazzed. The windows flexed and bowed, building toward a chorus.

And then it stopped.

Mid-note.

There was a squeal of feedback, and then yelling. There

were sirens churning from the bottom of the hill. Dalton and Chuff pushed their way to the tiny window. On the back lawn, a full-scale brawl was taking place. The Balls seemed to be getting the best of it. Along with some random sploets, they had various Kokrocks and Pinker Caskets backed against the stage. Chugg, leading the charge with a broken table leg, yelled, "Touchdown!" Fists were flying, headlocks were cinched, wild movie-style kicks missed wildly. The sirens came whirling up the driveway. There were authoritative yells, a synchronized slamming of doors, and then Snouts everywhere.

"That *idiot!*" Chuff growled. He pushed Dalton aside and submarined from the room. Dalton watched Snouts coming out of the bushes in waves, rounding up fighters, swinging billy clubs, and flashing handcuffs. Jenny One leaped into the fray, clearing a path that had to be for Cassiopeia, but Dalton couldn't see her. Or Macy. Lu Lu Footer was yelling at a plainclothes in the middle of it all, demanding her rights. Dalton knew it was a knock-heads-now/demand-rights-later sort of situation, but Footer stood firm above it all, the pitch of her voice nearly avian. Kurt Tarot's van wheeled out of the driveway in a patch of gray rubber. A cruiser tried to follow it but hit a Face Boi Mercedes that was backing out instead.

THE PRIVATE DICK HANDBOOK, RULE #42
Never be ashamed to take the back door like a thief,
hide in the woods like a coward, and let heroes explain
bail to their own parents.

The staircase was quiet. Dalton slipped through the kitchen, where the Euclidians were still deep into their game, "Phoebe

Cates! Badfinger! Kerensky and the White Russians! Charles Bukowski! The Coriolis effect!" It was clear sailing to his scooter, which, amazingly, hadn't been knocked over. Clear sailing, that is, except for Hutch. Who stood by the back bumper with his arms crossed.

"So how's the investigation coming, Dick?"

Dalton acted resigned, palms up, giving a little smile, and then took off at an angle across the lawn, with Hutch right on his heels. They wove through Snouts and struggling cliques, past Chugg being held down and clubbed, past a clutch of Rotten in Denmark miming *Guernica*, until they came to an open area just before the tree line.

"Lee Harvies!" someone screamed. There was a single rifle shot. Or maybe an explosion. A Des Barres, running in terror, slammed into Dalton, turning him around. Hutch was closing, about five steps away. There was a second *clang*. And then he felt it. Like being punched. In the chest. Punched by a very small, very high-velocity piece of metal. He felt himself falling. Then he felt nothing at all.

CHAPTER 21

FLASHBACK II: TIME IS FALLIBLE, HEROES LIVE OR DIE

Landon had been gone for more than fourteen months. It was the summer before Dalton's junior year. He'd handled five or six cases and transferred schools at least three times. The money was coming in, but it was going out just as fast. His father still wasn't working. Turd Unit was his usual one-man terror cell. On a humid Wednesday, Sherry Rev knocked over the mailbox on her way to work, drove through the neighbor's flowers, came home from the grocery store with three bags of mini nondairy creamers, and finally just took to her bed. Turd Unit sensed that something was up. For days he'd hung out quietly in his room. Dalton at first just gave his mother space. Not only because he figured she needed it but because he didn't have time to deal. For one thing, he was neck-deep in his first real girlfriend, a no-nonsense Whiskey Lick with short black hair and a husky laugh. Not to mention his ongoing infiltration of a stolen-bicycle ring. But when he'd come home and all the lights were off, the same dishes on the kitchen table that had been there over the weekend, he went up and knocked on the old study door, despite having zero clue what he was going to say.

"Go away," Sherry Rev said. She and Dalton's father had long since been sleeping in separate rooms.

"It's me, Mom. Can I come in?"

"No."

Dalton turned the knob and entered anyhow. The room was dark and airless. It smelled like shampoo and graham crackers. Sherry lay in bed, the covers pulled entirely over her. Dalton clicked on a reading lamp and dragged a chair next to the lump of sheets he assumed was her head.

"What's going on, Mom? Turd Unit's down there licking old candy wrappers. Dad looks like he hasn't moved in days."

"Those that can't care for themselves must perish," said her muffled voice. "It's the law of natural selection."

"Somehow I think downtown Tehachapi has different rules than the Galápagos."

"This is a family of failed apes," Sherry insisted. "We're good with crude tools, but we can't hunt to save our opposable thumbs. I'm sorry, but we simply don't seem to have vital-enough genes to merit passing on. I've decided it's just as well that we allow our line to wither off and die."

"We're not failed. We're...in flux. Dad will—"

"No, Dalton. That's the thing. Whatever you're about to say he will do, trust me, he won't."

Dalton cleared his throat. "Well, okay, Landon—"

"Halfway around the world."

"True, but at least Turd Unit—"

"Maniacal. Unparentable."

Dalton shifted uncomfortably in the chair. "That's all a little

211

grim, Ma, don't you think? I mean, you can't just give up, can you?"

Sherry Rev was quiet for a moment.

"Actually, I can. Besides, being a fossil won't be so bad."

"Yes, it will. It'll suck." All the patience drained from Dalton's voice. "You need to stop feeling so sorry for yourself."

Sherry Rev tossed off her blankets and glared at her son. She stuck a pinky nail between her teeth and adjusted the wet architecture of her braces. "And what do you know about feeling sorry?"

"Probably nothing," Dalton admitted.

"Have you ever sent a boy off to war? A boy you birthed from between your own screaming loins?"

"Definitely not."

"Have you ever raised an *enfant terrible* so ter-ee-blay that even his own teachers are terrified of his little red head?"

"Again, no."

"Proves my point, doesn't it? About the whole you-knowing-things thing?"

"You just won another case, Ma. I stand corrected."

Sherry threw a pillow at Dalton. "Don't patronize me. There's nothing worse than being patronized by someone who doesn't shave. Not to mention wearing a four-dollar tie. You look like an undertaker."

Dalton picked up the pillow and put it back on the bed. Undertaker? That was actually pretty cool. He tightened his Windsor knot. "Ma, can I make you a pot of tea?"

Sherry Rev sighed. "Yes, please."

Dalton went down and put together a tray of silverware and the ceramic tea set. He arranged some cookies on a plate and picked a flower from the yard and put it in a water glass. When he came back up, his mother was sitting at her bureau in a robe. She looked at the tray and then at Dalton, wiping her eyes.

"Thanks, honey."

"Sure."

They appraised each other through the ornate mirror.

"You haven't sat there and looked at me like that since you were ten. You were trying to work up the courage to ask me to stop holding your hand on the way to school. It was, apparently, embarrassing you in front of your friends."

"Yeah, sorry about that. If it makes you feel any better, it wouldn't embarrass me anymore."

"It does, actually. Make me feel better."

"Although that may be less a function of my maturity than the fact that I no longer have any friends."

Sherry laughed, putting on lipstick. She leaned close to the mirror, holding one hand steady with the other.

"So what now?" Dalton asked.

Sherry blotted her lips, then picked up a compact. "I suppose I traipse out a few stock phrases like *come to terms* or *soldier on*, or something to do with pulling up bootstraps. I'll grudgingly accept Landon's absence in an abstract way that mostly involves not really thinking about it. And then a month or so from now, I'll take you aside and kiss you on the forehead and thank you for helping me through this."

"You will?"

She nodded. "Unless I forget. In which case I won't, but you'll be able to tell by my forgiving-of-your-bad-grades demeanor that I still appreciate it."

213

Dalton looked at his mother, half made up, disheveled, a mischievous grin on her face. He wondered why he so rarely took the time to consider how excellent she actually was.

"Mom?"

"Yes?"

"Can I, uh, sit over there with you? Like, maybe hold your hand for a while?"

Sherry looked amazed. Then shocked. Then sensing a trap. "Do you really want to?"

"No," Dalton said. "Not at all. But if I do, it'll be so like the end of a cheesy movie where the doe-eyed son learns to come to terms with his angrily beautiful psychologist mom, that for a few minutes it'll seem like we both deserve an Oscar."

Sherry laughed again, this time louder than before. "Get out of here! I have to get dressed. My god, who knew my son was going to be such a walking cliché?"

"Pretty much everyone," Dalton said. "They're always like, *Hey, there's that hard-boiled kid from across the tracks. The one with stars in his eyes, feelings on his sleeve, a crazy dream, a checkered past, and a heart made of solid gold.*"

Sherry Rev slid over. Dalton sat beside his mother and took her hand in his.

CHAPTER 22
REVIVE ME HIGH

Dalton opened his eyes. It wasn't heaven. It might have been hell, if they had interrogation rooms in hell, which they probably did. He was handcuffed to a chair in front of a folding table with an ashtray and a tape recorder. Up on the cinderblock wall was a calendar from 1982, a corkboard full of rusty tacks, and an ancient security camera whose red eye blinked derisively.

Estrada came in the door. He loosened his tie and tossed something that landed with a loud smack on the table. It was a yearbook.

"Am I dead?"

"It's negotiable," Estrada said. "But not yet, no."

"How come every time I pass out, when I wake up I'm looking at you?"

"Who would you prefer?"

"I'm not sure, but whoever she is, she doesn't have a mustache."

"You must be okay—your sense of humor's intact and still lousy."

"I got shot. I felt it." Dalton pressed his hand to his sternum, looking at the huge purple bruise between his nipples. The skin remained unbroken.

"You weren't shot. You were hit with a piece of shrapnel."

"Shrapnel?"

"Well, a piece of microphone to be exact."

Dalton coughed. "Even if that made sense, it makes no sense."

"There was no shooting. No bullet. One of the band's microphones overheated."

Estrada held up a blackened stand, the twisted metal base of the microphone still screwed onto one end.

"Then what knocked me out?"

"Nothing knocked you out. You fainted, tough guy."

THE PRIVATE DICK HANDBOOK, RULE #43
Unless you're a Russian general's daughter who hangs
out in the parlor, receives eligible bachelors for tea,
and is prone to the vapors, fainting isn't a good look.

Estrada held up the yearbook. "For some reason you had this stuffed down the front of your shirt." There was a hole in the cover. Inside, a piece of metal had obliterated the picture of Lenny Poole, a Face Boi sophomore who'd won Nicest Glutes. "Lucky it was there. Might have done some real damage otherwise. If you didn't have. Something hidden. Like a thief. In your shirt."

Dalton pretended to marvel at the hole, sticking his finger in it.

Estrada held up the compressed mic fragment, the size and

shape of a ball bearing, and then dropped it into Dalton's palm.

"You were under observation in the infirmary most of the night, out cold. Had nothing to do with that bruise. Doc says you were just tired."

"All *night*? What time is it?"

"It's Saturday afternoon."

"You call my parents?"

"Not yet."

Dalton nodded gratefully. "I owe you one."

Estrada smoothed his mustache. "Questions. Answers. Favors. They all come around in the end."

"Am I under arrest?"

"No."

"Then why am I handcuffed?"

Estrada produced a key. Dalton rubbed his wrists.

"And why was Hutch chasing me?"

Hutch barged into the room, laughing. "'Cause you ran, perp. Big-time Private Dick like you should know better than to take off running with officers of the peace in the vicinity."

Estrada gave his partner a tired look.

"Also, you bag of hair, we've been wanting to have a chat. But, like most perps, you're hard to find. We get a call, party out of control turning into a full-scale riot, what do you know, guess who I run into? Not only that, we got you nailed for suspected theft, a clear-cut sixty-one forty."

"What's a sixty-one forty?"

Estrada rolled his eyes.

"Hot book," Hutch said, with slightly less verve.

"*Book* thief?" Dalton laughed. "Nice collar, Hutch. They're gonna give you a captain's shield soon."

"Thief's a thief," Hutch said, with a half pout that reminded Dalton a little too much of Turd Unit.

"How do you know it's not mine?"

"All the inscriptions are addressed to a girl. You named Lu Lu? Huh, Private Dick? You got a special private name?"

"Forget the book," Estrada said, annoyed. He slid it toward Dalton. "Give it back to her when you're done with it, okay?"

"Okay."

"Better yet," Estrada said, "let me borrow it. Seems to work better than Kevlar."

Dalton chuckled. Hutch scowled.

"Listen," Estrada said, straightening his cuffs. "We just want to check in on a few things. I did you a solid, you do me a solid."

"What few things?"

"Wesley Xavier Payne."

"I thought the case was closed."

"Yeah, well, we have some new information. Little birdie told us you might too. We want to compare notes."

"Like what information? What little birdie?"

"You first," said Hutch. "And never mind who our sources are."

Dalton laughed. "Sources? You mean Honey Bucket? Slip a C-note in her nylons and she tells you anything you want to hear?"

"Just get us up to speed," Estrada said wearily. "Huh? So we can all go home and watch the game?"

"You mean I should act like they do in all the cop shows where the poor mope being squeezed finally tells what he knows, and then they toss him in a cell anyhow?"

"Trust me, that's not—"

"There's two ways to insult a Private Dick," Dalton interrupted. "And the second one is to say 'trust me.'"

"Fair enough," Estrada said. "So don't trust me and just listen."

Dalton nodded.

"We hear you had a body in your basement. We hear it was duct taped. We hear it looked a whole lot like—"

A sergeant opened the door and poked his head in.

"Not now!" Hutch barked.

"Sorry, sir. The kid's bail has been posted."

"How? He's not even under arrest!"

"The party that posted bail is waiting in the lobby," the sergeant said, winking clumsily. "That same party is making a lot of noise? Um, about lawyering the kid up? About the kid being interrogated underage and without family present?" The sergeant cleared his throat, palms out. "Just thought you'd want to know this party is tossing around a lot of convincing legalese along the lines of contacting the newspaper and—"

"Yeah, yeah, yeah," Estrada said, standing. "You can go, Rev."

"Wait a minute!" Hutch said. "He hasn't even told us—"

"He can go," Estrada said, staring at his partner.

Dalton got up and walked toward the door. "Who is it?" he asked the sergeant. "My mother?"

The sergeant looked over his shoulder. "If that's your mother, kid, you got more troubles than I thought."

CHAPTER 23
KISS FIST, EAT FLOOR

Dalton signed nine pieces of paper before being given his personal belongings. The sergeant dumped a manila envelope on his desk and read them off one by one, "Penknife, check, three nickels, check, six thousand dollars in cash, check. Notebook entitled *Private Dick Handbook*, check. Envelope filled with poetry, check. Index cards with mysterious block handwriting, check. One slightly damaged yearbook, check."

"There was a key," Dalton said. "In my pocket."

The sergeant went down his list. "No key."

"I'm positive. Small. Silver. A number 9 on it?"

"You want I should go ask the detective?"

"No, don't do that. I guess I, ah…I guess I left it at home."

Dalton signed another four papers and then was walked to the gate for release.

"Oh, wait!" the sergeant called, turning over the envelope one more time, as a small silver key slid out. "You mean this?"

Dalton almost laughed. Almost.

"Yeah, I mean that."

He pocketed the key, trying to figure out what he was going to tell his mother on the other side. But it wasn't Sherry Rev waiting.

"You!"

"Me," Elisha Cook said as they buzzed Dalton out.

"But why?"

Elisha Cook held a finger over his lips. "Come this way." They walked down the hallway, past offices and racks of brochures with titles like *Not Doing Tempting Crimes: A Primer* and *This Is an Egg, This Is Your Brain, and This Is 10 to 20 in Leavenworth*.

"We have some very important matters to go over schoolwise. However, I don't feel comfortable…discussing Harvard in this place. My car is outside."

"I don't feel comfortable either," Dalton said. "Mostly because I gotta hit the splashbox. I'll meet you at the car."

Elisha Cook raised an eyebrow but said nothing, continuing on through the double glass doors. Dalton went back around the corner and crouched by the brochure rack, waiting until the sergeant turned to file something. Then he sneaked back through the buzzer gate he'd left slightly ajar by stuffing a yearbook page into the bolt slot. He tiptoed along the wall, hid behind a file cabinet until another Snout walked by, and then slipped through a heavy green door that had OFFICERS' LOCKER ROOM stenciled in gray paint.

Inside it smelled like sweat and cheddar. There were towels and jockstraps all over the floor. There were shelves of billy clubs and walkie-talkies and uniforms stuffed in cubbies. Near the showers were three parallel rows of lockers. Dalton hid behind the first row, numbers 99 to 66. There were two Snouts getting dressed on the other side, talking about last weekend's Salt River game.

"That Chuff kid is one tough bastard. Took the team onto his back single-handed in the fourth quarter."

"I know it. That last drive was a thing of beauty. Up the middle six plays in a row. Took real stones. Then, you know…"

The other cop joined in.

"Chuff to Chugg…touchdown!"

They slapped five. Dalton ducked behind a big laundry cart, waited a beat, and then slid over to the next row, 65 to 32. It was empty. The cops' voices started to fade as they headed toward the door. Dalton crept to the final row and found locker number 8. Not 9. Eight. But it had to be a mistake, since the nameplate read HUTCH HUTCHERSON.

Dalton slipped the key into the slot. It fit perfectly. He turned it, but it didn't want to go. He tried again. No good. He tried number 9. This time, the key wouldn't move at all. Dalton laid his forehead against the cool metal of the locker.

THE PRIVATE DICK HANDBOOK, RULE #44
The only people who need a key are
Francis Scott and girls with drugstore diaries.
Stop being a murse and improvise!

Dalton waited until the Snouts were gone for sure. Then he punched the long rectangle of fire safety glass with a Hutch-smelling towel wrapped around his fist, grabbing the ax mounted to the wall behind it. He hefted the weight, trying to calculate distance and torque, and then swung the blade at number 9, levering it into the gap just above the bolt. He widened the space between the door and swung again, popping the lock. Empty. He did the same thing with Hutch's. It didn't want to come as easily, and Dalton had to swing twice more. A fourth hit sprung it open, just as an alarm went off.

REEE-EEER, REEE-EEER, REEE-EEER.

There was a red canvas duffel in Hutch's locker. Dalton grabbed it and closed the mangled door.

In the parking lot, Cassiopcia Jones *scree*d up in her red Jaguar as Dalton clomped over.

"Get in!"

He slid into the passenger seat as the alarm was joined by multiple sirens.

Cassiopeia turned her head as they passed Elisha Cook, who was waiting for Dalton beside an enormous black Diktatorat LE. The car had to be thirty years old but was in pristine condition—a huge steel boat, painted hearse black. Elisha Cook looked up and saw Dalton in the Jag, confusion on his face as Cassiopeia took a left out of the parking lot and accelerated away.

"I think we just drove away from my scholarship."

"Yeah, he's not going to like that. Oh well, there's always state school."

"I was sorta getting used to being Ivy League material."

Cassiopeia pointed to the large red duffel bag between Dalton's feet. "I didn't see the sergeant counting that back as part of your personal effects."

"You were watching?"

"Behind the chair in the lobby. I was pretending to read pamphlets."

"Of course."

Cassiopeia downshifted. "I presume all those alarms going off were the result of your need to visit the bathroom?"

"Yup."

THE PRIVATE DICK HANDBOOK, RULE #45
When you've run out of excuses, acting like a little boy on a long car trip who's had too much lemonade never fails.

"I further presume that your wriggling out of the only window in the police station without bars on it, and then dropping fifteen feet to the pavement like a thief with the Hope Diamond stuffed in an examination-unlikely crevasse is also related to said alarms?"

"Check out the vocab on Cassie."

"Just answer the question, crackstar."

"The Snouts have a locker room. You know, where they change into their uniforms? I'm thinking a locker room full of lockers in the best-guarded place in town is pretty much the perfect place to stash something for a while."

"The key fit?"

Dalton looked at it. "Nope. I was sure it was going to, but it's the wrong one. A silver herring. I had to use an ax."

"Resourceful."

"Thanks."

"And it was in Hutch's?"

"It was in Hutch's."

"Interesting."

"Yeah, I need to think about that for a minute."

Cassiopeia began to slow down, approaching a crowded intersection. "This just gets weirder and weirder."

"Speaking of which, how did you know I was in the Snout Hut in the first place? And where'd you scare up Elisha Cook to spring me?"

"I saw Estrada load you into the back of a cruiser at Footer's, but they never checked you into the hospital, so where else would you be? As far as Cook goes, who did you want me to call?" Cassiopeia pretended to pick up a phone, lapsing into Sherry Rev's voice. *"Oh, hi, Cassie! You say he's got his dumb ass arrested again? Oh, my. Well, I guess I'll finish baking this cake and then I'll cruise on by and bail Dalton out. Thanks for calling!"*

"Fair enough," Dalton said grudgingly.

Cassiopeia went back to her normal voice. "I was driving around, trying to figure out what I was going to do, since half of the Caskets and most of the Balls got arrested at Footer's too, and I happened to see ol' Pinstripe hanging around outside school, even though it was closed. He looked like a hobo trying to decide which windowsill to steal a pie off of. I thought he might, just might, be willing to play Uncle to the Rescue."

"You have to grease his palm?"

"Nope. He agreed right away."

Dalton pointed to the sheet lying on the dashboard. "You didn't grease him, what's that expense form for?"

Cassiopeia handed it over, along with a stack of paper-clipped receipts. "Costumes. Makeup. Gas. Singing lessons. I've had some serious expenses, boss man."

"Don't call me that."

"Okay, boss man." Cassiopeia took a left off the main road, pulling into the parking lot of Doggie Diner—We Make Wieners You'll Bark For! She backed in between two trucks, which provided cover while allowing them to watch the road and the parking lot's entrance at the same time. She left the key half-turned and maxed the A/C.

"Four hundred dollars for makeup?" he said, thumbing the receipts.

"Hey, Dalton? You taken a look at me lately? This Bride of Foxxenstein routine isn't cheap. Besides which, you know my mom doesn't even let me wear eyeliner. That means I have to wash it all off every time I go home, and then start all over again as soon as I get back in the car."

"Okay, okay, but a Jaguar? I mean, are you serious? What's this thing cost a day to rent?"

Cassiopeia shook her head. "Think, boss man. Frau Cassiopeia *Jones* doesn't drive no Ford Escort. You want me deep cover, you got me deep cover. That means no skimping on the outfits, and maybe a few other perks befitting the leader of a certain very upscale clique."

Dalton knew she was right. He folded the expense form and the receipts and stuck them into his wallet. "Well, Estrada sure bought Cook's bluff. He fell all over himself to let me go. So, yeah, I appreciate you getting him to spring me."

"You don't sound too convinced about it."

THE PRIVATE DICK HANDBOOK, RULE #46
No good Dick ever works alone.
But most good Dicks sure as farck wish they did.
These days it's almost impossible to find good help.

"That's because if I get any more enthusiastic, you're gonna ask for a raise."

"Now that you mention it."

"Don't even think—"

Cassiopeia held up a finger to shush him, looking at her watch. She silently counted down from ten, saying "Now!" just as two Snout cruisers and an unmarked shot by. Five seconds later they were followed by Elisha Cook's Diktatorat LE.

"Nice call."

"Snouts are predictable," Cassiopeia said. "It's the first thing you taught me."

"The first thing I taught you was how to French kiss."

She made a mock shocked face. "Is that what it was? I thought you were doing a tonsil exam."

"Hilarious," Dalton said, pulling out the index cards he'd found in his helmet.

"Why have you been leaving me those stupid notes? Anyone could have read them. Um, remember protocol? Like how you're supposed to send IMs? Through the encryption link?"

Cassiopeia looked at the cards in Dalton's hand. She flipped through them slowly, reading the big block letters.

"For one, you should know that's not my handwriting, syntax, or grammar. I haven't put anything in your helmet. Not even your head. For another, I haven't sent any encryption since your 'Mustang Sally' routine, and that was because you wouldn't talk to me."

"Yeah," Dalton said. "Because Mole was right there, and I didn't want to blow your cover. Besides, anything Mole hears, so does every kid at Salt River."

"Speaking of your head, exactly what are you doing with the Payne girl? It's not up to me to tell you about professionalism.

Or, um, ethics. But, Dalton, it seems like you've let her get way too close."

"It's business. Digging for information. Manipulating scenarios. Believe me, I'm just meeting my client's needs. *Our* client's needs."

"Uh-huh."

"Speaking of which, looks like you've done a nice job getting under Tarot's skin. Way under. I mean, burrowed in like a deer tick."

Cassiopeia was about to fire back but then stopped herself. "Listen, with all these fake arguments in the hallway, I can barely tell when we're really arguing anymore."

"You're right. Sorry. What have you got for me?"

"That microphone, for one thing." Cassiopeia opened a folder, handing him microphone schematics and electrical specs. "It didn't just explode on its own. Someone rigged it."

Dalton, as always impressed by her thoroughness, looked at the sheets detailing ohms, capacity, and wattage.

"There's nothing in a microphone that would make it come apart like that, no matter how hot it got."

"A firecracker?" he guessed. "A couple of M-80's?"

"Probably. But that's no kind of prank. If I'd been singing when it went off…"

Dalton put his hand on her shoulder. They both stared out the window for a while.

"I found Chuff. Upstairs. Just as you started your set."

"And?"

"And he was in one of the bedrooms."

"Did you run the plan by him?"

"Not really time to."

"Why not?"

"He was on top of Macy."

"Oh, my," Cassiopeia said. This time she put her hand on his shoulder. "Was she complaining?"

"Not at first. Not until he got a little too rough about it."

"Men, I swear. What hole did y'all crawl out of, anyway?"

"I'm not sure," Dalton said, not bothering to deny that there was one to crawl out of.

"Well, don't blame her just yet. You don't know what you'd do or say to get that monster off you."

Dalton nodded. The urge to beat Chuff with a mallet welled in him like dirty bathwater.

Cassiopeia tore off her wig. The short black hair underneath glistened with sweat. She grabbed a towel from the floor and used it to swab off about a pound of makeup. Her light brown face was thin and flushed. She was pretty without all the goop, but not the ridiculously exotic swan she'd been a second before. It was a relief to see her plainly. To see her normal features, just another sharp-eyed girl without her cheekbones accentuated or long lashes batted and framed by a neon wig.

"Oh my Bob, am I tired of wearing this crap. I don't know if I can do it anymore."

Dalton considered how all he had to do was loosen his tie to be officially decostumed. It was hard to blame her. Especially as she reached into her shirt and slipped a clasp, pulling out an enormous set of tan neoprene breasts. She heaved a sigh of relief, her shirt now four sizes too big. She was an entirely different person. She was, once again, the person he knew. Had known.

"You won't have to do it much longer," Dalton said, wanting to believe it. "Hopefully tonight it's over. You can return all this stuff, shut down Foxxes."

She laughed. "That's the one thing I *don't* want to do."

"That clique has just spun out of control. But in the best possible way. Turns out the girls of Salt River were hungry for an excuse to butch up and practice some karate. This has been an exercise in empowerment and collective feminism. They're not going to want to give it back now."

"They're not going to want to give *you* back. Especially those Jennys. You may have to move to Vermont and marry all three of them."

"There's only one Jenny."

"Excuse me?"

"Jenny. There's only one. The triplets thing was my idea. She's like Superman, slips into the splashbox and keeps changing her costume."

"No effing way."

"Yup," Cassiopeia said proudly. "Recruited her after the volleyball team disbanded. She was so perfect, I thought, *Where am I going to find more than one?*"

"Man, you're good. You really have a future in this business."

"Thanks, D." Cassiopeia slipped off her leather skirt and began pulling on some jeans. Dalton politely turned his head.

"Oh, it's like that now, is it?"

"Like what?"

"You really *are* into this Payne girl, aren't you?"

Dalton wondered why he and Cassiopeia had ever stopped

seeing each other. There was the prom thing, sure, and the constant arguing and mountain-high sarcasm to go along with the river-deep lust. There was the not getting along, and the lengthy silences. But it wasn't really any of that.

THE PRIVATE DICK HANDBOOK, RULE #47
Because no one smart ever sleeps with his partner, that's why. Did Spade hook up with Archer? Did Barney hook up with Fred? Did Nick hook up with Nora? Let alone Asta? Did the guy in the movie about robot trucks that transformed into truck-bots hook up with the girl in the movie about robot trucks that turned into truck-bots? Okay, bad example.

"So, are you going to look in the duffel bag, or what?"

"It's in there," Dalton said.

"Are you sure? I mean, you looked, right?"

"Nope. But I know."

"How do you know? What if it's, like, softballs and cleats?"

"I just do."

Cassiopeia leaned over and pulled the zipper back, exposing many, many rubber-banded stacks of folding green. "Oh, my." She ran her hands through the money, lifting the stacks and letting them fall again. She laughed, digging even deeper, and pulled out the gun that was at the bottom. And then pointed it at Dalton.

Their eyes met and held for a ridiculously long time.

"Is this the part where you tell me to get out of the car? I mean, is this the part where it dawns on my dumb ass that our

231

partnership is over and Tarot has brainwashed your little brain into thinking you really wanted the cash for yourself all along?"

Cassiopeia pulled the trigger. A tongue of flame licked out the other end.

They both laughed. She tossed the gun on his lap.

"I missed this thing. Didn't think I'd ever get it back."

Cassiopeia reached into her purse. "I've got something even better for you."

"What?"

She handed him a piece of computer paper. It said:

$C_{17}H_{21}NO_4$ (1R,2S)-2-(methylamino)-1-phenylpropan-1-ol

"Great. What is it?"

"A formula of some kind. Maybe."

"Yeah? So?"

Cassiopeia licked her thumb. The piece of paper underneath was the sheet music to "The Ballad of Mary Surratt."

"I got to thinking about these lyrics after you showed them to Kurt at the practice room. He didn't want to play the song for Footer's gig, but I talked him into it."

"That was a shocker. But why?"

"Because, Dalton," Cassiopeia explained, "if you were a *real* singer, you'd know that music is nothing but math. Any given song is really just a bunch of notes. But it's not the notes that are important — it's the intervals between them."

"Intervals?"

"The distance. Like, the number of steps to get from C to

G. Any song is essentially a mathematical pattern, counting the steps. But lyrics can be a pattern too."

Dalton smiled, catching on. "Poetry is pentameter. A Plath told me that. And Tarot said his words had been moved around…"

"…because Wesley moved them."

"The suicide note isn't lyrics, it's a code! Both songs are codes!"

"Right. I ran the lyrics through some encryption programs. It just kept being gibberish. Then I did some searches and found a type of encryption the army used back in World War II. It's been retired because it's totally basic. You could crack it with an abacus. But guess what it's called?"

"I have no idea."

Cassiopeia smiled. "Euclidic Geometrical Masking."

"No way."

"Way. It's a basic letter substitution pattern. If you put in Kurt's lyrics, it doesn't mean anything. If you put in the lyrics as Wesley adjusted them, first 'Exquisite Lies' from the suicide note, and then 'The Ballad of Mary Surratt,' that formula is what you get."

Dalton looked at the paper again.

$C_{17}H_{21}NO_4$ (1R,2S)-2-(methylamino)-1-phenylpropan-1-ol

"Did I say you were good? You're better than good. You're fan*tastic*."

Cassiopeia blushed.

"So I guess it's up to me to figure out what it's for."

"Thank Bob. I thought you were going to give me that job too."

"No, ma'am. You've already more than earned your keep."

"Speaking of which," Cassiopeia said, turning back to the red duffel, "how much of this do you need for Landon's armor?"

"Why?"

"So we know how much is left. For us."

Dalton shook his head. "I have to get it all to Inference. And then collect my percentage. I have until midnight tonight to wire whatever I have to Ukraine."

"But you'll still be short. You don't have to take that money to Inference. Just send it."

"I can't do that. You know I can't."

Cassiopeia threw back her head in frustration. The lead on her pencil broke. "No, I don't know you can't."

Dalton was fully aware that if he was the excuses guy in the movie with the drunk coed, he was also the excuses guy in the movie where you want the hero to take the money and stop pretending to have a conscience. The bottom line was, at some point over the last year, Dalton had decided that ethics weren't malleable. They couldn't be changed to fit different situations. If something was ever wrong, it was always wrong. He planned to put the money from Wesley's envelope back in the duffel before he turned it over to Inference as well. Because a million cruel-ending noirs had proved that there was no way to take dirty money and make it clean. No way to spend ill-gotten cash without buying the consequences. If he'd earned it, fine, it was back in circulation like anything else. But he hadn't earned it. Dalton knew if he were sitting in an audience watching the movie of his own life, right this second he'd be throwing popcorn at the screen and yelling, *Take the money, fool! What, are you kidding with this probe routine? Grow a sac and TAKE. THE. DAMN. MONEY!*

Lex Cole once said having a conscience was the true religion of the born sucker. Having a blanket conscience allowed suckers to live dull, empty lives and not feel guilty about missing out on what they really wanted deep down. He said it was a justification to grow old cowering away from all the things their true natures desired.

"I know you think you can't," Cassiopeia said. "But this is racket money. It's not like you lifted it from some old lady's savings account. Landon and his unit need it way more than Inference or Chuff does."

"I know."

"If you know, King of Contradictions, then why not just do it?"

"I'm going to tell you something. It's something I don't want to say out loud, but I'm going to anyway. And I'm going to because you've stuck your neck out so far on this case that I owe it to you."

Cassiopeia was about to make a joke about what Dalton owed her, but she changed her mind, nodding solemnly instead.

"Believe me, I'm tempted to just take this cash. But some part of me knows, just like I knew the money was in the duffel to begin with, that if I use the dirty end of it, if I *steal* it, Landon is going to get killed. The armor won't protect him. It'll do the opposite. He'll put it on and it will taint him. He'll wear it and it will mark him."

Cassiopeia said nothing.

"Karma or whatever? Luck? Religion? Who cares what it's called or what people believe in. I know, in the very center of my stomach, that I have to send him something clean. All the way around. No shortcuts."

"Okay," she said. "I get it."

"You sure?"

"Yes."

He was about to lean over and hug her, when he looked at the clock in the dash of the Jaguar, which read 1:56. "Farck! I'm gonna to be late!"

"For what?"

"Meeting with Tarot and Chuff."

"That's now? Like, right now?"

"Yeah, in five minutes. And it's at the kids' playground. All the way across town."

"No problem."

Cassiopeia Jones popped her wig on sideways and gunned the massive engine, nearly sideswiping the enormous plastic dachshund head mounted on a pole outside of Doggie Diner, before roaring off into traffic.

CHAPTER 24
TERMS OF ESTRANGEMENT

Cassiopeia dropped Dalton off after he'd gone over the plan a final time.

"Are you sure this is how you want to do it?"

"It's the only thing I can think of that might actually work."

She revved the engine. "I'd wait around for you, but I've got to prep."

"It's okay," Dalton said, half in love with the determination in her eyes, clear and natural and unforced. And the other half remembered what a failure it had been the last time he was half in love with her. "Besides, we can't take a chance on someone seeing you out of costume."

"I feel very naked like this."

"I'll bet."

"It's liberating to be naked," she said, driving away.

◎

Dalton walked across the playground. Dark clouds loomed over the trees as a slight mist began to fall. Kids screamed unabated. Moms sat tiredly on benches, texting one another or handing out cheese sticks. Beyond the sandbox, older kids were tossing Frisbees or hiding the plumes from their cigarettes. Girls and boys entwined found a marginal privacy behind the tall grass. A snack shack was open in the corner, impatient kids twenty deep, all of them rubbing quarters and staring malevolently at the person in the front of the line.

Dalton waited by the swings. He took a deep breath, running through his speech one last time, wishing the Sit 'n Spin were a teleprompter. Chuff came first, from across the field, his bulk forming a long shadow that scythed across children and parents in turn. He approached Dalton with a smirk, stopping five feet away.

"This better be good, fish. Where we left it last night? Not satisfactory, I have to say. I might even need to grab you like a chicken bone, make a wish, and extract a refund."

Before Dalton could answer, three little kids ran over and began *vroom vroom*ing with their toy trucks, burying Chuff's feet in mounds of sand, instinctively attracted to him in the same way they were to Barney or Grimace.

"It *is* good," Dalton said. "If by *good* you mean likely to make you a lot of money and simultaneously remove your archnemesis. If not, it probably sucks."

Chuff laughed. "You've got a way with words, fish, I'll give you that. You really should be a sploet. Maybe I'll pull some strings and get you in."

"Just play your part, okay? Tarot thinks you're already on board."

"Don't worry, I can handle my end."

Tarot came from the east, almost seeming to glide on a slick

238

of distaste, hands shoved deep into leather pockets. No kids approached him, instinctively repelled by his sour countenance in the same way they knew to avoid poison sumac or leprosy. In fact, they cleared the area, laughing and playing one second, then bailing like someone spotted a turd floating in the deep end of the pool.

"So here we are," Dalton said.

Tarot yawned. "Not for long." The shirt under his trench coat read THROUGH A SCANNER PINKLY.

"Yeah, make with the plan, Stan," Chuff said.

"It's a job. A heist."

"So pull it yourzelf. Why am I here?"

"Muscle."

"So pull it with Chuff. Why am I here?"

"Numbers. I need both cliques for it to work. And so do you, given all the arrests at the party."

They both grunted.

"How many Balls got picked up last night?"

"Too many. And most of the ones that weren't arrested have been grounded."

"Caskets too?"

Tarot nodded grudgingly.

"So manpower's at a premium. We all need each other. Which, as it turns out, is the only thing likely to keep everyone honest anyway."

"Why should I want to be honest?" Chuff asked.

"Change of pace," Dalton said as Tarot noticed the red duffel between his feet. Dalton had intended to bury it in the sand, but he hadn't had time. Chuff noticed Tarot noticing.

"What's in the bag?"

"Money. It's packed with folding green."

Chuff laughed. Tarot rolled his eyes.

"Listen, you guys want your own duffels full of cash? What I have in mind is a score that'll make your rackets seem like carp feed. I mean, how many girlie mags can you sell in a semester? How many cracked iPods?"

They both shrugged defensively.

"Exactly. This will set both cliques up with enough cash so that you don't ever have to worry about a takeover. You'll each have an army *and* a bankroll. One job. One night. And then you're set. For life. Or at least until graduation."

"We do need a new van and a PA."

"We do need new equipment and helmets."

"Okay, good," Dalton said. "Truce. Shake hands and we'll go over the details."

Neither of them moved. A dad walked by with his son. "Nice game last week, Jeffrey."

"Thank you, sir."

"Chuff to Chugg…touchdown!" the kid said, slapping Chuff five.

Tarot made vomity sounds.

"Eff you, Assy Assbourne."

"The game player playing his games." Tarot yawned. "The zeventeen-year-old who plays with his balls."

THE PRIVATE DICK HANDBOOK, RULE #48
Arabs, meet your new friends, the Jews.
Jews, meet your new friends, the Arabs.

"Hard to believe me and Assbourne used to be buddies," Chuff marveled. "Isn't it, fish?"

Tarot's expression changed, just slightly.

"All up through sixth grade."

"Shut up," Tarot said.

"Sleepovers, candy bars, rides to school. Kurt over there used to have a flattop and a milk mustache. He used to collect baseball cards. He used to—"

"SHUT YOUR CAKEHOLE, YOU BLOATED CARDI-GAN!" The gaggle of moms and nannies looked up nervously. A few kids dropped their toys. Dalton laughed like it was all a big joke, putting his hand on Tarot's shoulder and waving to the parents. "Laugh!" he hissed through his teeth. "Before some nervous mom calls the Snouts." Tarot gave a sickly smile. Chuff did a fake ho-ho-ho, holding his belly as the moms went back to their cell phones.

"Kurt always did have self-control problems," Chuff said quietly. "I guess it was right around the time they put him on Ritalin we had our first falling-out."

"Yeah," Tarot shot back, the skull in his tongue bobbing frantically. "And you know what Jeffrey used to do? Before he realized he could put his bulk to use crushing smaller boyz into the end zone dirt? Theater. Oh, yes, he was terrific onstage. You should have seen him in hiz tights, *Hamlet* this, *Hamlet* that. And not just Shakespeare. Singing. *Musical theater.*"

"Yeah, and you know what *Captain Z*'s real name is?" Chuff pointed at Tarot's forehead. "*Kurt Tarot?* Are you kidding me? Like, where did he find that name, the Disgraced

Magicians Union? Issue number sixty-three of *Green Lantern*? His real name is—"

"Don't," Tarot warned, arms extended like a bat's wings, the leather jacket spreading out behind him.

"His real name is Herbie Lum."

The two of them flew at each other.

"STOP!" Dalton yelled as they grappled, pushing them apart. Chuff barely moved, but Tarot took a step back, almost tripping over the edge of the sandbox. This time the moms stood, getting their strollers and bottles together, the little kids all repeating, "Shut up shut up shut up! Lum Lum Lum Lum Lum!"

Tarot glowered. "You have broken a zolemn vow, Chuff. It will not be forgotten."

"You two want to mature up and get this thing done?" Dalton hissed. "This is your last chance."

"Listen to the new fish, Herbie. Let's make some money, and you can cast spells on me later."

Tarot's eyes burned steaming holes in Chuff's neck, but he said nothing.

"So what are we boosting?"

"Everything."

"Everything?"

"All of it. TVs. Electronics. Jewelry. Lawn mowers."

"Yeah, and where do they have all that stuff?"

It was a good question. Where did they have it all, plus hundred-gallon tubs of marinara sauce and fifty-packs of discontinued toothpaste? Where did they have all that, and also happen to be the place that fired Dad and refused to pay his health insurance?

"BoxxMart."

"Impossible."

"Ridiculous. It's like a steel fortrezz."

"Yeah," Dalton said, revving up to the unintentional genius of it himself. "That's why we need both cliques. BoxxMart has four separate entrances. Each one needs to be covered. We need drivers. We need guys hauling and loading. We need a guy monitoring the police band. We need guys on the roof to clear any Lee Harvies. We need guys down the street watching the exit ramps and the entrances to the parking lot."

"Terrific," Chuff said. "So we set all that up. Is someone gonna just knock on the door all Jehovah's Witness and ask can we come in?"

"I've got an entry code."

"How?"

"My old man worked there fifteen years. Before he got canned I used to hang out all the time, watch the employees use the swipe machine. It takes an employee card, but a lot of times the strip wears away or gets scratched, so there's a numerical override. I have it memorized."

"And we just waltz in?"

"Nope, that only gets us in the foyer. Then there's thirty feet of linked security gate you have to open manually from inside."

"Who's gonna do that? The security guard? You gonna ask him real nice while he's dialing the Snouts?"

"Nope. I'm gonna hold my piece on him while he does what I tell him to."

"No good," Tarot said. "You can't zhoot through safety glass."

"Won't be shooting through it. I'll be inside."

"How?"

"I'll be persuasive. Meanwhile, the Balls go first, start pulling goods off shelves. Caskets wait in back, ready to load the dozen band vans you're going to borrow or steal from the practice space. After they're full, the vans take off like they're on their way to gigs. They drive across the state line and meet at my fence. He buys the whole load at forty cents on the dollar, prenegotiated."

"Forty cents?"

"That's a good price. The fence has to turn around and move the stuff himself. He's got to store vans full of hot merch until he can. He's got to file serial numbers. Meanwhile, all we have to do is drop it off, get paid, and walk away. You two kick the proceeds down to your people however you want."

"And how do you know this mysteriouz fence?"

Good question, Count Blackula.

"Worked on a case for him once. Tracked down a stolen butterfly hairpin."

"What about cash registers?" Chuff asked. "BoxxMart's got forty of them, easy."

"No good. The money goes into a hydraulic tube up to a counting room in the rafters. Double steel doors. Even if you had the tools, it would take too long to get in. We go for goods, split the money three ways, that's it. Until then, truce. No more bloshite."

"Got to hand it to you, fish, it's not bad."

"You got a cheater?" Tarot asked.

"I got a cheater."

"Not that toy?" Chuff said. "Not the lighter?"

"*You* thought it was real." Tarot laughed, holding up his hands in mock fear. "Oh, pleaze don't shoot me, sure I'll clean off your scooter, just don't shoot!"

"Eat me."

"Pass."

"So we go tonight. Midnight. Either of you doesn't show, it's off. And that's it, my end is finished. No second chances. And no extra cliques. Just Balls and Caskets. Agreed?"

"I'll be there," Chuff said over his shoulder, already walking away. Tarot said nothing, striding in the opposite direction.

And then it was just Dalton.

And his red duffel bag.

CHAPTER 25

RIVER SHALLOW, MOUNTAIN LOW

He stood by Route 6, thumb out. There was no sign of the Snouts or Elisha Cook's Diktatorat LE. Even so, Dalton remained ready to jump into the bushes if they came by.

Cars zoomed past for an hour or more before a red one finally stopped. It wasn't a Nova. The passenger window rolled down. "Guy!" Mole said. "You need a ride or what?"

The Kia pulled back onto the road, doing a steady twenty miles an hour.

"So I woke up and started calling around to see what I'd done last night, you know? The whole thing is, like, a movie effects blur. Am I hungover? Guy, you have no em effing idea how utterly hung I am. I feel like I'd been rode hard and hung up wet." Mole laughed and popped open a plastic bottle of Rush with his teeth, draining half of it. "This is the only stuff that helps." He swilled the second half and then tossed the bottle out the window, dried spit caked in the corners of his lips.

"Where'd you get that?" Dalton asked, grabbing an empty

bottle off the floor and sniffing it. It smelled like the ammonia swab in a chemistry set.

"Bought a Coal Train's final stash. Said he'd been saving it for band tryouts but needed the money. Anyhow, I was calling around and everyone was like, whoo, dude, can you party or what? They're all like, MOLE THE BOTTOMLESS HOLE! and LESTER THE INGESTER! And then someone starts being like, and oh hey, that new fish? Buddy of yours? That dude got shot. He's carcassed. I'm all calling the hospitals, these nurses answering the phone all bored, blah, forms, blah, files, *Nope, we don't have a record of any young Dean Martin admitted with a gunshot wound, now leave me alone so I can get back to my crossword.* But then I call this other dude and he goes it's true, the scooter kid got ventilated. He got pinched, along with half the Balls. So I got in Mom's Kia and punched it over to the Snout Hut to see if you were either muerto or muy bien."

"Thanks."

"Yeah, but you weren't there. Nada Rev. Was I about to give up? No sir. No way. Well, actually, sorta. But just long enough to swing by home for a snack. And then *there you were*, all tall and cool by the side of the road, standing with your thumb out and your big red bag, and I'm all, I wonder if Coolio needs a ride?"

"I did," Dalton said, looking in the side mirror, where a long line of cars had already backed up behind the barely moving Kia. "I do."

Mole reached between the seats and twisted open another Rush. "Hey, so what's in the red duffel, anyhow?"

Dalton had slung it between his feet, forcing his knees so far up, his chin practically rested on them.

"Laundry."

"No, seriously. What's in el duffelo?"

"A hundred grand."

Mole laughed. "Okay, fine, you don't need to tell your old friend and possible lifelong sidekick if you don't want to."

Dalton shrugged.

"But I know you got something going." Mole tossed another empty out the window. Faster cars laid on their horns and gave him the finger as they roared by. "I can practically smell it."

"Yeah, actually, I do. But I'm not going to tell you."

"Guyfriend! Why not?"

"Listen, Mole, I want to apologize for getting you involved in this stuff to begin with. You don't need to be a part of what's coming down, even if it wasn't going to be a disaster."

Mole wiped his bloodshot eyes. Three trucks tore around the Kia, beeping and swerving.

"Nice of you. Thinking of me and all."

"Yeah."

"Speaking of which, I saw Macy. She really wants to talk."

"She does?"

"Something happened at the party, huh? You try to kiss her or what? Push the envelope? Lorenzo your Lamas? Not a smart move. That's a girl who needs to go slow, and I should know."

"Why should you know?"

Mole's face was pale. There was sweat on his forehead.

"If you want, we could cruise by her place, you could ask her."

"No, bring me to Footer's."

"Hair of the dog, huh? A little unfinished business?"

"My scooter's there. I hope."

◎

Mole pulled the Kia next to Dalton's ride and revved the engine. "Love you, man."

"Okay."

"Okay? *Okay*, guy? What's that all about? Where're the warriors expressing their true feelings in a manly but totally expressive way before going into battle?"

"We're not going into battle."

"Yeah, we are. It's written all over you like a book."

"Go home, Mole."

"Know what, guy?" Mole said, before slowly driving away. "You need to get in touch with your emotions."

◎

The scooter didn't start on the first or second try. After the third backfire, Lu Lu Footer came out to watch, sitting on the steps above Dalton's head. She was wearing a tight terry-cloth bathrobe and no makeup. Eighteen feet of unshaved legs were crossed over a pair of cheap rubber slippers. She looked like a different person.

"You went upstairs. I told you not to go upstairs."

"You lied about Wes Payne. I didn't tell you not to, but you did anyway."

Lu Lu retied her robe. "Maybe. But I didn't lie in any way that really matters."

"Maybe not that mattered to you. That's when it's easiest to lie."

Dalton handed her the old yearbook. She looked at the hole in the cover, sticking her finger in it.

"Where'd that come from?"

"Long story. Just look inside."

Lu Lu flipped through, read the inscription, then tossed it onto the lawn, which set off the sprinklers.

"Doesn't prove anything. Besides, I—"

"You kissed Wesley Payne."

"What?"

"Were you his girlfriend or not?"

Lu Lu looked at Dalton, shocked. She shook her head. A little too quickly, he thought.

"You sure?"

"Uh, yeah, I'm sure."

"Well, I just thought—"

Lu Lu's eyes narrowed. "I'm the one who should be asking questions here. Like about you rifling through my room."

"Are you mad?"

"Mad like crazy or mad like angry?"

"Both."

"Neither. After that party? What I am is off Yearbook. I'm off activities. I'm so busted my father's talking military school. My mom's out right now giving most of my clothes to Goodwill. None if it seems to matter a whole lot at the moment."

"Tough break."

"Maybe it's for the best," she said, crossing her legs. "It's more comfortable dressing like this. And I was getting tired of being called a Spirit Bunny."

"You should hear what they call me."

"I know what they call you. I called you the same thing when I saw you went in my room."

"I'm a Private Dick. What did you expect when you let me in the door? *Hey, don't go up there!* It's like asking a mosquito not to hover. Besides, I needed to rule you out for Wesley."

"I didn't kill him and I didn't date him."

Dalton reached over and picked up her yearbook, pulling out the drawings of Kurt Tarot sucking blood from Wesley Payne's head. Already wet from the sprinkler, the ink ran down the paper in bloody rivulets. "What about these? Hidden away. Suspiciously."

Lu Lu seemed to consider lying but changed her mind.

"I sent them in. I had them printed on purpose."

"Evening some kind of score? Or someone pay you to?"

She rubbed her eyes, working up to admitting what was right in front of her. "I sent them because I wanted to wake people up! You said yourself everyone acts like they'd forgotten Wesley already, like he was never even at Salt River. I wanted to shock them into remembering. I wanted the yearbook to matter for something. To actually have a purpose, even if I had to piss people off to do it."

"Did you draw them?"

"No, they came in anonymously. We get a lot of junk like that. I thought it was disgusting and was ready to toss them when I realized using the shite might be even better."

"I believe you."

"You do? Why? No one believes anyone at Salt River."

"There're only two things for certain in life. Death and rackets. So, Wesley's death was probably meant to birth new rackets."

"I don't get it."

The scooter backfired again. Dalton was about to explain when an enormously tall man stepped out the front door in no-nonsense tan pants. "Is there a problem here?"

"No, Dad," Lu Lu said, smiling grimly. "Unless you count being grounded for the next six months."

"Do you think this is funny, Louise?" The man glared at Dalton. "Because, trust me, we can make it funny. We can ramp it up a whole other level of hilarious."

"No, Dad, it's not funny."

"Nine grand in damage! We go away one night and suddenly every cop in town is camped in my backyard. What would have happened if we were gone for a *week*?"

Dalton wasn't sure if he was expected to answer. The man scowled, then snapped his fingers twice next to his thigh as if he were calling a dog.

"I'll be right in," Lu Lu said.

The man looked at his no-nonsense watch and then pointed to its no-nonsense face. "You got ninety seconds to get your nose deep into an algebra text, Louise. You're not? Then we move to plan B. Trust me, you do *not* want to find out about plan B."

"Yes, Dad."

The man went back inside. Dalton commiserated silently.

"You saw the letters, huh?" Lu Lu whispered, a flush of red

starting where the robe opened at her chest, working its way up her neck. "Under my mattress?"

"What letters?"

"You know exactly—"

"What letters?" Dalton said again.

Lu Lu stared at him, finally nodding. "Thanks."

He shrugged.

"I interviewed a guy who went to Salt River a long time ago. He'd been in jail almost ten years. I thought it would be a good angle for the paper's Spring Redemption theme and, you know, we just started writing each other. He told me about all the old-time cliques, like Tattooed Love Boys and the Orphan Age and Yale Fauxs and Keir Dulleas. There was, like, a Sinatra clique called Night and Day, and a Nixon clique called Bebe Rebozos. It was really interesting. I actually felt like I was learning something. And then, I guess one thing led to another, because—"

"No need to explain," Dalton said. "I'm called a Private Dick for a reason."

Lu Lu looked at him gratefully. "Anyway, I should get inside."

"Yeah, you should."

The scooter's motor caught with a yelp and a sigh. Lu Lu stood and stretched, practically reaching the sun. Dalton opened the duffel and handed her two stacks of bills, ten thousand total.

"Give it to your dad in a couple days. Say you've been saving from bake sales or something. Say you want to use it to cover the damage to the house. Might help him wrench the stick out his butt an inch."

Lu Lu Footer looked at the money in amazement before taking it.

"Who are you, Dalton Rev?"

"Still trying to figure that one out myself," he said, then put down his visor and pulled out onto Route 6.

CHAPTER 26
A MAN OF WEALTH AND TASTE

Albert Payne answered the door with purple gums.

"Sure did leave in a hurry last time, huh?"

"Sorry, sir."

Albert waved the apology off and then flopped onto the couch in front of his big screen.

Macy was at her pink desk, doing homework. Dalton was expecting her to be furious, but when she saw him in the doorway she ran up and threw her arms around his neck.

"I'm so sorry, I'm so sorry, I'm so sorry," she said over and over, only pulling away when she realized he wasn't hugging her back.

"Don't be like that. I know, *okay*? I know I've been handling this *all* wrong. I've been acting like a *crazy* person."

Dalton said nothing.

"I admit it really... *really* pissed me off what happened the other night. I mean, taking stuff from Wes's room without telling me? Even if it's just some poem. And then, I mean, have you ever seen *Gossip Girl*? Have you even read a chick book in your life? God, Dalton, you can't just pull away like that!

Not after you made me act all like I wanted to...I mean, who makes someone all *vulnerable* and then just pulls away? It's cruel. I swear, it's almost like you were just trying to prove something."

"Prove what?"

"That I actually liked you enough to get in bed with you! Okay, yeah, you passed the test. *Con-grat-u-la-tions*."

"That's not why I—"

"But I *know* you wanted to also. There was something going on between us even over the computer. You just get so wrapped up in your head, *what's professional, what's ethical*, you're all gridlocked. And you tell yourself there's a reason for it besides just being scared."

"I'm not scared of anything."

Macy scoffed. "Anyone who says *I'm not scared of anything* is scared of, like, everything."

"Whatever," he said, knowing she was so right it hurt.

"You can trust me, Dalton, okay? You need, for once, to *trust* somebody."

"That what you told Chuff at Footer's?"

Macy looked at him in disbelief.

"You saw what happened." She half turned away. "Did you not see what he was like?"

"Yeah, I heard what he was like before that too. I heard what you were like. I was at the door. I only came in when it went sour."

Macy put her face into her hands, then pulled them away angrily. "You gave that girl my pin, okay? Even so, I went up there with Jeff to tell him it was over. That I was done with him. But then he got all touchy. He wouldn't stop. He started to scare me and wouldn't let me out of the room. I wasn't being nice to him—I was trying to get him to let me go!"

"Uh-huh."

Macy wiped the corners of her mouth. "Please, Dalton, you have to believe me."

"No, I don't."

"Yes, you do!"

She put her lips against his and gently pressed. She ran her hands up and down his arms and through his hair. At first he resisted, cautious and cool, but soon he found himself kissing her back. Eventually she let go, straightening her dress and breathing heavily. She took a step into the hall, trying to gauge the sounds from the television downstairs.

"I think Dad's asleep." She winked, and then tripped over the duffel bag. Dalton had to hold out an arm to keep her from falling. She looked down at her feet.

"What's in there?"

"A hundred grand. Or so."

Macy laughed.

Dalton levered the bag into the room, then got on one knee and unzipped it like a suture.

"Oh my Bob!" Macy got down next to him and ran her hands through it. She lifted stacks of the cash and smelled them deeply.

"Where did you find it?"

"Not at Tarot's."

"What does that mean?"

"It means I think I know who killed Wesley. It means I think this case is almost over. It means you and I are going to be settling up soon."

Macy stared. "You *know*?"

"Almost. I'll be sure by tonight. When I am, you'll be the first person I tell."

"Tell me now," she said, eyes unnaturally bright.

"Not until I know for sure."

"That's so…that's so…" She was about to say something more, but stopped herself. "What are you going to do with the money?"

"Give it to Inference. Collect my percentage."

Macy gave the cash another sniff before standing.

"But why?"

"Why what?"

"Why give it to her? It's dirty. She'll just make it dirtier."

"What else should I do with it?"

"Us."

"What us?"

"Us leaving with it, that's what. Getting out of this place. Away from Salt River. Let's take the money and go somewhere."

"Just like that? A bag of folding green shows up and you're ready to fold up and split?"

"Just like that. In case you haven't noticed, Salt River really sucks."

"Say I thought it was a good idea. Say we took off tonight. Where would we go?"

"I don't know and I don't care," she said, doing a mock actress's voice. *"As long as it's with you."*

Dalton thought about what he was going to do with the money. What he *had* to do with the money. Then he allowed himself to think about what he *could* do. It felt like a betrayal, but there it was. Greed. Lust. Venality. It couldn't be stopped.

"What about school? Graduating with a degree in Euclidian? All your clubs and activities?"

"What about it? Wesley is gone, and every single thing in this town is a reminder of what they did to him. How they crucified him. I'd soak the whole place in diesel and light up a carton of Luckys if I thought I could get away with it."

"A hundred grand isn't five million," Dalton said, wondering who he was trying to convince. "And it's hard to pay for things in cash. Rent, bills, a car…people get all suspicious. You have to worry about someone stealing it all the time. You have to stash it in lockers and worry about losing the key. Money like this, all bundled up and out in the open, is an albatross."

"No, it isn't! It's freedom. It's a free hall pass. It's a ticket away from here. Don't you think I deserve that? Don't we both?"

"Even if we did, what happens when it runs out?"

"We get jobs. Like everyone else in the world. We'd have each other, a little apartment, a little head start."

Dalton thought about Landon, the morning he'd gotten on the bus for boot camp. His new buzz cut, his face like an egg-white omelet, terrified but trying to make jokes. Signing the papers and acting cool, sweat glistening in his hairline. Sometimes you had to lie to yourself. And sometimes you had to face the truth.

Dalton reached into the bag and handed Macy a stack of cash. "Here."

"What's this?"

"I was lying. I don't know who killed your brother, and I probably never will. I'm dropping the case and returning your fee in full."

Macy tossed the money on the bed. "Oh, don't be like that."

"Be like what?"

She sidled over. She bit his lip and his ear, pressing herself against him.

"I know you, Dalton Rev. After all this? I can see through that mask like it was Saran Wrap. Do you really want to say it's all over and go back to being cool and stoic and alone? Take more cases and solve more mysteries? It's such a crutch. I've *seen* you. You're not that person at all. It's a movie character. You're not tough, and you're not even particularly good at what you do. It's the act that you love. It's acting that you're *way* too good at."

THE PRIVATE DICK HANDBOOK, RULE #50
Could that be true? Not could it, wasn't it?
Wasn't it definitely, totally, completely true?

"So stop reading your lines. Improvise for once. This is a real chance. Take it."

"Take what?"

"Take me," she said, lowering her voice. Her left eye blinked three times. "And I'll take you."

Dalton made a mental list of all the things about himself no one should want to take. It started and ended with him never doing what the movie audience was throwing their popcorn and begging him to do.

"Promise?"

"Promise."

He stared at Macy, at her complete self-possession.

"Let's fail out of Salt River," she whispered. "Let's think about having kids and then not have them. Let's travel and give each other joke Christmas presents. Let's get fat and get old and then die."

"Die?"

"Together."

Dalton bit her neck. She tasted like fresh lime.

"All right."

"Really?" She somehow jumped without leaving the ground. "Let's go!"

"Tomorrow."

Macy looked sorely disappointed but didn't say anything. She forced a smile back onto her face and waited.

"I have something to take care of tonight. Just stay home and mind your own business, okay? Pack only what you really need. Tomorrow we get on the scooter and leave Salt River to the cliques."

"Good." She pressed her mouth back onto his, finding the right fit, lips in perfect, soft alignment. They stood there, losing themselves in it.

After a while he moved back. "I have to go. Stay here and be ready."

"I will. I am."

Dalton picked up the duffel and gently closed her door. He

walked down the steps, peeking in on Albert Payne, who was snoring in front of the TV. Next to him was a bottle of home-made wine. Dalton walked through the kitchen to the basement door. The heavy hasp lock was hanging open. He slipped through and turned on the light. On a big table at the bottom of the stairs was Albert Payne's fermenting equipment. Barrels and flasks and measuring cups and empty jugs rimed with dried grapes. He poked around the crates and dusty equipment until he came to the back of the room, where there was a large metal storage case.

Q: How much you wanna bet?
A: A lot.

Dalton fished in his pocket and pulled out Wesley Payne's key. He walked over to the case and stuck it into the lock. It fit perfectly. And when he turned the key, the lock turned with it.

CHAPTER 27
REVIVE ME HIGH

They both watched Dalton Rev, dressed in a black shirt with a black tie, sneaking across the massive BoxxMart lot in a military crouch. The night was dark and quiet, only the creak of cyclone fence flexing in the wind. The store was an airplane hangar poured into a cement trough off the interstate, next to welding shops and auto repair places and a low-slung recycling plant that smelled like burned hair. Dogs barked, their volleys echoing pointlessly. Lights flashed from cars on the faraway overpass, lending a strobe effect as Dalton jogged the last hundred yards, flattening his back against the brick entrance. Next to the tall glass door was a numerical keypad whose back-lit keys could be seen as tiny pixilations all the way across the lot. Dalton punched in a series of numbers and waited. It didn't work. He tried it again. The timelock hissed, and the bolts drew back.

"He's in," Chuff said, standing behind the first of eight vans that idled in the shadows at the far end of the compound.

"Not yet," Tarot said. "The gate is ztill down."

They watched Dalton grab the metal and shake it. In the

booth, a security guard stood and walked toward him, holding up his hands. Dalton pulled out his piece and held it level.

"Guezz he found a gun after all," Tarot said, peering through binoculars.

Chuff grabbed the binoculars away and watched Dalton threaten the guard. The guard, his cap pulled low over his face, nodded and hit a red button on the wall. The gate began to lift. Tarot grabbed the binoculars back and watched as Dalton racked the chamber. A report rang clearly all the way to where they were standing. They both saw the security guard fall.

"Holy shite," Chuff said. "That murse shot the guard. Like, for real."

"Good," Tarot said, giving the signal to Mick Freeley, who then gave the signal to the rest of the Caskets. The vans started backing up.

"*Good?*" Chuff said, looking pale.

Tarot grinned. "One less thing to worry about. You ever stop playing with your ballz long enough to go to the movies? The only reason to tie someone up is so they can find a way to get loose and be a hero. If you shoot them right away, there's definitely no sequel. Let's go."

"I know, but—"

"What are you going to do, Jeffrey, cry like you used to when I took your lunch money?"

"Farck off and drive," Chuff said, holding on to the running board as Tarot's van pulled away with a chirp. Three minutes later they were at the loading dock, where a dozen Balls crept out of the shadows to drag metal ramps over the back bumpers. Five minutes later, the huge steel gate opened, Dalton holding the control that operated the lift chains.

"Hurry. We got less than an hour before the next shift checks on their buddy."

Balls streamed into the store. Caskets got the vans ready.

"Didn't know you had those kind of pearls, fish," Chuff said, miming a pistol and firing off a few rounds.

"Just go grab a TV," Dalton said grimly. "And make sure it's hi-def."

Under an hour later, all eight vans were loaded full of equipment, electronics, computers, CDs, watches, and pallets of cold medicine. Chuff nodded with approval. "Smooth operation, fish. Tell you the truth, I wasn't sure you could be trusted."

Dalton was about to answer, when Chance Chugg ran up with a case of frozen pies. He guzzled a big mouthful of Rush. "Now?"

"Shut up," Chuff said, and then looked at Dalton. "Maybe we just do this straight, huh? Forget the double cross and get out of here while the getting's good? That's the smart play. Cash in, save the ultraviolence for later. Why complicate profit?"

"Now?" Chugg asked again, his pupils turning counter-clockwise, dried spit caked around his lips.

Chuff turned toward him angrily. "What did I just—"

"Now!" Dalton said loudly, backing up.

Chugg let out a war whoop. "Touchdown!"

"No, wait!" Chuff yelled. "NO!"

"Why is that idiot yelling?" Tarot demanded as a dozen

Balls and Couldabeen Contenders poured from behind a set of Dumpsters and surrounded the Caskets. They'd brought a pallet from Sporting Goods, big Whiffson golf bags, each one holding clubs, drivers, three woods, and nine irons.

"Betrayal, Jeffrey? What a surprise."

Chuff shrugged, too late to turn it around now. He chose a pitching wedge and swung it over his head like D'Artagnan.

Tarot threw off his leather jacket and yelled, "*Kashmir!*" Several dozen Airplane Gluze and Kokrocks swarmed out of vans that screeched up to the entrance. The Caskets had a pallet from Auto Parts, and each one was armed with a socket wrench.

"You weasly farcker," Chuff said as the alarm went off.

"Takes a farcker to know a farcker," Tarot said, throwing a looping right that caught Chuff full on the jaw. It would have felled a horse. It would have felled a statue of a horse. But Chuff barely moved. He poked around inside his mouth with two fingers, pulled out an incisor, and smiled, flipping it in the air. Before the tooth hit the ground, he slammed Tarot with a hydraulic right, the crunch of which echoed around the high-ceilinged room. "*OOOOH*," everyone said, on both sides, the noise elemental in its purity. The Balls and Caskets, plus the rogue cliques they'd recruited, crowded around, forming a natural arena. Chants of "Chuff!" and "Tarot!" competed for primacy as the two behemoths descended on each other.

Dalton backed away, his piece in his waistband, the Crowdarounds too engrossed in the fight to stop him. Chuff had Tarot on the ground, pounding him with massive lefts. Tarot spun on his back crabwise, pulling something from his boot and hitting Chuff with it. Blood fountained in a cinematic arc, and then Tarot was on Chuff's back, appearing to bite his neck. The Crowdarounds went apeshite.

Dalton ran through Patio Furniture, Frozen Goods, Lead Crockery, Gum and Candy, Beef and Ham, Power Tools, and Essential Herbs before reaching the dozen perpendicular aisles that brought him to the front doors. He lowered the steel gate and relocked the front, jogging back across the vast lot. His scooter was stashed under the ramp he intended to use to make his escape.

Dalton put the key in the ignition, wondering when the Snouts would show up. Balls and Caskets would be arrested, most of them for the second time in two days, some of them for good. It was over.

"Where do you think you're going, party boy?"

She was wearing a tight leather dress and high heels. She was wearing full makeup. Her hair was newly dyed and spiked straight up. She looked so smoking hot, it took his breath away. She looked about twenty-five. She looked like a Dutch model. She looked like the acid queen of all Foxxes.

"Hi, Dalty, honey. How's your heist going?"

Dalton looked at the little gun she held, a snub-nosed one that was almost as cute as she was. He looked at the way she stood, legs spread and hips cocked, aimed right at him.

She was the A-bomb.

She was disco atomic.

Dalton took off his helmet and looked right at Macy as she said:

"And better yet, where's that little ol' duffel bag of yours?"

CHAPTER 28
IF IT HADN'T BEEN FOR THE MEDDLING OF YOU DAMN SKIDS

Macy reached into her bustier for a lipstick, reapplying heavily. "Where's the cash?"

"Yeah, guy," Mole said, walking over from his mom's pinging Kia. He reached out to hold Macy's hand, but she pulled it away to steady her aim. Mole settled for kissing her on the cheek. His hair was slicked straight back. The goatee was gone. He was wearing expensive glasses, rectangular, that made him look like a European architect or an eccentric poet laureate. He even looked a little thinner. "Where's that big stack of folding green with my name on it, yo?"

Dalton laughed, short and ugly and bitter. "You two? Seriously?"

"Yeah, us two," Mole said. "You got a problem with that?"

"No problem at all," Dalton forced himself to say.

Macy's eyes narrowed. Mole took a step forward. "What, did you really think you and she were going to breed? Not likely. Euclidians stick with Euclidians. Keeps the brain line pure."

"Brain line?"

"That's right, fool. It's called eugenics. Take a class. Look it up, yo."

"Frisk him," Macy said. "And stop saying *yo*."

"I can see his gun. It's the fake."

"Frisk him anyway."

"For what?"

"For a treasure map," Macy snapped. "And any guns that aren't fake, and my butterfly pin, and anything else incriminating."

Mole nodded and then punched Dalton in the stomach as hard as he could. Which was really, really hard.

"Oooh, bet that hurt," Macy said.

"Yeah, me too," Mole said, blowing on his knuckles. "I'd bet almost a hundred grand."

Dalton bent over. Drool hung from his mouth as he struggled to breathe. He could see red lights coming hot from way off on the overpass. There were no sirens yet, but there would be soon. There were tears in his eyes. Some of them were from being punched. He wiped his face as Mole gave him a quick pat-down.

"What makes you think she's not playing you like she played me? Huh, Lester? You special or something?"

"Yeah, I *am* special, you purse. Only, you could never see it, could you? You have any idea how much work it is to play the clown? To be the asshat everyone gets to feel superior to? Like I wanted to be your sidekick? Are you kidding? You should be begging to be *my* sidekick!"

"Just get the hairpin," Macy said. "Hurry."

"Yeah, Lester, hurry," Dalton prodded. "Take instructions from someone else for a change."

"That divide and conquer crap?" Mole punched Dalton

again. "That shite only works in the movies. In bad movies about ineffectual bad guys who talk, talk, talk until the pretty boy comes up with an escape plan. Well, we're not going to talk. We're going to punch instead."

Mole swung, hitting Dalton in the shoulder blade. He'd never been punched in the shoulder blade. It ached. His stomach ached. His chest ached. His eyeballs ached. He was a cuckold and a fool. Mostly because he'd always known. The Lex part of him was furious for being a sap. But the Dalton part had held out. And the Dalton part had lost.

"Yeah, well, no matter how the script goes, this *is* a bad movie. It's a buddy film where the moron traitor buddy wears a mustard-stained Hawaiian shirt and then when he's concentrating on his victory donut, gets dogged by the femme fatale."

Mole looked down at his shirt, which was expensive and not Hawaiian. Even so, there did seem to be a mustard stain.

"You think she likes you for you? You think she's gonna just split the cash down the middle?"

"Yeah, I do. You know why?" Mole twisted his fingers under Dalton's nose, wriggling them like the church, steeple, and all the people. "Buffy Bucharest and Albert Payne were knocking boots in motels the whole time we were growing up. They'd lock us in the car and toss in some crayons and a juice box. We've been, like, hatchback soul mates, yo. Macy and I were always going to be together. Hell, it's a long shot, but we might even be brother and sister."

Dalton gagged.

"Stop saying *yo!*" Macy hissed. "And get his stuff so I have a clean shot!"

"I been reading about it, like, royals and all, back in King

Arthur times," Mole continued, pulling off Dalton's boot and looking inside. "They say inbreeding has gotten a bad rap. They say it actually makes your kids even smarter."

"Like Rush makes you smarter?"

"*Exactly* like Rush," Mole said, kicking Dalton in the thigh. "Except not soda and not in a bottle. And being DNA instead of liquid."

He handed Macy Dalton's lighter-gun and key ring. She held out the number 9 key.

"Look familiar?" Dalton asked.

"Clever Dick," Macy said, sticking it in her purse. "Did you find the pin, Lester?"

Mole frowned. "What's with that thing, anyway?"

"It's just a souvenir. Or I guess you could call it a trophy."

"But why do you want *his* trophy?"

"Because I don't want yours," Macy said, pulling her hand back and conking Mole in the forehead with the butt of the gun. He fell like a tray of lasagna, out cold.

"I mean, really, does he *ever* shut up? He couldn't have possibly thought that I…that I…ah, well. Euclidians will be needing a new sub-clique soon. I think I'll call it Natural Born Suckers."

"Count me in," Dalton said, edging toward her.

"Oh, yeah, sweetie, I already have." Macy raised the gun, causing him to stop. "The red duffel?"

"Or what?"

"Well, let's see. I'll shoot you, for starters. And then keep shooting you. And then shoot you even more."

The sirens began in earnest, a long train of Snout cruisers flashing and nearing the exit ramp. Dalton turned as the battle between Chuff and Tarot spilled off the loading dock and into the parking lot. Various Balls and Caskets had paired off and joined in. Mick Freeley stood on Chance Chugg's chest, kicking him in the neck. Merchandise was smashed all around them. A mix of screaming and begging and cheering droned over the blacktop in waves.

"Couldn't have planned it better myself," Macy said, backing into the shadows under the ramp. "Oh, wait, actually I did plan it. Hiring you, Private Donkey, was the essential first step. *The problem solver!* Hah. More like the Catalyst. Know what that *means*, Harvard boy? Wesley was more or less forgotten, the money was gone, it was over. Now Caskets and Balls are going to be arrested for robbery, and, with any luck, your murder. Finally, Euclidians will have the best racket *and* run the school, thanks to you."

"That was it all along, huh? Take over the reins? Be top dog?"

"Be top cat! Get back our seed money and move a few tired clique bosses out of the way. It's time for a Euclidian revolution. Salt River is *ripe* for new leadership."

On the far end of the parking lot, Snout cruisers screeched at the edge of the brawl. Cops poured out, clubs raised.

"Duffel," Macy said. "Now."

"I don't have it."

"Bloshite. I know it's close, since you were gonna take me away with it. Remember?"

"Yeah, I remember saying that. But I wasn't ever going anywhere with you."

Macy shot a round at his foot. The bullet *pang*ed off the pavement. Snouts had their hands full cuffing Balls and Caskets, minor sploets and Kokrocks running for the hobo camps behind the recycling plant. They were grabbing kids like bears in a salmon stream, forcing them facedown on the pavement in rows. They didn't seem to notice the sound.

"Where's the money?" Macy asked again. "I am so not kid—"

"Russia."

"Russia?"

"Little country between China and Poland."

Macy fired again. This time over Dalton's left shoulder.

"Ukraine," Dalton said, wincing. "It's where they make body armor. That armor's going to the Middle East Front. To my brother's command. I shipped the money UPS two hours ago. What can Brown do for me? Well, for one thing, overnight enough cash to semireputable arms dealers halfway around the world."

"No."

"Yes."

"You didn't."

"I did."

"You FISH STICK!"

Dalton pulled the now-empty duffel from inside his jacket. "But it wasn't just money in here." He rooted around inside, throwing handfuls of leftover bills onto the ground. Macy got down on her knees, grabbing at them with her free hand.

"There's this, for one thing. It's an exquisite lie, all right."

"What is?"

"Wesley's suicide note." Dalton held up the paper with the deconstructed stanzas and the translated formula.

Macy stood and snatched the translation away. "A code? He hid the formula in that *stupid song*?"

"Wesley didn't trust you with it."

"I can't believe I bought for a second he'd really listen to Pinker Casket."

"Too much Rush makes it hard to concentrate."

Macy smirked. "No, it doesn't. It makes it really easy. And by next week, every student at Salt River is going to be begging for things to get easier and easier."

The Snouts were beginning to get control of the situation. Some of the officers were looking over at Dalton, who appeared to be talking to a shadow. One pointed and another spoke into his shoulder radio.

"Last chance," Macy said, rooting through Mole's pockets for the keys to the Kia. "Where is the money, really? I know you didn't mail it anywhere. You probably don't even have a brother. Your whole sensitive ethics routine is such self-serving bloshite. Even your *angle*'s an angle."

Dalton reached into the duffel and pulled out something small and flat, about the size of a deck of cards. "Didn't see this in there before."

"Give it to me," Macy demanded, backing toward the Kia.

"Looks like Wesley's wallet," Dalton said, flipping it open. He pulled out two dollar bills, a school ID, a business card from the Salt River Police Department, and a picture. "What's this? Wesley's mysterious girlfriend?"

"Do you really think I won't shoot you? Do you really think that?"

Dalton held the picture up. It was a wallet-size glossy. It was a smiling face. It was a picture of Jeff Chuff, QB. Dalton looked at Macy.

"*You* killed Wesley Payne."

CHAPTER 28 ½
WHAT, YOU'VE NEVER SEEN A FRENCH MOVIE BEFORE?

Macy Payne took off her high heels and walked barefoot through the wet grass. The white paint of the yard markers stuck to the soles of her feet. Up ahead, her brother, Wesley, walked with a stepladder over his shoulder.

"But you *have* to tell me where the formula is, Wes."

"I can't. I destroyed it."

"Oh, you did not," Macy said, glaring at his back. Wesley stopped under the goalposts and threw a red duffel bag on the ground. He unzipped it in one motion and pulled out a length of rope and three rolls of duct tape.

"Think, okay? Do you see the effing corner this puts me in? Inference has the money in her safe. Balls already matched our share. The bank is rolled. They're expecting production."

"We're not producing any more. Period. It's *addictive*."

"So people *really* want to buy it," Macy said. "What's wrong with that? I mean, this is a racket no one's ever thought of before. And *we'll* control it. If we don't, someone else will. It might as well be Euclidians."

"No, that's exactly who it shouldn't be. Euclidians should be the ones to shut it down."

"Do you know how long it took to set this up? While you're tinkering with your chemistry set? What, are we going to go to Inference and tell her, *Oh, sorry, changed our minds, can we just give everyone their money back?*"

"You're right," Wesley said. "Can't do that at all. Which is why we're calling the police. If Inference goes down, it won't matter if Euclidians are in power, because there will be nothing left to take over. Which is how it should be."

"Who are you to decide how the school should be?"

"Someone has to," Wesley said quietly. "Salt River is a shithole."

"Salt River is fine," Macy said. "It'll be even better when we start cashing in."

"Every penny we've made off Rush so far is being donated. I've already got it set aside." Wesley threw a rope over the goalpost and tied a knot. Then he unfurled the sign he was going to hang for everyone to see in the morning.

POPULAHS FUND-RAISER FOR SPECIAL-NEEDS YOUTH—SIGN UP NOW!

"Donated? You can't do that, Wes! It's *my* money too. Besides, calling the Snouts? Are you kidding? Where do you think Inference got the go-ahead from to begin with? They're totally in for a cut."

"I don't believe that. There has to be *someone* in this town who's not corrupt."

"Well, start believing!" Macy said, her left eye starting to blink. She put one hand over it, forcing it to stop. "This is a real chance for Euclidians. To put people in charge who *should* have been in charge all along."

"Can you stop speechifying and give me a hand?" Wesley raised the heavy poster board.

Macy held the sign while he duct taped rope along the stanchion to hold it in place.

"Listen," he said soothingly. "You definitely earned your end. Okay? That little brain in there is totally worthy of Euclidian status. The test batches and financing couldn't have happened without you. But I guess I never thought the stuff would actually work, so I didn't take the time to think through the consequences."

Macy tried to ignore her brother's compliment but smiled despite herself.

"You've seen how people get when they drink Rush," he continued, giving her a sideways look. "Um, especially since you tripled the dosage without bothering to tell me? Total bloshite move, by the way, but at least it opened my eyes. Rush isn't a racket—it's a death sentence. A long and slow one. Thank Bob the last batch is almost gone."

Macy shrugged unhappily. "The only thing I see is cliques wanting to spend. Lined up at the lockers, pushing and shoving to buy more. And more. And more."

"What about those Crop Crème girls? Tried talking to one of them lately? Or Jeffrey. Have you noticed how paranoid he's gotten?"

"Since when did you grow this big fat conscience, Mistah Populah?"

Wesley held out his arms. "Since I realized how farcking

fake all of this is. Freshmen come and seniors go and the only things that stay are Inference and rackets. Climbing on the backs of lesser cliques is worse than meaningless. It's cruel. Euclidians don't deserve to be in charge if Rush is what it takes to get them there."

"What about all your big talk about changing things from the inside? How else does it ever happen without getting your hands dirty? You can't just wave signs about fairness or justice like some whiny Barefoot. You have to be strong enough, or rich enough, to demand that people listen."

Wesley slipped and lost his balance, almost falling off the stool. Macy didn't move to steady it. "It's already decided. Jeff is for giving the money back too. He's going to give Balls to Chugg and concentrate on acting again. And then we're going to State together in the fall."

"Oh, really? You and Goliath gonna share a room? Hold hands like everyone's favorite freshman couple?"

"They're a lot more…open-minded there. It's not like Salt River."

"You fool! It's exactly like here. They'll run you off campus."

Wesley frowned. "Maybe. But at least there we won't be lying anymore."

"Jeff isn't giving that money back."

"Ask him," Wesley said, taping the other end of the sign. "He'll be here in a minute."

"I already did."

"What's that supposed to mean?"

"I asked him how he'd feel if the other cliques knew," she

said acidly. "How he's going to get kicked off the team. How he's gonna have to buy a beret and a black skirt and become a Plath for the rest of the year."

Wesley paled, trying to smile. "No one will believe you."

"Probably not. Who would ever believe a lowly Euclidian spreading rumors about Balls and Crop Crème? Who would believe the crazy kid sister of Wes Payne?"

"That's not what I meant."

"It's exactly what you meant. And you're right."

"About what?"

"About no one believing me. Unless I had photos." She held up a set of contact sheets. Telephoto shots. Of Jeff and Wesley near the football field. Pretending to argue. Jeff pretending to shove Wesley behind the porta-potties. So they could make out with no one seeing.

"You *wouldn't*," Wes said. The stool wobbled again.

"Yeah," Macy said. "I would."

"I'd believe her if I were you." Jeff Chuff walked out of the darkness and put his arm around Macy.

"What are you *doing*?"

"It's called cutting a side deal, Wes. It's called looking at your cards and knowing you're beat."

Wes Payne's face was almost entirely without color. "Beat at what?"

"You and me? No way. Never happened. This whole cash back rebate deal? You heard what you wanted to hear."

Wesley fought to speak calmly. "I heard what you *told* me, Jeffrey."

"I know..." Chuff trailed off until Macy squeezed his arm.

279

"That cheddar's not going anywhere, Wes. Shite's invested. Production and distribution. We need to secure the materials and go from there. We *need* that formula."

"It's almost like," Wes said, in a low voice, "it's almost like you've been poisoned."

"Poisoned?" Macy laughed, putting her hand in Chuff's shirt.

"It's not too late," Wesley said, ignoring his sister. "We can—"

"We can't."

Wesley rubbed his neck, up on the stool, completely lost. "I thought—"

"That's the problem!" Chuff forced himself to yell. "I realized…Macy and I realized…that you've been thinking *for me*. So Rush is addictive? It's nothing compared to power. This time next year elevator doors will open, and Rush will flow through Salt River like Kubrick blood. Euclidians and Balls will be beyond rich. I'd be…I'd have to be a fool not to get in on it."

"You'd be something, all right." Wes held the rope above his head, looking down at Jeff and Macy holding hands. "You're already there. Both of you. At the bottom floor."

"The Rush formula," Macy told her brother. "I want it on my desk. Next to my pink pencil holder. I want it by tomorrow morning, or these pictures are all over school."

"Do it," Chuff said, unable to meet Wesley's eyes.

"I don't believe this is you," Wesley told Jeff. "All ball, no brain. Confused with greed. Emotionless."

"Believe it," Macy said. "Chuff would duct tape Chugg to an A-bomb for a hundred grand."

Wesley cut down the sign with a penknife. "Okay. Tomorrow."

Macy led Chuff away. "I knew all along *I* was the kid with the special need." Their laughter echoed across the field, dying beneath the bleachers.

When they were gone, Wesley Payne made a decision. Monks had lit themselves on fire to protest war. Single men had stood in front of tanks, refusing to let them pass. But making a difference also meant making sacrifices. Macy was his fault. He'd apologized too often for her. Deluded himself that she would get better. She would never get better.

Wesley gathered up his things and drove home. He wrote down the formula, staring at it for a long time. It was too dangerous, even on a piece of paper. It needed to be hidden somehow. Hidden in plain sight. Hidden so that it could be decoded when the time came, if only as proof he was telling the truth.

Wes bit his fingernails, then got up, plastic crunching under his foot. It was a CD case. He reached for it and the lyric sheet fell out.

In plain sight.

He wrote ten pages of longhand, explaining how the racket was going to work. The delicate balances needed in the chemistry, the protocols he'd devised to maximize production. All of the damning truth. Then he got some of his father's tools from the basement. It was one a.m. by the time he got to school. He had just enough time to get to the police station and back before the first buses arrived at six.

It was better to be a symbol than be alone.

People talked endlessly about their beliefs, but very few put theory into practice.

Being popular was a yoke *and* a currency.

But it was his to spend freely.

Wesley Payne retied the rope to the goalpost, next to four rolls of duct tape, and then carried his red duffel bag full of tools to the window outside Principal Inference's office. He hit it with his elbow, shards of glass tinkling lightly across the floor.

CHAPTER 29
I SENT THE MALCONTENT

"You killed Wesley Payne," Dalton almost whispered.

Flares of red darkened Macy's face. "No, I didn't!"

"You might as well have. You talked your own brother into killing himself."

"That's not how it's going to read to the cops if you're not around to tell them," Macy said, backing through the shadows. "I mean, technically, I guess you could say that I didn't leave him a lot of choices and he took the weak one. The cowardly one." She tried a hard laugh. "Plus, like you, he just wouldn't give me the money."

"Big mistake," Dalton said, following her. "On both our parts."

"Okay, so I didn't think he'd actually...I mean, listen, he could have just handed over the formula. He could have... everything would have just..." She wiped her eyes and took a deep breath. The hard-girl face fell like a curtain. "Farck it. I tried to toughen him. But it didn't take. Never does with true believers. That's why no one likes them. He killed himself to spark some mythical revolution, and people barely noticed. His death changed nothing."

"That's right," Dalton said. "Reason it all out. Play me a song about how it's all someone else's fault. About how everything's meaningless so you don't have to feel guilty about what you did. Wesley's death changed nothing, not even you."

Macy started to blink. Just her left eye. First like Morse code, and then in shuddering triplets. She put her palm over it and pulled a bottle of Rush from her purse, taking a huge gulp. She finished the bottle and threw it at Dalton's feet. He watched it bounce away.

"Wesley goes and drills Inference's safe and takes the money just so you can't have it. You believe that? A guy pulling the rug out from under his own sister? And then, you know, here I come along and do the same thing? That's really got to hurt, huh?"

Macy shrugged, her teeth chattering.

"How *did* Wesley get upside down?"

Macy flinched, her fingers under the Kia's door handle. "He didn't. I just told you that. Told you to keep you. Poking around. Annoying people. Your greatest. Skill."

"Chuff wasn't forcing himself on you at Lu Lu Footer's, was he?"

"No." Macy wrapped her arms around her body as if she were freezing. "That was just good. Acting. Jeffrey is. Multi-talented. We saw you sneak into Footer's room. Sure, Jeffrey needed some…prompting. But I still have those. Pictures. Couldn't have you guessing. Too much. Before you found. The money."

A group of Snouts began walking across the lot. Macy saw them coming and shook her head violently. Her eyes cleared, dried spit in the corners of her mouth. She reached in to start the engine. Dalton took a quick step forward. Macy jerked the gun up, pulling the trigger, as a BoxxMart security guard with a bloodstained shirt kicked it out of her hand. Macy tried to get in the car, but the guard grabbed her by the wrists.

"About time," Dalton said.

"I thought you two might need a word alone," the security guard said, then took off his hat. Except it wasn't a him.

Macy stopped struggling. "Wait a minute. You two *work* together?"

Cassiopeia waved genially. "Hi."

"Of course," Dalton said. "It's Rev and Jones Associates. You don't think I'm dumb enough to work alone, do you?"

Macy stomped her foot like a child. And then did it again. And again. Her heel broke off and skittered across the pavement.

"Is *that* what our name is?" Cassiopeia asked.

"It is now."

"Partner?"

"Full partner."

Cassiopeia nodded and began unbuttoning her security guard uniform. Underneath, she was wearing a T-shirt that said THE VELVET UNDERGROUND IS THE ONLY BAND THAT MATTERS. Three Snouts arrived at the cyclone fence, lifting up the corner where Dalton had snipped the tines.

"Dalton, honey," Macy said, shifting gears. She was deep in a Rush overload, suddenly talking too slow, her lids drooping. "I'm sorry. Okay? Listen, it's not too late. There's still time. I. You and I. We could still . . . Dalton? I'm."

"You're what?" He wanted the answer. He didn't want the answer.

"Look," she said. "Look at me."

He did.

"I. Love. You."

Cassiopeia punched Macy in the stomach. Not too hard, but hard enough.

"Unprofessional," Dalton said as Macy bent over and threw up half a gallon of soda.

"Sorry, but I can't listen to that Euclidiarrhea anymore. Besides, it'll save her from getting her stomach pumped. Not to mention she's the one who put the M-80 in my microphone."

The Snouts walked into the circle of light. It was Hutch and Estrada, along with six uniforms struggling to carry a battered Chuff, hog-tied like he was about to be roasted on a spit. They set him down with relief.

"Welcome, gentlemen," Dalton said.

"Good to see you in one piece, Rev," Estrada said.

"You too, Detective."

Chuff looked up at Cassiopeia, craning his neck painfully. "But I saw you get shot. The fish blasted you."

Dalton pulled out his gun and pulled the trigger. A tiny flame danced as Cassiopeia instinctively rubbed her ketchup-stained chest.

"So who do we have here?" Estrada asked.

Dalton pointed to Macy. "She'll be taking the fall for Wesley Payne. You'll find his wallet on her, along with a chemical formula that she and her brother used to manufacture the crude liquid accelerant they've been selling at Salt River.

There're a few cases of it left in the basement of her father's house, in a metal cabinet, along with the equipment used to cook it. It's set up for large-scale production. The key to the cabinet is in her pocket, has a number nine on it."

"Excellent," Estrada said.

Dalton pointed to the still-dazed Chuff. "I know it's hard to believe, but LeadWig Wittgenstein there is the main backer of the Rush enterprise. You'll find the basc components on the pallets he was trying to steal, primarily a combination of cold medicine, seltzer water, and Flavor Flavah."

"Bathtub crank, eh?"

"Not quite that potent," Dalton said, "but close."

A cruiser parked next to Mole's Kia, followed by an ambulance. Two EMTs picked up the still-unconscious Mole and cuffed him to a gurney. A lady Snout put Macy's arm over her shoulder and helped her, trembly legged, to another cruiser.

"Dalton?" she slurred. "Babylove?"

He watched as she was plopped unceremoniously into the backseat. Part of him wanted to help her in. Part of him wanted to kick the door closed.

"So, have you found that money, by any chance?" Estrada asked.

"Last I saw, the cash was in Hutch's locker."

"No *shite*?"

"Nope."

Estrada exhaled deeply. He nodded sadly. He brushed his mustache contemplatively. Then he pressed the SEND button on his radio, about to tell more dress blues to come over and arrest his partner.

"Which is exactly where you put it," Dalton added, holding

up Detective Estrada's business card. The one he'd found in Wesley Payne's wallet.

"*What?*"

"Wes Payne gave you the money. Before he killed himself. Ran the whole enterprise down for you, formula, production, all of it. Who would have thought you'd see it as a road map to get in on the racket yourself, instead of arresting Inference and everyone else involved? Who would have thought it was you who was going to bankroll the next batch?"

"Ridiculous," Estrada scoffed.

"It's true," Chuff groaned, from the ground.

"What, like anyone would believe what this perp says?"

"I'll sign a deposition," Chuff said, allowing himself to blubber dramatically. "Whatever it takes to make up for what I did to Wesley."

Estrada kicked Chuff in the stomach on general principle.

"Or, who knows, Estrada?" Dalton said. "After you saw Wesley's confession, maybe you did go to arrest Inference. And maybe while you were doing it, she used her leadership talents to walk you down another path. Maybe you and she started having one-on-one meetings, planning out how things could go if they were handled the right way. That version'll sound better to the judge, I'm sure. Honest cop led astray by the femme fatale. Even if you had the fatale's stolen money all along."

"Are you through?" Estrada said, backing up. He smiled at Hutch. "Do you believe this?"

"Out of the closet and onto the tier the same day," Chuff said, coughing blood. "Hey, Estrada. Maybe we'll be cell mates."

"Look, Hutch, he's got a gun!" Estrada yelled, pointing at Dalton and reaching for his piece, but Hutch slipped it out of the holster first.

"What are you doing? Shoot!"

Hutch grabbed Estrada's wrists and turned him around roughly, before cuffing him. "Your girlfriend Inference is already in jail. We found her in a motel out over the state line with twenty grand worth of office supplies. She rolled over on you, buddy."

A sergeant ran over. "Detective Hutcherson? We've got most of them cuffed and Miranda'd, but the rocker seems to have gotten away with a vehicle full of goods."

"Well, Officer," Hutch said. "You think you might want to put out an APB on a big rusty van that has *Pinker Casket* spray-painted on the side in huge red letters, or should we just let him go?"

"Yes, sir," the sergeant said, jogging away.

"We'll get him," Hutch told Dalton, and then stuck out his hand. They bumped knuckles.

"You Dicks are *working* together?" Estrada yelled.

"I called Hutch first thing, when I took this job," Dalton said.

Hutch nodded. "I used to moonlight security at BoxxMart way back. I've known Dalton and his brother since they were little kids, playing around on the crates, waiting for their dad to punch out."

"Couldn't have gotten in the front door without him," Dalton said. "Let alone the security gate. I would have had to really shoot a guard, which, you know, is pretty much against Private Dick operational standards. Let alone the law."

Hutch smiled. "Nothing to it once we got it cleared with the captain."

"Speaking of ethics," Dalton said, massaging his jaw where Hutch had hit him. "That time in the nurse's office? You were a little too convincing, you know what I'm saying?"

"Yeah, sorry about that. But Estrada sure bought it, didn't he?"

"Bought it enough to stash the money in the cops' locker room until things cooled off. When they didn't, he put it in your locker to frame you."

"Not very ethical," Hutch said. "That's not how a buddy treats a buddy."

"I want a lawyer," Estrada said.

"You'll get one, you purse," Hutch said as a Snout van pulled up, full of cuffed Caskets and Balls. Hutch shoved Estrada in with them, banging his head on the roof and forgetting to say "Watch your head."

"What about the money?" Chuff asked as seven grimacing officers lifted him up and rolled him into the cruiser.

"Yeah," Cassiopeia said, running her hand over her short, bristly hair. "Where's that folding green at, Dalton?"

CHAPTER 30
WILL THE REAL JETT RINK PLEASE STAND UP?

Dalton looked at Hutch. "You may need to cuff me too."

"Why?"

"Because that money's gone."

"What money?"

Dalton held up the empty red duffel.

"Oh, you mean the bag the suspects all keep referring to that was never officially recovered?"

Dalton nodded.

"It's a true investigative mystery. Now, I did hear a wild rumor that some Russkies just got a little richer. And maybe Landon got a little safer. But that's all I know about that. Rumors. I mean, otherwise, far as I understand, it's still missing."

Cassiopeia looked at Dalton. "I thought you weren't cool with that. Landon getting it that way, I mean."

"Macy was right about one thing. *Acting* scared, or superstitious, is a way to avoid making hard choices. So, yeah, I sent the full boat to the Russians. Eff it. Armor is armor, period.

Money isn't clean or dirty. It's a tool. What was left over I donated to the fund Wesley started. The thing for special-needs kids at Salt River. And that's that."

Dalton turned to Hutch. "Kosher?"

"No idea what you're talking about." Hutch got in the car and started the engine. "Didn't hear a word."

Dalton motioned for him to roll down the window.

"One other thing."

"Shoot."

"How did Wes Payne's body get into my mother's laundry room? Especially a month after he was dead?"

"Yeah. I've been looking into that pretty much since you called. It's a total blank."

Dalton stepped closer and lowered his voice. "What's going to happen to Macy?"

Hutch looked at him without blinking. "What do you think?"

"I know. It's just…"

"It's just what?"

"Nothing."

"You wanna do something, kid? Call her a good lawyer. Aside from that? My advice is forget her. She's gonna be gone a long time."

The cruiser peeled toward the entrance ramp.

When they were finally alone, Cassiopeia looked at Dalton.

"Need a ride?"

"Nah, I got my scooter."

"I still don't get why they didn't arrest you."

"For what?"

"Shooting a security guard and all."

"Oh, yeah. That. I did, didn't I?"

"Yup."

"Listen, Cassie—" Dalton began, as Ronnie Newport ducked under the hole in the cyclone fencing. He walked over and stood next to Cassiopeia. Then dipped his finger in the red blotch on her chest, licking it. "Can't believe people still eat Flavor Flavah after the Shanghai recall."

Cassiopeia put her arm around Newport and kissed his cheek.

"Are you *serious*? You two too?"

Cassiopeia nodded happily. Newport shrugged, expertly slicking back his pompadour.

"Why didn't you tell me, Cassie?"

"Guess we weren't sure ourselves."

"What about the Ginny Slims? You ever take a look in his backseat?"

"I'm not *with* them. I take care of them," Newport said. "The way Wesley asked me to."

"Take care of them?"

Newport looked embarrassed. "I helped Wesley come up with the first batch of Rush. Years ago, playing around with his Lil' Egghead set. I had no idea he'd see a racket in it. But I still feel partly responsible."

"For what?"

"The Ginny Slims used to be Crop Crème," Cassiopeia explained.

"Until they started drinking Rush all the time. Wesley didn't know how addictive it was, at least not until Macy and Mole were cranking it out by the gallon. He tried to get the Ginnys to stop, but they wanted to lose weight, they wanted to be funny, they wanted to stay up and study, they wanted to concentrate harder. And after a while...they got a little off-brand. So I told Wesley I'd keep an eye out for them."

"Were you keeping an eye out for me?" Dalton asked. "Picking me up and driving me around?"

"I took you to the people you needed to see. So I pretended they wanted me to get you there. Bottom line, I figured you were the best hope to finally put Wesley to rest. It had to be someone from outside. Someone clean. Everyone else, all of us at Salt River, are guilty as hell one way or another."

"So why didn't *you* do something about Macy?"

"Honestly?" Newport said, looking away from Cassiopeia. "I was scared."

"There's nothing wrong with that," she said, rubbing his back. "It's normal."

"You don't understand. All those times over at Wesley's house, hanging out, even when we were younger? I was scared to death."

"Of Wesley?"

"Of *Macy*, man. Of that crazy little Euclidian chick. I mean, you ever look into her eyes? Like, way deep down?"

"Yes," Dalton said.

"She's a blank well. Even when we were little, man, I wouldn't turn my back on that girl. No way. I wouldn't leave her alone with my cat. And Wesley was the only one who could keep her in line. And when he was gone?" Newport let out a low whistle.

Cassiopeia took a few steps forward, leaned over, and kissed Dalton's cheek. "See you back at Tehachapi on Monday?"

"Who knows? I guess I do have to transfer somewhere. I've got things to think through first."

"Ivy Rev?" Cassiopeia said. "Dalton League?"

He shrugged, suddenly feeling utterly, completely empty.

"Well, don't think too long," she said. "I've got a lead on a new case."

"We'll see."

"Okay. Call me." Cassiopeia took Newport's hand and led him away. Dalton watched her go. Holding someone else's hand. Again. They made it about twenty feet before he spoke up.

"There's one last thing."

They turned together. Cassiopeia looked at Dalton expectantly.

"Yeah?"

"Lee Harvies."

"What about them?" Newport said.

"I have this feeling. Like, there I was in that Yearbook dark-room, looking at all those pictures you took for Lu Lu. Tele-photo shots, long lenses. Almost sniper shots. Then I'm thinking, you know, I'm not sure there is a Lee Harvies clique."

"There's not?"

"No, there's not. I think it's just one guy."

"Huh."

"I think it's you."

Cassiopeia laughed. Newport didn't laugh. She turned and grabbed his arm. "You're not, are you?"

Newport reached into his back pocket and pulled out the Jason mask, slowly putting it on. Up close, you could see that the anarchy symbols weren't painted over the eyes; they were made with strips of duct tape.

Cassiopeia put her hands on her hips. Newport took the mask off and casually tossed it on the ground. "I was totally going to tell you."

"*When?*"

"Same time you told me you weren't really the leader of Foxxes but some plant working as a Private Dick."

"Fair enough," she said reluctantly.

"But also when I was sure that knowing about it wasn't going to put you in any danger."

"I saw the negatives in the Yearbook darkroom," Dalton said. "How did you take shots of yourself?"

"Ever heard of a tripod? How about a timer? I figured if anyone started getting suspicious, the fact that I'd been the only one to photograph Lee Harvies sort of let me off the hook. Especially after Macy and Mole stole all the Yearbook computers."

"Okay," Cassiopeia said. "But why Lee Harvies?"

"It's another thing Wesley and I came up with. Years ago. Talking about how to change Salt River. At first, Wesley was all for speeches. Like assemblies where he explained how things could be different. How the cliques could treat each other with respect."

"Good luck," Dalton and Cassiopeia said simultaneously.

"I know, right? I mean, after a while, he realized that high-concept stuff wasn't going to change anyone's mind. It may have even made it worse. So then he thought just by being a real live example, not trying to convince anyone of anything, people might start to follow him. That it might rub off."

"And?"

"Well, it worked a little. Populahs stopped being all about

looking good and posing in the hallways. But pretty much everyone else kept up with the rackets. So then Wesley decided nothing would ever change at Salt River without a major reduction in violence."

"Makes sense."

"Yeah, except his idea was to use the theoretics of violence to do it."

"What does that mean?"

"Sowing dissension. Confusion as a means of crowd control. Fear of violence as a tamping device. He came up with the idea of Lee Harvies as mythic figures, like Zorro. A symbol. And then the fear of them leading to a kind of unspoken truce. At the time I really didn't even get what he was talking about."

"And you do now?"

Newport scratched his sideburns. "Wesley was my best friend. After he died, I wanted to make up for being a Populah. For the stupidity of Crop Crème. The day after the funeral, I stood there in the hallway thinking about all his usual speeches. The bankruptcy of our lives, the worthless things we think are important, seeking each other's approval or trying to impress each other with crap we buy and wear around like it matters. Suddenly it stopped being gibberish. I mean, me being all cool and Steve McQueen, who cared? I realized I could do something to make things better."

"With a rifle?"

"You weren't around back then, Rev. It was out of control with everyone strapped all the time. I went to Inference. I went to the Snouts. They did zip. Then I remembered this Lee Harvies thing Wesley was talking about. Scare guns away with guns."

"Except there's no way that works. You're going to miss eventually. Shoot someone by mistake. It's too random. Too dangerous."

"Yeah, I know. I almost gave up on it. Until I realized there really didn't have to be any guns."

"There didn't?"

Newport laughed. "What do you think? You walking around with that lighter? You're the best possible example. People believed in the idea of your gun, whether it was real or not."

"There never were any bullets," Dalton said, the brilliance of it dawning on him. "You never fired a single shot, did you?"

"I got to thinking about my telephoto lenses and how taking pictures was a lot like pulling a trigger, especially at long distance. Then I thought about how my brother and his buddies play paintball. And how real his rifle looked. Except red paint looks more like paint than blood. No one was going to buy it was real. And then I thought about the experiments Wesley and I did with Flavor Flavah, and how it looks a whole hell of a lot like blood, like, to the point people were even believing it was Euclidian blood. Except it's stickier and smells worse. So I figured out a way to put it in the paint capsules."

"Blood that smells like vinegar," Dalton said, thinking about the Kokrock City in the nurse's office insisting he'd poked himself in the leg with a pencil. "People practically convincing themselves they've been shot."

"The weirder something is," Newport said, "the more likely people are to believe it. Or at least not question it. I mean, if you say you saw the Virgin Mary in your dreams, no one cares. You say you saw her face on your tortilla? The news trucks can't find you fast enough."

"You believed there were three Jennys," Cassiopeia said.

"It's inspired thinking, I have to admit."

"Yup. Stop violence with ketchup. It could get, like, real popular. Span the country, schools handing out little restaurant packets. It could —"

Cassiopeia entwined her fingers with Newport's, and he stopped talking, relieved. She started to pull him away.

Dalton took the playing card with the guy's face glued on it out of his back pocket and held it up. "I found this chasing you on the roof yesterday."

"Almost got me too."

"So who is it?"

"The jack of spades."

Dalton didn't laugh.

"Leon Czolgosz."

"Bless you," Cassiopeia said, pretending to hand him a Kleenex.

"Who?"

"Guy who shot President McKinley in 1901."

"Oh, yeah, of course. And, um, what about him?"

"He was a Polish anarchist. After he was arrested, supposedly they found a quarter in his pocket with the year 2288 stamped on it. Some people think he was a time traveler. Wesley thought it was the perfect detail for his dissension plan. To throw the cliques into a panic. Typical Wesley, no one could have cared less. He was like one of three people in the world who had ever even heard of the guy. And the other two are McKinley's great-granddaughters."

Cassiopeia rolled her eyes. "We should go. Okay, Dalton?"

Dalton looked at his partner, out of costume. Beautiful with her short hair, plain clothes, and tired eyes. Part of him wanted to say no. To refuse to let her walk away. To insist she stay with him. And he was pretty sure some part of her wanted him to. Or was at least wondering if he finally would. If that part in both of them still existed enough to fight over.

"Okay," Dalton finally said. "Go."

Cassiopeia nodded. She turned and pulled Ronnie Newport's hand gently as they walked to the gleaming Nova parked out on the street.

And then the lot was empty.

And Dalton was alone.

CHAPTER 31
KISS POINT BLANK

Dalton sneaked into his room after two a.m., lay on his bed, and for the first time in years didn't spread out broken dishes. He thought about Macy. For about fourteen straight minutes. Then fell asleep.

He got up four hours later. The only one awake, he made eggs and toast and a phone call. The person who answered was delighted to hear from him. Dalton hung up and went outside and cleaned the garage. He washed his mom's car, and then Landon's Kawasaki. He weeded the driveway and then mowed the back lawn. When he was halfway done with the front, there was a tap on his shoulder. It was his father. Dalton kicked off the mower, wiping blades of grass from his neck. Scanlon Rev sat at the edge of the lawn. Dalton sat next to him.

"You've been busy."

"Work helps me think."

"What're you thinking about?"

Dalton considered telling his father about Macy. About the raw strip mine that was his stomach. He wanted to ask what you did when you thought you knew someone, when you let down your defenses and let them see a part of you that you didn't even know was there, and then it turned out you didn't know them at all. He wanted to ask what you did when there was no way to scream loud enough or run fast enough or punch something hard enough. When there was just another morning and just another lawn and not a single thing to look forward to. Ever.

"Nothing. School stuff."

Dalton's father let out a little laugh. "Which one? You transfer so much, I can't keep them straight. There was Darlington High and then Voight Kampff Tech…and then Upheere High before you even went to Tehachapi…"

"I'm picky," Dalton said.

"You're a Private Dick."

Dalton looked at his father, one eyebrow raised.

"You think I don't know how to turn on a computer? You think I'm so crazy I don't know where that money's coming from?"

Of course they knew, Dalton thought. His mother too. Who was he kidding?

THE PRIVATE DICK HANDBOOK, RULE #51
Assuming your parents are stupid usually makes an ass of U and ME. Not to mention anyone who spells *you* like *U*.

"You're not crazy, Dad."

"Comes and goes," Scanlon said. "Mostly comes."

Dalton nodded.

"It's not easy letting your son take the reins," Scanlon continued, and then winced, holding his back as he readjusted his posture. "But I did. We took your money, which I figure pretty much means I have no right to pass judgment."

Dalton hadn't really thought about that before. How much pride his father must have swallowed over the last year.

"If you don't want—"

"It's not about what I want. It's about our family and what's best for us. It's not about ego. We all have to sacrifice. Some of us more than others. You're old enough to realize that family is the most important thing there is. Maybe the only thing."

Dalton knew his father was talking mostly about Landon. "I haven't been giving you all of the money."

"That's okay. A boy has expenses. Car, girls, beer."

"No, it's not that." Dalton was about to tell his father that he'd gotten an e-mail back from Ukraine. The money had arrived and the shipment had gone to the Middle East Front. But when Dalton saw the look on his father's face, the effort it was already taking him with the pain in his back to just sit there, he couldn't do it. Whether the pain was real or not didn't matter. If his father thought it was, it was.

"Yeah, you're right, Dad. A guy's got to screw around a little bit, huh?"

"I know I did enough of it when I was your age," Scanlon said with a laugh. Then he used Dalton's shoulder to awkwardly stand.

"Dad?"

"Yeah?"

"I think I'm going to go to Harvard."

Scanlon looked off toward the houses along the pine ridge above them. He didn't say anything for a while.

"I'm sorry, bud, but we can't afford it."

"Mom filled out an application. Without telling me, actually. Somehow I got a scholarship."

"Part or full?"

"Admissions guy said full. Anyway, I have to meet him in an hour to nail down the details."

"Studying what?"

"Writing."

"Writing?"

"Yeah."

"Well, we could still use you around here. You know that."

"Yeah, I know."

"But I'm proud of you, Bud. If you really want to go, I say show those Ivy League pussies where it's at."

"I will, Dad."

"At least it's not the goddamned military."

Scanlon Rev hobbled back inside to get some pudding and turn on the news.

Dalton put the lawn mower and Weed Decimator 9000 back in the garage and was about to head upstairs and take a shower, when he heard a loud noise down in the laundry room. It definitely wasn't his mother.

"CAN YOU DIG IT?" a voice asked.

"WE CAN DIG IT!" other voices answered.

Dalton eased open the door to the basement and crept down the stairs. Turd Unit stood on the washing machine addressing a bunch of other little kids. There must have been thirty of them.

"Turd Unit?" Dalton said. "What are you guys *doing*?"

Turd Unit leaped off the washing machine like a stage diver. The outstretched arms of other little boys caught him and set him down gently. He stood in the middle of them, and they turned as one. Dalton was about to laugh, but the look on Turd Unit's face seemed to warn against it.

"What exactly are you guys doing?" he asked again, more quietly this time.

"Oh, I dunno," Turd Unit said. "We thought we might wrap some duct tape around Tiny and swing him from the pole for a while."

All the kids laughed.

"Tiny?"

A big, heavy kid lumbered from the shadows and stood in the light.

"What is he, twenty five?"

"He's got glandular problems," Turd Unit said. "So shut up. He's sensitive about it."

Tiny took two strips of duct tape and stuck his lips through them. "Recognize me now, wise guy?"

The kid was big enough to have looked like The Body. The right shape, the right size, the right lips.

"No way."

"Yes, way," Turd Unit said. "Totally yes, way."

"But how did you even get him up there?"

Turd Unit snapped his fingers, and immediately all the kids jammed into action. Like a well-rehearsed machine, they had the big kid off his feet, ankles duct taped together and hanging from the pipe above the dryer in about nine seconds. The big kid smiled at Dalton, flipping him the double birds.

"But why? And how did you even know about that?"

"I've been reading your case files," Turd Unit said. "Duh! How hard do you think it was to crack into your lockbox? Anyway, we wanted to give you a test. See if you had any pearls. See how difficult a rival you're going to be while we're climbing up the clique chart. And you know what? I gotta say, big bro, the results are in, and we figure it's not going to be too hard. In fact, I think we pretty much just go straight to the top."

"Top of what?"

"We are Generation Terror," Turd Unit said.

"WE ARE GENERATION TERROR!" all the boys said as one, their little soprano voices in a frenzied pitch.

"You have to be effing kidding me."

Turd Unit walked over and calmly handed Dalton a piece of paper. It was blank except for the title and two boxes:

SALT RIVER HIGH
CLIQUE CHART

GENERATION TERRUR

Other Students

Dalton looked at his little brother quizzically.

"You cliques are old news," Turd Unit said, his flaming-red hair even more flaming than usual. "You've gotten fat and weak and corrupt. We are the next wave. Gen T's time has come, and you're either going to step off, or we're going to step you off. Plain and simple, we're taking over."

This time Dalton did laugh, but not for long. Thirty little faces looked at him somberly. Then Turd Unit pulled out a gun. A little gun in his little hand.

"What's my name?"

"Turd Unit."

"What's my *name*?" his little brother demanded again, raising the gun to point at Dalton.

"Okay, okay, Kirk."

"Kirk?"

"Sorry. Kirkland."

"Kirkland?"

"Sorry. Kirkland Rev! Your name is Kirkland Rev!"

"That's right," Turd Unit said. "Leader of Generation Terror."

Dalton stared at his little brother.

"SAY IT!"

"You are Kirkland Rev, leader of Generation Terror!"

"And this is my clique."

"And this is your clique!"

Turd Unit lowered his gun. He handed Dalton an index card. On it, in familiar block letters was written:

BANG! DUCK! OOPS, TOO LATE!

DUH.

Dalton stared with amazement.

"*You* were the one leaving me those notes?"

Turd Unit smiled. "Yup."

"But why?"

"I told you, I read your case files. You weren't connecting the dots. Plus, you know, I was bored. Mom says the doctor says I have ADD. You know what that stands for?"

"Attention Deficit Disorder?"

"No. It means Absolute Dictatorship, Dude. It means I was born to be in charge. And also, you know, sort stuff out."

"Uh, yeah, I can see that now."

"Good. I'm glad you're on board. Frankly, I wasn't so sure you'd be amenable."

"Listen, I have to go," Dalton said, feeling dizzy. "I have to meet a guy."

"Yeah, about this whole you leaving thing? I'm afraid we can't let you do that."

"*Let* me?"

"That's right."

"What are you going to do? Shoot your own brother?"

"No, I'm not."

Dalton couldn't deny feeling a sense of relief.

"But they are." Turd Unit snapped his fingers. Thirty little boys raised their arms and pointed thirty little identical guns.

"Holy shite, Turd Un...I mean Kirkland! Is your melon watered?"

"Sorry, big bro, but we can't allow our secret to get out until we're ready to make our move and consolidate power."

"What power?"

"I'm sorry, but there is no compromising with Gen T. It's in the rules."

"What rules?"

"The first rule of Generation Terror is there is no Generation Terror."

"Don't," Dalton said.

Turd Unit snapped his fingers again, and thirty little fingers pulled thirty little triggers.

Dalton closed his eyes. There was a loud series of bangs, point-blank. Dalton opened them to see thirty little lighters, with thirty little flames poking out.

"Oh my Bob."

Turd Unit burst out laughing. "Stiff Sheets carped his unders! Stiff Sheets carped his unders! Get him some soap! Get him a rag! Stiff Sheets carped his unders!"

All the little boys howled with laughter, holding their stomachs with their non-gun hands and clapping each other on the back, bumping knuckles and slapping five. Tiny brought out sticks and a big bag of marshmallows, and they all started roasting them at the end of their lighters.

"Man, I totally had you," Turd Unit said, rubbing tears from his eyes.

"You did, little dude. You really did."

"Mole told me all about your lighter trick at breakfast. Found these things for sale on the Internet. Got a great bulk deal. That guy's okay, you know it?"

"If by okay you mean dangerously psychotic, then, yeah, sure he is."

"So go to your thing," Turd Unit said, dismissing Dalton

with a wave. "We have to finish our meeting. And, anyway, you don't want to be late for your stupid college."

"Wait, how do you know about—" Dalton began, and then waved his hand in the same way. "Never mind."

He started up the stairs.

"Seriously, though?" Turd Unit called from below, his little face utterly deadpan. "I'm telling you, bro, in five years, we're totally going to rule Salt River High."

CHAPTER 32

WHEREVER YOU GO, THERE YOU ARE

Dalton parked his scooter at the mall, next to the enormous black Diktatorat LE. He walked in and sat on a bench across from Elisha Cook overlooking an elaborately cherubed fountain full of dank pennies.

"Right on time."

"Yes, sir."

"I take it everything with your...detainment is now sorted out? I hear Detective Estrada is facing some very serious charges."

"Unlike almost every other job I've ever worked, this one seems to have wrapped itself into a neat little ball."

"Except for Mr. Tarot?"

"How do you know about that?"

Elisha Cook tapped the newspaper neatly folded on his lap. The headline said YOUNG DRAC GETS AWAY WITH APPLIANCES.

"Yeah. I guess he was smart enough not to take all the stuff to the fake fence Hutch set up. They waited for him all night."

"Well, I'm sure it will resolve itself soon."

"Speaking of which. Thanks for bailing me out, or what-ever. Sorry I had to run off on you like that."

Elisha Cook sniffed. "It was...unexpected."

"Anyway, I've thought about it a lot."

"Thought about what?"

"I've decided I want to go to Harvard, after all."

"I see."

Dalton took a deep breath, relieved with the finality of it. "I'm ready to get out of this town, do something different. I'm ready to, you know, write."

"Ah, yes," Elisha Cook said. "The creative life."

"I've got a lot of ideas. New stories, characters. A new direction in style. I feel like I need to be pushed, you know? Like, out of my comfort zone? I mean, maybe even poetry. Really get out there and find my voice."

"The thing is—" Elisha Cook began, and then stopped.

Dalton waited. Some kids went by on skateboards. One of them gave Elisha Cook the finger. The fountain burbled. A security guard came by on a motorized scooter, eyeballed Dalton, and then eased away.

"The thing is—"

"You've pulled the scholarship, haven't you?"

Elisha Cook opened his mouth, but nothing came out.

"I guess I should have known it was too good to be true. Is it because of the arrest?"

"I haven't pulled the scholarship."

"Oh," Dalton said, with palpable relief. "That's, um. Great. So what then?"

Elisha Cook smoothed his mustache carefully. He cleaned his fingernails. Shoppers walked all around them, moms and daughters, dads and sons, all of them with bags full of stuff, vacuum-sealed and vacuum-packed.

"There is no scholarship."

Dalton sat back. He suddenly felt old and heavy, laden with rusty weights. He felt exhausted by the ridiculousness of having believed in it in the first place.

"There never was, was there?"

Elisha Cook sighed deeply. "I told you that I went to Salt River a number of years ago, did I not?"

"Yes, you did. And even a mediocre Dick would have made more of that information. He would have done a little research, instead of just hearing what he wanted to hear, lapping it up like a thirsty dog."

"Perhaps."

"So you're a Scam Wow? Or, what, you work some sort of bribe thing?"

Elisha Cook shook his head. "I do not want any money."

"Then what *do* you want?"

"Before my matriculation from Salt River, I was the leader of the Harvard Fauxs, a now-defunct clique."

"Fohs?"

"Fauxs. We were boys who went around telling everyone we knew that we'd been accepted to Harvard, when, in actuality, few of us had even applied. Let alone gotten accepted. That was the entirety of our racket. There was, of course, a competing Yale Fauxs."

"But why? Where's the percentage in that?"

"I'm still not sure. Nevertheless, as the years went by I seem to have kept up the pretense."

"So you don't work for Harvard at all?"

"I'm afraid not. In fact, I live right here in town. With my mother."

"Which is why you're always here. Instead of Massachusetts."

"Precisely."

"Again, something a decent Dick should have viewed with a shiteload more skepticism."

"I imagine so."

"You need to get yourself a white jacket," Dalton said. "You need to find a corner in a rubber room."

Elisha Cook nodded. "I have been, shall we say, extensively evaluated by psychology professionals over the last few decades."

In front of them, a little girl tripped and spilled her smoothie across the floor in a splash of red. She got up, bawling. A woman came over and yanked her by the hand, leaving the slick for someone else to deal with.

"The story of the world, is it not?" Elisha Cook observed. "Misfortune, tears, an evasion of responsibility. It's the math of the human condition. We just play it out again and again, in ways big and small."

"That's a fortune cookie," Dalton said. "Not a philosophy."

"Perhaps."

"Tell me how you got my application. I know my mother really mailed one."

"After the Fauxs disbanded for good, most of us moved to towns where Ivy League schools are. We got jobs working as waiters and clerks, telling people we were taking extension classes. We are all congenital liars, you see. And some, being better liars than I, managed to get jobs in various admissions offices. One such gentleman, a Woodrow F. Strode, sends me the names of young men and women who were rejected from our area."

"Then you go around pretending to offer them scholarships?"

"Sadly, yes."

"So I was rejected by the actual Harvard outright."

"Yes."

"I've been going nowhere all along."

"There's always community college. There's still time to apply."

Dalton closed his eyes, trying to get his head around it. "Looks like I'll be taking cases again."

"You do seem to be rather adept at it."

"And you seem to need some serious help."

"I do indeed. In fact, I was wondering if you were for hire."

Dalton stood, looking at Elisha Cook with disbelief.

"Please?" Cook said, the facade of erudition melting into a low sallow note. "Help me?"

"I can't. You need a whole team of Dicks to cure what you've got."

Elisha Cook nodded, his eyes misty.

In *Standing on the Marrow-Sucked Bones of Tomorrow*, Lex Cole had slapped at least two crying men. *It's possible*, Dalton thought, *that it's time to stop doing anything Lex Cole did.*

"If it helps," Elisha Cook said softly, "I truly did very much enjoy your stories."

Dalton ran his hand through his hair, shorter and closer

cropped, his new school cut. "You know what Voltaire once said?"

"No, what did Voltaire once say?"

"It's better to be stupid and French than just stupid. And, unfortunately, Mr. Cook, you're not French."

Dalton began walking toward the exit. He abruptly stopped, pulling something out of his waistband. Elisha Cook flinched, holding up his hands. Dalton pointed the notebook at him like a gun, said "Pow," and then tossed it onto his lap.

"What is this?" Elisha Cook asked, pulling off the rubber band that held the pages of the Private Dick Handbook together.

"Some rules to live by. Maybe you should study them."

Dalton turned again and walked toward the door.

"Where are you going? If I may be so bold as to ask."

"To the cemetery."

"What for?"

"I'm going to go pay my respects to Wesley Payne. As far as I can tell, he's the only one in Salt River who deserves them."

THE PRIVATE DICK HANDBOOK, FINAL RULE
They'll think you're crazy if you talk to the dead, but most of the time the dead are the only ones who listen.

THE GLOSSARY

Asshat |azz het|
noun
1. One of those insults that really has no meaning but for some reason just sorta feels right. Either that, or you're wearing Stetson pants.

Assy Assbourne |azzy azbourne|
person
1. Big-haired and hopelessly addled metal singer who used to front Black Sabbath but now spends most of his time as the intermittently coherent punch line of a truly depressing reality show. Rumored to have once bitten the head off a bat, a rumor that held no truth whatsoever but resulted in the sale of about nine million more albums than just wearing tight pants and makeup would have.

Barnaby Smollet |'burn u be smo let|
person
1. A notorious and long-standing member of London's Hellfire Club, Smollet is also the author of the marginally successful and many-volumed Lexington Cole detective series. Called an "infidel" and a "rake" by his literary nemesis, Percy Eaton-Hogg, Smollet seemed oblivious to both reviews and critique, happily churning out one Cole novel per year until the end of his life. The series, reviewed variously in the *Times* of London as "puerile slop," "books for people who hate to read," "the franchise that put *no more* in *moribund*," and "thoroughly distasteful brain static," still managed to find a reasonable, if hard to identify, readership.

Bebe Rebozo |'bee bee ra bozo|
person
1. Aside from Spiro Agnew, the most damningly and alliteratively named of the Watergate conspirators and their ilk. Rebozo was a financier up to his cleft in all things seamy during the long reign of Richard Nixon. They apparently went sailing together a lot. The name Spiro Agnew can be rearranged to spell Grow a Penis. The name Bebe Rebozo can be rearranged to spell Zoo Beer Ebb.

Bertolt Brecht |bert olt brekt|
person
1. The world's most boring and strident playwright, usually beloved by the world's most annoying and humorless theater professors.

Bitches Brew |beet chez broo|
noun
1. The seminal Miles Davis recording of 1970 that is now, in retrospect, almost universally agreed to have been the gravitational and theoretical nexus wherein

318

jazz, funk, and rock met in a throbbing hell-broth of grooving wail and spanky dissonance. Essentially the recording that ruined the music industry for just about everyone else, since in comparison they suddenly seemed relentlessly mediocre, if not outright inert. Akin to guzzling shellac just before being aurally trepanned. Of course, like anything truly original or challenging, it was widely hated at the time of its release.

Bite Me Totally Neckless |boit meh tot lee nik lus|
noun

1. The third volume in the populous and megaselling vampire series written by Fanny Moroni, *Neckless* is widely revered by generations of young girls and moms alike, from cheerleading to menopause. The series concerns the adventures of desperately beautiful but painfully shy tween vampire Jordan Schwartz and her search for eternal love. Or, at least the right sweater and something fun to do on Friday night.

Blackula |vlak ku-lah|
adjective

1. Having bushy and ludicrous sideburns, usually in conjunction with an unfortunate tendency to wear black.

Blah Blah Blagatha Christie |bla ga tha kris ti|
person

1. Mystery writer Agatha Christie's even less interesting older sister, Blagatha, wrote lots of books where a roster of plausibly guilty characters gather in a fireplace-laden room so the detective can explain why each didn't commit the crime, until the one who did pulls out a musket, and then the high-strung maid stabs him in the neck with a hat pin.

Bloshite |blow shy it|
adjective

1. Not true.
2. Patently false.
3. Complete carp.

Bolshevik |bhol sheff ic|
adjective

1. So old-school, it's ancient.

Bovine Spongiform |beau fine spong a ferm|
noun

1. Known as BSE, or mad cow, this neurodegenerative disorder is the better-documented cousin of lupine spongiform, or "werewolf dementia." Primarily the

result of factory farm profit vectors that include introducing pesticides, hormones, antibiotics, and the ground spinal tissue of other animals into the feed of cows, otherwise primarily herbivores. The lupine version is mostly a result of preferring Jacob to Edward and is most frequently seen among fervid preteen girls driven to "were-distraction," in which they forget to bathe, refuse to eat, deflect pointed questions, and sit on their beds in a numb haze for entire summers staring at the phases of the ripening moon.

BoxxMart |bahks murt|
place
1. Need a seventy-five–pound barrel of Mexican pretzels? Need a tube of Meatless Snack Paste the size of a dachshund? In the market for a nine-piece set of chrome Celery Mounts? BoxxMart, known on the street as "Boxxie M's," is your place.

Burger Barn |boo gah bahn|
place
1. The home of That Phat Burger, Farmer Ed's Field Chum, Duck Nougat, and Triple-Dipped Dipping Tails. Also, a gratuitous previous book in-joke for detail nerds, reference geeks, and conspiracy dorks. Is Chad Chilton the manager? He will be once Whimple gets the can.

Caesar |'seēz ər|
person
1. Someone who thinks they're in power, when they aren't or don't deserve to be.
2. Caesar, Gaius Julius (100–44 BC); Roman statesman or something.

Calculus |'kalk yə ləs|
noun
1. The classroom process during which Stained Sweatshirt continually makes fun of Always Raises His Hand, to the point that Hand-Raiser stops volunteering answers and draws in the margins of his textbook for the rest of the semester, while Stained Sweatshirt settles into a newfound sense of purpose.
2. Mathematics & logic: a particular method or system of calculation or reasoning.

Carcassed |'kar kised|
adjective
1. In big trouble. Screwed. Doomed. In some cases denoting actually having been stomped to jelly.

Cardigan |kar degg in|
noun — pejorative
1. A preppy fish stick.

Carp |'kar pe|

adjective

1. Not particularly believable.
2. Bloshite.

Cary Grant |kery grent|

person

1. Famous actor whose real name was Archibald Leach. His characters spent a lot of time rooting around in George Washington's nose at Mount Rushmore. Known to run sort of cockeyed and look good in a suit. The only man in the history of cinema for whom the words *debonair*, *mid-Atlantic*, *screwball*, *leathery*, *constipated*, *virile*, and *hat-tastic* all apply in equal measure.

Casket of Amontadildo |'kes ket av a mont a del doe|

noun

1. Where Eddie Allan Poe hid his battery-operated implements.

Catwalk Ninja |'khat wulk nhyn jhuh|

noun

1. Don't stare. Don't make any quick movements. Do not touch her leather skirt. If she says move, move. If she says eat your own nose paste, eat your own nose paste. Her name is Jenny. Your name is Mudd.

Charlie Sheen |chur lee she|

person; adjective

1. The worst of a bad lot of Sheens, this uniquely American monument to wasted opportunities, rampant narcissism, bad acting, chin overload, the horrors of nepotism, and smug satisfaction continues to lower the bar of a cultural discourse that already thinks *So You Think You Can Dance* is a form of philosophical inquiry. And yet, oddly, Sheen-*fils* does provide an almost Intelligently Designed, perfectly banal yin to Jon Cryer's neutered post-Duckie yang every Monday night on CBS. If there's two men there, it's a mystery to this viewer, but it's certainly clear whose nub provides the extra half. As the jowly Colonel Kurtz says to young Martin Sheen after a long journey into the darkness that is the Nung River: "All things come to pass and all debts are ultimately paid." In this case, that probably means a half hour in a small room with Denise Richards.

Cheater |chē tər|

noun

1. Any kind of handgun, especially one that's easily concealed.
2. A person who acts dishonestly in order to gain an advantage.

Chernobyl |cher no bill|
place
1. See, what happened was, the Russkies got a little lazy with the safety protocols at one of their nuclear plants and then the whole thing sort of overheated and had to be covered with about a million tons of concrete to avoid irradiating most of northern Europe and then President Reagan had to get sort of mad about it and insist they start paying as much attention to the fissile coolant as they do importing crates of knock-off Levis.

Chitty Chitty |chit ee chit ee|
adjective/noun
1. A dangerous place where lots of shooting happens.
2. Dick Van Dyke's favorite car.
3. *Chitty Chitty Bang Bang.*

Cinnabon |sin hey bahn|
adjective
1. Someone with a posterior of oceanic movement and breathtaking dimension. Example sentence: "Holy shite, did you see the junk Inference is dragging around in that red dress? She walks like two hogs fighting in a grocery bag! Homegirl is one grade-A Cinnabon!"

The Clash |da klash|
noun
1. The only band that matters.
2. Immediately and illegally download every single one of their songs (except "Rock the Casbah") over a peer-to-peer file sharing network now.
3. When the record company lawyers start hammering at your downstairs door, tell them "Only knobs pay cash for the Clash!" Guaranteed to stand up in court.

Cobra Cobretti |koh bra ko bret ee|
person
1. Just another classic role in the long and storied Stallone pantheon. Cobretti is so effing tough, and has so much bristly stubble, that he almost manages to act his way into Brigitte Nielsen's leather pantsuit—but then some cannibal biker stabs him, in the provolone.

Cosmonaut |kas mo not|
noun
1. A Russian astronaut. Or a monkey in a Sputnik. Or a girlie cocktail with a nautical theme.

Crackstar |krak stər|
noun
   1. A person who makes sarcastic jokes or insults, and does it very well, i.e, "cracking wise."

The Crunge |krunj|
noun
   1. The name for that look on your face when you ask someone what they do for a living and they say, "I'm a writer," and you say, "A writer?" and they say, "Yeah. I mean, I take care of people's cats, but I also write plays," and then you say, "Plays?" and they say, "Yeah," and you say, "About what?" and they say, "Cats."

Dagwoodie |'dag, whoŏ dee|
noun
   1. Mortifyingly having to hold your biology textbook in front of your jeans when a Foxx walks by.
   ALTERNATE:
   1. Throwing a rodney.
   2. Steve Winwood cover art.

Dangle |'dayn gul|
noun—pejorative
   1. Someone hard to love.

D'Artagnan |'dee are tan yan|
person
   1. French guy who was hell with a cutlass and also really knew how to haybale a wench. The fourth Musketeer.

Deano at the Copa |'dee know at da co pah|
noun
   1. Dean "Deano" Martin was a singer your grandmother probably loved, who sang like he was doing an impersonation of a life-sized martini glass gargling pomade. The Copacabana was an old-school nightclub in Manhattan where Pacinos and Goodfellas and Sopranos of every stripe hung out and left bad tips for the hatcheck girls.

Death of a Salesman |'deth off a cels mun|
noun
   1. A play about Willy Loman, famous sad sack, written by Arthur Miller, famous husband of numerous blonds.

Dick Flavor | 'deck flah vah |
noun
1. The type of Private Dick you would prefer to hire.

Diego Rivera | 'die ay goh riff er a |
person
1. Iconic Mexican painter, muralist, and avowed Communist. This, of course, was back when being a Communist meant you supported the right of your sharecropper uncle to own a tractor. Rivera was known to render a mustache in fresco now and again, as well as having notoriously big appetites. He also liked to knock out the occasional mural with his wife, Frida Kahlo, who was relatively unknown until the mid-nineties, when she enjoyed an inexplicable renaissance in the form of refrigerator magnets, dorm calendars, farmers' market T-shirts, and ironic postcards.

Diktatorat LE | 'deck tah tah rat el ee |
noun
1. Long, sleek, and black, the Diktatorat LE sedan is the preferred vehicle of third-world dictators, elderly Polish émigrés, the hearse-obsessed, and those wishing for personal or political reasons to average under six miles to the gallon.

Disco Atomic | 'dees ko a tom ek |
noun
1. A girl so unbelievably smoking that she makes nearly any guy within a hundred-mile radius of her radiance immediately come to the brute realization that he's spent his life foolishly and without true reward.
2. Disco rodney.

Dongtower | 'dahng t'wer |
noun
1. A mythical place from which the obviously self-satisfied look down upon their lessers.

Dragon Rider Series | drag ann rhi dah ser es |
noun
1. They're dragons! They're scaly! They breathe fire! They knock stuff over with their tails! Some of them are really wise! Some of them are evil! Sooner or later the wise ones are approached in their mountain lairs by some cloak-y dude with a long white beard and gnarled staff about coming together to fight a common evil, and then a dashing young prince kills the dragon that wears an eye patch with an amazing arrow shot, and then all the little elves in the village dance around the fire except the surly, fat, comic relief elf, who sits under a tree swilling grog from a pewter stein while mumbling rude things into his multiple chins.

Dr. Phil |dok tah fil|

person

1. Who gives advice anymore, anyhow? Do this, do that. Tell her you like her casserole. Tell him his snoring doesn't bother you. Recent polls show that 97 percent of Americans say we should form a mob, storm Dr. Phil's Pedantic Advice Castle with torches, shave his mustache, rub him down with pork fat, and then throw him into a moat teeming with starving piranhas. Want some advice, Doc? Use the aerodynamics of that waxed head to help you swim faster.

Easter Island |'e stah ah lant|

place

1. Also known as Rapa Nui, this island is farther from any other landmass than anywhere else on Earth, which is excellent in and of itself. Add to that the fact that the island is ringed with massive carved stone statues of bemused heads? Awesome. The statues are so big, it's almost impossible to imagine how the indigenous tribespeople could have moved them into place with Stone Age tools. Like, it almost had to be aliens. Or Kirk. Or Khan. Either way, it makes for the best episode of *In Search Of* since the one about Bigfoot.

Ed Lecter |ed lek tah|

person

1. Hannibal the Cannibal's older brother, known on the streets alternately as "Ed the Marrow fed" or "Eddie the Transfusion-ready," Lecter *frère aîné* owns a small bar in downtown LA called The Overlook Pub and Single Girl's Disappearing Place that enjoys a certain renown for its affordable tapas menu. A notorious wearer of argyle-scented cologne, Ed is said to regularly forget young Hannibal on the family's Secret Santa list. His lone film credit comes from a small role in the Cannes-feted indie darling *Blood Guzzling Stranger II: Welcome to Conveniently Isolated Summer Camp.*

Em Effer |ehm f ah'|

noun—pejorative

1. [trans.] Mother Copulator.

Entrenched |en 'tren ched |

verb

1. [trans.] To be in a long-term and pointless relationship, usually since the first week of school, with a guy or girl who stopped even bothering to look good since you're there pretty much every day and there's no one left to impress.

The Fack Cult T |duh fa cult ee|

noun

1. The name of the clique of teachers, administration, and school staff. All teachers are Fack Cult, but some are more Fack than others.

Farck, Farcking, Farcker |'phark|
adjective, noun, verb, adverb, you name it
1. What do you think it means? Grow a sac already.

Fat Man and Little Boy |'phat mun n lee tle boi|
noun
1. The names of the two bombs dropped on the civilian populations of Hiroshima and Nagasaki respectively.

Feedback Queen |fheet bak kween|
noun
1. Half-hippie, half-metal kid who likes long screechy guitar solos and thinks anything even vaguely resembling a melody or chorus is a total sellout.

Fish Stick |'fish ˌstik|
noun—pejorative
1. A total stiff, loser, bore.

Flavor Flavah |'flay vo flay va|
noun
1. A brand of clear, inorganic syrup used as a taste booster and general food topping. Slogan: "The Natural Flavor Enhancer!" Claims to have no trans fats despite the fact that it's 93 percent trans fat and 96 percent bacon-based. Somewhat famous for its desperately catchy advertising jingle: "Put it on cereal, put it on toast, put it on anything Mom shoves in front of you most! *Flavor, flavor, flavor, flay-vah!*"
2. Cousin of that guy who wore a big clock around his neck.

Folding Green |'foal d'n ghreen|
noun
1. Cash. Money. Dinero. Moolah. Smackers. Simoleons. Franklins. Filthy lucre. Cheese. Pesos.

"Freebird" |'frē burt|
noun
1. "Freebird" is the title of a song. The band that played it is still touring, even though they all died in a plane crash in 1977. This seeming contradiction does not change the fact that for years there was always someone in a crowd at any given show who would yell out "FREEBIRD!" either ironically or with genuine hope, mostly because it's sort of a twenty-six–minute hillbilly onanistic solo-jam extravaganza. And also because people holding six-dollar lite beers tend not to be particularly original.

Free Range | 'fuh rhee rayn juh |
adjective
1. Braless (applies to all females and certain mansiere males).

From Crayons to Perfume | 'fram kray enz tu perfume |
phrase
1. Oh my Bob, did I, your minimum-wage glossary-entry writer, have a crush on Lulu back in the day. Yeah, Lulu, who sings the theme song of *To Sir, with Love*. Sidney Poitier acts in that one, playing the cool teacher who connects with the tough inner-city kids, but Lulu, man, up on that table belting it out? It was instant sheer love. "From crayons to perfume" is the best line in the song.

Full of Spleens | 'fu lah splah en ez |
adjective
1. Not telling the truth.
2. Packed with extra internal organs.

Gat | 'ghat |
noun
1. A gun.

Get Ventilated | ghet 'vent hil at ed |
verb
1. To take a bullet. To be shot. To open some extra breathing room through the miracle of random ballistics. Hey, remember that movie *Ballistic: Ecks vs. Sever*? Man, not only was that movie really, really stupid, it also made no sense at all. Even the title is hopelessly convoluted and annoying. The feeling here is that Antonio Banderas was never a good idea in general.

Get Your Nose Open | 'ghit yer nos op enn |
phrase
1. Be overly interested in, have a crush on, head over heels over and unwilling to listen to reason about.

Gimcracks | 'jim krakz |
noun
1. Cheap jewelry. Baubles and bric-a-brac.

Glark | 'gah lurk |
adjective
1. The sound your throat makes when something's caught deep in there, like, say, a dried gob of Flavor Flavah. Or the words "I love you too, Mom." Or, like, "Hey, thanks for putting me through college, Grandpa." But, also, when the girls are

practicing with the carrots in the Ridgemont High cafeteria. Or when that guy you know with eyes like a dead haddock decides he's going to show off by eating three cheeseburgers before you've even finished half your pimento loaf, and then you think he's joking when he turns purple but after a while you realize the burgers got caught in his throat, but you don't do anything except stare, and Haddock keeps going *glark...glark...glark*, and then that weird kid who hasn't said four words since fourth grade rushes over and gives Haddock the Heimlich and a long tube of undigested cheese-bun comes out of him whole and he breathes with relief, and then people clap and someone does a story about Silent One in the school paper and two months later he ends up going to the prom with that ridiculously hot Finnish girl just because he was the one who got up off his ham and acted first.

Godot |'gah doh|
person
1. *Who you gonna call?* No, wait, that's not it. *Who you waiting for?* Yeah, that's the one. Venkman? No, Beckett. The Stay Puft Marshmallow Man? No, French existentialism.

Grow a Sac |'groh uh sak|
phrase
1. Man up. Cowboy up. Be courageous. Get 'er done. Stop whining. Tough it out. Have some stones. Rub some mud on it and get back in there, son.

Guernica |'gwere nee ka|
noun
1. Picasso's famous painting about the bombing of civilians in the small Basque town of Guernica during the Spanish Civil War.

Hand Gallop |'hä nud gal urp|
noun
1. What they used to say would give boys hair on their palms. Or make them go blind.
   ALTERNATE: **Tongue Gallop** |'tahng gal urp|
1. Take a guess. Rhymes with *flow knob*.

Hedda Lettuce |hed uf 'let is|
noun, *Lactuca sativa*
adjective—pejorative
1. Not very smart.
2. Hedda Hopper's less talented sister.

Hong Kong Phooey |häng käng 'pfhoo ee|
adjective
1. Describing a situation that goes totally haywire and ends poorly for everyone.

Huffed Up |'hof ed ap|
verb
1. Confronted. Stood up to.

Insertable |en ser ta bahll|
adjective—pejorative
1. A total probe.

Jett Rink |zhet rink|
person
1. James Dean's character in *Giant*, who possibly sported the coolest hair in celluloid history.

Jimmy Hoffa |'jee mee huff uh|
person
1. Former Teamsters boss whose body and head disappeared and will almost certainly never be found. He's rumored to have been deconstructed and then poured into the concrete footprint of Giants Stadium in the Meadowlands, New Jersey. Apparently, he pretty much thought he was indispensable among people for whom he was pretty dispensable, especially Aldo "Two Times" Carnesecca and Morty "The Hatchet Killer" Bastrianno.

Joe "Mama" Besser |'yo ma ma bess a|
person
1. Legendary drummer who spontaneously combusted onstage.

Joe Strummer |'jo stram ur|
person
1. Lead singer and guitar player for The Clash. Don't like him because you think liking him somehow makes you cool by association, LOVE him because loving him makes you want to find a length of lead pipe and smash your TV into tiny non-VH1 bits.

Johnny Rambo |'jon e ram bo|
person
1. Provolone Stallone at his leanest and meanest. First, he saved a small town from Brian Dennehy's appetite, and then he saved eighties-Vietnam from a dangerous influx of fairness, intelligence, and historical perspective. It turns out, ideologically, steroids are more effective than Communism. "He'll eat things that'll make a billy goat puke."

Judas |'zhu das|
person
1. Dude got a bad rap, was apparently only following orders.

Ka-Ra-Tay |kah rhuh tay|
noun
1. The way you're supposed to pronounce *karate*. Mostly stands for all the different iterations of the martial arts, but tends only to really work in the movies and on your eight-year-old cousin.

Knob |nhob|
noun—pejorative
1. Relative of the nub. Impugning of size. Not needing any extra space in the front of your 501's.

Krispy Kreme |kree spy kreeme|
noun
1. The Donut's donut. A big, steaming, massive, calorie-packed, deep-fried, sugary wad of oil-soaked dough that is occasionally also stuffed with lardy custard. People drive across state lines for these babies, buy a couple dozen at a time, and then scarf hard, washing them down their muscular esophogi with 128 ounces of Mountain Dew. Not recommended for diabetics, the ripped-abs crowd, or those likely to be bothered by the ethics of eating something which, if lit on fire and hooked up to a generator, would slowly release enough kinetic energy to power most of Eastern Illinois for a month. **See also: Cinnabon.**

Krugerrand |crew gur end|
noun
1. A one-ounce gold coin minted in South Africa and known to be popular among thieves, embezzlers, derivatives traders, and Nevada politicians; since they have no set value, each coin's worth is directly tied to the overall bullion market.

LeadWig Wittgenstein |led wig wit gen styn|
person
1. The very dumb finger-sniffing younger brother of famed Viennese philosopher and author of *Tractatus Logico-Philisophicus* Ludwig Wittgenstein. Rumored to have invented Snausages.

Lesser |'lhez zer|
noun
1. Just what it sounds like, as in "You are my lesser, and I will now treat you as such."

Level of Suck | 'leh vul ahf suk |
noun
1. A quantifiable, mathematical scale rating based on the internationally used one-to-ten formula enabling disparate parties to find common ground in their assessment of a person, place, or thing.

Lexington Cole | 'lehx n' tan koal |
noun
1. A briefly popular but now mostly obscure fictional detective who helmed a poor-selling but long-lived series of cheap pulp novels read mostly by winos, grifters, vacuum salesmen, and the sort of lifetime academics who make a career decrying the dearth of good literature in public. Lexington Cole is known mostly for his biting cynicism, bare-knuckled pugilistic skills, world-weary womanizing, and impeccably ironed slacks. Among the most popular titles in the hundred-odd-volume series were: *Rubble Blood Clang*, *The Ventimingian Caper*, *Her Shark Is Worse Than Her Bite*, and *You'll Never Die on My Watch Again*.

Lorenzo Lamas | lur en za lam a |
person
1. Oh, the hair. Oh, the ropy guns. Oh, the acting chops. He was awesome on *T.J. Hooker*. What do you mean, What's *T.J. Hooker*? It's the cop show that destroyed Shatner's girdle. What do you mean, *Who's Shatner*? He's the guy who defeated Khan and also yelled it repeatedly. What do you mean, *Who's Khan*? He's the wrath-filled waxed chest played by Ricardo Montalban. **See: Adrian Zmed.**

Lurid | 'loŏr id |
adjective
1. Unbelievably and utterly cool.

The *Lusitania* | loŏ si tā nya |
noun
1. A passenger boat in the Cunard line torpedoed by the German navy in 1915, considered the instrumental act in bringing the United States into WWI. Most historians agree that it was an absolute tragedy the German navy didn't have the aesthetic wherewithal to torpedo Leo DiCaprio while he was standing on the bow of the *Titanic* instead.

Mad Max | med mex |
movie
1. Possibly the greatest movie ever made. You got Mel Gibson, back when he was young and not totally batshite, going totally batshite after these mean killer

331

bikers who sort of nonchalantly kill his family, and then he chases them all across the Australian outback with a big black car and eventually runs a few of them over a couple of times. The bad guys' names are the Toecutter, the Night Rider, and Johnny the Boy. Isn't that enough? The sequel to this film, where the scariest guy in the whole movie wears assless leather pants and feathers on his shoulder pads, is called *The Road Warrior*.

Marshall Stack |mur shel steck|
noun
1. The Marshall company makes really, really loud amps. If you balance a head on top of a couple of really large speakers, there's your stack. Picture Jimi Hendrix standing in front of a wall of amps. Picture your eardrums blown out in the seventy-sixth row.

Melon Watered |mel un wha turd|
verb [trans.]
1. Taking a hard one to the skull.

Middle East Front |'med dle est frant|
noun
1. Pretty much from Oman to Algeria, and all terrorist strongholds in between. We need to fight them there, so that we don't have to fight them here, on the streets of downtown Akron.

Milton Friedman |mil ton freed man|
person
1. King of the Chicago school of economic theorists/imperialists, he brought his own dispassionate brand of shock-monetism to Chile under the dictator/torturer Augusto Pinochet. Not only did he put the laissez in laissez-faire, he died wholly uncomeuppanced. Not to mention rich.

Mission Proboscis Brown |meh shun prob az iz brun|
noun
1. Euclidians and other hand raisers who have their nose so far up Fack Cult's T that they've actually come full circle and are now sort of giving them a hard time.

Moloko Milk Bar |'mal ak o milk bah|
place
1. Where Alex hangs out to listen to Beethoven.
2. The place guys who name their bands after any phrase in *A Clockwork Orange* should be permanently incarcerated.

Mr. Tibbs |mist ah tibs|
person
1. Sidney Poitier played him in the great sixties movie *In the Heat of the Night,* a movie in which Archie Bunker is a sorta likeable villain, and Sidney is one serious badass who's all like "You better call me Mr. Tibbs, and you better mean it!" Yes, we are aware that there is a glut of Sidney Poitier references in this glossary.

Nymphette |'nihm fett|
person
1. Cousin of Boba Fett. Runs a little corner grocery on Dagobah.

Occam's Razor |ok hams ray zor|
noun
1. A crusty old dude who said "When you have two ideas, the simpler one is better." Sure, it's obvious now, but this is back when people were still eating raw chicken with their dirty fingers and thought sneezing was a way to expel the devil, or at least an allergic reaction to a Dave Matthews violin solo.

One-Cheek Sneak |'wan chik snik|
noun
1. Thinking you're going to cut a silent one during the chem test and letting go of more than you planned.
ALTERNATE:
1. Carped Your Unders.

On the Scuff |ahn thuh skəf|
adjective
1. Running a tab, getting credit, owing money.

On the Slum |'ahn thuh sluh muh|
adjective [attrib.]
1. Girls from higher-end cliques hanging out at parties with guys a few rungs down the ladder.

Packing a Saint |pok ing uh saynt|
adjective
1. Pregnant.

Perv Idols |'purv ah dos|
noun
1. Possibly the best underground band of the early nineties, led by hipster poster boy and antigrunge icon Ely Kyburg, who plays drums, scat, yella rock, screaming

leads, and carnival rhymes. Best song is "Courtney Hole." Second-best song is "Necrofeelyouup."

The Pesterton Boys Young Gentlemen's Tales |'pest ur ton boyz|
title
1. A much beloved middle-grade book series that follows the travails of brothers Joey and Jimmy Pesterton as they solve crimes and undertake capers in the small town of Plock's Mill, Iowa. While derided by some as "a neutered fifties anachronism," and "books that made me long for autism," the Pestertons still enjoy brisk sales while continuing to find lost cats, thwart mustachioed traveling salesmen, and helping the owner of the Plock's Mill Five 'n' Dime identify shoplifters.

Phallick |fal ich|
adjective
1. Shaped like what your sister's Ken doll isn't sporting.

Pinkertons |'penk u tonz|
noun
1. The Pinkerton National Detective Agency. A firm that made its name by foiling a plot to assassinate President Lincoln, the Pinkertons became the group of choice to be used as strikebreakers against miners and farmers and other such groups who had the audacity to demand wages and food and a slightly amended on-the-job death rate. The early antecedent of Blackwater.

Pinky Tuscadero |'peen key tusk er der a|
person
1. Never heard of Fonzie? It's just as well. Pinky was the Fonz's girlfriend on *Happy Days*, this show that was on TV forever back when your mom was still enthralled with the first Boston album. Pinky wore pink leather hot pants and drove cars in Smash-up Derbys and got killed or something in this one episode that coincided with her getting dropped from the show.

Pleather |'pleh thah|
noun
1. Plastic-feeling imitation leather that was popular among hipster college students, drag queens, hungry artists, and ironic punks. If you see some in a thrift store, snap it up at any price; it's coming around again soon.

Pompadour |'pom poo door|
noun
1. Sort of the hair Fonzie wore; a big greasy flip-up of slicked locks that Elvis rocked hard and no one really has since except the Stray Cats and Governor Blago.

President Forehead |pre sa dent fo het|
person
1. He was a male cheerleader at Yale but managed to make an entire country think he was a regular southern dude by buying a million-dollar ranch in Texas and cutting a lot of brush with a chain saw while gullible reporters took pictures. Then he went and played a round of golf, betting Rummy twenty bucks a hole that the gopher in *Caddyshack* was real.

Private Dick |prhy vatt dik|
noun
1. A detective for hire.

Probe |'pah rha obe|
adjective—pejorative
1. Completely insertable.

Prodigal Son |'prah dag al sun|
noun
1. Remember how your older brother Kirk slammed the porch door and took off with all his stuff crammed into the back of his Toyota hatchback and lived in San Francisco for a few years without ever once calling Mom, and then out of nowhere returned and moved into the attic room and started mowing the lawn without being asked and suddenly it was like he and Dad could sit and watch painfully ironic hospital shows with Zach Braff in them and not have raging arguments about the remote anymore? Well, Kirk is prodigal.

Proust |prust|
person
1. A Remembrance of Smaller Glossaries Past.
2. Marcel Proust is a famous French writer, mostly famous for being a hip reference in the *New Yorker* or punch line in Woody Allen movies, but who no one actually ever reads anymore. His stuff is pretty dense. Old Marcel is also sort of famous for almost never getting out of bed, which leaves plenty of time for scarfing freedom fries and fey rumination.

Pull Your Coat |pul yhor koat|
verb
1. Explain something, give information, show the ropes.

Purse |pərs|
noun—pejorative
1. A whiny little pussy, crier, snitch, or mommy-boy.
2. A sum of money given as a prize in a sporting contest, esp. a boxing match.

ALTERNATE: **Murse** |mers|
1. A "man purse."

Rasputin |'raz pew tahn|
person
1. The "Mad Monk." This Russian mystic was rumored to have supernatural powers and is thought to have heavily influenced Czar Nicholas II to the point of bringing down the Romanov dynasty. Rent *Anastasia* for further research. "R-dog," as he was known by the Russian peasantry, was stabbed, shot, and poisoned by his many detractors, but survived. Eventually, a group of nobles drowned him in the freezing Neva River, but some people think it didn't really take.

Readers of the Beats |rəa drz a thu beehts|
noun
1. Guys who carry around copies of *On the Road* or well-thumbed Ginsberg chapbooks in an attempt to appear deep and enigmatic.
ALTERNATE: **Yawners of the Beats**
2. Those not falling for flashy literary tricks or the notion of profundity through addled spelling and bad grammar.

Ricardo Montalban |rik ur doh mun la ben|
person
1. **See: Lorenzo Lamas**.

Rimwipe |'rhim why pah|
adjective—pejorative
1. A less than stellar personality.

Rita Moreno |'rē tuh mer en oh|
person
1. She won a Best Supporting Actress Oscar in the Natalie Wood version of *West Side Story* but distinguished herself in several saucy stints on the ultimate down-on-his-luck-private-dick TV show, *The Rockford Files*.

The Rubicon |rhoo ba conn|
place
1. The stream in northeast Italy marking the boundary between Italy and Cisalpine Gaul, which Julius Caesar and his troops crossed, violating Roman law and plunging Rome into civil war.
2. Also, a great name for a car shaped like a fat little boy. Introducing the new Ford Rubicon coupe! *It's perfectly round so you don't have to be!*

Rumpus |rhum phus|
noun
1. Commotion, action, problem, beef.

Rush Soda |rhush tso da|
noun
1. Uncredited but highly sought-after homemade beverage. Usually found in reused water bottles or sports-drink containers with the labels ripped off. Utterly caffeinated beverage that appears to be more caffeine than beverage. Typically has *RUSH!* written on it in black Sharpie. Rumored to be addictive. In a good way.

Saipan |'cy pen|
place
1. The largest island in the Northern Marianas archipelago.

Sheer Gravy |shir gray vee|
noun
1. Largesse. Free stuff. Extra goodness you didn't expect.

Shibboleth |'chib o luth|
noun
1. A word used to verbally test the identity of spies, soldiers, or foreigners. If you're a night sentry and someone approaches your post, for example, you might say, "What is the frequency, Kenneth?" not because you thought the soldier on the other side would actually know the frequency, but because if he cannot correctly pronounce *Kenneth* without an accent, you start shooting. The word *lollapalooza* was often used by American soldiers as a shibboleth during WWII.

Shorthairs |'schort airz|
noun
1. Those which one should neither pluck nor shave, but by which one may, in the end, be dragged around.

Sitting on Your Ham |sett in' on yah hem|
phrase
1. Being lazy. Coasting. Parking your donk at the end of the bench and refusing to move. Trading up three jeans sizes in one semester. Ordering a pair of McGriddles to go with your order of four McGriddles. Flipping channels. Chillaxin'. Adding a few more broken lamps to the pile of junk that's already flowing out of your big ol' steamer trunk.
ALTERNATE: **"Get up off of that ham right now, young lady, and come help swab your brother!"**

Sleep with Danger (Mother May I?) |sle pah wif dan jur|
phrase
1. Oh my Bob, Tori was so good in that.
2. Doing something outrageous and possibly illegal.

Slide |slīd|
verb (past: slid|slid|) [intrans.]
1. Sex.
2. Move along a smooth surface while maintaining continuous contact. Ex: *Same thing.*

Snooper |cnu puhr|
noun—pejorative
1. A guy who sneaks into your room and goes through your drawers, finds something embarrassing, and shows it to everybody.
ALTERNATE: **Creeper** |kree puhr|
1. A guy who sneaks into your room, goes through your drawers, finds your underwear, and keeps it. Also see: Fat man on Internet chatting as goth girl named Kendra who just got in a big fight with her stepmom about navel piercings.

The Snouts |'sah knout|
noun
1. Cops. See also: Police, Fuzz, Le Flic, the Man, the Filth, Pigs, Po-lice, Five-O, the Constabulary, the Federales, Johnny Law.
ALTERNATE: **The Snout Huts** |'sah knout hyut|
noun
1. Cop shop. Po-lice station. Downtown. The lockup. The brig. The stripey hole. Attica. The cooler. Inside. Suge's pad. The Turkish bath. Motel Six years without parole. The pokey. Maximum.

"The Spanish Inquisition" |spensh qui sitsh un|
noun
1. A skit by the comedy troupe Monty Python rumored to be based on a real historical event, where Cardinal Ximenez tortures someone with a dish rack and a "comfy chair." If you ask your uncle Morty about it this Thanksgiving, he will immediately launch into the world's worst English accent and recite all the dialogue from memory, causing not a single person to laugh, and resulting in Aunt Alice storming into the kitchen to eat her way through an entire tray of leftover Stove Top Stuffing.

Spinderella |speen da rhel la|
noun
1. A girl with a reputation for lying, thus giving you "the spin."
ALTERNATE: **Spinderfella** |speen da fel la|

1. A politically correct inclusion of the reverse gender slur that no one actually ever uses, but will make certain people feel better. Or at least less likely to sue.

Splashbox |'splash bôcks|
noun
1. Bathroom.
ALTERNATE: **Lungbox** |lǝng bôcks|
noun
1. A splashbox people are known to smoke in.

Sploets |'spah low etz|
noun
1. Guys who write haiku about the Super Bowl and odes to the '27 Yankees.
Ex:
Joltin' Joe hit the ball
And then ran so very fast
His team scored and then they
Won

Stanley Kubrick |coo brook|
person
1. Notoriously perfectionist film director who made a handful of films that count among the greatest of all time. *The Shining*, in which an old hotel's elevator doors repeatedly open to release thousands of gallons of blood, is essentially a series of indelibly frightening images some writers are relegated to carrying around for a lifetime as a result of having seen it at far too young an age. Poor Scatman Crothers gets it at the end. He could easily also have been named Catman Scrothers.

Stylish |'stī lish|
adjective
1. The opposite of its usual meaning, typically said with acid irony.

Take a Sniff |tek uh shniff|
verb
1. Leave quickly. Being told to leave.

Tear a New Clasp |tare ah nu klasp|
verb
1. To lay into someone verbally, or dress someone down.

Thank Bob |thuh anq bhap|
phrase
    1. What you say when you want to lard some appreciation on a higher power, but realize it's probably not something that's important enough to bother the deity with. "Thank Bob, you remembered to bring the mayonnaise."
    ALTERNATE: **"Oh my Bob!"**

Tuned Up |twooned op|
verb
    1. Given a beating.

Tunguska Event |ton gus cah iv int|
noun
    1. An explosion in Siberia in 1908 that knocked down 80 million trees over 2,200 square miles and is thought to have had five times the power of a thermonuclear bomb. While most scientists agree the blast came from a meteorite or comet, there are those who think the source was alien, with a Heavy Raider crash being the most frequently espoused theory. If that is the case, the blast is more than 74 percent likely to have been Cylon in nature.

Uddersuck |uh der sahk|
adjective—pejorative
    1. Really, really bad.

The Velvet Underground |vev et un dah grund|
noun
    1. The band for people who think every other band blows. These people are pretty much right. Hey, man, they had a female drummer in 1965.

Vines |vhines|
noun
    1. Nice clothes.
    1. A ridiculously sharp outfit.

Voltaire |volt air|
person
    1. François-Marie Arouet (November 21, 1694–May 30, 1778). Quite possibly the coolest, funniest, most bad-arse French Enlightenment figure you've never heard of. The original crackstar. Seriously, everyone should have a Voltaire poster above his bed.

War Paint |whoor paynt|
noun
    1. Makeup. Usually tending to be on the heavy side.

Where's the Opera? |'warez thuh hop rah|
phrase
  1. What's your hurry?
     ALTERNATE: **Who's Singing Opera?** |whoze cing ing hop rah|
     phrase
  1. What's the big rush?

Whiskey Lick |whus kee lek|
noun
  1. The state of being way too hot.

Why Can't You People Understand What I'm *Going Through*?
|y kent u pe ple un ne stan wha I gone throo|
phrase
  1. After many, many years of study, like a demi-glace made from boiling down
     thousands of meat bones into a delicate spoonful of complimentary sauce, this
     sentence has been scientifically proven to be the single phrase in which the
     entirety of the awkward, mortifying, painful, hormonal, vain, transparent, over-
     weight, undersexed, and ultimately ludicrously impossible experience *that is
     human adolescence* can be distilled.

Wilson Pickett |'wul sen pek et|
person
  1. Shake that thing. The man who put *raw* in *raw*. The man who put *raspy* in *raspy*.
     The man who put *soul* in *soul*. Stax of wax. Download him now.

Yalta |yahl tah|
place
  1. Where Donna Summer, Bruce Willis, Stalin, and one of the Jonas Sisters met to
     decide the fate of modern Europe after World War II.

Zoot Suit |zute sute|
noun
  1. High-waisted, tight-legged, pegged hipster vines that were the Members Only
     jackets of the 1940s. Seriously wide lapels and padded shoulders. Killer-diller
     drape shape with a watch chain dangling down like the hippest Pachuco
     around.

Zounds |za ow nahs|
noun
  1. How Kurt Tarot says "sounds."

Danielle Steel Creative Writing Scholarship Application
Story #1, "The Leaves Always Scream the Loudest"
By Dalton Rev

It was twelve o'clock on a Tuesday afternoon and the darkness was absolute. Ash felt his way across the bedroom floor until he found the bottle of brandy that Counselor Dan kept under the bed. He popped it open and took a long swig, coughing half back up. His throat burned and he felt queasy. So he forced down another gulp. Counselor Dan wouldn't mind. Mostly because Counselor Dan and Counselor Sue and all the rest of the adults had disappeared a week ago.

Along with the electricity.

And the sun.

There was a scream and then a crash. One floor below, the remaining campers scratched and tore and rooted around. "Mom!" they yelled, over and over. "Mom mom mom mom mom!" Pubescent baritones mixed with late bloomers' pinched sopranos, both dwarfed by the turbinelike rage of the Band of Girls. Within the cacophony, Ash recognized the voice of Merril, a redheaded kid from Montpelier. Merril's parents had paid $1,400 for a Teen Reconnect Weekend Package that ended just as Ash's You Will One Day Be a Parent Too support group began. They'd smirked at one another knowingly, forced to deal with teen/parent power issues through elaborate role play and fat-free snacks.

Ash's parents had signed him up for an entire summer's

worth of classes. They also gave Counselor Dan power of attorney before flying to the Caymans on a snorkel and mojito junket. Merril, who just a few days ago had seemed totally normal, was now down there hooting like a demented toad, his voice rising in agonized fifths. It sounded like he'd completely lost his shite and totally didn't care anymore. Actually, no one really cared anymore. Especially now that most of them had stripped naked. And used the mud in the yard for body paint. And torn the furniture apart to make clubs and spears. And tied the fat kid caught hoarding Ring Dings to the desk in the lobby, the same fat kid who kept moaning and crying and begging to be released, or at least given some water.

Ash finished the brandy as banging resumed against Counselor Dan's door. At first it was just a few fists, and then a frenzied dozen. Voices cursed and railed, fingers grappling for purchase, chanting in unison.

"Ash Ash Ash Ash Ash!"

They slammed themselves against the heavy oak door Ash had blocked with a pair of dressers and then nailed the dressers in place using seven of the nine arms from an enormous teak statue of Shiva that had once dominated the lobby. But even that wouldn't hold much longer.

"Ash!" *Bam.* "Ash!" *Bam.* "Ash!"

It had been a week since the darkness fell.

"Kill!" *Bam.* "Kill!" *Bam.* "Kill!"

Or never lifted.

It had been seven full days since the entire camp had woken to an absolutely black morning, since the students and staff and faculty had been forced to admit that the sun had simply failed to rise.

And maybe never would again.

The Winding Hills Family Healing Retreat sat in a remote clearing in the lush Champlain Valley. Ash had spent most of the summer in Teen Yurt #6 with a bunch of other stiffs who were in for the long haul, not the weekenders whose parents actually stayed and participated. Counselor Dan was perpetually barefoot. Much of his counsel came through displays of juggling and pointed mime. Counselor Todd did yoga at dawn, grunting and expelling curdled seitan breath in a desperate bid to achieve Kundalini. Counselor Sue weighed in at over two bills, permanently sunburned in sour-smelling batik, the neckline of which allowed her unfettered and gigantic mams to blink freely in the dappled morning light.

Ash's parents had agreed to Winding Hills after he'd been nailed for graffiti. Actually, tagging the proscenium of the Lutheran church in the center of town. Ash got the full book, the judge sentencing him to an entire summer. The judge was also the pastor at the church. What Ash had spray-painted, for reasons he still didn't quite understand, in huge red block-letters, was JESUS SAVES SOULS AND REDEEMS THEM FOR VALUABLE CASH PRIZES. The judge was not amused. Neither were Ash's parents.

"You're lucky," Ash's dad had pronounced. "You could have been sentenced to military school."

"We're cashing in our air miles," Ash's mom said. "We'll see you in September."

So Ash attended classes, took nature walks, participated in

yoga marathons, and made embroidered buckskin pouches. There were pamphlets, videos, talent shows, trust exercises, anklets, and parchment cookbooks. There were psalms, Vedas, and Upanishads. There were Tae and Quan and Do.

At least until the darkness fell.

Or never lifted.

A week ago, on a morning that marked Winding Hill's thirtieth anniversary of rehabilitation and spiritual renewal, the entire camp had woken to find the sun had simply failed to rise.

At first, it just seemed odd. Despite an internal distress alluded to by percussive, bean-curdish flatulence, Counselor Dan and the staff laughed it off, gathering all the kids and parents around the fire in the lobby, eating apples and playing board games by candlelight.

"Could it be an eclipse? Anyone have an almanac?"

"A big forest fire would do it. Do you smell smoke?"

"Some guy in a uniform will drive up in a Jeep and explain, right?"

Ash had the feeling, even from the very beginning, that no one was coming. He didn't know what was going on, but it had the feel of permanence. He'd told as much to Lucy, a weekender he'd been flirting with during sandal-making class. Ash took her by the hand and led her into the pantry, whispering.

"I think we should try to get out of here."

"We?"

"Yeah. You and me."

"And go where?"

"Anywhere. Just not...here."

Lucy had huge dark eyes and short hair. Her skin was brown and smooth. She was elaborately and pinkly lipsticked. Ash had an overwhelming desire to kiss her.

"I'll think about it," she said, letting go.

The following morning, still pitch-black at eleven, the camaraderie, the feeling of a snow day off from school, began to wear away.

"Is it daytime?" Counselor Bruce asked.

"I don't know," Counselor Gina answered. "I can't see my feet."

"Bet you can smell them, though," someone said.

A pot of cold oatmeal was passed around, to a general grumbling among the parents.

"I want to talk to someone about getting my deposit back!"

There were scattered "Hear! Hear!"s that gave the lobby a parliamentary feel. Counselor Dan tried to calm and assuage. There was talk of gift certificates.

"I hate to say it, but my money's on nuclear winter."

"If this doesn't stink like an alien invasion, I don't know what does."

As if in confirmation, a metallic whine rolled over the hills. It was a mortgage broker from Houston who'd brought his three daughters for sessions on Understanding Dad's Needs Through Interpretative Dance.

"C'mon, c'mon, c'mon, *c'mon!*"

The starter of his Explorer ground mercilessly. None of the car engines would turn over.

"Stop, Daddy!" his daughters begged. "*Please* stop!"

The smell of ozone filled the air. Everyone had long since given up on the cars. And everything else electronic or mechanical.

By day three, the speculation ceased. Families began to pair off, speaking in whispers. Deals were made, plans discussed, handshakes clenched, teens ignored. The shy, ill equipped, and ally free retreated to dark corners. The world was a dark corner.

On day four, the adults ran into the woods.

"Are they going for help?"

"Does this mean they forfeit their granola ration?"

Soon the drumming started. Angry rhythms thrummed throughout the valley. There were hoots and wails, keening voices acting as counterpoint.

"What *is* that?"

"It sounds like, what's that word? *Feral.*"

Every hour or so, someone's daughter would skulk outside and yell from the front steps.

"Mommy, can you hear me?"

"Dad? Daddy, are you coming back?"

"Counselor Tom? Are you listening, Counselor Tom?"

There was no response. The black tree line was barely discernable, without the slightest hint of the moon. The drumming continued day and night, until it stopped. For good.

On day five, all the females got together, forming an alliance called the Band of Girls. They donned large towels like robes.

Baptisms were performed in the hot tub at regular intervals. Their male acolytes prayed and fasted on the porch. Lucy was one of their leaders. It was then that Ash found a hammer and nails, snuck upstairs with a few provisions, and heavily reinforced the door.

A sudden glow reflected off Counselor Dan's window. Ash put his face against the cool glass, peering outside. The ancient oak in the front yard crackled like an enormous match. The lawn was illuminated, a ring of figures in robes holding hands and dancing around the tree like a giant maypole. Their robes fluttered in the breeze, a lurid nudity beneath. There seemed to be characters written on their bodies, red scrawls, flesh hieroglyphs. They set up a table in the middle of the circle, covering it with garlands and black leather carved from the lobby sofa, while chanting "ASH! ASH! ASH!"

The Band of Girls carried a shrouded woman on their shoulders, tying her down to the table before gyrating around her. Fire tore into the upper branches of the tree, popping and squalling as greenery ignited. The entire compound was illuminated in an orange haze, as if giant Klieg lights had been trucked in for a movie opening. It pained Ash's eyes after days of moldering in the dark.

A cry went up as the shroud was pulled off the prostrate girl. It was Lucy. She wore a bikini made of braided vines. Sparks leaped off the tree and began to rain down onto the roof. The corner of the porch spat flames. The banging at Counselor Dan's door increased. It sounded like they were using a ram. Ash opened his window, breathing shingle.

"Lucy!" he yelled.

The teens below fell silent, the dancing and chanting stopped. Merril stepped forward, wearing a crown of elk horns that had been mounted above the reception desk. He approached the table where Lucy was strapped, standing over her with a blade ripped from the lawn mower. He raised it in both hands, intoning something vaguely Latin.

"Lucy!" Ash yelled again.

She looked up at him and winked.

Merril brought down the blade. Ash turned as Counselor Dan's door finally gave way. Six hooded girls broke in, panting, holding torches made from bone. Ash stepped onto the throne he'd made of Counselor Dan's books, most of them texts from various classes and symposiums. It was a literate mound, a thousand years of wisdom, numerology, kabbalah, I Ching, Samuel Johnson, Nietzsche, and the collected works of Shel Silverstein.

"Kneel!" Ash commanded.

There was a prolonged scream from outside. Fire licked at the windowpane. The girls looked at one another. Ash groped randomly for the heaviest volume, coming up with one about a girl who moves to a small Northwest town and falls in love with a vampire. He brandished it, the black and red cover glowing eerily in reflected firelight.

"KNEEL BEFORE ME!" Ash said again.

The girls looked at the book. They looked at Ash.

And then obeyed.

A. God exists, exactly like it says in the Bible. We'll all be judged in heaven when we die, and a certain percentage of us will be cast down to hell.

B. God exists, which is proven by the fact that I am here to write this sentence. God recognizes that my mere existence is the best possible way of honoring him. He will welcome me in heaven whether I go to church or not because I am generally a good person.

C. God exists, but it turns out he's the one Amazon River cannibals worship. We've been praying to the wrong guy all this time, and Uglathuthlu is seriously pissed about it.

D. God exists, but he's some math nerd and we are his battery-powered action figures. He watches us with scientific disinterest, recording everything we do in a giant celestial laptop.

E. God exists, but we are so yesterday. He's busy creating the rest of the universe. Once in a while, while fielding prayers from a brand-new planet full of cactus-shaped people, he remembers us fondly.

F. God exists but is some sort of catalytic electrochemical stew not capable of thought, emotion, or profundity. The Stew has no investment whatsoever in our lives.

G. God exists and is indeed a bearded man on a throne, but that man is cold, confused, and scared. He would very much like it if some cosmonaut flew up to heaven and told him what he's supposed to be doing.

H. God not only exists, he actively hates us. Everything that has happened throughout the course of human history is a cruel joke of his devising, particularly the Spanish Inquisition, ATM fees, and Fergie.

I. God doesn't exist. The universe is vast and unknowable. Everything within it is cold brute logic. The fact that there is life on Earth is mere mathematical happenstance. Eventually the sun will run out of hydrogen, and our planet will freeze. Nothing awaits us but eons of silence.

J. God doesn't exist. We are products of evolution and we shall continue to evolve. In ten thousand years, who we are now will be as strange and distant as Neanderthal man seems to us today. We may yet go on to develop impervious metal skin, sprout downy angel wings, or consolidate into giant heads floating in vats of saline solution, whichever natural selection sees fit.

K. God absolutely exists. He is us. We are god. All things that breathe or think or even move, like wind or water, are integral parts of the celestial being that we are collectively. At some point we will learn to worship ourselves.

L. We do not exist. Our nonexistent selves dreamed up our non-existent god to make our lack of existence more palatable.

M. Alien gods showed up in 1952 in a pie-shaped landing craft to explain the pyramids, but the government killed them.

N. Alien gods showed up in 1952 in a pie-shaped landing craft, looked around for a while, and then left in disgust.

O. Alien gods showed up in 1952 in a pie-shaped landing craft, looked around for a while, bought a house in Orange County, and started working on their tans.

P. Art Tatum's left hand is the hand of god. Pele's right foot is the foot of god. Selma Hayak's booty is the booty of god. Stephen Hawking's brain is the brain of god. Natalie Portman's ankles are the ankles of god. H. L. Mencken's vocabulary is the vocabulary of god. Billie Holiday's voice is the voice of god. Miles Davis's cool is the cool of god. Your mom's heart is the heart of god.

Q. The Greeks were right. The stars are gods. The constellations are meaning. Everything spiritual and true was lost when the Romans started building bridges and aqueducts. Hail, Minerva.

R. God exists, and in all his heavenly mercy is about to step in and help me here since I have eight more letters to go and ran out of funny stuff somewhere between E and F.

S. God exists. The Devil exists. Our souls hang in the balance. In the meantime, shut your yap, *Deal or No Deal* is about to start.

T. Someone invented the tuba. People spend years in their rooms trying to learn to play it. Some of them do, putting together notes in pleasing sequences. We all generally understand and respond to the same arbitrary construction of rhythm and melody regardless of culture or geography. Tuba exists. Mozart exists. There is god in that randomness alone.

U. A child's skinned knee. A fresh lime. Ice on a hot day. Boots that fit perfectly. A book you can't wait to finish. Lying on the rug while your parents talk about their jobs. Your grandmother palming you a twenty. The smell of coffee. A movie you really want to see that turns out to be worth seeing. Washing grease off your hands after figuring out how to fix something yourself. Your girlfriend's neck. Your boyfriend's stomach. Waking up and having an hour more to sleep.

V. *God* backward spells *dog*. *Devil* backward sounds like a word for being really mad. *Vatican* backward sort of sounds like that metal band Savatage. *Muslim* backward sounds like a brand of baby food. *Confucianism* backward sounds about the same as *Confucianism* forward. *Pray* backward sounds like an old-timey cowboy answering in the affirmative. Words are meaningless. Divisions are meaningless. Labels are meaningless. If god is truly god, we are truly one.

W. hy am I writing this?

X. In some religions the letter *X* is holy. Everyone prays to Gox.

Y. Turns out god is about treating other people with respect and kindness. If you never once prayed, never were baptized, never were circumcised, never faced Mecca, never recited the Vedas, never achieved Zen, and never took communion, but spent your entire life simply being kind to those around you, whoever is waiting will almost certainly approve no matter what rituals you chose to observe.

Z. Ultimately, there will soon be ten billion people on this planet, most of whom have contradictory views of faith, worship, and afterlife. God exists for those who need him to, in whatever incarnation. God exists for those who don't need him, mostly as a source of nervous conjecture about whether they're making a huge mistake by spurning him. Tens of millions of people have lived and died before us, and when they died found out if their beliefs were right or wrong. Or, they found nothing at all. Either way, we still wake up every morning. Until we don't.

KISS ME ONCE, KISS ME TWICE, YOUR FINAL BREATH SMELLED VERY NICE

A LEXINGTON COLE MYSTERY
by Sir Barnaby Smollet

#53 in the series. First edition. 232 pgs. Fade Publishing, New York, NY, 1961.

CHAPTER ONE

The hippie was right where he was supposed to be.

Sprawled out on the floor.

Underneath Lexington Cole's knee.

Lex grabbed a shank of hair and smashed the hippie's head into the oak planks. Again.

"Okay, okay, man, I'll talk!" the kid sniveled, pulling a cellophane of dope from his dirty dungarees. Lex Cole made a fist, pistoning it into the kid's privileged belly an extra time. Just for good measure. The hippie was dirty. At least enough to pass muster on the street. But Cole knew he was a fake, on the slum, probably just dropped out of his second year at Choate. For one thing, he sported two rows of perfect dental work. And a smooth leather wallet. And a belt buckle that cost more than most longshoremen made in a month. Lex slipped the baggie into the inside pocket of his suit coat. He'd do more careful testing of its quality back in the hotel tub. In the meantime, the hippie would talk, all right. He'd do exactly what he was told. Or it'd be time to find some pliers and try out a little emergency field orthodontia.

The Rad Panthers were holed up in an apartment across the hallway. Lex had been staking it out for weeks. The Rads had sent a series of letters to the *Times.* The kind with the words cut out from the style section and then glued to notebook paper in a way that no one with an ounce of criminal talent had done since the Lindbergh baby. The letters, barely comprehensible "power to the people" rants, threatened to start blowing up schools and police stations across Manhattan. That is, unless their leader, Seldridge Mallet, was immediately released from custody. Cole didn't really care if they blew up schools. They'd just build more. Or police stations. One less copper was one less copper. Lex especially didn't care at all if Seldridge Mallet rotted in jail. He was a guy born for the podium, born to rail against the status quo with his Lenin goatee and cute turns of phrase. He talked about the way people treated each other. The way things could be better. Free lunches. Free elections. Equal rights. Problem was, once the downtrodden Mallets of the world got a little power, they became carpetbaggers just like all the rest. The pretty talk became garlands on a dead Christmas tree. They made deals, shook hands, skimmed contributions. They became the pigs they were supposed to replace. All Mallets were equal, it's just that some Mallets were more equal than others.

Lex hated politics. And slogans.

There were jobs to do.

And there were the men who did those jobs.

Smoothly and professionally.

That was it.

Lex was here to get paid and get out. And what he'd been paid for was to grab the little kidnapped debutante the Rads had been doing God knows what to since they'd plucked her off the streets uptown, in full daylight, two weeks ago. Lex needed to hightail her back to Park Avenue, where her extremely wealthy father was falling all over himself to pay Lex off with a Samsonite full of Krugerrands. And now, two weeks and endless neck stubble later, his patience was about to be rewarded. If he happened to foil a bomb plot in the meantime, so be it. He wasn't losing any sleep over anything but the industrialist's daughter, a rude little minx named Seraphina Willeford. Lex looked at her yearbook photo one last time. She stared at the camera with bee-stung lips and gray eyes like icebergs bobbing in the North Atlantic. She had eyes that men would crash their hulls into and sink, again and again, and be happy to do it. Eighteen, with a thousand-dollar handbag and a knowing smirk. Lex figured she'd probably been in on her own abduction, was hoping to fleece Daddy for enough folding green to spend sophomore year sunning herself in Biarritz.

Either way, the hippie was the key.

Lex had caught him skulking on the fire escape, dragged him into the stakeout room for questioning, and squeezed him hard. The hippie confessed right away that he and the Willeford girl were classmates. The Rads had run out of dope, or their usual connection had burned them, and now they were looking for a new delivery boy. And guess who that new delivery boy was going to be? Lex would knock, offer his wares, and then use the hippie as a shield while he gorilla'd into their midst. He had everything he needed: a very big gun, a very bad headache, and a very heavy set of onions dangling in his immaculately ironed slacks.

Lexington Cole smiled, as he always did when a solid plan finally came together. He lit a cigarette, the smell of stewardess perfume lingering on the back of his hand. His close-cropped steel-blue hair glistened in the morning light. His body, wiry like wound cable, almost flexed back in on itself. Twin .44 autos hung reassuringly in the holsters under his arms. The hippie began to weep.

All in all, it had been a good morning.

To be continued...

The Junkie with Two Bad Habits

The Luger That Said I Love You

And Her Burning Rage Lit the Way

The Blues Ruse and the Bloody Shoes

Not for All the Feldspar in Belgrade

The Hollow-Pointed Cerebellum

Never Trust a Taxidermist

Daddy Met a Lady, Mommy Died Alone

A Contentment in Harlem

Hide, Cannibal, Hide!

These Two Hands Born to Smack

The Judas Fruit

Ask the Zebra, Answer the Stripes

The Fat Man Warbles at Midnight

A Spinnaker to Starboard, a Shiv to the Ribs

And Whose Corpse Shall Claim Dominion?

The End of Everything Is G

A Dirge, a Dirigible, and a Dirty Lie

The Butcher Buys a Loaf

In the Court of the Granite Mandarin

The Torture Mechanic

One Small Step for Man, One Giant Step for Pan

The Gypsy Who Could Only Sort of Dance

SALT RIVER HIGH **CLIQUE INDEX**

THE BALLS: Comprised of Salt River's football team, except the punter and some freshman scrubs. Wearers of no-irony crew cuts, shoulder pads without shirts, and cleats for kicking the fallen and cleatless. They play only one sport at Salt River, and it's not field hockey. Mortal enemies of Pinker Casket. ▶ **LEADER:** Jeff Chuff, QB ▶ **RIGHT-HAND MAN TO JEFF CHUFF:** Chance Chugg, WR ▶ **QUOTE:** "Chuff to Chugg…touchdown!" ▶ **RACKET:** Girlie mags, by-the-sip water fountain, game tickets, autographs, pay-for-play bathroom use. ▶ **GROUPIES: SIS BOOM BAHS:** Milk-fed, long-legged leaders of cheer. Big hair. Aggressively dim. Can't spell *pom* or *pom.* Make up sixty percent of the Booze 'n' Fondle dating pool. ▶ **SUB-CLIQUES: COULDABEEN CONTENDERS:** Good enough to compete, damaged enough to avoid competing, e.g., the girl who was smarter than everyone else but now fails all her classes; the super-arty kid who gave up drawing and now mostly picks his nose; the seven-foot guy who quit basketball to write sploetry. **SCAM WOWS:** Ferret-faced huckster clan. Members wear matching Bluetooth headsets and tight polo shirts. They'll buy or sell your mother. Seriously, is she available for purchase? Most are also sploets. Writers of sports poetry. Poetry about sports. What? Chuff does it. So what? No way, it's cool. It's about sports. Shut up. It is not. No, I mean it. I swear, you better shut your cakehole before I come over there.

PINKER CASKET: The rockingest, thrashingest band on campus. Loud and dark and droning. Plays all pep rallies, proms, and school events, although probably most appropriate for funerals or virgin sacrifices. The yearly battle of the bands isn't a battle, it's a slaughter. Most popular songs are "There's a Shocker in My Locker," "Sex Nuke," and "The Devil Went Down to Georgia, No, Not That Georgia, the One That Was Part of the Former Soviet Union Whose Capital Is Now Tbilisi." Mortal enemies of the Balls. ▶ **LEADER:** Kurt Tarot ▶ **RIGHT-HAND MAN TO KURT TAROT:** Mick Freeley ▶ **QUOTE:** "If you can't play an instrument, why even have a name?" ▶ **RACKET:** Knockoff iPods, bootlegged MP3s, ripped DVDs, suspect electronics, and not-punch-you fees. ▶ **GROUPIES: DES BARRES:** Spandex toe to neck and willing to de-spandex as required. Tend to be in love with the sensitive drummer, who's actually more half asleep than he is sensitive. Most secret inner desire is to get a Marshall Stack tattoo. ▶ **SUB-CLIQUES: KOKROCK CITY:** Guys who spend the majority of their time claiming to have heard of the latest trendy band way before you did. Anyone who sells more than ten albums is a sellout. Anyone whose second album sounds even slightly different from the first is a sellout. Includes indie, glam, metal, punk, rude boys, go-go, hardcore, and thrash. **AIRPLANE GLUZE:** Frequent wearers of a perm-mullet hybrid. Lots of PARTY HEARTY bumper stickers. Lots of CERTIFIED SEX INSPECTOR T-shirts. Congenital utterance of "huh?" Includes Garage Rockers, Jam Banders, Zep Heads, Random Noodlers, Stinky Phishers, and Feedback Queens.

YEARBOOK COMMITTEE: Controls all social events. Controls all captions and candid shots. Kingmakers for all student government and student council slots. ▶ **LEADER:** Lu Lu Footer ▶ **QUOTE:** "You want a quote, buy a yearbook." ▶ **RACKET:** The status inherent in being in print, and the favors delivered accordingly. ▶ **SUB-CLIQUES: MOST LIKELY TO HAVE NICEST TEETH:** If you keep smiling, eventually someone will take your picture.

SMOKE: Enjoys muscle cars, smoking, and leaning against brick walls enigmatically. Prefers nonfilters. ▶ **LEADER AND ONLY MEMBER:** Ronnie Newport ▶ **QUOTE:** "Hey, you got a light?" ▶ **RACKET:** Transportation, yearbook photography, being the man behind the lens. ▶ **GROUPIES: GINNY SLIMS:** Ronnie Newport's inexplicably dim backseat posse. Big on laughing too loud, headbands, ripped jeans, glossy lips, and stiletto boots.

FOXXES: Hot Chix and Whiskey Licks. All Foxxes can more than hold their own, and frequently do. Wearing the best vines and dressed to the nines. ▶ **LEADER:** Cassiopeia Jones ▶ **QUOTE:** "Go ahead and mess with me. Please." ▶ **RACKET:** Unknown but highly lucrative. ▶ **GROUPIES:** None. Unless you count every guy at school. ▶ **SUB-CLIQUES: CATWALK NINJA:** The Foxxes' highly mysterious bodyguard triplets, with lightning moves to match their racy leatherette. Thighs to die for. Sometimes referred to as "Jenny," but rarely to their faces.

CAPE SILVERSPOON: Rich girls who are, amazingly, also popular. Not as smoking hot as Foxxes but with spending power to work around it. Too much of a cliché to have a leader, too boring to even describe. Yeah, blond; yeah, perfect; yeah, big house and sculpted calves and two-grand pumps. Not big fans of Proust. ▶ **QUOTE:** "Whatever, lesser. Go get me a diet Rush." ▶ **RACKET:** Dad's wallet. ▶ **GROUPIES:** You gotta be born into it. ▶ **SUB-CLIQUES: FACE BOI:** Groomed, attractive, naturally muscled, and unencumbered with the baggage of excess personality. They enjoy driving Silverspoon to the mall or a movie like the expensively sweatered gentlemen they are. Formerly Lax Brahs with flow, but since they cut the lacrosse budget, it's all about abs and three-stage acne solutions. **GIRLZ WITH TWO FIRST NAMES:** Tiffany Michele. Amber Jennifer. Sadie Lynn. Cari Natalie. Hannah Bella. Exotic nomenclature allows them to be a subset of Cape Silverspoon without having sufficient access to Mom's credit card to otherwise qualify. **BULL LEMIA:** One purged meal and a designer handbag away from graduating to Silverspoon. Oh so in love with that Face Boi who would probably notice them if they could only stop eating Cool Ranch Bloritos. Time to do another thousand leg lifts.

LEE HARVIES: Self-appointed regulators of who is or isn't strapped at Salt River. Shadowy group with no known leader, cause, racket, or purpose, except firing at random. Sniper skills are without parallel, as there has yet to be a Lee Harvies–related fatality. Are either disrupting the herd, or herding the herd. When rare Lee Harvies sightings are made, they're usually running from the scene, wearing a Jason-style hockey mask with silver anarchy symbols painted over the eyes. They always leave behind a single playing card, the jack of spades, where the jack's face has been replaced by a portrait of Leon Czolgosz. ▶ **LEADER:** None. ▶ **QUOTE:** "I'll give up my gun when they pry it from my cold, grassy knoll." ▶ **RACKET:** None. They can't be bribed. Or bargained with. Or even identified.

FRESHMAN GIRLS: Sigh. ▶ **RACKET:** Causing sighs.

ROTTEN IN DENMARK: The theater department. Constantly quoting Brecht. Prone to porkpie hats and Kansas prairie dresses. Members know all the songs from *Cats* and two-thirds of the songs from *Rent*. Since third grade have been beat up at least one-fourth of the time because of it. ▶ **LEADER:** Whoever's got the most lines that day. ▶ **QUOTE:** "Give me a minute to get into character." ▶ **RACKET:** Improv tips. ▶ **GROUPIES:** The occasional soon-to-be-arrested visiting playwright who has graciously volunteered his scraggly-bearded time for one-on-one instruction. ▶ **SUB-CLIQUES: FOOTLIGHTS:** Kids who really, *really* want to be in a play but never make it through an audition without crying and saying, "Okay, sorry...sorry... okay, let me start again...I just...I just...sorry. I have it. I can totally do it. Let's just start over. Can we start over? From the top?" They tend to hang around dejectedly backstage before eventually agreeing to spend the weekend painting backdrops. **GIRLS WITH UNNECESSARY Y'S:** Aspiring dancers like Cyndi, Jyll, Alyce, Chrys, and Lysa. Women who refer to themselves as *womyn*. Aspiring spokesmodels like Susyn, Lynda, Jordyn, Bryn, and Cameryn. Aspiring trophy wives like Kyra, Mylissa, Tyne, and Skyler.

CROWDAROUNDS: Pretty much everyone at school is a charter member. If there's action, they crowd around. They gawk and laugh while basking in utter relief that they're not the one being picked on. Everyone talks derisively about Crowdarounds, which is ironic, since pretty much everyone is one. ▶ **LEADER:** None, or they wouldn't be Crowdarounds. ▶ **QUOTE:** "Be quiet and watch." ▶ **RACKET:** Vicarious immersion. ▶ **SUB-CLIQUES: TEXT MOB LOL:** OMG! D U just C wht hppnd? Tht wuz Cr8zy! LOL! Did U C Skyler's hair???? Gross! R U cming 2 School 2day? Im txting in my homework since mom got doc's note sez my thumbs r inflamed. LOL.

EUCLIDIANS: Sure, *nerd* is a cliché, but nerds are a reality and revenge is inevitable. As Moses or someone once said: "The nerds will inherit the meek." Mostly fingertip-sniffers, Fack Cult daughters, corduroy wearers, and that kid who plays with his Robot Lion Fist™ action figures while making a *preer preer* sound through his nose during lunch. ▶ **LEADER:** Possibly Stephen Hawking. ▶ **QUOTE:** "Some people like to study, okay? Get over it, mouth-breather." ▶ **RACKET:** Test scores, term papers, video game unlockables, tutoring, high-grade Wite-Out, and Finish Your Sudoku for You? ▶ **GROUPIES:** Occasionally a wayward Plath with a few wine coolers under her belt, but not really, no. ▶ **SUB-CLIQUES:** None, except for the natural loose affiliation with various New Skids.

NEW SKIDS ON THE LOOM: More a poorly dressed amoeba than a true clique, New Skids is a nebulous catchall for the socially stranded. Encompasses most species of geeks, kingdoms of nerds, and phyla of dorks, including but not limited to: debating geeks, activities geeks, code-writing nerds, geeks with dice, nerds with long stringy hair, and Elvis Costello glasses–wearing dorks, as well as all other variants of sit-alones, snorty laughers, movie dialogue reciters, the helplessly flatulent, the NASA obsessed, pretty-horse drawers, the willfully unpleasant, virtual-girl fantasizers, those with yellow breath, the cat-hair-covered, Nerf herders, the daily velour-swathed, and those having fully retreated into elf realms. ▶ **SUB-CLIQUES: PLATHS:** Girls who write aching poetry in their algebra book margins about razors, virgins, and the eternal love of Germanic vampire overlords. Are known to rock the occasional beret, along with the occasional stained sweatpants. **COAL TRAIN:** Marching band wieners. Tuba lards. Flautists. Triangle dingers. Auto-harp toters. Sniffers of fuzzy-tipped drumsticks, owners of spit-caked clarinets, and donners of fringy polyester uniforms. Tend to spend countless hours on the bus trying to interest people in their quadraphonic recordings of *Bitches Brew*. **BAREFOOTS:** Random shouting vegans and the petition-wielding patchouli-soaked. Peace yellers. Justice demanders. Tofu garglers. The mud-flecked. **STEEL-TOE DYSTOPIA:** Wearing distressed leather and fingerless gloves, they spend many hours on the couch envisioning themselves with architectural stomach musculature, an indefatigable sword arm, and a high-tensile mullet. They lust for the Take-Charge Apocalypse Female, who tends to prefer to do her fighting in something tight and low-cut and will soon come to lead them to the promised land, which in this case is the remnants of a heavily irradiated Las Vegas.

THE FACK CULT T: The faculty and administration: young, idealistic math teachers; old, broken, sweater-vested history teachers; gym teachers driven insane by the parade of hopeless delinquency; secretaries; various staff; substitutes, lackeys, librarians; cafeteria workers; and the dude who drives the Roach Coach. ▶ **LEADER:** Principal Inference ▶ **CO-LEADER:** Miss Honey Bucket, school registrar ▶ **QUOTE:** "Do you have a hall pass? No? Well, then, do you have ten dollars?" ▶ **RACKET:** Power corrupts. Absolute power equals absolute cash.

THE BODY: Don't think about Wesley. Don't talk about Wesley. *Shhh.* Who? What body? I have no idea what you're talking about, and even if I did, do you think I'd talk to *you* about it?